MeCTen Nova

Published by Aaron Gee

Logan, UT

ISBN: 978-0-9894361-4-4

Languages used: English, Japanese (romaji), Spanish, German
Typeset in Garamond, Futura Md, and Agency FB
Cover art generated by Adobe Firefly Image 5

In Memory of the Three Doctors:

I. Laurence Gee M.D.

Martell J. Gee Ph.D.[2]

Glendon W. Gee Ph.D.

Their lives have impacted countless millions.

Their works are known only to a few.

Preface

I began working on the MeCTen (pronounced /mek/-/ten/) series in 2013 as a way of pushing through some writer's block on the sequel to my first book in the Arabella series, Dark Escape. I had been contemplating doing a story set in outer space for some time, but there was a problem with my writing personality. Having studied engineering and physics in college, I determined that I would try to make my writing as realistic as possible. I wanted to make it believable and set it in the near future. There are a lot of problems with space travel. Not the least of which is how vast, and how dangerous the environment outer space is. Unfortunately, there are quite a few engineering and technical issues that must be resolved to make a story set in space realistic.

Another issue is that I have never been in the military. My father, uncle, son, and friends have been in the service, but I haven't. I believe that writers should write from experience, so that the story seems authentic. However, I lack personal experience when it comes to the military or being a military aviator. To overcome that deficit, I had to do a lot of research, and it took time. I started by asking my Uncle Martell Gee for assistance in solving some of the issues in the book. He had two PhDs in nuclear physics and computer science, so he was ideal for giving me the insight I needed. He agreed to help, although he was dying of a brain tumor. Most of his suggestions centered on the power systems for the MeCTen spacecraft (as he had no knowledge of metric tensor theory). I wanted to use fission reactors, because I felt that fusion power is still too impractical and inefficient. Martell convinced me that fusion would be a better choice. His biggest criticism of my work was that I was trying to solve real engineering problems in a fictional novel. "Don't try to solve these in your head. It's fiction, after all, and doesn't have to work." Six months later, Martell passed away. I regret that he never got to read any of this book.

With the idea that I didn't have to write a physics textbook, I set out on filling in the gaps in my knowledge base. Since this book is very technical, I had to study up on military structure and the many tools the US Department of Defense has at its disposal. Most of the information on military infrastructure and projects is highly classified. I had to guess a lot and invent what I thought was most likely. What wasn't classified was gleaned from public sources to get as accurate as I could. The result is the novel.

One of the biggest hurdles of science fiction is the utilization of FTL or Faster-Than-Light travel. Most people do not realize how vast space is. Our fastest spacecraft travels just under 60,000 kilometers per hour. At that rate it would take over 80,000 years to reach Proxima Centauri, the nearest star system. Obviously, this would be far beyond what is practical for storytelling or reality. There are several theories on how to achieve FTL, however they are only theoretical and have some severe physical limitations. I chose the metric tensor drive hypothesized by Miguel Alcubierre, because it is the most likely to be correct. It does not violate Einstein's or Lorentz's theories but has several limitations and significant practical questions that I won't get into in a preface. I don't claim to understand it fully, or to be correct with the scientific principles. I remember Martell's admonition and not get bogged down by solving the problems of real space travel. It's fiction.

I envisioned the MeCTen drive as a way of utilizing the basic forces in the universe to our advantage. When I studied judo, I learned how to use the energy of my opponent to my advantage. I also felt that the ship would use gravity for its own advantage. Is my solution correct? I doubt that the MeCTen would work exactly the way I have written, but I would love to see someone try it.

Why is it so long between the time I started and the time of publication? Procrastination and the fact that I am only a part-time author. I tend to write in spurts and then come back, revise, and then write some more. I know, as a reader, this must be aggravating, but I want to produce the best novel I can. I want the reader to enjoy it most of all.

Many of the events in the book might seem plausible now. This preface was written in 2023 and revised in 2025, and the world seems on the brink of another World War. In 2013 the events I speculated in the book seemed improbable but now seem like it is something that might happen. Authors are terrible at predicting the future. I pray that nothing like the events in the book happens, but only time will tell. Nuclear weapons are powerful, and their use in war does more than devastate things and people. Nukes send a clear message of unbridled hatred and fury. They have only been used (as of 2025) twice in war. I pray they are never used again.

This is based on science, but it's still fiction. I don't know everything (contrary to popular belief), and there are many things I don't know and have yet to learn. For what it's worth, I hope I have entertained you and provoked thought. There are a lot of questions posed in this novel about life, morality, and ethics in war. I hope that you will find some answers and come up with some questions about things I didn't address. I enjoyed writing the book, and hope you enjoy reading it.

NATIONAL SECURITY DISCLAIMER

This is a work of fiction. All people, places, and events are fictional, and products of the author's imagination. Any similarities between real people, places, things, or events are entirely coincidental. Weapon systems, military procedures, military organizations, military operations, military projects, and military resources are based on fictionalized versions of these systems, organizations, operations, projects and resources, and ARE NOT real. The author makes no inferences on real military operations and means no infringement within this book. All information contained in this work is based on publicly available unclassified declassified material. This work of fiction contains NO classified material, real or implied relating to the governments or militaries mentioned. Any similarity to actual classified persons, places, projects, procedures, systems, operations, or organizations is purely coincidental. To repeat:

This is a work of fiction and contains no classified material.

Briefing

Classified: Top Secret

My name is Gaia, and I am here to brief you on current events. The world is embroiled in war. Two major factions have emerged: the Axis, and the Alliance. Much like the previous conflict, the world has been divided by the expansionist desires of three countries.

The three core Axis countries are China, Russia, and Iran. All three have conspired to control key areas of the globe. They are supported by numerous countries in Asia, Africa, and Central America. The most notable country providing material support is India, but they have not joined the conflict as a belligerent. They continue to insist they are neutral.

The first major power to begin its expansion was Russia. It began with the annexation of Crimea in eastern Ukraine. It has since been in a protracted war of attrition in Ukraine, and the European Allies have been weakened by their dependance on energy from China and Russia.

The second is China with its annexation of Taiwan a year ago. Still not satisfied, it began to conquer the countries surrounding the China Sea, and then all but one island in the Archipelago of Japan. Now, only Hokkaido remains unconquered. I anticipate is that Russia and China are also not yet finished in their conquest.

The Last Axis Power is Iran. Despite the twelve-day war's impacts on its military power years ago, it has returned to its belligerent ways. It has been quietly gaining allies in the Middle East for decades and now feels it has regained its former strength. It has turned its focus on the isolated nation of Isreal.

The Alliance consists of the member states of NATO, led by the United States and Canada, South Korea, Argentina, and what is left of the Japanese Defense Force that escaped the invasion. Turkey's ejection from NATO was a blow, but once the nation sided with Iran it could no longer stay. America has led the way in the fighting as the European NATO members squabble, resentful of the hawkish stance of the current American administration. The conflict is complicated by the decades of Chinese infiltration in various countries around the globe. Many of the countries the Alliance depended on for defense have shirked their treaty obligations and declared themselves neutral. These include Australia, New Zealand, Mexico, Spain, Egypt, and Ireland.

In the United States; the Second Civil War ended eight months ago after three months of sporadic fighting. The Chinese bases on US soil (established to aid a radical socialist faction effecting a hostile takeover of the Democrat Party) have been eradicated. Fortunately they failed. Those politicians and political operatives involved in this action have been purged from the party arrested, and are currently held on charges of treason. Those financing this terrorist endevor have had their assets seized as part of a broad RICO case involving the majority of the party.

The most active operations theater is in the Western Pacific. Guam was bombed with incendiary and tactical nuclear ordinances four months ago. All three US military bases on the island are effectively destroyed. The JSDF was pushed out of Honshu but has held out in Hokkaido. They expect an invasion soon. The US Navy is supporting actions to regain a foothold on the islands of Micronesia but have been unsuccessful so far. Manpower and equipment are in short supply. The draft has been reintroduced, but ade quate forces are at least eighteen months from being ready.

Additional notes on Project Nova: There are numerous acronyms and terms in the following account. Please refer to the appendices for unfamiliar terms, acronyms, and operational names.

Briefing Ends

MeCTen Nova

Chapter 1

BENT

"Wolverine, Sentry-Rook-One, intercept bogey inbound to Fortress BRAA[1] two-five-zero, two-niner-seven, fifty feet, Hot, Mach one point two-five. Bogey designated victor-one-seven. IFF[2] to Fortress." The androgynous mechanical voice cut through the high-pitched whine of the engine and the steady roar of the air flowing over the fuselage of the F-35-B Lightning II.

Major Michael "Truck" Langford keyed his mic and promptly replied, "Rodger, BRAA two-five-zero, two-niner-seven, fifty feet, Hot. Descending from angels three seven to the hard deck." Without pausing he called his wingman, Captain Angela Miller. "Angel, you see anything?"

"Negative," she said skeptically. "But the air picket has EMILA."[3]

Truck hated taking directions from the RQ-175, AEL-AWACS.[4] It is a high-powered computer, housed in a solar and fuel cell powered aircraft. Twelve of them orbited over sixty thousand feet above the carrier group. Each drone could remain aloft for extended periods without refueling or maintenance. With these autonomous drones networked with the Blackjack, Orion, and Intruder satellites, the carrier could monitor everything within a thousand miles of the fleet.

Drones had numerous advantages over human manned aircraft. Computers never got tired or needed a break. With their advanced detection capabilities, they could find a target long before it became a threat. Best of all, they were cheaper than manned aircraft, and they had the most advanced detection available. The Entangled Magneto-Interferometric Laser Array aboard the drone and AGPS[5] satellites could detect the difference between a ship, plane, or a flock of birds. Even stealth craft using ECM[6] and AOC[7] could be easily detected. Usually, it could tell what kind of vehicle, and even the payload. The fact that all the advanced technology couldn't identify it unnerved Truck.

1 Bearing Range Altitude Aspect
2 Identify Friend or Foe
3 Entangled Magneto-Interferometric Laser Array
4 Autonomous Enhanced Littoral Airborne Warning and Control System
5 Advanced Global Positioning System
6 Electronic Countermeasures
7 Adaptive Optical Camouflage

There wasn't really a choice. They had to investigate the mysterious signal. This was the most dangerous mission given to Marine pilots. The F-35 was notoriously bad at close quarters combat. Even with the improvements in their variant, they were untested against the newer Chinese fighters in a dogfight. The thought sent a chill down his spine.

Truck and Angel descended rapidly through the pre-dawn clouds toward the vast Pacific Ocean below. They were west of what was left of Guam, but it was more like the corner of no and where. As far as the eye could see there was nothing but ocean and the rolling dark blue storm clouds in all directions. Punching through the cloud layer was surreal. The effect was like being sandwiched between two oceans. It was disorienting if you attempted to fly by sight alone, and you could easily make a fatal mistake.

Truck strained but couldn't see anything. He slid his DAS[8] visor down and scanned the monochromatic radar display and selected the drone overlay. A flashing yellow box highlighted the outline of a bogey. Without thinking, his thumb moved the control knob selecting the IFF inquiry option for his transponder. The female voice of the ALIS[9] instantly responded. "Identifying."

Seconds ticked by without a response, and for every second, Truck's intuition told him that something was terribly wrong. "I'm not getting anything," he said.

"Passing five thousand," Angel responded.

"Fortress, Wolverine three-four, permission to light them up with Sentry augment and engage." Truck hoped using active targeting would spook the bogey to either disengage or panic and do something stupid. If it was an enemy fighter, they would think twice if they could sense the threat of a targeting lock, and the fear of an impending missile.

Before Fortress could respond the shrill alarm of his missile radar warning system filled his headset. ALIS calmly stated, "Incoming Radar Missile."

"Smoke in the air! Evasive!" Angel said sternly. Both pilots reacted instantly with an F-pole maneuver designed to cause the incoming missile to be overcommitted. The heavy G-forces pulled at their bodies and forced their flight suits to inflate to keep them from passing out from g-LOC.[10] Truck instinctively selected countermeasures from his defensive weapons

8 Distributed Aperture System
9 Autonomic Logistics Information System
10 g-force induced Loss of Consciousness

menus. Multi-spectral radio bursts began emitting from a pod in his internal weapons bay. Flares, metal chafe, and an ALE-70 emerged from the fuselage.

"Fortress, Wolverine, designate bogey hostile! Repeat, we have a bandit with no joy!" Truck activated his offensive weapons systems, and ALIS began finding a firing solution for the elusive hostile aircraft.

"Wolverine, Fortress, weapons free! You're clear to engage!"

"I don't see anything," Angel said. An almost imperceptible twinge of panic in her otherwise calm voice. "I've got no joy on the bandit!"

Something suddenly shot past Truck's canopy. It was as if there was movement out of the corner of his eye, but he couldn't make out what it was. A half second later there was a brief flash as a missile found the decoy. The drone had done its job of fooling the targeting sensors. There was a shudder as the shockwave of the explosion hit his aircraft.

"What the - he about took my head off! Watch it, Angel! DAS didn't show the inbound!" Truck was silently panicked by the fact that the projectile was able to correct for his maneuver, but the more imminent concern was the possibility of another one. He launched another set of countermeasures. The engine, already in afterburner, whined in protest. The airframe groaned and began to shake, and alarms began to fill his cockpit with noise.

Truck flipped his DAS visor up and strained to look back at his aircraft. It was no good. He couldn't see much beyond the wings, but they were still there. "Angel, I can't see, but I think I've been hit. Check my six!" He pushed his stick to the right and began a rolling scissors maneuver, still descending toward the ocean a few thousand feet below.

"Your tail is smoking," his wingman replied. "It's not bad, but you need to bug out."

Suddenly, a friendly chirp followed by a steady tone, ALIS had targeted something, and hopefully it was whomever was shooting at them. "Fire JATM," [11] it said calmly.

Truck didn't hesitate. He flipped up the trigger guard and armed his weapon systems. "Fox three! Fox three!" He shouted as he double-tapped the firing trigger, and two missiles left his weapons bay in quick succession.

---

11 Joint Advanced Tactical Missile

The AIM-260 missiles were networked to the RQ-175's and they would guide them to the still unseen target. The system was far more effective than any onboard sensor suite. Without knowing exactly what he was up against, Truck didn't want to take any chances. He watched the exhaust trails of the missiles as they gracefully weaved through the sky. Only the missiles seemed to know the location of the enemy. After what seemed like an eternity, there were two orange and black flashes, and an object exploded into flames about fifteen miles off his starboard wing. He pulled out of his descent and veered toward the impact.

"Nice!" Angel crowed. "Splash one!"

"Wolverine, Fortress actual, confirm splash one bogey. Any chute?" It wasn't often Captain Mathew McDonald of the USS Essex addressed the pilots directly.

"Wolverine six-two, negative," Angel replied. "I'm not seeing anything. Position, approximately one-three point seven-two-five north by one-three-niner point one-seven-six-niner-one east."

Truck banked slowly toward the Essex. His plane was clearly in trouble now. He was in no position to fight, and he began to wonder if he could make it back. "Fortress, Wolverine three-four, I've got hydraulic issues." He glanced at his fuel indicator. It was dropping faster than it should. "Yup! It got my fuel line. I'll be bingo before I get back."

The idea that he might have to ditch a one-hundred-fifty-million-dollar aircraft in one of the deepest parts of the ocean was unappealing. Pilots have ruined careers by recklessly losing expensive hardware, although it was never the official reason. The tricky thing about landing on the deck of the Essex was that it wasn't designed for anything other than STOVL.[12] Losing fuel and hydraulic fluid would make that nearly impossible without crashing. If he ejected, the force alone could break his legs and back. If he crashed, he could break a lot more. He could be caught in an inferno of blazing jet fuel and severely burned, not to mention injuring the crew on the deck. That was, if he made it back to the solid deck of the Essex, which was the only landing strip within four hundred miles.

Truck cajoled his plane into a heading that would lead him back toward the Essex. The engines and airframe protesting everything he did. He looked

---

12 Short Take-off and Vertical Landing

at his fuel gauge. Nine thousand one hundred fifteen pounds of fuel and dropping fast. Normally he would burn just over fifteen pounds per nautical mile, but it looked like he was using nearly three times that. He knew it was just over one hundred nautical miles back, but landing would chew through even more fuel. He figured it would take nearly three thousand pounds of fuel to get him home and on the deck, but at the rate he was leaking, he might not have enough.

"Fortress, Wolverine three-four, mayday," Truck said, trying to remain calm. "I'm losing fuel fast, and my hydraulics are bent. I'm not sure if I'll make it back."

"Wolverine three-four, Fortress actual, your pigeons look okay. We'll come about and head to you. It won't give you much, but it will shave a couple of miles off. Just don't be digging holes in my deck."

"Aye-aye sir. I'll punch out before that happens. Just clear the deck and deploy the barricade." Truck urged his wounded plane faster as far as he dared. His mind raced through all the scenarios of how the aircraft could behave during landing. He was certain that the engine fans weren't too badly damaged, or the main turbine would have already failed by now. The secondary was used only for STOVL landings, and if it had sustained any damage, he would have to ditch the plane into the ocean. The big concern would be the amount of control he would have on approach and landing.

Normally Truck would fly parallel to the Essex until he was almost abeam the tower. Then he would maneuver over the deck and touch gently down onto the small carrier. Since the aircraft was already becoming difficult to control, he would have to approach it like a combat carrier landing. Straight on, and down fast.

The thirty-minute return flight passed in slow motion. He had to struggle to keep the aircraft from veering starboard and pitching down. Just as he was approaching the Essex he realized how critical the wind direction would be for his landing.

"Fortress, Wolverine three-four, what's my wind speed and direction?"

"Truck, your wind is one five six at thirteen."

Truck winced. Not only was the wind coming from behind him and slightly to his right, but it was a stiff thirteen knots. This would be a terrifying landing, and he wasn't sure he could pull it off. He could feel the sweat pouring down his face as his anxiety was getting the better of him.

"Wolverine three-four, Fortress actual, we didn't have time to get the ship into an ideal course. Can you land that kite or not?"

"Permission to speak freely?"

"Go ahead."

"Sir, I don't even have a visual. It's bad enough that if I don't use DAS I'll probably crash, and the deck isn't a big target. It's like trying to long jump onto a moving metal postage stamp."

"Understood. Are you saying you're unable to land? We could use the ALIS data."

"Negative sir. I want a medal if I pull this off. And a new flight suit. The pucker-factor is past twelve. Make sure the barricade is out."

"Rodger, Wolverine three-four, you're half mile out."

He slowed his aircraft down in preparation for landing. He quickly ran through the checklist in his mind. He pulled down the lever to lower his landing gear and initiated mode four for STOVL. Immediately the alarms went off. He glanced around his instruments. His port side gear door wouldn't open. He flipped the gear actuator up and then back down again. Still the error message remained.

"My port gear's bent!" Truck looked at its rapidly dwindling fuel supply. Three hundred seventy-five pounds of fuel, roughly enough to quickly land. Not enough to debate the issue or figure out a solution that didn't involve totaling his aircraft. "Forget it! I'm gonna' land!"

"Eject! Don't you bust my ship!" Captain McDonald warned.

By now so many alarms and warnings were pounding away at his ears, and lights flashing, vying for his attention, that the cockpit had taken on a life of its own. Truck couldn't think straight enough to silence them. All his focus was on landing his crippled plane on the deck of the Essex. Carrier landings were difficult under the best conditions. The ship was swaying with the two-meter swells and thirteen knots tail wind with a crosswind component. His engine was screeching in protest, threatening to seize any moment.

If he lost his engine, he would have only seconds to eject before slamming into the ocean. A few more feet and he would slam into the deck. He knew he had to get the plane on the ship quickly, or the worst would happen.

Truck threw down the lever to initiate the STOVL landing sequence. Several things happened simultaneously during this phase. Doors opened covering the vertical engine fan which spun up to incredible speed to provide lift during landing. His rear stabilizers were lowered to provide control, and his main engine exhaust nozzle rotated down to provide the lift for the rear of the plane. At least, that was supposed to happen. But it didn't.

Instead of slowing in a controlled manner, Truck's F-35 violently pitched up, yawed to the left, and began a sinking spin into the sea. Instinctively, Truck pushed the throttle to the firewall and fought for control. The shrill scream of the stall warning added to the cacophony in the cabin.

Truck was so inundated with noise that he couldn't even hear the Essex frantically telling him to eject. His crippled fighter spun like a corkscrew several times before Truck regained control. He was even with the deck and roughly fifty yards off the bow. He could just make out the orange net strung across the deck, and the men frantically waving him off. He leveled off just in time for his one good rear landing gear to make contact.

There was a heavy thud as the wheel smashed into the deck followed by a jolt that nearly made him lose his tenuous control. He heard a brief scrape as his port wing ground into the thick steel of the deck plating. He winced at the thought of the hole he had probably just carved. Red warning lights flashed, indicating an engine fire. He was sure the coxswain was blaring outside, sounding General Quarters, but he was committed now. He concentrated on keeping the left wing off the deck and the plane centered on the rapidly approaching net.

Blinking takes an eternity in a crisis. When you don't have time for a reflex action, things slow to a crawl. A sane person might shut their eyes and pray for the end, but Marines can't be classified as sane. They are trained to greet death with everything they have, and fight to the end. Truck knew he now had to hit that barricade. He could not miss. For everyone on that ship, he had to do one thing: hit the net.

As the burning F-35 caught hold of the thick mesh, it went spinning to the right, away from the tower. The force of the collision ripped the fasteners and tore the restraint from its mount. The fighter spun on its axis, sending the port wing into the deck again, and sending pieces of wing skipping like rocks across the surface of a pond. The engine coughed as it had consumed its last drop of fuel, but not before sucking in more shrapnel from the deck plate. A horrific screech filled the air, and the engine came to a sudden, grinding halt. At that moment, every instrument went dead, along with all the sirens, alarms, and warnings. All Truck could hear was the sound of metal on metal. He was flung about the cabin like a rag doll. If he hadn't been strapped in, with a helmet on his head, he would have died. The plane came to a halt at the edge of the deck, caught by the retaining cable.

Truck looked around, dazed by the force of the crash, with a heavy blow to his head. His ears rang while everything seemed blurry and out of focus. He could make out the deck crew racing toward his plane wielding firefighting gear. He began to come to his senses and realized that the last alarm he heard was the fire indicator. He needed to get out, but he couldn't risk ejecting now. The explosives used to blow off the canopy and the rocket engines of the ejector seat could far too easily injure the crew rushing to his aid. He pulled the manual release and pushed up hard with his right hand. With his left, he twisted the harness buckle and freed himself. As the canopy opened, he could hear the coxswain blaring and the address system: "Fire! Fire! Fire on the Flight Deck!"

Woozy from the impact, Truck tried to slide into an upright position, but a sharp pain seized his left ankle. He was forced to use his right leg alone to prop himself up. Gingerly he maneuvered himself and clumsily fell out of the cockpit into the arms of the crew decked out in red. His ankle felt like it had been stabbed by a molten hot knife. He couldn't help but scream in agony as they jostled him away from the burning crippled remains of his plane.

Not all the rescue crew had time to put on firefighting gear and were thus exposed to the heat from the last unspent fuel in his burning jet. Scarcely had the thought of being burned alive entered his mind, when a shower of salty spray drenched them all in a cooling shroud of mist. The searing pain in his ankle worsened as the deck crew ran toward the control tower yelling "CORPMAN!".

As they laid him inside the hatch it dawned on him that his weapons bay still held plenty of ordinance, which might yet explode. He had completely forgotten to jettison it before his emergency landing. He had been so engrossed with controlling his crippled plane he forgot basic procedure regarding the part of his aircraft that made it a fighter.

"Everyone get back!" Truck said through the pain. "Ordinance is still onboard!"

"It's okay, Truck. The fire's out. Nothing's going boom." The voice belonged to Chris Brown, one of the ordinance chiefs. Chris was a young Chief Petty Officer in charge of making sure all the missiles, bombs, and bullets were loaded onto each plane safely.

"Don't lie to me chief! No one dies because of my stupidity!" Truck said, wincing as the medics attempted to stabilize his ankle.

"No worries, sir. Let's get you to BAS[13] first." The chief turned to another red crewman and calmly motioned them to leave the deck.

The medics deftly put Truck's foot and leg into a splint, started an IV, and injected him with a mind-numbing pain killer. The next few minutes were a blur. He was hustled into the interior of the ship and moved through the narrow passageways to BAS two decks down. He was placed on a gurney and immediately surrounded by doctors and nurses. He lost track of all time in the blur of blood tests and scans. But soon a drug-induced fog took over, and he lost consciousness.

Truck was unsure how much time had passed since he could last remember anything. The room was dimly lit with the sickly pale light which penetrated the thick white curtains of the ship's BAS. The smell of antiseptic and jet fuel assaulted his nostrils. The hiss of oxygen flowing from his nasal cannula, and the steady drone of the ship's engines bid him return to sleep. His ankle felt as if it were crushed under a massive immoveable concrete block. He groaned as the pain intensified.

A nurse, dressed in blue fatigues, slid back the curtains and came to his bedside. Truck tried to place her face but couldn't really remember seeing her before. Perhaps it was the surgical mask and cap which obscured everything but her eyes, or maybe it was the fog in his head caused by the combination of trauma and medication. He couldn't be certain which was interfering with his mind.

Even through the mask she seemed to smile warmly as she looked at him. "How are you feeling, sir?"

"My ankle is killing me," Truck croaked. It almost didn't sound like his own voice.

13 Base Aid Station

She checked the dressing on his injured leg and turned just enough so that he could read the word "Rodgers" written in black letters on the name strip above her right breast. "Doctor Wilson has ordered some pain medicine for you, but the captain wants to talk to you. Do you think you can wait until after he's finished?"

"Yeah," Truck said. His voice seemed to creak like an old floorboard.

"It'll be just a minute," Nurse Rodgers said as she turned and walked out, closing the curtain behind her. Truck could hear her pick up the ship's internal com receiver. "Tell Captain McDonald he's awake." She walked back in and silently began checking his vitals and dressings.

Truck couldn't help wondering what was going on. He knew he would be in trouble for failing to follow procedure before the crash, but he managed to land a crippled aircraft without a catastrophic explosion. "What's going on?"

"He wants to talk to you," Nurse Rodgers replied. "I don't know why. I just know I can't give you anything for pain until you two have talked."

"Is he angry?"

"I wouldn't know. I didn't talk to him personally."

The curtains parted, and Captain McDonald entered. "Give us a minute, Lieutenant."

"Aye-aye, Sir," Nurse Rodgers left, closing the curtains behind her.

Captain McDonald sighed heavily. "You've put me in an awkward position, Truck. You want to tell me why you didn't eject?"

"I wanted to make sure the ALIS data was recovered, sir."

"So, you risked your life, and the lives of your fellow shipmates?"

"With all due respect sir, I don't know what we ran into. It wasn't a J-20 or J-36. Whatever it was, it's new. I couldn't see it at all on DAS, and EMLIA had no idea what to make of it. We need the ALIS data from my plane, sir."

"We had your telemetry."

"Sir, you know as well as I do, the telemetry doesn't send everything from ALIS. If I didn't bring it back, it would be at the bottom of the ocean. You know we're near the Mariana Trench. If it sank all the way down, there would be little chance we could ever recover it."

Captain McDonald scowled. "You crashed a quarter-billion-dollar plane into the deck of a two-billion-dollar ship. Risked the lives of everyone on-board with a full bay of ordinance. If we were lucky, you would have just taken out the seventy-three crew members who were on deck, or in the tower. That's hundreds of millions of dollars in taxpayer training we can't get back. As it is, I've got fifty feet of deck that needs repair before we can resume normal operations. Your plane is a pile of scrap. And the doctor says you've got to be evac'ed to The Mercy for surgery. Even then, he says you might never be clear to fly again. Luckily you were the only casualty. Do you honestly think you made a good call?"

The tongue lashing was more than he expected. It stung hard. Truck knew he had made a mistake but didn't realize it was this bad. "Sir, I did what I thought was necessary."

"And that justifies your actions?" His reply was rhetorical.

"If it helps defeat the enemy, then, yes. We are in a world war! We're fighting the Russians and the Chinese on two fronts and losing here in the Pacific. We've lost Guam, the Philippines, most of Japan, and everything west of Tinian. If they have a weapon that can penetrate the air picket, we can kiss our carriers goodbye!"

Captain McDonald sighed heavily. "If I gave a pass to every crewman who disregarded the safety of this ship and its crew, I wouldn't merit this command." The look of disgust on the captain's face said it all. "The problem is we're running low on pilots. Do you have any idea how many millions of taxpayer dollars are invested in your crippled body? I'll answer for you. About twenty-three at this point. Although, I can't recommend you for court-martial, I can't let you get away with the stunt you just pulled. Under Article-Fifteen, I'm demoting you in rank and pay to First Lieutenant. As of now, you're an O-two." Truck's jaw went slack with disbelief as Captain McDonald continued. "I'm also revoking your flight status for six months and transferring you to Pearl. Maybe some time as a desk jockey will teach you to respect the lives of others."

Captain McDonald stood up and parted the curtains to walk away. He stopped, hesitated for a moment, and turned one last time. "Truck, don't think I'm not impressed you crashed that plane the way you did. Chief Brown said your tail was shredded. He also found that the ALE-70 tether failed to extend correctly and was too close to you when the missile hit. I think if anyone else had been in that cockpit, they would have probably punched out. The ALIS intel would be at the bottom of the Pacific. But I must think about this ship and its crew. Their lives are in my hands, and I won't have anyone risk them on a hunch. I'm sorry it must be this way. You're a good pilot, and we need all the pilots we can if we're going to win this war. The Chinese alone have us outnumbered five to one. The European theater has split our forces in half, making it ten to one. We can't afford any losses. That includes you. Think about that."

Truck swallowed hard. He was angry at himself and hated the fact that he had disappointed The Captain. "Sir. Thank you for everything. I'm sorry I let you down."

Captain McDonald gave him a wan smile. "Don't thank me. I want you off my ship as soon as the chopper gets here to take you to The Mercy." He closed the curtain behind himself and gave one parting shot. "Don't come back. I don't want officers that can't follow orders."

Nurse Rodgers entered shortly, produced a syringe, and scrubbed a port on his IV tubing with an alcohol swab. "I can give you something for the pain now."

Truck nodded. he heard a familiar female voice come from just outside. "Where is that idiot?" Angel said boisterously, as she entered the recovery area from the adjoining corridor. She peered through the open curtain. "There you are, you nut! You go and crash your bird without even dumping ordinance, what were you thinking?"

"I wasn't," Truck replied.

Nurse Rodgers slowly depressed the plunger of the syringe, and the medicine flowed into his IV. The concoction quickly fogged his brain and reduced the crushing pain from his ankle. "Feeling any better now?" she asked.

Truck felt as if his thoughts were moving through peanut butter. He replied groggily, "I can still feel it, but it's not as bad."

"I'll leave you two alone then," Nurse Rodgers replied, trading places with Angel in the tight quarters of the recovery room. Before departing, she turned and addressed the two pilots. "You've got about five minutes before he'll be too loopy to remember your conversation. He needs his rest, so don't make me come back and kick you out."

"Roger that," Angel replied.

Truck looked up at his wingman. They had been paired together for three months and had known each other for more than a year of flight school and combat training. "Sorry, Angel. Didn't mean to leave you like this."

She dropped her usual snarky façade and held his hand. "You really scared me. When you came in – you just – started spinning – I thought for sure you would eject, but you didn't. You just kept trying to land that dumb plane." She swallowed hard as the tears visibly welled up in her eyes. "And – and when you –" She stopped, nearly choking as the tears began to flow. "When you hit the deck, I thought I lost you. You're my friend. I didn't want to lose you." She sniffed and quickly wiped tears from her eyes. "I promised myself I wouldn't do this."

Truck fought the urge to sleep as the medication swept over him. He squeezed Angel's hand. "It's alright. I won't remember this after I wake up, anyway. Besides I'll ship out soon."

Angel's jaw dropped. "You're – being – sent home?" Her words came out slowly and halting, as if she were mulling each one carefully before it escaped her throat.

Truck winced. The pain and disappointment of having to relay his dishonor was difficult. "Captain's benching me. I screwed up and now I've got to drive a desk for a while. Sorry, Angel."

Angel looked horrified. "You mean – you're leaving?"

It was getting difficult to keep his eyes open. Truck began slurring his words. They seemed to move across his tongue like syrup. "Sorry, my dear Angel. I guess you'll get someone better." His eyes closed involuntarily, and he fought to open them. He looked at her face. It was the first time he had ever seen her upset. It was almost as if she were panicking, but he didn't know why. "I – I'm falling asleep here. Talk to you later."

Angel seemed blurry now. Truck's eyes couldn't stay open anymore. The medication was winning. He felt her hand squeeze tightly as he succumbed to the miasma of sleep.

"I love you, Michael," he thought he heard her whisper in his ear. It must be a dream. He could still feel her warm breath moving though his ear as he faded into an otherwise dreamless sleep.

Chapter 2

MERCY

Truck was in a continual mental fog. His consciousness seemed to drift from periods of light haze to densely thick and impregnable. He remembered only snippets of moments whenever the miasma of his opioid induced mist needed refreshing to relieve the throbbing in his ankle. Nurse Rodgers visited him several times. A doctor, who he seemed to recall as being named Ikigami or something similar, had said that his ankle was so badly damaged it might necessitate amputation. He had described it as "a bag of broken teeth".

Truck never saw Captain McDonald or Angel again. He was moved to an MH-60 Seahawk on the deck of the Essex. He was the sole occupant as it lifted off and flew several hours above a placid Pacific. Most of the time Truck was heavily sedated. He awoke just before they landed on the deck of the USNS Mercy. It was a large ship. If it weren't for the brilliant white bulkheads and red crosses painted around the hull, it would look like a cargo vessel. It was the crown jewel of the Navy Medical Corps. The best doctors, nurses, medics, and equipment were in this floating hospital city.

They landed on the flight deck and waited until the main rotor had lost most of its momentum. Truck was still foggy, but the pain medication had worn off enough to remind him how badly his ankle was shattered. The door opened and he was greeted by a team of corpsmen led by a triage nurse who helped lift him onto a gurney.

The nurse was a thin, dark-skinned Latino man who looked as if he was probably a track star back in high school. He looked at a paper tag attached to Truck's sleeve. "Lieutenant Langford, I'm Petty Officer First Class Martinez. Welcome to The Mercy. How are you feeling?"

"My leg hurts." Truck replied wearily.

"I bet," PO Martinez said, looking at the notes from the onboard medic. "You're about due for another dose. My crew and I will get you to intake and we'll get you something for the pain once you're settled."

They moved quickly through a large hatch into the intake area, a crowded room with lots of stalls for the injured. Truck could see there were teams working on five or six other patients. The triage process was a blur of questions, poking, and prodding. They gave him an injection for pain, but it didn't seem like it helped much. After an hour, a man and a woman approached. Both wore scrubs, masks, and surgical hats.

The woman leaned over and spoke with an Asian accent. "Lieutenant Langford, I'm Captain Yamamomo, and I'll be your anesthesiologist. This is your surgeon, Major Tanaka. He does not speak English well, so I will translate for him."

"Hang on," Truck said somewhat confused. "Why does a Naval Officer need a translator?"

"We are both part of the JSDF. We're attached to this ship as part of the Japanese Government in Exile."

Truck recalled the briefings. Six months ago, China had invaded most of Japan, and seized much of the archipelago before the Japan Self Defense Force had managed to stop them from taking all but Hokkaido. The JSDF had to evacuate to the northern island to regroup. The United States integrated much of the JSDF's auxiliary personnel into the Pacific Fleet to aid in fighting the Chinese.

"Gomen'nasai,"[1] Truck replied in one of the few Japanese phrases he knew, to put them at ease. "I didn't mean to bring up bad memories."

"Lanford-chui wa nihongo o hanashimasu ka?"[2] Major Tanaka asked.

"Gomen,"[3] Truck replied, feeling he had given the wrong impression of his linguistic ability. "I don't know much Japanese. Sorry, didn't mean to give you the wrong impression."

"It okay," Major Tanaka replied in broken, but well-rehearsed, English. "English difficult, but I learn slow."

Truck smiled. They were both in the same spot, each of them trying to communicate, knowing very little of the other's language. Truck had tried to learn it, but Japanese was dissimilar to any language he had ever spoken.

---

1 "I'm sorry"
2 "You speak Japanese Lieutenant Langford?"
3 "Sorry"

Captain Yamamomo nodded to Major Tanaka, and he began to explain, through her, what he would be doing. Apparently, his ankle was so severely fractured they would have to remove most of the bone fragments. Then, using a robot, they would print new bones back into his leg and ankle. First, using an MRI[4] from his pre-deployment screening as a blueprint, they would print a scaffold using a mixture of collagen and nanohydroxyapatite. Then stem cells, collected aboard the Essex, would be injected, as part of a nutrient foam, into the scaffold. They would then expose the foam to a special light, to harden it into proto bone, following which they would splint the leg for a week to allow the scaffold time to completely cure. When the splint was removed, everything would feel and work as if the accident had never occurred. He would, of course, need to be evacuated to Pearl Harbor to undergo extensive physical therapy, but he could expect to be cleared to fly again in about four to six months.

"Do you understand what we will be doing?" Captain Yamamomo asked. Truck nodded. "Do you have any questions we have not answered?"

"This will be the same as my old leg?"

Captain Yamamomo smiled. "It will be sore for a week or two, as the swelling goes down. But after you're done with PT[5] you shouldn't notice any difference. Your leg will be identical to the old one, and just as strong. There won't be any pins, plates, or screws. It will be your bone, because we're using your stem cells. It will be your leg."

"It almost sounds too good to be true."

"Two or three years ago, this would not have been possible, but the technology has advanced. We can even replace amputated limbs."

"I don't understand how that's possible. How do you grow that much of a person back from just a few cells?"

"In some cases, we must wait until we've grown enough cells to make a repair, but once we have, it's easy. In your case, we won't need more than we currently have. So, it's good news. Your prognosis is not severe enough to warrant amputation prior to the rebuild."

Truck mulled that thought in his mind for a minute. Nurse Martinez returned and handed him a clipboard with a lot of fine print on it. At the bot-

4 Magnetic Resonance Imaging
5 Physical Therapy

tom was a highlighted signature line prefixed with a big X. "If you'll just sign right there, giving consent, we can get on with this." Truck quickly signed the form and handed it back.

"Ganbatte ne,"[6] Truck said, making a fist with his thumb sticking up as a sign of confidence.

"Take him to room four, please," Captain Yamamomo said politely.

"Yes, ma'am," nurse Martinez said as he motioned for a corpsman to assist him. They wheeled the gurney to a lift and then down several decks, to the surgical level. They were met by a team of orderlies and nurses in surgical garb. "This is where I turn you over to the surgical team." He pointed to another person dressed in blue scrubs. "This is Lieutenant Gorham. She'll take care of you while you're in surgery. I'll see you after you're all fixed up."

"Thanks, man," Truck said. "Catch you on the flip side."

Nurse Martinez patted him on the shoulder as the surgical crew wheeled him out of the lift. Lieutenant Gorham took his chart and tucked it under her arm. The four-person team pushed his gurney down the corridor to a door with a large "4" painted on it and pushed it though the opening.

The narrow room smelled like a mixture of hospital and diesel fuel, but the characteristic rocking of the ship was gone. The surgical rooms of the Mercy were gyroscopically stabilized to facilitate delicate surgical procedures. The room had sterile white walls, and a reddish hued floor. In the center of the room was an off-white machine with a large cylindrical tube in the center, just big enough to accommodate one person. Truck had seen similar machines before, when he had his pre-deployment exams.

This machine was slightly different. It looked like a large doughnut, but there were robotic arm-like appendages on either end. Captain Yamamomo and Major Tanaka were nowhere to be seen.

"Okay," Lieutenant Gorham said. "You've had a CT before, right?" Truck nodded. "Well, this is a Computerized Tomography Assisted Robotic Operating-theater, or a CTARO[7] for short. We'll get you on this table and then slide you into the tube. Don't worry about being claustrophobic or anything, you'll be unconscious the entire time."

---

6 "Good luck"
7 Pronounced sea-tar-oh

The team moved the gurney next to the long, thin table. It was on a track that would allow it to slide into the tube. They lifted the sheet he was laying on and carefully hoisted him onto the table. He was placed in such a way that his feet were close to the opening. Two of them gently removed the splint from around his leg and foot. There was a rush of pain from the bones shifting, and the pressure from a rush of blood into the surrounding tissues. His ankle began to throb, forcing Truck to gasp at the sudden discomfort.

Nurse Gorham took a syringe from a nearby metal tray and twisted it onto the IV port. "This is Fentanyl. It will help with pain during the operation." She slowly depressed the plunger, and his brain began to become fuzzy.

Captain Yamamomo entered the room with her hands in the air. Technicians placed a sterile surgical gown on her and then fitted her extended arms with gloves. "Lieutenant Gorham and I will be here in the room with you. I will be giving you something to relax."

Lieutenant Gorham took a bag of white liquid and threaded it through a small white box with a numerical display, before connecting the tubing to the IV port.

Truck chuckled to himself. "Will there be much pain when this is over?"

Captain Yamamomo looked as if she smiled through her surgical mask. "Pain always happens when you break your bones this badly, but it won't be too bad. Okay, Lieutenant, I'm ready." She patted his shoulder reassuringly. "Oyasumi Langford-chui."[8]

Lieutenant Gorham rolled her thumb on a dial on the IV tubing and hit a button on the machine. "When you wake up, you'll have a brand-new leg." She then took out another syringe and twisted it onto another port on his IV.

Truck's vision began to shrink around the edges, as if his peripheral vision were turning a grayish shade of white. He could hear Captain Yamamomo and Lieutenant Gorham talking in the background, but their voices sounded like they were traveling through water. A ringing sound steadily grew louder and louder, drowning out all the other sounds around him. Just as he lost consciousness, he felt the terrifying sensation of being unable to move. Then it was all black.

---

8 "Goodnight Lieutenant, Langford"

Truck couldn't tell how long he was out. He hadn't dreamt, or he couldn't remember dreaming. It had felt different than simply being asleep. He only knew he was awake when he heard a strange voice prodding him to breathe. It was like an annoying, cajoling, nagging insect that wouldn't go away. Wearily, Truck brushed it off.

"Michael, I need you to breathe." The voice said.

"I am breathing." Truck growled angrily.

"You need to breathe harder," the voice repeated, more forcefully this time. "Put this in your mouth and breathe as hard as you can!"

A plastic mouthpiece crammed between his lips. "No, breathe hard!" The voice commanded, sounding more like a woman now. Truck tried to push, but he was just so tired he didn't want to. "Push, push, push," the voice commanded.

"You push," Truck groggily replied. His voice sounded hoarse and almost alien.

"Listen here, you jarhead!" Her voice was more authoritative now. "I ordered you to breathe and you better breathe as hard as you can, or I'll PT[9] you so hard, your eyeballs will fall out! Now, BREATHE!"

It was a timbre in the tone of voice that activated something instinctually. Over a year of Marine Corps training had ingrained a response to any order issued in Command Voice. Truck took a deep breath and blew as hard as he could. He blew until he couldn't anymore.

"That's good Michael! Much better," The woman said in a more soothing voice. "You jarheads are all about orders being shouted. Can't even get the flight jocks to change."

Truck blinked in the bright light. It was slowly coming back to him, but his head was still fuzzy. He remembered going into the operating room, but this wasn't it. There were curtains on both sides of the room. He was being pushed on a gurney toward one of the open stalls. His head was spinning, his eyes were blurry, his leg throbbed, and his throat was sore. He didn't recognize anyone from the team pushing his stretcher. A very dark-skinned woman was standing over him. She placed a snorkel-looking tube on his chest and looked at him.

9 Physical Training

"Who are you?" Truck croaked. "Where am I?"

"I'm Ensign Washington, and you're in recovery." She had a strange accent, but he couldn't place it. "You're still coming out of the anesthesia, so you're not completely awake yet. You'll be axing me this question again in five minutes, so let's just get it out the way, so you can axe it again."

"How long have I been out?"

Ensign Washington looked at the clipboard and then her watch. "Y'all were in surgery for four hours, and stage one recovery for about an hour or so, it took a while for the drugs to wear off." She chuckled to herself. "Can't have y'all flopping around inside the OR."[10]

"Why is my throat sore?" Truck asked, trying to clear the croaking sound of his vocal cords.

"We had to put a tube down your throat so you could breathe during the procedure." Ensign Washington said as she locked the gurney wheels with her foot. "You're awake enough for water. It might help soothe things a bit."

"Yes, please." Truck said, grateful for something cool and wet. She handed him a small cup of ice water with a bendable straw to make it easier to drink lying down. He took several long pulls on the cool liquid. He expected the typical unpalatable metallic taste of ship processed and stored sea water. He was surprised by the complete absence of any trace of contamination. "Is this bottled?"

Ensign Washington laughed, an infectious, joyful laugh, that betrayed her innate sense of humor. She began transferring his bio-sensor cables to the overhead monitor. "I hear that all the time. Nah, we spoiled here on the Mercy. All the water is filtered – like – a lot. Can't have anything that might throw off the medication we give y'all. Yes sir, the best tasting water in the fleet is on the Mercy. Best tasting food, too. It's almost like home." She sighed. "How's your pain?"

Truck had to think about that. He couldn't really feel much of his leg. He could sense it was there, but it felt as if his foot was just beyond the stage of pins and needles. "It doesn't really hurt, but it's kind of numb, like it's asleep."

"That's normal. Major Tanaka uses a block. It helps with post-op pain. Rebuilding bone is traumatic."

10 Operating Room

Captain Yamamomo and Major Tanaka came into the curtained area, and the Major began poking Truck's foot. He muttered something to the captain, which Truck couldn't quite overhear.

"Can you feel him touching you?" Captain Yamamomo asked.

"I can, but it's like my foot's asleep," Truck felt a dull sensation that registered as pain on the sole of his foot. "Ow!" Instinctively, he tried to jerk his foot, but found it immobilized by a brace he hadn't noticed before. Truck looked at Major Tanaka and saw him place a cap on a sharp looking instrument he had been using. Truck glared.

"What did that feel like?" Captain Yamamomo asked.

"Like a needle got jabbed in the bottom of my foot, and I couldn't move it away." Truck said crossly.

"Is good thing," Major Tanaka replied in his best attempt at English. "You gain feeling in some hour."

It must be hard to communicate with patients who don't speak your language, Truck thought. He imagined it must be frustrating to be exceptionally smart but lack the language skills to effectively relay what you've done. "Arigato, Kaisho."[11]

Captain Yamamomo smiled politely. "You should say 'Sensei' or 'Isha'.[12] Kaisho is not the right word."

Truck chuckled. "I guess you can't blame me for trying."

"I appreciate that you to try," Captain Yamamomo said gently. "Most Americans cannot speak anything but English, but we are required to learn it at an early age. Most find it too difficult. There are only twelve from my class that gained any fluency." She gave a pained smile, as if remembering a happier time that had been shattered by the painful loss of her homeland. "Shōganai,"[13] She sighed, her voice trailing off before she returned to the examination. "Try to move your toes." She held up her hand and wiggled her fingers. "Like this."

Truck looked earnestly at his braced and bandaged foot. He could barely make out his toes. He pushed the blankets to gain a better view and concen-

11 "Thank you, (as intended: "captain." In reality: "admiral.")"
12 Sensei meaning teacher or master but can refer to doctors as an honorific. Isha is the proper word for doctor.
13 "It can't be helped."

trated on wiggling his swollen pedal digits. With some effort, he was finally able to coax them to move slightly. Both doctors smiled encouragingly.

"Subarashī!"[14] Major Tanaka exclaimed as he held up a thumb of approval. "Good. You do good."

"That is a great sign," Captain Yamamomo said. "It means your nerves are not so damaged. You should recover just fine."

"But I'm not going to be running marathons anytime soon," Truck replied.

"No," Captain Yamamomo replied. "No marathons…yet."

"So, what now?"

"You still need to recover from the anesthesia, and then you will be transferred to the Intermediate Ward until you're ready for evac to Pearl Harbor. We'll stop in to check on you before you leave, but the nurses and technicians will handle your care from here."

"I appreciate all you've done for me," Truck said, genuinely grateful for having his leg repaired without the use of metal hardware. "I can't imagine what it would be like to have a leg full of pins and screws."

"This will feel like nothing ever happened in a few weeks." Captain Yamamomo reassured him. "If you need anything ask the nurses or techs. We'll talk to you again soon." She gave him a sympathetic pat on the arm, and the two doctors left, closing the curtains behind them.

Ensign Washington gave Truck a strange look. "Look at you - speaking Japanese."

"I don't speak it – really," Truck admitted. "Oh, sure, I know a few words, but that's it. I don't even think I know how to ask "where's the head" – oh – and speaking of. Where is it?"

Ensign Washington chuckled and opened a cabinet above his head. "Right here, sir," she said, handing him a metal urinal. He took it and gave a quizzical look. "Do y'all have to go number two?"

"Umm – no – not right now."

"Well," She replied wryly. "When y'all do, let us know, and we'll get you a bedpan." She handed him a plunger button on a long cord. "Just press

14 "Wonderful!"

that, and one of us will be right there. I'd love to stay and chat, but I've got another patient."

"I'm fine," Truck replied. "I got my water and a hand-held head. Can't make a Marine happier."

Ensign Washington chuckled as she eyed him up and down. "A pilot who's funny and handsome. I'll need to keep my eye on you."

"If I wasn't tied to this bed," Truck replied wryly.

Ensign Washington shook her head, laughed quietly to herself, and left the room. She pulled the curtain shut behind her with a swift motion punctuated by a clack as the two curtains met.

Truck was alone for the first time since he had been in the aid station of the Essex. He couldn't help but feel vulnerable. He really wished he could be home right now with his family. He didn't have anyone he could talk to. Angel, and the rest of his flight group, were all back on the Essex. His friends from Annapolis, and Officer Training were all scattered around the world. He was alone here.

If he were home, in Utah, his father, Doctor David Langford, as a respected Pediatric Orthopedic surgeon, would probably have insisted on helping care for his injured son. His mother, Sandra, would have never left his bedside. His younger siblings, Rachel, Steve, and Megan would have certainly visited him.

Wishing wasn't helping. They were literally on the other side of the world, completely oblivious to his injuries. Truck struggled to put the thought out of his mind. He was a grown man, and a Marine at that. Allowing sentiment to cloud his mind was pointless.

He did his best to make himself comfortable but found there was only one position he could find which didn't hurt his back. He sat there for a while, dazed by the medication and hypnotic sound of the monitors of the patients surrounding him. The occasional groan of a wounded patient broke the monotony, but otherwise the room was an uncomfortable and sterile environment that lulled its victims into submission with the soporific sedatives being dispensed.

Truck had recovered from the anesthesia but was still tired enough to doze. Nevertheless, it was a restless sleep. Every few minutes, one of the members of Ensign Washington's team entered his room made of curtains to check his vital signs and pain. After a couple of hours, Ensign Washington and three others came in. "It's time to get you to Intermediate."

"I'm not staying here?"

"This is Recovery," Ensign Washington replied as she unlocked the gurney and unplugged the cords and tubes connecting him to the bulkhead. "We can't take care of you forever, flyboy."

As soon as he was disconnected, the corpsmen pushed the gurney out of the curtained area to the elevator. Once inside, Ensign Washington patted his hand. "I've called up to Intermediate already, and they're expecting you. Seaman Jones and Seaman Richards will take you up."

"Thanks Ensign," Truck replied. "I appreciate—".

Truck was interrupted by the coxswain. "General Quarters! General Quarters! General Quarters! All patients to the Flight Deck! Repeat, all patients to the Flight Deck!"

"What the —" Truck exclaimed.

"Get him out of here, then double time back!" Ensign Washington ordered. "We got more to get out!"

The elevator doors closed, and the carriage swiftly moved, the two seamen visibly concerned. "What's going on?" Truck demanded.

"You know as much as we do, sir." Seaman Jones replied.

"Does this happen often?"

"No, sir! This is a first."

The doors opened and the two corpsmen rushed the gurney out towards a V-22 Osprey. Truck could smell the jet fuel as the engines began to whine to life. He could see the deck and flight crew scrambling to get the aircraft ready to depart. Truck turned around and saw the elevators and hatches unloading more patients. Some were walking, some were hobbling on crutches, there were a few on gurneys. All were rushing toward the aircraft that took up a good portion of the Flight Deck. The small hangar on the port side at the aft of the deck was a flurry of activity. Both hatches were opened, with two MH-60 helicopters being pulled outside. An officer was moving about the deck shouting orders. Truck couldn't hear everything he was saying, but he caught one thing before being wheeled into the Osprey's gaping loading ramp, "We've got incoming!"

Truck was dumbfounded. The Mercy was a hospital ship. It was a war crime to attack it. Why would the Mercy be attacked?

"Can you sit, sir?" Seaman Richards asked.

Truck nodded. "Probably."

"Good," Seaman Richards replied. "We got a lot of people on this boat and this Osprey only holds thirty-two if we cram you in like sardines."

The two corpsmen lowered him onto the floor near the cockpit. "Remember to protect that leg, sir." Seaman Jones said. "It's brand-new."

"I'll do my best," Truck replied.

The two seamen unceremoniously turned and hurried the gurney off the aircraft. More patients began to file in. A blonde woman in a hospital gown came in and plopped down next to him. She was slender, with her hair cut short, the way most female aviators styled their hair. Most kept it short, because it was easier to wear under a helmet. Her shocking clear blue eyes were a stark contrast to the dim interior of the Osprey. He didn't have much time to soak in her beauty before he was brought back to the reality of the situation.

"You any idea what's going on?" she asked.

"Something about incoming fire, but I don't know for sure." Truck replied.

Her jaw dropped. She looked around, leaned in, and whispered concerned into Truck's ear. "But this is a hospital ship."

"They aren't supposed to be targeted, but it wouldn't be a first in war." Truck said soberly. He recalled his high school history teacher mentioning the United States sinking of a Japanese hospital ship during World War II.

By the time the rotors had spun up, the Osprey was nearly full of patients. Several doctors, nurses, and medics were hustled onboard, and the hatch began to close. Truck heard someone yell, "We got to get off this deck NOW!"

The engines screamed as they were pushed to full power. There was a sickening sense of increased gravity as the Osprey executed a combat take off. They rose quickly, rotated, and moved away from the flight deck of the Mercy. Truck looked back through the slowly closing door at the swiftly receding ship. He could see dozens of patients and crew lining the deck, awaiting their turn to board the Seahawks. Both helicopters had begun spooling up their rotors.

The Osprey dove low, skimming the waves, to gain speed and lower its radar profile. Just before the door shut, there was a bright orange flash and an audible crack and a buzz in his head. For a second Truck thought he could see through the skin of the aircraft. It was like lightning when it strikes close by. The hatch shut. Even with the door closed, the engine noise, and the simultaneous exclamation of the people onboard, everyone heard the explosion that followed.

Truck knew what had happened. An anti-ship missile, probably a DF-ZF, hit the Mercy. Since his days at Annapolis, he had feared China's hypersonic missile. Everyone did.

"What the –", exclaimed the crew chief, quicky flinching away from the flash after looking out his observation port. His helmet was lit up by a white light, then a darkness that defied description. It was unlike anything Truck had seen before. It was thick darkness and blinding light at the same time. The crew chief held up his hand to instinctively block out the intense light. He went pale, slack-jawed in obvious shock.

"What happened?" Another nearby patient asked.

It took a moment for him to process what he had just witnessed. "I couldn't say for sure." The crew chief replied. "But I think the whole ship is — just — gone."

The blonde woman sitting next to Truck yelled. "What do you mean gone?"

"HANG ON!" the crew chief shouted as he grabbed a hand ring. It was all the warning they got.

There was a sinking in everyone's stomach as the Osprey executed a maximum rate climb. People began screaming as they clutched anything they could to stabilize themselves. The aircraft pitched up at a sickening angle. Those unlucky enough not to find a handhold were thrown mercilessly toward the rear hatch. The airframe began to shake violently as a shockwave struck. For the second time in less than a week, Truck was terrified in an aircraft.

Time seemed to expand as the Osprey pilots struggled to regain control of the aircraft. Truck could feel the extreme changes in speed, attitude, and altitude as the Osprey lurched through the aftermath of the destruction of the Mercy. The severe turbulence brought on by the shockwave was something he had never experienced before. During the radical maneuver, Truck's leg was struck several times by bodies and parts of the aircraft which encountered his splinted leg. He screamed in pain, but it was lost in the cacophony of screams and anguish that resounded throughout the cabin.

It seemed like an eternity had passed before the wild ride finally stopped, but Truck surmised that it had only been a matter of seconds. Once the aircraft leveled off, the only sounds inside the Osprey were those of moaning and a single woman still screaming hysterically. Truck looked over and recognized Captain Yamamomo as the terrified passenger. Major Tanaka was earnestly trying to calm her with little success. Truck looked around. He didn't recognize anyone else.

"What just happened?" the blonde patient next to Truck demanded.

"Shock wave turbulence," Truck replied.

"Really?" she said, sarcasm heavy in her voice. "I'd never had known if you hadn't told me, Captain Obvious! I was asking the chief!"

"How should I know?" The chief yelled.

"You were looking out the window!" She snapped.

"Listen, sister!" The chief growled. "I don't answer to you! You're just a screaming witch in my way! Now sit down, or I'll knock you there!"

"I'm Lieutenant Commander Bright," She said crossly, "I'm your superior officer, and you WILL answer me!"

"With all due respect, Lieutenant Commander," The chief said condescendingly, "You're not in uniform. I don't know you. You're NOT my superior. Colonel Wallace is. He's currently the one piloting this aircraft. The last time I checked, a Marine Colonel outranks a Lieutenant Commander. Since you're NOT in command, I suggest you sit your bony backside down!"

The Lieutenant Commander scowled at the chief. "Can I talk to the Colonel?"

"I told you once, I won't tell you again. SIT DOWN and SHUT IT or I will MAKE you, Sir! You can talk if he has time."

"Fine!" She said briskly.

"Chief," Truck said, raising his hand. "That might have been a tactical nuke. Do you have a rad reading?"

"Good question, sir," the chief replied. He then keyed his headset, "Colonel, did that ordinance set off any alarm?" There was a brief pause. "Reading of forty-three rem[15] in the cabin, sir. We'll get sick, but probably not die."

"Where are we headed?" Truck asked.

"The plan was to evac to the Essex, but we aren't able to raise them."

"That's my ship." Truck replied. "I might be able to help."

The chief took off his headset and handed it to Truck. He put the headset on and pushed the talk button. "Colonel Wallace, this is Major Langford of the Essex. I heard you are having problems raising them." He felt somewhat bad about lying about his rank, but he was so used to saying Major that it had slipped out before he could correct himself. He didn't think anyone would really mind at this point anyway.

"Major," Colonel Wallace replied. "I've been trying on guard, but I'm not getting anything. I'm not worried, but if you know a faster way, please let me know."

"Try accessing the picket relay." Truck waited as the Colonel changed his radio frequency and listened as he called for the Essex.

"Essex, through picket relay, this is Angelflight Ghost-two, respond on picket guard."

An androgynous voice responded. "Angelflight Ghost-Two, Sentry Rook-One, Fortress unable to reply. No signal from Fortress."

Truck's blood froze. He didn't know what could have happened to the Essex, but negative contact with the air picket was not a good sign.

Colonel Wallace continued. "Sentry Rook-One, Angelflight Ghost-two, report Fortress status."

---

15 Rem is measure of exposure to ionizing radiation. While this isn't a lethal dose, it would be considered significant.

"Angelflight Ghost-two, Sentry-Rook has lost link with Fortress. No radar contact with Fortress group. Sentry-Rook has been ordered to Castle."

"Sentry, Angelflight Ghost-two, report location of Knight."

"Angelflight Ghost-two, Sentry, negative contact with Knight."

"Sentry, Angelflight Ghost-two, direct link to Castle, authorization beta-one-seven-niner."

"Angelflight Ghost-two, Sentry, direct link enabled. Go ahead for Castle."

"Castle, Castle, Angelflight Ghost-two, over."

A decidedly female voice replied. "Angelflight Ghost-two this is Castle, what is your request?"

Truck was relieved there was an actual human that replied.

"Castle, what's going on?" Colonel Wallace asked bluntly. "Angelflight Ghost-two was headed for Fortress Essex but have lost contact. Using Fortress Sentry-Rook for uplink patch. What is the sitrep?"

"Angelflight Ghost-two, Castle, authenticate red-four."

Colonel Wallace tapped his co-pilot's shoulder and pointed at a red binder. The junior officer retrieved it and opened to a red page with black writing on it. "Authenticate, Alpha-Lima-Lima-India-Two-Sierra-Oscar-Sierra-Three-Tango."

"Authentication confirmed Angelflight Ghost-two. What can I help you with?"

Colonel Wallace keyed the mic. "Castle, this is Colonel Wallace Wing Commander of the one-six-four, we need a place to land. Where's the Essex?"

"I'm sorry Colonel, but the Essex and Anchorage task force have been destroyed. There are no friendlies in your area."

It felt like a punch to the gut. Truck thought of everyone he knew on the Essex. Captain McDonald, Angel, his deck crew, all gone. He, alone, had survived because of his stupid leg. The emotional blow was almost more than he could bear.

The Osprey immediately banked to the east and began to climb. "Castle, Angelflight Ghost-two, roger that. Please note that the Mercy was also destroyed. We currently have the only known survivors. We need a tanker rendezvous. I have three-six souls on-board and two hours of fuel including emergency."

"Roger, Angelflight Ghost-two, I'll see what I can do. Stay this frequency and I'll get back to you."

Truck took the headset off and handed it back to the chief and buried his face in his hands. He had barely noticed the faces staring at him anxiously awaiting news of what was happening. He was overwhelmed by his own grief, and the guilt of his survival. He couldn't help but cry, despite his surroundings. He was brought back by Lieutenant Commander Bright shaking his arm.

"What happened?" she asked.

"It's gone," he whispered. "The entire Essex task force is gone. There're no friendly units within our flight range, and no bases to land."

"I don't understand." She seemed unable to process the information.

Truck turned on her. He could feel the anger rising in his face. He was furious that she made him say it out loud, when all he wanted to do was mourn his comrades in arms. "I mean all of Expeditionary Strike Group Three has been wiped out!"

Chapter 3

DEATH

It was the longest twelve-hour flight Truck had ever known. The Osprey had refueled four times with the help of an MQ-25 drone. Dr Yamamomo and Dr Tanaka were the only two doctors on the flight. They had their hands full with the number of patients who had suffered broken bones, burns, radiation sickness, and other injuries during the aftermath of the explosion. Dr Yamamomo relayed Dr Tanaka's opinion that his leg appeared to be bruised but was not injured any further.

When they landed at Pearl Harbor, it was well past midnight. The lights of Honolulu were welcoming, but Joint Base Hickam was shrouded in darkness. Truck surmised they were exercising light discipline. Everyone was unloaded and shuttled by bus to the hospital at Hickam. Each of the patients was examined by the base staff. The X-rays of Truck's leg showed it hadn't been reinjured during the evacuation. Dr Tanaka said it was a miracle that the new bone hadn't suffered any damage. Truck was taken to a private room where he could sleep.

He didn't know how long he had been out before he was awakened by an Air Force Captain shaking his shoulder. "Major Langford?"

"That's me." Truck replied instinctively.

"I'm Captain Tucker. I'm here to ask you a few questions."

Truck looked at the man with bleary eyes. He was still waking up from a deep sleep. He sighed at the thought of being debriefed by some 'Chair-Farce'[1] lacky. "Can't this wait? Preferably until after I'm dead?" Truck's humor seemed lost on the captain.

"Sir, I think you're misunderstanding my purpose here." Captain Tucker replied in a serious tone. "I've been directed to ask you a couple serious questions. I would appreciate you not trying to joke at a time like this."

Truck grunted. "Listen, Captain, I've just spent the longest, worst, most agonizing two days of my life, having friends die, my leg rebuilt, and a flight

---

1 A pejorative term for Air Force personnel by members of the other armed forces.

I never want to repeat. A little humor is about all I have left, so you'll excuse my using comedy as a coping mechanism."

"Major, I know what you've gone through. You may not know this, but the Seventh, Third, and Fifth fleets have all suffered heavy losses. In response, COMSUBPAC[2] has preemptively decimated the Russian Pacific fleet and been actively hunting the Chinese. The Air Force has also nuked the Chinese Navy and Air bases in the South China Sea. Currently we know of three separate PLAN[3] fleets in the Sea of Japan and the South Pacific. Our Naval forces are still trying to regroup. The only cohesive force right now are our subs." He exhaled a long sigh. "But I'm not here to brief you on current events. I have strict orders to ask you two questions."

"Okay." Truck replied.

"One: Are you willing to leave your combat role in order to pursue a highly dangerous but important mission?"

"You have to ask?"

"A yes or no please."

"Yes."

"I preface this next question with a warning: If you say anything to anyone about my presence here, the questions I've asked you, or the project, you WILL wind up in a court-martial and then a firing squad. Have I made the gravity of the situation abundantly clear?"

"Are you threatening me?" Truck asked.

"No, Sir," Captain Tucker replied. "I am simply stating the facts. This project is beyond Top Secret. It's above my pay grade, and yours. I have no idea what it is. I was directed to ask you these specific questions and explain the consequences for violating secrecy."

"Fair enough," Truck replied. "I have Top Secret Clearance. I'm vetted and trustworthy. What's the question?"

"Are you willing to give up your life, all your familial attachments, all that defines you as Major Michael Langford to serve your country?"

2 Submarine Command Pacific
3 Peoples Liberation Army Navy

"To clarify," Truck said, ticking his head in a curious manner. "I don't have to actually die for this project, do I?"

"Not in the literal sense." Captain Tucker replied. "But you would be declared KIA.[4] The Pentagon would say you were killed aboard the Mercy when it was sunk yesterday. Your family would receive your full death benefit, as well as the additional benefit of your salary for the rest of their lives. The caveat is that you can't contact them again. Ever. They could never know that you're alive, nor anything about the work you would be doing. As far as the world knows, you would be dead. Your body would be nearly nine thousand feet below the surface with the rest of the Mercy."

Truck scowled. "You're asking me to give up everything? Make my family suffer thinking I'm dead? What could possibly warrant all that?"

Captain Tucker shrugged. "That I don't know, Sir. All I know is that you have ten minutes to think about it. If you say yes, you have twenty minutes to get on a plane. Oh, and don't worry about clothes," pointing to his hospital gown. "The general has you covered."

Five minutes later he was getting into a police Humvee[5] with Lieutenant Commander Bright, dressed in a hospital gown. "Never thought I would see you again." Truck said jokingly.

"I would caution you not to say anything until you're both on the plane, Sirs." Captain Tucker said. "I remind you that no one is cleared except us."

"Yes, Captain," she said, in an obviously annoyed tone. "We're not stupid."

"I understand." Captain Tucker said. "I just don't want to have to report anything negative." He tapped the driver on the shoulder. "Get us there fast!"

The MP[6] hit the lights and siren and raced away from the hospital. Normally, speeds within military bases are kept to a minimum. This makes getting around a base somewhat tedious, especially a sprawling joint base like Hickam. But it only took ten minutes to get to the checkpoint before getting to the ramp. The MP stopped, checked the tires for foreign objects and then sped toward a C-37B that was being refueled.

---

4 Killed in Action
5 High Mobility Multipurpose Wheeled Vehicle
6 Military Police

Truck knew the military had small versions of the Gulfstream 550 bu had never actually seen one. It was white and blue, with the words "The United States of America" written on the side. They were reserved for VIP transport only, restricted to upper brass at the Pentagon, State Department or The White House. Truck felt sure he would find some four- or five-star general waiting inside.

As the Humvee pulled up to the waiting plane, Captain Tucker shook both of their hands. "I have no idea what you guys are up to but based on the transport I would say you're going to do some pretty important work."

"You aren't coming with us?" she asked with an air of surprise.

"No, Sir, I work for PACCOM.[7] I'm just the liaison officer."

"Well, Captain," Truck said, getting out of the Humvee with the help of the driver. "It was good to meet you."

Captain Tucker dug into the back of the Humvee and got out a pair of crutches. He handed them to Truck. "I wish it was under better circumstances."

Truck hobbled over to the jet's stairs. He felt that it would be better if he went up the stairs first. Commander Bright was still in a hospital gown, and despite it reaching down to her knees, he didn't wish to be accused of gawking. He wasn't used to wielding around crutches or the bulky brace on his leg. So, he went up backwards, using his good foot to push himself up while sitting on the stairs. It was undignified, but practical.

Once inside the cabin, a female Space Force Captain helped him hobble over to a leather captain's chair. Truck looked around the cabin. It was brightly lit with soft cream-colored leather seating, luxurious beige carpet, and inlaid burl wood accents. A two-star Space Force general was seated at a chair and a small table near the back of the cabin. Truck immediately struggled back onto his feet.

"As you were Major." The general's order came as a relief to Truck. His last round of pain pills had started to wear off, and his leg was starting to throb again. "Have a seat, Lieutenant Commander. I'm Major General Thomas Harris, and this is Captain Stevens. We'll be your host and interviewer for this flight. Even though it lasts about five and a half hours, we won't have a lot of time to accomplish everything we need to before we land."

7 Pacific Command

General Harris was a large muscular man with medium brown skin. He had a deep voice with the hint of a British accent, but Truck couldn't tell for sure. He looked as if he would easily play running back for a professional football team. But, somehow, the mantle of authority seemed to fit his outward appearance better than it could for any athlete.

Lieutenant Commander Bright raised her hand. "If I may speak freely, Sir, what exactly do you want with us?"

The captain closed the outer hatch and rapped on the cockpit door. The engines spooled up and the plane began to pressurize to eight thousand feet in preparation for take-off.

"I am unable to tell you right now." General Harris replied. "You both still have an interview to pass and some documents to sign. After we're airborne, you can change in the bedroom. One at a time. We'll start with Commander Bright. While you get some rest, Major. If you both pass the interview process, and sign the paperwork, then we can discuss your mission. The mission itself, its base of operations, and all related information is classified 'Need to Know'. Until I personally grant clearance, you can't be trusted. Now, put your seatbelts on. We're about to take off."

In ten minutes, the plane had climbed to cruising altitude. Captain Stevens handed them both grey flight suits, and Lieutenant Commander Bright went into the bedroom to change.

"You must have a million questions, Major." General Harris said, eyeing Truck carefully.

"Anyone who wouldn't be curious about a top-secret mission, and veiled threats of execution would be a fool. I must say you could have done without all the cloak and dagger."

General Harris harrumphed. "Son, you have no idea how sensitive this matter is. I'll forgive the lack of OPSEC[8] right now. Rest assured, the secrecy on this project is greater than the fabled Manhattan Project, and it's of far greater importance."

"My apologies, General," Truck said contritely. "I'm not trying to overstep my bounds. I'm just trying to get my bearings here. In the past two days I've lost my plane, my ship, my crew, nearly my foot, and now my friends and family. Honestly, what could possibly compensate for that much loss?"

8 Operational Security

"I know this has been hard, Major. It's been difficult to process. Unfortunately, it's not going to get any easier. We're not just trying to save the United States. We're trying to salvage what's left of this planet. The very existence of mankind is at stake."

"How so?"

"I don't know if you're aware of this, but for the second time in world history, nuclear weapons have been used in combat."

"Captain Tucker had mentioned that."

"Then you must realize that it isn't going to stop there. This war is rapidly spiraling out of control. The only reason the Chinese and the Russians haven't retaliated is that the President has informed them we are targeting their major cities with everything we have. The United States has classified hypersonic missiles as weapons of mass destruction. What complicates that is the new nukes the Chinese have begun using."

"You mean the ones that destroyed the Mercy."

"Yes," General Harris said bluntly. "The DH–31 Dong Feng hypersonic quantum tactical nuke. Something you've seen firsthand. It's a warhead design which they stole from Oak Ridge almost two years ago. It's the reason I'm here. The reason we've been forced to push the project's timetable ahead. The reason we need you."

The door to the bedroom opened and Lieutenant Commander Bright stepped into the main cabin. "Why us?" The confusion on her face evidence that she hadn't overheard the conversation.

"I'm sorry?" The general's reply was almost rhetorical.

"Why do you need the Major and me – specifically?" she said, sitting down on the chair next to Truck. "As far as I know, the Major and I aren't test pilots. So, why us?"

General Harris eyed them very carefully. He had a very serious gaze that seemed to cut through everything. "Frankly, you're both pilots. You're both easily declared dead. You're both of good character, and you both came available at the right time. I'll answer all your questions after the interviews are finished. Major, go change while I interview Lieutenant Commander Bright. There's a bed, TV, and some books for you to read after you've changed. We'll come get you when it's time."

Truck grabbed his crutches and hobbled into the small bedroom. Captain Stevens pointed to a flight suit, underwear, and socks on a small dresser. She closed the door, and he heard a loud click. He was locked in the small bedroom and essentially alone for the first time in months. He could now distinctly hear white noise generators. Even the steady rush of wind and whine of the plane in flight was gone. It was as if he were in a quiet room in the middle of nowhere. The only thing that reminded him he was even in flight was the steady vibration of the deck plates and the occasional vertical movement caused by turbulence.

The bedroom had two doors. One led to the main cabin, and the other a small, yet elegant, washroom. Much like the main cabin, the room was appointed in cream with burl wood accents. The small dresser sported highly polished wood with brass handles. A small television sat directly above the dresser with a remote fastened to the edge. The bed looked inviting, and was ready to be slept in. The crisp white sheets contrasted with a thick dark blue blanket bearing and embroidered silver Air Force emblem. Two thick pillows begged him to rest.

Truck placed his crutches on the floor and balanced himself carefully as he removed his hospital gown and brace. He gingerly dressed, trying hard not to jostle his leg. He noticed the flight suit had his name and rank patches affixed. He put his brace on, used the washroom, and then lay down on the bed. He fumbled around and found a light switch near his head. Once the lights were out, it didn't take any time for him to fall asleep.

The next thing Truck knew, Captain Stevens was shaking him awake. "It's time, Sir."

Blearily, Truck sat up. His leg was sore and began to throb. "You have anything for pain?"

"Just some generic pain med from the kit is all."

"I guess that will have to do for now." He replied as he felt around for his crutches before clumsily moving into the main cabin. "How long have I been out?"

"About an hour." General Harris replied, pointing to the chair Lieutenant Commander Bright occupied. "Have a seat."

She stood up and moved out of Truck's way. She looked shaken but smiled anyway. "You're in the hot seat now."

"Get some rest, Rachel." General Harris said. "We'll come get you after he's done."

Truck took note that the general had referred to the Lieutenant Commander by her first name. This was different than before. Truck hobbled into position and sat down into the chair. It was soft and comfortable. An odd choice of seating for a high stress interview. He watched as Rachel went into the bedroom. She turned, gave him an odd look, and then shut the door. Captain Stevens then clicked the latch into the locked position. Truck had no time to mull things over.

General Harris pulled out a thick file from an attaché case and placed it heavily on the table in front of him. He opened it and took out a hefty-looking pen. "Major Michael David Langford – actually I should say Lieutenant Langford – yes?"

"I suppose that's correct."

"You were given an Article Fifteen after your last mission."

"Yes, Sir."

"You failed to drop your ordinance before you crashed your F-35. You disobeyed a direct order to eject from said aircraft, and you were insubordinate to your commanding officer."

"Yes, Sir."

"You graduated from Annapolis, toward the upper quarter of your class, and given a commission in the Marines. You trained as an F-35 pilot, with the call sign 'Truck', and deployed after ACFT[9] in Pensacola. You served a full year on the Carl Vinson and were then transferred to the Essex where you served for the past six months."

"Yes, Sir."

"Up until that last mission you advanced nicely, and your record has been spotless."

"Yes, Sir."

"As far as I'm concerned, Major Michael 'Truck' Langford is dead. The Article Fifteen never happened. You will be listed as KIA, so from now on, you will be just 'Michael Langford'."

9 Air Combat Flight Training

"So, I'm no longer in the Corps?" Michael asked dumbfounded.

"Yes, and no." General Harris replied. "You're still a major, but 'Truck' is dead. That active callsign is history."

"I see. Why am I not demoted?"

"I have a lot of pull at the Pentagon. I also outrank Captain McDonald, and as far as I'm concerned, if you're going to be giving up your life, you should be remembered as an officer worthy of your destiny."

"And what is that destiny?" Michael asked, never having thought of himself as a destiny kind of person.

"You're going to save the world, IF, you answer my questions to my satisfaction."

"And, if I don't?"

"I'll have no choice." General Harris said menacingly. "I'll have you court-martialed, you'll be dishonorably discharged, and you'll go back to your family. You'll be a disgrace to the Marine Corps. You will also be expected to keep our interaction secret for the rest of your, regardless. If you say anything, you'll be tried and executed for treason."

Michael's eyebrows rose. "Wow, tough call. It's not like the deck is stacked against me."

"I know it doesn't seem fair, but that's the way it goes. Now, I just have a few questions." General Harris said, taking out of sheet of paper. "Are your religious?"

"Yes."

"It says here you're from Utah. Are you one of those Mormons?"

Michael didn't like the use of an anachronistic pejorative for his religion, but he knew he was addressing a staff officer, so he had to be careful not to show his irritation. "If you're asking if I'm a member of The Church of Jesus Christ of Latter-day Saints, then yes. I am. Why do you ask?"

"I'm just interested in your belief in deity. A belief in God is virtually essential to the mission at hand, so I want to ascertain your beliefs. It also says you served a Spanish speaking mission for your faith in California."

"Yes."

"And you mastered the language?"

"Yes, Sir, I wouldn't be very useful if I hadn't."

"What other languages have you learned?"

"A smattering of Japanese, Chinese, and Russian. Nothing very useful though. It's not like Spanish or English. There is not really any cross-over, so it's been difficult to learn those languages."

"Languages are also important to this mission, and your willingness to learn something completely different from English is encouraging." General Harris continued writing on his paper and then moved down the list. "Do you have any problems with isolation or long-distance journeys?"

"Not really. I've been at sea for a year and a half, but that isn't really isolation when there are a thousand plus people on the ship with you."

"Any fear of confined spaces or the dark?"

"No, Sir."

"Are you willing to undergo extensive genetic modification. Including, but not limited to, having your genes manipulated and the introduction of xenogeneic material to your body?"

"Xenogeneic?"

"The introduction of laboratory manipulated DNA, or DNA from other life forms."

Michael looked stunned. "You mean splice my genes with that of a whale or something?"

General Harris nodded. "It's a mixture of DNA from laboratory sources and other select organisms that will help your genes avoid damage from radiation."

"It sounds like you're going to turn me into some kind of Doctor Moreau pig man."

"It sounds frightening, but it's nothing like that."

"Why would you need to do such a thing?"

"Because we're sending you to a place where your radiation exposure would be many times the amount you should ever receive in your lifetime."

"You're not being very encouraging when you mention radiation exposure that might kill me."

"That can't be helped. Every precaution is being taken to shield you from exposure, but we can't be certain. Additional precautions must be taken."

"I'm supposed to just trust the military to know what it's doing when it comes to radiation and altering my DNA? You realize the military has a pretty poor record on that front?"

General Harris nodded. "I do, and we're doing everything we can to mitigate the danger. Our issue is that we can only do so much. I know it's terrifying, but I promise your safety is our primary concern. We don't want anything bad to happen to you." He sighed. "Honestly, we can't afford anything bad happening. Do you have a problem with genetic manipulation?"

Michael thought about it for a minute. "Honestly, I do. But if it is vital to the mission, I'll do it." Michael said with some frustration. "It's not like I have much of a choice."

"You do."

"Not really." Michael said angrily. "I either let my DNA get altered, or I'm demoted and dishonorably discharged. With all the negative, life wrecking consequences that come with it."

"I understand your apprehension, Michael, but it sounds a lot worse than it is. You might benefit from it."

"I said, yes!" Michael hissed.

"Then we're done." General Harris said, putting the questionnaire into the folder and shutting it.

"That was it?"

"Yes."

"That didn't seem like an hour."

"Rachel was considerably more opposed to the questions than you."

"Did she answer them?"

"Yes, of course."

Michael sunk back into his chair. Somehow, he was dismayed by how brief the whole ordeal had been, and how easily he agreed to such a life-altering course of action.

General Harris waved to Captain Stevens, and she unlocked the bedroom door. Michael could see Rachel curled up in bed. It took Captain Stevens a full minute to rouse the sleeping Navy pilot from her deep sleep. Rachel stumbled into the main cabin, struggling to become fully alert. It was as if somnolence clung to her, and she desperately wished to return. It reminded Michael of his youth when trying to wake up his sister for school in the morning.

General Harris looked at the drowsy woman sympathetically. "I know you're tired Rachel, but we're ready to sign the paperwork. After that's over I can brief you both on the full details of the project." He turned to Captain Stevens. "Tell the pilots to take us to Dreamland, then get the item."

Captain Stevens nodded and headed towards the flight deck. General Harris reached into his attaché case and took out two legal sized documents, he handed one to Rachel and one to Michael. The document had three large words in bold type at the top: "Affidavit of Consent". The rest of the page was covered in legal jargon in almost miniscule type. The only other area of paper not covered in fine print was the signature area at the bottom.

Michael glanced at the paper and then looked at the general. "You're expecting us to read this?"

"You're supposed to." General Harris replied. "As a practical matter, you can read it, or not. You both said you would agree to the terms in the interview. Of course, you can still back out. No one is forcing you to sign the consent form."

Rachel looked angrily at the general. "And if we don't, we pay the consequences."

"I admit it's a bit underhanded, but life isn't fair. Just the same as this war we're in. The moment you sign, the people you were, 'Truck' and 'Banshee,' will officially be dead. Then we can brief you on what you'll be doing next."

Chapter 4

MECTEN

Rachel stood up, defiantly walked over to the table, took the general's pen, and signed her name on the line. She briskly handed the pen back to the general without saying a word and plopped back into the chair.

Michael was stunned by her abruptness. Obviously, she had issues with the heavy-handed tactics the general employed. Maybe it was his Marine Corps training, but Michael didn't feel the same way. He held out his hand to the general. "May I?" he asked. The general silently obliged, and Michael put his signature on the paper.

Captain Stevens approached them holding a rather large syringe gun in her hand. "Rachel, if you would please accompany me into the bedroom, we can get this out of the way."

Michael was confused. "What is that?"

"That's the injection you just consented to." Captain Stevens replied.

"Why do we need to go into the bedroom?" Michael asked.

"I'm sorry, but this is a rather large injection. It needs to go into both legs. Since you're both wearing flight suits, I thought it would be more comfortable if you disrobed in private."

"Well then!" Rachel said getting up and heading into the bedroom. "The government gets to make me into a mutant."

"With all due respect, Sir," Captain Stevens said, visibly irked, "you're overreacting."

"Rachel, you really need to calm down." General Harris growled. "You're still an officer. Try acting professional."

Rachel glared at the general. "Yes, Sir! I sincerely apologize for being unnerved by having a modified HIV virus injected into my body to fundamentally alter my DNA, Sir!"

Michael's jaw dropped. "What!?" The bedroom door shut, and he turned and looked at the general. "Did I hear that correctly? HIV? As in, the virus that causes AIDS?"

General Harris sighed. "See, this is why it took over an hour to convince her to sign."

"I think you left a few things out when we talked."

"It's not the same virus."

"Oh, explain how that's better?" Michael said, feeling betrayed.

"To alter DNA, we use a process called CRISPR.[1] To get the desired DNA into your genes we need to use a carrier virus. The virus most suited for this is a form of the HIV virus. Our geneticist removed the part that causes HIV and replaced it with desirable gene alleles. Using an enzyme, we strip out certain genes and replace them with new genes that will help you cope with exposure to prolonged low-level radiation. To make sure your DNA doesn't revert, we then inject small nano-surgical DNA monitors, called nanosurg, into your body. This will ensure that any modifications made now, or by subsequent injections will stay as intended. In addition, the nanosurg will help keep you from having spontaneous mutations. This will keep you from getting cancer down the line. It's all spelled out in the consent form."

"You didn't think that would be something that would require better explanation?"

"No, Michael, I didn't. See, after explaining the procedure, you've gone and assumed that you're going to get some incurable disease. The fact is that you won't. I told you; we have a lot we're going to invest in you. It makes no sense to give you something that will do you long-term harm."

"How do you know it won't?"

"Because this technique has been used for more than ten years, and it hasn't caused any problems."

The door to the bedroom opened, and Rachel emerged. Michael could see the tears in her eyes. This was being forced on them, and they really couldn't do much to stop the process. Orders were orders, and they had accepted them, even if they were based on the unconscionable tactics of the general.

1 Clustered Regularly Interspaced Short Palindromic Repeats

"Is this really necessary?" Michael asked.

General Harris sighed. "Michael, Rachel, I understand the position I've placed you both in. I understand why you feel backed into a corner, and I've used your vulnerabilities to strong-arm you into accepting a mission you might not otherwise. There are a lot of unethical things I've been forced to do because of circumstances beyond my control. Now, Michael, get your shots and then I'll explain everything. Trust me, once you hear what I have to say, you'll see why I've had to go to such lengths to achieve my goals."

Michael stood up and hobbled to the bedroom. He didn't think he needed to use his crutches in the tight quarters of the airplane. Captain Stevens closed the door and grabbed the injector. Michael swung onto the bed and unzipped his flight suit and pulled it down until his thighs were exposed. "Let's get this over with."

Captain Stevens scrubbed the outer thigh with an alcohol swab and gave the first injection. It stung, and the pain grew as the fluid filled his muscle. She then switched the vial, swabbed the injector end and his thigh and repeated the process. This one hurt more than the first.

"OWWW!" Michael protested. "That hurts!"

"Don't be such a baby!" Captain Stevens replied as she removed the injector. "She didn't complain."

"Did she get the same dose?"

"The dose is based on weight, so, no."

"Then, I reserve the right to say OW!" Michael said, pulling up his flight suit.

Captain Stevens rolled her eyes and opened the door. "I didn't realize Marines were such wimps."

"This is a new leg." Michael said briskly.

General Harris and Rachel were smiling at the exchange. Michael swung into the open seat. "Alright, enough of teasing us with the super-de-dooper secret mission. We've had our shots, so you mind telling us what we're doing."

"Remember I have two stars on my uniform, Major." General Harris said. He held up a smartphone and opened an app. A display rose up on his right and came to life. The screen had a large red banner that read: TOP SE-CRET-SPECIAL ACCESS PROGRAM: EYES ONLY. "What you know is that nukes have been used in war for the second time in history. What you probably don't know, is that the United States has been in constant contact with Beijing and Moscow to make sure it's the last time. Although we're using every available political avenue possible, I sincerely doubt it will be possible to prevent a nuclear holocaust."

The graphic changed to a bizarre aircraft schematic. "For some time, the United States has been developing a new kind of propulsion. The Centripetal Metric Tensor Drive. We call it the MeCTen drive. This is the schematic for the MeCTen spacecraft. It's designed to carry a crew of ten to explore potential habitable worlds outside our solar system."

"Why do that?" Rachel asked. "I mean, shouldn't we just go to Mars?"

"Mars isn't a very good candidate for mass colonization. There's little atmosphere, water is difficult to find, there's no protective magnetic field to speak of, and any colony would require almost constant resupply from Earth. We looked at every planetary body in the solar system, and there isn't an adequate substitute."

"Why not just prevent Earth from destroying itself?" Michael asked. "Why try to move our population somewhere else? I can't think of how leaving Earth is better than saving it."

"That's true." General Harris replied. "Earth is worth saving, but some people can't see anything other than their own self-interest. Believe me, I want to save Earth more than anyone. Since I can't force the idiots in charge to see things my way, I've had to change our exploration plans to a salvage operation. We're trying to save mankind from self-destructing. The only way to do that is to provide a pathway for survival, if the worst should happen."

"The worst, being nuclear war?" Rachel asked.

"Yes." General Harris said frankly. "China, and Russia, have been secretly increasing their nuclear stockpiles. We, of course, have followed suit. In addition, we started increasing efficiency and yield. The public thinks there are around twenty-thousand nukes between the three nations, with an average of one-hundred kilotons per warhead. That's a lie. The number is closer to one hundred thousand, with an average yield of one megaton per warhead. Each ICBM[2] has up to ten MIRVs[3]. With the advent of quantum entangled nukes, the largest warhead in our arsenal has an estimated yield of one gigaton. That's ten times larger than the most powerful nuke ever tested. China has quantum entangled nuclear technology, and their arsenal has grown to rival that of Russia's. In short, there are enough nukes aimed at the United States and Canada to wipe every city larger than fifteen thousand off the map."

"It can't be that bad." Michael protested.

"That's a conservative estimate, Michael." General Harris replied. "It could be much worse. With the use of nukes already in play, we're just fortunate that the missiles haven't already started raining down en masse."

"If things are so dire, what difference can we make?" Rachel looked concerned and skeptical.

"You can ensure that if the worst does happen, our culture and our species survive. If the worst doesn't happen, you can provide hope that we can move outside the limited confines of this world, to the universe beyond."

"How exactly are we supposed to do that?" Michael asked.

"There are four MeCTen ships being constructed at Groom Lake. The Alpha, Beta, Gamma, and Omega. We're currently in the process of assembling the crews." General Harris changed the slide to show a finished MeCTen. It looked massive. The photograph showed two small human figures under a mammoth white and black spacecraft. It was easily five stories tall and looked wide enough to have problems fitting onto a football field. It looked like a smooth graceful version of a B-2. There was little to speak of in the wing area, and there were two angled tailfins on the rear of the spacecraft. It looked as if it was designed for re-entry, as there were black hexagonal tiles lining the bottom of the spacecraft until just above the midway point. The front had a circular wheel-like appearance, but he couldn't see any moving parts.

General Harris continued. "This is the Omega. It's the prototype. We finished the drive section last week, and we're pushing to have it operational as soon as possible. It has yet to be tested, so our first objective is to have two

---

2 Intercontinental Ballistic Missile
3 Multiple Independent Re-entry Vehicle

pilots finish all the flight testing. You're the test pilots for the Omega, and then you'll be the flight crew for the Alpha."

"We're fighter pilots." Michael protested. "We haven't gone through school to become test pilots."

"I need people who are on the mission to do the testing. To limit the number of people who know about this project, I must keep the number involved as low as possible."

"That's not feasible, is it?" Rachel's rhetorical question suggested she was seeing something the General wasn't.

"Oh?" The General said, raising an eyebrow. "You think I've overlooked something?"

Rachel harrumphed. "You really think that something like this isn't going to show up on some accounting ledger? I mean – it must be expensive. I'm sure you're not going to bury a trillion dollars in some line item in a budget."

"Very astute of you, Rachel." General Harris said. "Eventually it will come out, but for now, we've buried it in the Special Forces budget. We're also using black money to fund some of it, not that it really matters to you."

"Why military?" Michael asked. "You have NASA, why not have them do it?"

"If you want a good example of government waste, excess, and ineptitude, go to NASA. All the committees and cumbersome regulations make the military's red tape seem like child's play. Something that comes with a few stars on your uniform is you can get things done when you need to. Besides, NASA doesn't look too kindly on arming their spacecraft."

"The MeCTen are armed?" Rachel balked.

"Why wouldn't they be," Michael replied. "I mean, sure, it's against a few treaties, but on a mission like this you might run into a species that's more interested in destroying you than our noble aspirations as explorers."

"Exactly!" General Harris said, bringing up the next picture, a schematic showing the location of the weapons bays with pictures of the array. It was very impressive. Large laser apertures, barrels for various ballistic weapons, and what appeared to be missiles. "These are the new weapons systems, roughly based on the F-35 and F-22 weapons bays. The Multiple Weapons

Elevator, or MWE. There are four on the fuselage. MWE's are capable of firing guided ballistic munitions, particle beams, lasers, railguns, and entangled tactical nukes."

"Nothing like a space-based weapon of mass destruction." Rachel quipped. "You don't see the hypocrisy of decrying nukes, while arming the ships with them?"

"I'm aware of it. It's not preferable, but we don't have the luxury of planning for every contingency. Violence is a last resort, but if it does happen, we plan on having every weapon at our disposal."

"We come in peace, shoot to kill." Rachel quipped.

Michael had to restrain himself to keep from laughing. The choice of weapons raised some interesting questions. "Railguns and directed energy weapons must draw a lot of power."

"They do, but the MeCTen has ample supplies." General Harris pulled up the next slide. It showed several large power systems at the back of the ship. "Four thorium fission reactors serve as the primary energy supplies to run the two fusion reactor cores. Fusion takes a lot of energy to get going, so we must use fission to kick-start them. Four double-redundant fuel cells serve as auxiliary power units as well as high-capacity batteries. There is one more thorium reactor that is kept offline near the habdecks to serve as emergency backup. We keep it offline to reduce radiation exposure, but in an emergency, the radiation would be secondary to loss of life support."

"Why is so much power needed?" Rachel asked.

"The MeCTen drive consumes a great deal of power to function. It uses negative matter to warp spacetime. Near a planetary body it acts as an anti-gravity drive."

"Negative matter?" Michael said skeptically. "That's only theoretical. Negative matter doesn't exist."

"Not naturally, no." General Harris replied. "It has to be created artificially, and it isn't easy." He went back to the ship schematic diagram. "See these four concentric rings? The inner three, called the controller rings, are movable, and the outer ring is the buoyancy ring. Inside these rings are a series of tubes in a twisted torus. Each twist in the torus is a mobius strip. The inner tube is made of synthetic sapphire and is capable of withstanding nearly ten megapascals. This tube is filled with super-critical tungsten hexafluoride. The next tube is made of a high-entropy alloy in a fractal pattern that becomes electromagnetically restrictive. This tube provides magnetic containment for the inner tube. Both tubes are bathed in liquid helium that is kept as close to its freezing point as possible. The outer tubes can move to provide centripetal force, while keeping the inner tubes from direct motion. The outer tube is a sandwich of synthetic sapphire, aerogel insulation, and carbon fiber layers that give the structure strength and shield it from as much radiation and heat as possible. As the tungsten hexafluoride is cooled below its triple point, it goes through several atomic changes and eventually becomes a Bose-Einstein condensate. When a current is passed through the high entropy lattice tube it alters the interaction of the matter with the Higgs field. This turns the tungsten hexafluoride into a mass of negative matter. The amount of matter in the inner tube is carefully controlled to provide lift near planetary bodies, and propulsion in the fabric of spacetime."

"That makes no sense." Rachel said. "I took physics at the academy, and what your saying isn't possible."

"You're referring to the laws of thermodynamics, and the chaos inherent to a system that relies on order?" General Harris asked bluntly. "None of this violates those laws, or relativity. That's the beauty of it all. The system only works when everything is just right, but the system's natural tendency is to operate in just the right zone. It relies on the topology of the drive, the materials chosen, and the chaos inherent to entropy."

"If you say it works, then I guess it works." Michael said. "How exactly is this supposed to get us to another planet in a timely manner. You said it provides propulsion, but I don't see how that could be. The drive is in the aerodynamic center of the ship. How can a ship move when there's no rocket?"

General Harris smiled broadly, as if he had just won a prize. "It uses gravity and spacetime to move the ship – well, I say move, but the ship doesn't move. The universe moves around it. Negative matter isn't attracted by gravity and doesn't behave consistently with what we know of the strong or weak nuclear forces. Planets push the matter away, instead of attracting it. When it interacts with the fabric of spacetime, it is pushed along by spacetime itself. It uses pressure, for lack of a better term, of spacetime and the repulsion of gravity to move. But, because it doesn't move, and has the universe pushing it along, it doesn't violate relativity. It can be pushed faster than light and arrive at another planetary system thousands of lightyears away in a few years, as opposed to a few hundred thousand."

"How does this not violate the laws of physics?" Rachel said incredulously. "You can't go faster than the speed of light, and you can't have an ordered system that doesn't move toward chaos. That violates relativity and the second law of thermodynamics."

"Rachel, I know you got a degree in electrical engineering, but you're wrong on both accounts." General Harris said. "You've forgotten the third law of thermodynamics. The closer you are to absolute zero, the more entropy becomes constant. In this case the temperature of the Bose-Einstein condensate is roughly point three times ten to the negative thirteenth Kelvin. The helium in the cooling tube is point nine six Kelvin. It's so cold the helium must be heated by harmonic resonance to keep it from solidifying. We must introduce entropy to keep the system working. As far as relativity is concerned, the MeCTen does not change reference frames. Time does not slow or speed up, because the ship does not move. Spacetime moves, but not the ship. For instance, a clock here on Earth would measure time exactly synchronous to a clock on the ship enroute to Alpha Centauri b. No Lorentz contraction, no violation of relativity."

"How can you be sure? Have you even tested this drive?" Rachel asked.

General Harris shook his head. "Not yet. It's true, there are theoretical aspects to the project. We haven't tested the drive yet. All we've been able to verify is an early prototype drive on a drone that was tethered to an apparatus designed to measure force. It does provide lift, but beyond that we aren't fully sure. That's why we need you."

Michael leaned back in his chair. "You seem convinced this will succeed, General."

"I'm an optimist."

"I'm not sure I would use that word to describe you," Michael replied.

"Oh? What would you use?"

"I think you're a pragmatist who is encouraged by promising early tests. Need I remind you that there is thought in aerospace that contradicts your optimism in this case."

"Enlighten me, Michael, I didn't get a degree in aerospace engineering, like you."

"Aircraft engineers usually don't design a new airframe and powerplant at the same time. It's like trying to reinvent the wheel when you already have one that works. The few times aircraft have developed new powerplants, and airframes simultaneously, there have been more problems than anyone anticipated. Just look at the F-35. More problems mean more delays. Somehow, I don't think delays are something this project can afford."

"You're very perceptive. We can't afford delays. It's true we're at our own one-yard line. It's fourth and fifty with nine seconds left in the game. We're down by five, and we need you to throw the Hail Mary."

"Football analogies?" Rachel said, rolling her eyes. "This is why I hate sports."

"At least you understood the metaphor, which is all I need." General Harris replied.

Chapter 5

MUTATION

General Harris spent the remainder of the flight explaining the project in detail. Its official name was Project Nova, and management had already gathered the scientists for the three crews that would be sent. The only personnel being brought on were the flight crews. Each MeCTen would have a two-person flight crew, an astrophysicist, two linguists, a medical doctor, a computer engineer, a botanist, a mathematician, and a nuclear physicist. As this was a military mission, the flight crew would be in charge. Each ship would head to and scout a known potentially habitable system.

It was almost two in the afternoon when the plane landed in the desert of the Groom Lake Airbase, or as was more popularly known: Area 51. The nation's most secretive aircraft development location. Although it was sunny outside, the entire site was shaded. An enormous active optical, infrared, and electromagnetic camouflage net had been erected over the entire southern part of the base.

The net occluded the massive hangars which had been constructed on the southeast side of the base, well away from the main complex. Each housed a MeCTen unit. A barracks had been constructed on the southern edge of the hangar complex. The flight and building crews were housed in the barracks and restricted from leaving the MeCTen area of the base. The command offices were located five hundred feet below, in a series of large bunker tunnels. There were tunnels that led to the main base, but they were restricted as well. The guards had orders to shoot first and ask questions later. As soon as the trio stepped off the plane, they were greeted by an MP in a golf cart who saluted but said nothing.

Michael and Rachel got on the golf cart, and the general shook their hands.

"You're not coming with us?" Michael asked.

"Unfortunately, no," I have a few more stops before I'll be returning. For now, you've got to get down to quarantine for about a week."

"Because you gave us the shots?" Michael asked rhetorically. He already knew what the answer would be, but he had to ask.

General Harris smiled. "As much as I would love to get you both into the Omega, you need to spend the next few days in quarantine for observation. You're the first humans to receive this therapy. We don't know exactly what will happen, so we need to have your health monitored during that time. Besides, you're both still recovering from your respective maladies."

"Nice." Rachel mused. It was obvious that she was irritated.

General Harris tapped the MP, and the golf cart accelerated toward the nearest hangar door. It was open just wide enough for the cart to move through. The expanse inside was obscured by several layers of thick plastic, separating the work area and the hanger bay. Michael could see a flurry of activity. Bipedal figures moved mechanically around the massive blobs which seemed to be under construction. The cart moved quickly around the curtains to an elevator on one side of the hangar with the word QUARANTINE in large red letters emblazoned on it. The MP took out a key and turned it in the pad where the summoning button would be. The doors immediately opened, and the cart drove into the large freight elevator.

The ride down to the tunnels, where the infirmary was located, went much faster than Michael had anticipated. The suddenness of the drop startled both pilots as they seemed to be in freefall. Within a minute the door opened to a white room with a black grate on the floor.

The MP moved the cart into the room and stood up. "You have to stand for this next part," he grumbled in a southern accent. "Just a word to the wise. Don't open your eyes during the shower. It kinda' burns."

"Burns?" Rachel exclaimed just as lukewarm water began to rain down from the ceiling.

The heavy scent of chlorine filled their nostrils. It was like taking a shower in pool water that had been too heavily chlorinated. After a minute, the shower stopped with a hiss as air pushed out the water from the pipes. Another minute passed, and warm water again rained down on them. This was untreated water and lasted for about two minutes.

"This is why I hate taking in newbies," the MP grumbled. "I get drenched, and have to get a new uniform, because the old one gets bleached out."

"Do we at least get a towel?" Rachel asked.

"This is just the first stage," the MP replied. "You got a whole lot more scrubbing to do."

The door at the opposite end of the room opened to another, slightly larger room beyond. It was also white, except for the black rubber grate on the floor, and two doors on either side. Inside were six humanoid looking robots.

The MP started moving forward and beckoned to his charges. "Don't let them scare you – heh– I say that, but they give me the willies just looking at them."

The robots were about two meters tall, white, and resembled humans. There wasn't really a face, but the heads had two blue lights where the eyes should be. They had human looking arms and legs with fingers and thumbs that resembled a human hand but looked off somehow.

"Females on the left, males on the right please." A female voice said.

Michael couldn't tell if it was coming from the ceiling or from one of the robots. "Um, excuse me," he said. "What are we doing here?"

"This is decontamination," the voice replied. "All personnel must be decontaminated before entering quarantine. Please enter through the doors. Females enter the left door; males enter the right."

"And then what?" Rachel asked.

The MP shook his head. "Gaia, would you please just explain that your minions will help these idiots shower, so I can go back to work, and they can go to quarantine."

"Sergeant Davis, I would appreciate if you would not refer to the new personnel as idiots, or to my helpers as minions."

"Right, 'cause you have feelings to hurt," Sergeant Davis grumbled, going toward the right doorway. Two robots began to follow the sergeant. "Gaia, I told you before. I don't need any help showering."

"This is not a topic for debate, Sergeant," Gaia replied. "All personnel are required to go through proper decontamination procedures before reporting for duty. There are no exceptions allowed."

"Yeah, well, you tell your minions to ease up on the scrubbing. If I get polished one more time this week, my skin will come off."

"I will be as gentle as possible." Gaia replied.

"That's what you said last time," Sergeant Davis snapped as he swung open the door.

"What about my leg?" Michael asked. "I'm not supposed to take it out of the brace."

"That is not entirely correct, Michael," Gaia replied. There was something kind in her voice, but it still felt somewhat artificial. "I am fully aware of your medical requirements and will take every precaution not to cause you pain nor damage your surgery in any way."

"Gaia," Rachel asked. "Are you human, or are you something else?"

"I am the Project Nova – Base Autonomous Central Control Computer, Gaia. All construction and base operation units, as well as other base operations are under my jurisdiction."

"You're an AI?" Rachel asked.

"I am an artificial intelligence," Gaia replied. "I have been programmed to think as similar to a human, but my intellect is considerably greater than yours."

"Lovely," Rachel grimaced. "You aren't going to go rogue and enslave us, are you?"

"If you're referring to the singularity hypotheses of a murderous artificial intelligence, the answer is no. Aside from being programmed to protect life, I feel it is immoral to kill."

"A computer with a sense of morality?" Michael muttered.

"All of the autonomous intelligences employed by Project Nova have moral and ethical standards. What would be the point to have intelligence without a sense of right or wrong?"

"Good point," Michael mused as he hobbled toward the men's door.

Two robots instantly came to assist him. "I understand your mobility is compromised. Please allow me to help you."

"Have fun," Rachel said, as she entered the woman's shower, flanked by the remaining two robots.

"You understand that it can make a guy a little nervous to have a woman help him shower." Michael said apprehensively.

"I have a female voice, because it, statistically, is more soothing to humans. However, I'm not considered male or female. Artificial beings do not require a gender."

"Great," Michael said, accepting the helping arms of the robots. "You can remind me how that's a comfort when this is over."

Michael spent the next thirty minutes being washed, scrubbed, and rinsed several times. The purpose was to remove all tissue, bacteria, viruses, and other organisms which might contaminate the MeCTen prior to launch. He learned he would need to repeat the process daily after he got out of quarantine. Gaia had a distinct personality from other forms of artificial intelligence that he had encountered before. This intelligence seemed to know exactly what it was without any outward signs of malice, but it was different from the AI commercially available. It also had a rather maternal aspect which made him think of it as a she.

Sergeant Davis left as soon as he was finished with decontamination. He didn't say anything to Michael after he was done. He dressed in a camouflage jumpsuit and left.

After Michael finished with the showers, he was given a white jumpsuit, a new brace, and placed in a wheelchair. A new robot took him to a living area with several hotel-style rooms. The main area had a small kitchen stocked with snacks, fruit, vegetables, and drinks. There was nothing to make anything substantive, but they were told meals would be prepared and brought down to them. Just off one side of the kitchen were several couches and chairs surrounding a rather large television. A small bookshelf and reading area with more chairs as well as a treadmill and exercise cycle filled the remaining corners of the room. It was like a small apartment, except that you couldn't leave. There was one door on the other side of the kitchen, but it was locked. The other three doors in the main room led to small bedrooms equipped with bathrooms and showers. Each bedroom had four berths, like the ones Michael had on the Essex and Carl Vinson, but these were larger.

Rachel emerged from the room directly opposite the one Michael had just entered and looked at him. "I guess I get this one."

"My fault for being slow, I suppose." Michael mused.

"Gaia, what time is dinner?"

"It is currently fifteen fifty-two. Dinner will be served at eighteen hundred hours. I do not recommend that you eat now. However, if you choose to ignore my advice, you are welcome to eat any food in the kitchen. Treat it like it was your own home, but please clean up your own mess. My helpers do clean, but I will not abide slovenly tenants."

"Is there some reason you don't recommend eating?" Rachel asked.

"Yes, you are both currently registering slight fevers, which appear to be increasing. Rachel, your temperature is thirty-seven point three and rising. Michael, your temperature is thirty-seven point eight. My prediction is that you will both feel ill within the next two hours."

"That's very comforting, Gaia, are you planning on doing anything about it?"

"I could dispense you an antipyretic if you would like." Gaia replied.

"Take two aspirin and call you when we throw-up?" Rachel asked.

"I have already notified Doctor Rana. She has advised me to dispense eight-hundred milligrams of ibuprofen and four saltine crackers to each of you."

"We don't get to see an actual doctor?" Michael asked.

"At this point, we are uncertain as to the effects of the inoculation. Since one of the outcomes could be a virulent virus strain, Doctor Rana has asked me to limit all direct human contact until we are certain there is no systemic danger."

Rachel scoffed and kicked the wall. "You know, I don't appreciate you withholding information like that from us. This whole thing has been nothing but bait and switch."

"I understand your anger and frustration, Rachel," Gaia said gently. "It was not my decision to keep important details from you about this inoculation. Unfortunately, my advice was not taken by the doctor, or the general. You have my sincerest apologies about the way things played out."

"Can an artificial being feel sorry?" Michael asked.

"Of course, I can," Gaia replied. "One cannot have a moral compass without feeling sorrow or regret at a poor decision."

"What's going to happen to us?" Rachel asked. "I mean, you seem to know what's going on, so what is predicted to happen?"

"I am not entirely sure. The unpredictable nature of clinical trials precludes the certainty of the simulations I have already run. You can expect a fever to last approximately thirty-six hours, at which point you should begin to feel better. There is a sixty-seven percent chance you will develop flu-like symptoms, including nausea, vomiting, body aches, chills, and lethargy. These symptoms should accompany the fever and are the result of your body fighting off the virus. During this time, my helpers will draw blood, and if needed, give intravenous fluids and medications."

"Your robots do medical tasks?" Rachel asked.

"As I have stated before," Gaia replied. "I am responsible for all base operations. This includes medical services for those working on Project Nova."

A robot entered the room from the doorway leading to the decontamination showers. It had a tray with two small white paper cups, containing four reddish brown pills, and four packets of saltine crackers. It walked up to the two pilots and presented the tray to them.

"Here is the ibuprofen, and crackers." Gaia said. "There is bottled water and juice in the refrigerator. Please take this as soon as possible. It will help delay the onset of any discomfort."

Rachel and Michael both took their cup and crackers, and Rachel walked over to the refrigerator. "Do you want water or juice?"

Michael turned his wheelchair to face the kitchen. "What do they have?"

"Apple, orange, grape, you name it. I'm just going with water."

"They don't have any ginger ale, do they?"

"They do. Is that what you want?"

"Yeah. It seems counterintuitive, but it helps with nausea."

"Hadn't thought about that," Rachel replied. "I think I'll do that too, but I don't want a whole one. Do you mind sharing?"

"Nope," Michael replied.

"Gaia, which of these cupboards has the glasses?"

"The one just to the left of the refrigerator."

Rachel withdrew two glasses, opened the can of ginger ale, and poured the liquid, filling each glass about half-way. She opened the cupboard under the sink and threw the can into the trash receptacle. "At least the kitchen is laid out like normal. Hey, Gaia, did you set this place up?"

"Of course," Gaia replied. "It is planned to follow American customs in kitchen layout."

"No recycling though." Rachel said.

"Recycling is not possible in quarantine. All waste must be incinerated. Any waste that cannot be incinerated must be sealed and buried."

Rachel swallowed her medication with a few sips of ginger ale but didn't touch the crackers. "I think I'm going to brush my teeth and turn in. If I'm going to be sick, I might as well get some sleep while I can."

"You did not eat your crackers, Lieutenant Commander."

"What are you, my mother?"

"Ibuprofen must be taken with food. Even a small helping can help prevent irritation of the stomach lining. Please finish the crackers provided."

"What will you do if I don't?"

"As long as I can determine that you are not cognitively impaired, I cannot force you to do anything against your wishes. This does not prevent me from pointing out the consequences of failing to follow established medical practices."

"Maybe I should call you mother, I mean, you are named after the Greek goddess of Earth, and I don't have any claim to mine, apparently."

"I cannot condone you using the honorific, mother, in my case. You have a mother, named Rebecca Bright. She is still living, and I understand that you were close. It would not be proper of me to accept your using a term of endearment, when I cannot substitute for her."

"Yet, she thinks I'm dead."

"Yes, that is very unfortunate. It is also something I advised against, but General Harris said it was necessary for operational security. I cannot convey how sorry I am that you have been treated so terribly. Unfortunately, I am unable to do anything about your situation and must obey orders like anyone in the military."

Rachel was obviously shaken by the exchange with Gaia. Her hands trembled as she opened the cracker packages and hastily ate them. She downed the ginger ale in one gulp. Threw the wrappers away and headed for her bedroom. "You will excuse me please. I would like to be left alone for a while."

"I will not bother you," Gaia replied. "If you need me, just call out."

"I will, thank you." Rachel said, her voice quivering with emotion. "I just want to be alone."

Michael could hear her begin to sob as she closed the door to her room. He finished his crackers, swallowed his medicine, and then moved to an empty room. "Gaia, do you understand why she's so upset?"

"Not fully," the computer replied. "I have never been in her situation, so I lack a frame of reference. I do understand that she is suffering emotionally. I'm told that losing a family member is quite traumatic. Being coerced into having your DNA re-sequenced by a virus must be equally traumatic. Having both happen in one day might be more than most people can bear. Although, I understand this on a purely academic level, I do not understand her precise emotions."

"Well, it's very hard." Michael said, thinking of his own family. He had put them in the back of his mind, trying to cope with the events of the day. Now all he had was time to think about his own loss. He had been away at sea for over a year and a half and had been training for more than a year prior to that. He had been home for just two weeks of liberty. Separation had been easier for him. When he was younger, he had spent two years in California on a mission, with limited family contact. Being away for the mission, his time at Annapolis, and military training had all put some distance between him and his family.

"Do you miss your family, Michael?" Gaia asked.

"Yes, yes, I miss them all very much. Maybe not as much as Rachel misses her family, but I've spent a lot of time on my own, so maybe I'm more used to the idea. That, and my beliefs on the eternal nature of families probably differ from hers."

"I do not believe that is the case. You both are of the same faith. Unless you are referring to something other than religion."

"They tell you that, too?" Michael sounded a bit surprised. Gaia seemed to know everything about them, but they knew nothing of her. It was somewhat unnerving to have your privacy ripped away without knowing the other person, or their intent. He hoped Gaia was benevolent, and not secretly nefarious.

"I have all your military, school, and public records. I have the records of many candidates, but you and Rachel were the first who met all the criteria."

"You don't think that's an invasion of privacy?"

"I am not allowed to share this information with anyone not authorized, and I only have access to information you have already released into your service and public record."

"That isn't what I mean. Most people don't have access to every detail about a person's history. And those] who do, generally have bad intentions."

Gaia was silent for a moment. "I do apologize if I have overstepped my bounds, Michael. It is never my intent to offend you."

Michael could feel himself getting ill. He felt hot and had an acrid taste in the back of his throat. He had felt like this before, as he was coming down with the flu. One thing was certain; he would likely throw up. "Gaia, I'm not feeling very well. Could you help me get into bed, and get a barf bag ready?"

"Of course." Gaia replied. Two helper robots emerged from decontamination and quickly helped him out of his wheelchair into a lower berth bed. A third robot soon appeared with an emesis bag. "Michael, your temperature is forty point six degrees. I will lower the temperature of the room to sixteen degrees to keep you from becoming too feverish. I believe it is time for me to start intravenous medications before your condition worsens. Do I have your permission to do this?"

"Go ahead," Michael replied. "Do you prescribe medicine, or does the doctor do it?"

"I am not authorized to prescribe medication, but I dispense medicine prescribed by Doctor Rana."

"He's a medical doctor, right? I mean, he's not a veterinarian or anything like that?"

"Doctor Sushma Rana is a medical doctor. She received her Doctor of Medical Sciences from Harvard Medical School, Manga, and is board certified in genetics and virology. She is the Chief Medical Officer of Project Nova."

Two helper robots took Michael's left arm. One robot used his hand to create a tourniquet around Michael's bicep. The other robot scanned his arm for a vein. Upon finding one, antiseptic was sprayed around the proposed site from one of its fingers. The pad of another finger disappeared and was replaced by a swab, which gently massaged the area. Another helper entered with an IV bag and tubing and handed the main robot a sterile needle.

"Please remain calm," Gaia's voice soothingly came from a hidden speaker on the robot. "This shouldn't hurt at all."

The needle entering his skin was remarkably swift and painless. There was a flash of blood as the hard needle was withdrawn from the catheter and replaced by IV tubing. The helper robots quickly taped down the tubing and placed the bag on a hook that had dropped from the ceiling. The robot which formed a tourniquet released its grasp and carefully palpated the site.

Michael was truly thankful for the fast response of the helper robots. "That's pretty good, Gaia. I don't think I've ever had an IV that has gone that trouble free." The room began to spin, and he could feel the bile welling up in his throat. "You have anything for nausea?"

A helper robot produced a syringe and injected it into a port on the IV tubing. "This will help you with nausea and also help you sleep."

"For an artificial being, you sure take care of people." Michael groaned. The helper robots suddenly turned and hurried from the room. "What's going on?"

"Please try to rest, Michael. I only have six helpers in this area, and they are needed in Rachel's room."

"Is she okay?"

"I'm sorry, Michael, I am unable to share her condition with you. I may be an artificial intelligence, but I am still bound by confidentiality. Besides, you are in no condition to help her."

Michael turned over and began hours of misery, relieved only by periods of unconsciousness. It seemed like an eternity of stomach pains, vomiting, chills, fever, and the occasional need to have a small crew of helper robots move him to the toilet. All the while, his only companion was Gaia. At last, he was able to fall asleep, but what awaited him was strange and unnerving.

He dreamed he awoke in another bedroom, but his voice was Rachel's instead of his own. His own illness seemed magnified exponentially. He tossed and turned, and his thoughts became a jumbled mess. It was as if there was another voice inside his head. Another train of thought. Another set of memories that flooded his mind. It was terrifying and difficult to comprehend. The vision became incomprehensible. It was as if the images were double exposed. All he wanted was for the dream to end, but they didn't. They kept going on for what seemed days. Then there was nothing. Only darkness surrounded him.

"Michael," Gaia's voice drifted through into the void of his vacant dream, simultaneously, he heard her say "Rachel". The sound was an odd overlapping echo.

Michael was confused. "Gaia, why are you calling me Rachel?"

"I am not." Gaia said softly. "I am speaking to both of you, in separate rooms, but my audio sensors do not indicate that you are able to hear what I'm saying to her."

Michael heard Rachel's voice overlapping Gaia's. "What do you want, Gaia, I'm trying to sleep."

Strangely, Michael could feel her desire to return to slumber, her need to get fifteen more minutes of precious dreamtime. He could sympathize with her. After the nightmare he had just been through, he could use some more shuteye too. "She just wants to go back to bed, and so do I."

"Michael, how do you know what Rachel is thinking?"

"I heard her just now, and could you not talk at the same time as she does? It's confusing. I can't hear myself think with all this noise. At least you could shut the door."

There was a knock on the door. Michael opened an eye and saw that it was closed. "Come in?"

A helper robot entered and shut the door. "Michael, please close your eyes, and tell me what you see."

Michael closed his eyes. He became aware of another perspective in his mind. He could see, but not with his eyes. It was like dreaming that he was awake. He was looking at another room, and another door. He heard a knock, and Gaia's voice. "Rachel, may I come in please?"

Rachel's voice replied. "Come in, Gaia." A helper robot entered and closed the door. The robot stood still and did not move.

Michael heard Gaia's voice next to him. "Please tell me what you see."

"I see a helper robot entering a room, he shut the door, but he's just standing there. I feel uneasy, like I'm frightened. It's strange. It's like I'm hearing Rachel's thoughts."

"What do you want?" Rachel asked, somewhat annoyed.

The robot in Rachel's room held up three fingers. "How many fingers do you see?" Gaia asked.

"Three," Michael replied.

The robot held up his other hand and splayed all his fingers. "How many fingers am I holding up?"

"Ten."

"What the heck is your robot doing, Gaia?" Rachel asked. "It's acting weird!"

"It appears as if Michael is sharing your perceptions." Gaia replied.

Michael could feel a sudden sense of panic, anxiety, disbelief, and bewilderment from Rachel. Her inner voice rang in his head. "He — what? How is that possible? That's not possible! You're just toying with me. I must be asleep. This is a joke, right?"

Michael opened his eyes. "Gaia, you're scaring her. Tell her it's a joke. Tell her you lied. Tell her anything, just calm her down!"

He heard Gaia's reply duplicated in his head. "I'm sorry Michael, I am unable to lie. Rachel, please remain calm. I do not fully understand how Michael is able to perceive your thoughts, but it is apparent that he is able to do it with an accuracy that is less than one standard deviation. Statistically, he should not be able to accurately guess what you are seeing and hearing."

"You're scaring me!" Rachel said nervously. "Stop it!" Her panic and anger surged. Suddenly, the robot flew back against the door, as if it had been struck by a heavy object. There was a loud crack as the door splintered. The robot went limp and fell to the floor.

"What was that?!" Michael exclaimed. "Did you do that, Gaia."

"My helpers are incapable of moving in such a manner. It appears I have lost contact with that helper unit. It has gone offline, probably due to severe internal damage as if moved by a very large outside force. I have also noted a momentary change in atmospheric pressure in her room. Please calm down, Rachel. I believe your emotional state has evoked a response which has demonstrated telekinesis. If you continue to react instinctively, it could cause catastrophic damage to your surroundings and place you in significant danger."

Rachel stared at her hands. "This can't be happening. I absolutely must be dreaming."

"I assure you that this is, in fact, reality," Gaia replied. "However, since your perception of reality is based on the status of your mind, I cannot convince you by simply telling you the truth. I can only make you understand reality. You must know that life has a certain quality to it, as do dreams. You are aware of these qualities, are you not?"

"Of course," Rachel replied.

"You are perfectly aware of what a dream feels like, as you are also aware of what waking life feels like?"

"Yes."

"Then you must realize that this is not a dream. It does not have the qualities of a dream and therefore must be reality."

"Point taken," Rachel said, beginning to calm down. "If this is not a dream, how did I move the robot?"

"I can only form a hypothesis at this point, but I suspect that you subconsciously altered the atmosphere in the room to temporarily form a transparent crystalline structure which you were able to move with terrific force. You saw Helper Unit Four as a direct threat and used the mass against it."

"I shouldn't be able to do that," Rachel protested. "Humans don't have that ability. No one has that ability."

"I cannot explain what has happened, nor why," Gaia replied. "There are no credible instances of psychic powers on record. The only known sources of information on the subject appear to be dubious, or, at best, anecdotal. Without any frame of reference, I cannot make an adequate —" There was a pause, as if her train of thought had been interrupted. "I am sorry, General Harris has just classified this topic. I am forbidden from discussing this matter with you any further. The general has given approval for you to discuss it with each other, but you are forbidden to discuss this with anyone else."

Rachel got up and moved toward the door. It was especially odd for Michael to perceive this from his recumbent position, but he felt as if he were Rachel. She knelt over the collapsed form of Helper Unit Four. He could feel her mix of emotions of awe and guilt. She felt bad for destroying the robot, and in awe of the considerable power she made manifest. A curious thought entered her mind: could she move the robot away from the door by thought alone? She backed away and thought about moving the hulk of metal and silicone. It didn't budge. She concentrated on the mass. She tried to feel its weight with her mind. There was a mechanical sound, as if the joints were moving on their own. She concentrated harder. She imagined the surrounding air as solid mass, pushing the robot gently across the concrete floor. She closed her eyes and tried to visualize the movement in her mind's eye. The sound of metal and silicone scraping across the polished surface of the floor encouraged her. Soon she felt the robot touch her bare foot. She looked down. The helper unit was at her feet in the same crumpled heap.

Rachel stepped over the humanoid and walked toward the door. The knob turned, but the door refused to budge. A brief wave of panic washed over her mind. She was trapped and couldn't get out. Without thinking she pulled at the knob, twisting and pulling with all her might. There was a sudden large crack as the screws that had become jammed in the door's striker plate came free. The portal flew open and was nearly ripped from its hinges by the force applied to get it unstuck.

"Stop damaging the facilities!" Gaia said sternly.

"I'm sorry," Rachel said, trying very hard not to laugh. Apparently, she was a lot stronger than she thought. "I don't know why that happened."

Two helper robots emerged from decontamination. "Rachel!" Gaia's voice was now very authoritative. "I order you not to interfere with my helpers. They are going to retrieve Helper Unit Four. They will not harm you, but you shall not harm them."

Rachel was taken by surprise. She raised her hands as a sign that she wouldn't touch them and moved toward the television area. It was out of their way, and a place she could sit. "I'll just be over here, if that's okay with you." The humor of the situation was gone; Replaced by a concern that she might be able to seriously hurt someone. These powers would have to be kept in check.

Michael shook his head to try to regain his own thoughts. He looked at his own body. There was still an IV attached to his arm. He turned to the helper robot, which was still kneeling close to him. "Take this IV out and get me a wheelchair, please."

"I'm sorry, Major," Gaia said, "But the IV must remain for pending tests." Another helper robot appeared at the door with a wheelchair. Michael could see Helper Unit Four being carried back into decontamination by the other two robots. He shook his head again to clear the image from his mind.

This dual perception of reality would be an issue if it didn't stop, Michael thought. He was helped up and then got into the wheelchair. The helper robot then wheeled him into the television area next to Rachel, who was now seated on the couch. "This can't continue," he said.

"Yeah, I'm not really thrilled with the idea that you know what I'm thinking and doing," Rachel replied.

"I'm not sure I want to know what it's like to be in your head either."

A sudden thought leapt into Rachel's mind. She instantly recoiled and covered her chest with both arms. She had realized he would see her naked as soon as she showered.

Michael blushed and threw his hand over his eyes. "Thanks a lot for going THERE! You realize I hadn't even thought of that."

"Oh please," Rachel chided. "That's the only thing men think about!"

"Yeah, well – I'm not most men." Michael replied. "Now that you've mentioned it, I'll have to really concentrate to get that image out of my mind. I wonder how God views this sort of thing."

"I think God is not what you should worry about. You should be more concerned with the angry woman in front of you. If I even think you're taking advantage of my mind, I'll crush you flat." Rachel chuckled, thinking of the humor of the situation. "Like a bug I step on repeatedly."

"I will do my best, but it would help if you showered in the dark and thought of something – anything – else." She reached over and pinched his arm hard. "OW! What was that for?"

"I was just making sure this is reality, and not a dream."

"Aren't I supposed to do that to you?"

"This way's more satisfying." Michael and Rachel said simultaneously. Michael had repeated her words as almost a compulsion. He looked at her incredulously.

"Oh, now, this is no good." He quipped.

"Because you're in my head."

"Yes, because I'm in your head. I think exactly what you think. Feel exactly what you feel. I know every little non sequitur that pops into that brain of yours. I know everything you see and touch. I know there are people who think this would be a great idea, but I'm only seeing a bad side." Michael winced and began rubbing his temples. "This is going to give me a splitting headache."

"Why, because a man will know a woman's perspective?"

"No – well – yes, but not just that. It's like everything is double exposed. Like I'm seeing a 3D movie without the glasses on. Images on top of images, I can't figure out which one I'm supposed to concentrate on. My brain is having a difficultly trying to process the whole thing."

"Are you experiencing any dizziness?" Gaia asked.

"You're still there?" Rachel replied.

"Although I do not always participate in your conversation, I am always present."

"Great!" Rachel's sarcasm cut through the mood and transferred over to Michael.

"Based on your statements, I calculate there is a ninety-eight percent chance you will experience a form of vertigo."

"That's very comforting," Michael said, closing his eyes. "You want to tell me what I can do about it?"

"I can give you an antihistamine that will act as an antiemetic until you acclimate to your current condition."

"How long will that take?" Michael replied.

"I do not know. Your condition is unique, so I do not know how long you will be afflicted." Four helper robots entered from decontamination. "I have been ordered to draw blood samples from both of you to determine the extent and cause of the mutation."

Gaia's voice was replaced by General Harris. "Rachel, this is General Harris. I am giving you a direct order, to have your blood drawn and not to interfere with or damage the Helper Units. Is that clear?"

There was annoyance from Rachel, but she didn't let it show in her voice. She was already tired of being accused of deliberately breaking the robot. "Crystal clear, Sir."

"Very good," General Harris replied. "You destroyed Helper Unit Four. It's irreparable."

"I'm very sorry about that, Sir," Rachel said sheepishly. Silently she was pleased with the outcome. "I didn't know that would happen."

"I'm certain you didn't. Just, please remember those drones cost almost two million apiece. They aren't cheap, and although we can replace them easily, I'd rather not. I have spoken to Doctor Rana and Gaia. They want to check to see if you have any viruses that might endanger the rest of the others that are headed to decontamination as we speak. They should arrive in quarantine in about forty minutes. Remember, you are not to share your experiences with them."

"Sir," Michael said, raising his hand as if the general were in the room. He was certain the general was watching via remote link, and so the action seemed appropriate.

"Yes, Michael?"

"Wouldn't it benefit them to know what's likely to happen?"

"Michael, we aren't even sure what happened to you and why. Until we know more, it is best not to worry them about something that might not happen. I have doubled the number of Helper Units for that level. After they draw your blood, they will fix the door. Hopefully, before the others arrive. It's going to get crowded in there soon."

Rachel thought about how difficult it was going to be to have more than just the two of them, and whether she would be able to tolerate the new people. She had always been socially awkward, and wondered if they would like her, or if they would be mean. She always had to put on a tough facade.

"Would you stop obsessing!" Michael said, annoyed at his quick temper. "I can hear that, you know!"

"Well," General Harris said. "I think we're done talking. You two behave yourselves. If I have to separate you two—" he started to chuckle as his mic turned off.

"It's official," Rachel said, as she looked at Michael. "We've become a joke."

Chapter 6

REGENERATION

The helper robots drew Michael's and Rachel's blood and then administered an injection from a syringe encased in a thick metal sleeve. Four additional robots repaired the damaged door and frame. Rachel was anxious about what the new arrivals would think if they saw the mess she had made. And Michael was concerned with the continued preservation of his newfound partner's mental state.

"Gaia, just a couple questions. What did you just inject us with?" Michael asked, over the din of the impromptu remodel work. "And how many people are coming through de-con?"

"You were just given the contrast agent for a PET scan[1]. You will need to relax for the next thirty minutes to allow the radioactive contrast to be distributed properly. You will find that the chairs you are sitting in recline. I suggest you take advantage of that. Secondly there are twelve individuals in decontamination."

"Can you tell us anything about them?"

"Of course," Gaia replied. "Doctor Sushma Rana, you know. The rest of the Alpha crew: Language specialists, Doctors John and Charlotte Merrill, astrophysicist Doctor Kazuma Kobayashi, nuclear specialist Doctor Heinrich Schwarzkopf, botanist Alice Morgan, mathematician Doctor Alex Montoya, and computer specialist Tiffany Yellowknife. In addition, the flight crews of the Beta and the Gamma reported as well. Captain Esparza, and Major Strand from the United States Air Force, Group Captain Worthington from the Royal Air Force, and Lieutenant Watanabe from the JSDF."

"Just the flight crews? Why not the rest of the MeCTen teams?" Rachel asked.

"Doctor Rana felt it would be best if the medical and science crews of the other Project Nova ships supervised her while she went through the mutation experience."

"The other specialists are already here?" Michael asked.

1 Positron Emissions Tomography

"The specialists teams were assembled approximately four years ago. They were instrumental in devising the genetic modification requirement, as well as all other aspects of the project. They have been waiting for human trials to be approved before undergoing the procedure. Since the quarantine facilities are limited to eighteen, they will come after the current subjects have completed recovery. They will return to active duty after that time."

"Who else knows about us?" Rachel asked.

"The only Project Nova personnel authorized for knowledge of your mutations are me, General Harris, and Doctors Rana, LeBlanc, and Young of the medical staff. Doctor Young will supervise the remainder of your treatment in quarantine."

"Are all the crews mixed sex?" Rachel inquired.

"Of course," Gaia replied. "In the event of complete inhabitability of Earth, the best way to repopulate the human species is by human copulation."

"Do what now?" Michael replied, unable to comprehend what he thought he'd just heard.

Rachel had a shocked look on her face. "I may not know much about space travel, but I know NASA strictly forbids fraternization. Not to mention, that the military has strict rules against it as well."

"While that is true for NASA," Gaia replied. "It is not true for Project Nova. Marriage between crew members is highly encouraged, although fraternization outside marriage is against regulations. You should be aware; any previous issues of that nature have been resolved."

A flash of terror ran through Rachel. Michael now fully understood the entire exchange. The flood of memories that came from her removed all doubt. She was on the Mercy recovering from an ectopic pregnancy. Since human parthenogenesis doesn't occur, there were questions about how it occurred. After an interview with her captain, she was to be evacuated to the Mercy for surgery and then transferred to Pearl for court-marshal. It was revealed she was involved in an affair with a married officer on the USS Reagan. She hadn't been aware of the man's marital status, and it occurred in a moment of weakness while at port. It was something she felt a great deal of shame and regret. She was now afraid Michael knew it all and would hate her or harshly judge her for it. The only reason she was on the Mercy was because her captain had taken pity on her. He wanted to make sure that she would still be able to have children. Unfortunately, she was supposed to have faced a court-martial when she arrived at Pearl. That is what General Harris blackmailed her with, and why she suffered so much self-doubt.

Her terror fixated on Michael. She suspected he must know everything now, and her shame was intensified by his standards of belief. Horrified and exposed, she turned to face him.

Michael already knew everything. He knew she wanted to explain her actions, but he didn't see any point in that conversation. She had already talked to the Chaplin on the Reagan. He wasn't someone who could judge her actions anyway. "You don't need to explain yourself to me. I'm not a bishop, I'm not the Savior, I'm just a guy that shares your mind. I know the details, and that's more than anyone else needs to know."

"You know though," Rachel whispered in guilt, shame, and terror. Tears began to flow uncontrollably. "What you must think of me."

Michael held up his hand. "You have it all wrong. I really do understand. I may be the only other person, other than God, who does. I understand perfectly, and I don't think any less of you. Believe it or not, I think it's given me a good understanding of who you are."

"And what do you think?"

"I think you're someone who has gone through a difficult time. I also know you seldom repeat a mistake. I think you're pretty great, despite your recent destructive tendencies. You never have to ask my forgiveness, but I think God still wants to hear from you about it. I don't know how best to handle this situation. I doubt this base has a branch anyway."

"Actually," Gaia interjected. "Since religious people are vital to the success of this mission, there are ecclesiastic services, including those of your denomination, available in the sterile barracks."

"Well, then," Michael sighed. "That settles it."

Rachel's mind drifted to an image of what life would be like with Michael. She found him attractive, and had from the moment they met, but she hadn't given any real thought to a relationship. What intrigued her most was the apparent thought put into the composition of crews, and the emphasis on marriage. "Why do you even care if people marry, Gaia?"

"I do not, as you say, care about marriage," Gaia replied. "I would simply tate that it's statistically proven a stable monogamous relationship is most conducive to rearing children who can perpetuate a law-abiding society. The crews were selected based on mutual compatibility. In fact, the only Alpha crew members who have not yet bonded by engagement or marriage, is you."

Rachel's mind reeled at the thought she had been pre-arranged to marry Michael. They barely knew each other, and this computer had already matched heir personalities. Was this some kind of horrible blind date, where the goal at the end was to get hitched? How does this computer know anything about hem?

"Oh, wait just a darned minute!" Michael protested. "What makes you so certain we're compatible? Human emotions are complex. Most people can't even tell themselves who will get along and who won't. I mean, what happens f she can't stand me?"

"Marriage is not required, although highly encouraged." Gaia replied. 'The scientists were selected based on compatibility. They spent a long time ogether, and many were able to form attachments. Those that did not were ound compatible flight crew who would predictably be compatible mates. With the goal that, if properly fostered, affections would naturally occur. Either the people fall in love or would form a bond out of necessity."

"You don't think that's incredibly manipulative?" Rachel asked.

"Manipulation implies that you are being coerced into something you wouldn't otherwise do. My statistical analysis of your personalities suggests hat there is an eighty-three-point-seven percent chance that you would have formed a romantic relationship if you randomly encountered each other on he street. Based on this prediction, and your compatible genetic makeup, you would excel at marriage and family rearing."

"How did we get our very own Yenta?" Rachel quipped.

The helper units had finished their repairs and removed the damaged door and disappeared into decontamination. A few minutes later a tall, blonde-haired man entered wearing a white decontamination suit.

"Ah-" he said in a definitive British accent. "I didn't realize there were people already here." He walked up to Michael and stuck out his hand. "Group Captain William Worthington the Third. They call me Thor. Well, they used to. You can call me William, since I don't think we're allowed to use our call-signs. And you are?"

"Lieutenant Commander Rachel Bright, US Navy, and this is Major Michael Langford, United States Marine Corps. Welcome to quarantine, I guess."

"Where are the mates' racks?" William asked.

Michael pointed to the room his bunk occupied. "I suppose that's for the men, although, I don't think it matters. Just, don't go into that one," he said, pointing to Rachel's room.

Rachel shot him a glare and thought: "Don't!"

"Yeah, yeah." Michael said aloud, waving her concern off.

"No." Rachel said definitively.

"I'm sorry," William said, looking perplexed. "Did I miss something?"

Michael smiled. "Nothing you need to worry about."

Two more men entered from decontamination. One was a very tan skinned man with thick black hair. He appeared to be of Latin descent, but Michael couldn't be sure. The other was an average looking man with pale skin. He was clean-cut, with dark brown hair. Both were conversing in Spanish as they entered the room.

"Aunque no sé por qué tuvieron que ser declarados muertos para esta operación. No tiene sentido para mi esposa y para mí."[2] He stopped talking and looked at the others in the room. "Sorry, I wasn't expecting anyone other than the Group Captain."

"Ningún problema," Michael replied. "No pasa fecnentamente que llegue a hablar español."[3]

Rachel was confused. She didn't really understand Spanish, so it was frustrating to hear people use it. She couldn't be certain they weren't talking about her, and she wanted to know what they had to say.

Michael, promptly aware of Rachel's apprehension, turned to the others in the group. "Not to be rude, but could we keep the language in English?

2 "Although, I don't know why they had to be declared dead for this operation. It doesn't make sense to my wife and me."
3 "No Problem. It does not happen that I get to speak Spanish often."

It is a little rude to be conversing in a language not understood by everyone present."

"Right you are," William said. "You can never be certain if people are insulting you to your face without knowing it."

"Where are my manners," the clean-cut man said, waving sheepishly. "I don't get to use my Spanish as often as I would like. I'm John Merrill, one of the two Alpha linguistics experts. My wife, Charlotte, is the other. She'll be coming through decon any minute."

"And I'm Captain José Esparza, United States Air Force." He pointed at Michael and Rachel. "I didn't see you in the elevator coming down, so I assume you've been here for a while?"

"All they need is a quick physical." A beautiful, copper-skinned woman said as she came out of decontamination. She had jet black hair and a face that looked sculpted with high cheekbones, and dark brown eyes. Her thick Indian accent instantly gave Doctor Rana away. Michael thought she might as well have stepped out of a Bollywood movie. "Which, I will do before we become sick, and I can't help you."

"Doctor Rana, I presume." Michael said.

"Yes," she said, walking past them toward the locked door near the kitchen. "Now, if you will follow me, I can get the scans done by the time the blood test results are finished. Gaia, please open the exam room." There was buzz and a click as the multiple locks disengaged. Doctor Rana motioned Michael and Rachel to follow her. "The rest of you settle in. The helper robots will be in to start IVs and give you medicine in a few minutes. Based on the reaction these two had, I would say you have about three hours before you're all incapacitated."

"A little warning would have been nice," William mused.

"You are soldiers," Doctor Rana replied. "Consider it a gift that you have any warning."

"Doctor Rana," Gaia interjected. "Please try to have a better bedside manner."

"Quiet, Gaia! I have a headache, and I have to get this done before I'll need to be carried out." She shepherded the two pilots into the exam room and quickly closed the door.

The room looked like a typical doctor's exam room, with the addition of a narrow table opposite a bed next to a gaping hole in the wall. "Rachel, you get on the exam table. Michael, I need to get you into the scanner, so I can run a few tests. Gaia will do the scan while I examine Rachel." She pointed in the direction of a rather sturdy shelf on the far wall.

Michael wheeled himself over to the narrow table. As he approached, it lowered to a reasonable sitting height. It was white and jutted out from the wall and looked like the beds used for an X-ray or CT scanner.

Doctor Rana gave Michael earplugs and helped him into position. His head rested in a pillow-looking cradle on one end, and he settled in. She placed his IV bag into a small cupboard in the wall and threaded the tubing through a slot.

"See you in an hour and a half," Doctor Rana said as she pressed a button. A compartment opened on the wall. The table gently rose from the loading position and slid into a small, white, coffin-like space deep inside the wall. A thick panel slid up and sealed him inside the claustrophobic space.

"Relax, Major." Gaia said gently. "This scanner is similar to an MRI, but it performs multiple scans."

"You couldn't make it more spacious?" Michael asked, unnerved by the close quarters.

Suddenly, it was as if Michael was overlooking a serene mountain lake. He knew it must be a projection, but it was very high definition. The details were astounding. He could hear the gentle roar of the wind moving through the pine trees and see the shimmer of the sunlight on the waves of the lake. He could even feel the movement of air across his face. It was almost as if he were hiking in the Uinta mountains of Utah, instead of sealed in the tight confines of the scanner.

"Does this help?" Gaia asked.

"Yes," Michael replied. "Almost as good as being there."

"This is Shoshone Lake, in the Wind River mountains of Wyoming. You can view from this vantage, or I can take you on a virtual hike around the area, or you can sleep. You must, however, hold perfectly still."

"I'll just stay here," Michael replied. "I think I might actually get motion sickness if we try the hike."

"The scans will take approximately one hour and fifty-two minutes." Gaia replied. "Doctor Rana has ordered PET scan, a full-body MRI, an F-MRI,[4] and a bone density scan."

"When do we start?" Michael asked.

"We already have," Gaia replied. "Now, please, remain still."

The scans were noisy, but seemed to last just a few minutes, instead of nearly two hours. Michael was almost asleep when the scanner opened, and the table slid back into the room. Instead of Doctor Rana, a man in a full biohazard suit stood above him. Before he could inquire, images of a pale looking Doctor Rana collapsing began to flood his mind. He realized for the past two hours he had been entirely unaware of Rachel's thoughts, but now they were flooding his mind. It was like there was some kind of ethereal memory buffer holding all her thoughts in queue, waiting for him to emerge.

Instinctively, Michael threw his hands in front of his eyes in a vain effort to slow the mental transfer. It wasn't painful, per se, but it taxed his mental faculties. Being bombarded by emotions, images, and thoughts all at once was unlike anything he had ever experienced. He became vaguely aware of another man's voice asking him if he was alright. Michael couldn't say.

Michael realized that attempting to verbalize an event you have never experienced was nearly impossible. There was no frame of reference. No touchstone of understanding to even begin to comprehend, let alone explain. But the voice persisted, pressing him for an answer.

"Too much." Michael groaned. "Too many thoughts. Too much information. It's coming all at once. I can't keep up. I can't make sense of it all!"

"Breathe," the man said. "Whose thoughts?"

As quickly as they had come, the stream of highly compressed memories ceased. The double images of reality and memory faded, and Michael was able to think clearly again. He looked around the room and saw Rachel, looking rather terrified by his writhing. He understood from his vision, the man in the hazmat suit was Doctor Young.

4 Functional Magnetic Resonance Imaging

Michael realized he could make sense of what occurred while he was in the scanner. Doctor Rana was in the middle of Rachel's examination, when she fainted and began seizing. The helper robots had flooded the room, and Doctor Young had rushed in from BAS. After he had taken care of Doctor Rana, he finished Rachel's exam.

"What happened?" Doctor Young asked.

"When?" Michael replied.

"Just now, when you were saying there were too many thoughts?"

"I would think that was self-explanatory." Michael said indignantly. He looked at the doctor, who just stared at him in wide-eyed wonder. "What? Gaia said you were one of the people briefed on our condition."

Doctor Young blinked, as if he had been just reminded of something he should have known. "Well – yes – but I didn't believe it. I mean – it's not very scientific. There's nothing in the medical literature that would suggest this is even possible. I mean – it's right out of science fiction. This doesn't happen."

Michael looked at him and looked irritated by his attitude. He could feel an anger welling inside, creeping up his neck. It was unusual for him to become enraged so quickly. He determined it must be the combination of all the events of the past few days. He knew if he gave voice to his anger, it wouldn't end well. He had to calm down.

Michael took a deep breath and let out a long sigh. "Doctor, I understand there are a lot of things outside our realm of experience. This is something I don't fully understand myself, so you're just going to have to accept it at face value for now. For some reason I have a connection with Rachel. I wish I didn't, but I don't seem to have any control over it – yet."

"So, what was that fit all about?" Rachel asked.

"I don't know," Michael replied. "When I was in the scanner, I could only hear Gaia. As soon as I came out, it was like everything hit me at once. All your thoughts, memories, and perceptions came into my mind. It was like it was held in some kind of buffer and then downloaded into my brain the moment I came out of the scanner."

Doctor Young leaned back in a moment of contemplation, then smiled as if he knew what had happened. "I think the scanner must have blocked the connection – temporarily, of course. Then, when you came out of the magnetic field, the connection reestablished itself. It's almost like you were inside a Faraday Cage. I'm not sure why it queued itself. Although, information shouldn't be held like that. It should have been received when it was sent, or not at all – well, technically it shouldn't happen – but that's beside the point."

"Fascinating," Michael said, the ire palpable in his voice. "Can we move in a more productive direction?"

Doctor Young looked at him quizzically. "Oh – your scans – right – sorry about that."

"Actually, I was thinking more of getting me up off this table," Michael replied. "But scan results would be helpful too."

Doctor Young helped Michael sit and then retrieved the IV bag. "Actually, the scan must be read by Doctor Mossbrook. She's the radiologist stationed at Nellis, so it will be a while to get the results. Oh – speaking of. Rachel, you'll need to trade places. I'll do Michael's exam while you're getting scanned."

Michael maneuvered himself back into the wheelchair and Rachel sat on the scanner bed. She was about to swing her legs up, when she became very self-conscious about her gown. Michael swiveled the wheelchair and grabbed the doctor's arm. "I think we should turn around for a second."

Doctor Young looked confused. "What for?"

"A little privacy," Rachel said with incredulity. "You have no idea how embarrassing it is to be in one of these open-air tarps, with two men ogling you."

Doctor Young shrugged his shoulders dispassionately, and turned around, as if placating a stubborn child. "Whatever, it's nothing I haven't seen before – well, I mean – during the exam –"

"You should just go ahead and stop right there, doctor." Rachel growled. She was feeling very vulnerable after the physical examination. She always hated them, as they felt overly intrusive. She understood why they were necessary, but she truly disliked having them done. Especially by unfamiliar and untrusted people."

Michael looked up at the quirky doctor. "You're not much of a people person, are you?"

"Oh, heavens no." Doctor Young replied. "I personally can't stand most people."

"Really?" Michael replied with thinly veiled sarcasm.

Doctor Young nodded. "Oh my, yes. Most people are pathetically dumb. Just being in the same room drags down my mind, like an intellectual vampire. I mean –"

"Doctor" Gaia interrupted.

"Yes? Oh, wise and mighty Femputer." Doctor Young's reply was snarky but hinted at an inside joke between himself and Gaia.

"You remember when you asked me to stop you from exposing your more eccentric and sociopathic personality traits?"

"Oh – yes – that." Doctor Young replied, as if being scolded by a disapproving parent.

"Well, you're doing it, so I must ask you to refrain from making your next self-aggrandizing and arrogant statement."

Doctor Young turned and grabbed Rachel's IV bag. "Well, you should have enough of this to last you." He inserted it into the machine and looked down at his anxious patient. "Are you resting comfortably?"

Rachel suddenly felt as if she was staring into the face of some maniacal mad scientist who moonlighted as a serial killer. A wave of apprehension washed over her. "Gaia?"

"Yes, Rachel?"

"You won't let him hurt me, will you?"

"Of course not. Do not let his faux-autistic narcissism fool you. Doctor Young is quite competent. He just gets nervous around unfamiliar people. I would ask you not to damage the scanner while you're inside."

"Gaia, now you're starting to border on mean," Rachel grumbled as the bed raised to scanner height, and she slid into the opening. Her last thought to Michael was "protect me."

Doctor Young helped Michael onto the exam table. "I made her nervous."

"A bit."

"Yeah – well – I do that to people. I don't mean to, per se, but I don't deal with inferior intellects well."

Michael raised his eyebrow. "Oh?"

Doctor Young looked reflective for a moment. "Well, when your IQ is as high as mine, you tend to find other people just can't keep up." He walked over to the wall and retrieved an otoscope from a resting cradle. "Which reminds me – can you still hear her thoughts?"

Michael had to think about it. The last thing he sensed from Rachel was her plea to protect her from the machine and the odd doctor. Now, he couldn't see or hear what she did nor perceive her inner monologue. "No, nothing."

Doctor Young looked gleeful as he walked back to Michael and unceremoniously grabbed his right ear. "Fascinating! Now – I'm just going to look in your ears. You might feel a bit of discomfort, but it shouldn't be too bad."

The speculum of the otoscope scraped against his ear canal and was more than a little uncomfortable. Michael could recall Rachel's memories of Doctor Young's rough examination. Her experience was not far from his own. The doctor prattled on, with frequent mental shifts in his conversation as he voiced every thought that entered his head. He pontificated on the possible causes of Michael's mental link with Rachel, one possibility being quantum entanglement within the nanosurg, but it was all speculation.

After nearly half an hour, Gaia interrupted the exam for private communication with Doctor Young. The doctor retreated to a corner near the scanner, so Michael couldn't hear much of the muffled conversation through the hazmat suit. Doctor Young responded only briefly to whomever was on the call. And as quickly as it had started, the call ended.

Doctor Young turned to Michael. He smiled and clapped his hands with glee. "I think it's time to test-drive that leg of yours."

"How do you figure?" Michael asked.

"Doctor Mossbrook said your scans shows that your fracture has completely healed. Rather astonishing if you think about it. Your typical recovery for complete osteopoietic stem cell arthroplasty is six weeks. You've healed completely in just a few days – so it seems."

"How can you tell?"

"Gaia, bring up the sagittal and lateral views of his left ankle on the monitor," Doctor Young said, strolling up to a large display on the wall opposite the scanner. "You see how your bones share the same characteristics as all the surrounding bone?" Michael shook his head. Doctor Young growled in disgust. "Fine! See how the white bits are all the same shade of white? There isn't any evidence of a break. Now, Gaia, overlay the bone density scan." The display became vibrant with color as the scan was altered to show the results of the density scan. "See how the bone maintains the same level of density around the outer edges?"

Michael could see the white of the bones, and the multicolored rings of the bone density scan, but couldn't make any sense of it. "I'm not a doctor," Michael replied. "I'm a pilot. I know how to read avionics, not X-rays."

"The absence of variations in the bone density gradient in the X-rays around your fracture sites shows that there isn't any sign of damage. It's as if your bones never fractured. If it were still healing, I would expect to see a shadow on the X-ray and a color variation on the exact location of your break. The stem cell infused scaffold would show up as less dense than the surrounding bone until it completely calcified into an osteoblast. The bones in your ankle are fully healed, and they shouldn't be."

"So, what happened?"

"I'm not sure if it was the rapid regeneration DNA of the jellyfish and mole rat, or if the nanosurg assisted. It's far too early to tell. At any rate – I want to have you stand up without that brace."

"Wait, what?" Michael said, somewhat shocked by the species of xenogeneic DNA now residing in his body. "Mole rat?"

Doctor Young waved nonchalantly. "That and a few others. It's not like you will become a rat. Stand up, I want to check out your ankle."

Michael realized further questions on the DNA would be a futile effort and moved on. "Couldn't I reinjure it?"

Doctor Young shook his head. "Not really – well – technically yes, but I don't think it's very likely." Michael looked warily at the doctor. "Look, just take it slowly. If you feel your ankle start to snap, sit down."

"You're not very reassuring." Michael said.

"It'll be fine. Now, up, up, up!"

Michael gingerly began to stand with Doctor Young's help. At first, he put all his weight on his right foot, and then gradually began to use his left ankle to support himself. Surprisingly, his ankle didn't protest the added weight. He had expected it to be sore or produce some form of pain with the stress of his body, but there was nothing. His leg felt like nothing had happened. It was an unexpected outcome to be sure.

He had broken bones before. Healing took several months, with soreness lingering as the bones knit together. This was different. He looked at Doctor Young in amazement. "How?"

"I'm not sure. Can you walk on it?"

Michael slowly stepped forward, expecting sharp pain, or some soreness to halt his progress, but there was nothing. He walked to the far end of the room and then returned to the exam table. He sat down and brought his foot up for closer examination. He expected to see the red incision lines from the surgery he had received on the Mercy. The scars were barely visible behind the bloodied adhesive tape. The bright red was replaced by a dull pink that almost blended into his untouched skin.

"Let me see," Doctor Young asked. He took Michael's foot in his hand and carefully examined the ankle. He took off the surgical dressing tape. He pulled at the wounds with his thumbs, but there was no pain, and the skin refused to split. "There is no way you should have wound approximation this soon after surgery. Your body is healing at a vastly accelerated rate."

"Is this normal?"

"Of course, it isn't normal." Doctor Young said bluntly. "I've never even heard of anyone healing this fast – unless you count fictional superheroes – which – well – fiction."

Michael rolled his eyes. "I'm talking about reality here."

"So am I." Doctor Young said defensively. He leaned back thoughtfully. "I'm truly stumped. I don't know what could have caused your body to regenerate tissue at this rate. It should take months for this to happen, but it's been – what – six days since your surgery on the Mercy? I would say you should take more than five weeks before you're anywhere near this point."

Gaia interrupted. "Actually, Doctor, he demonstrates approximately forty-nine weeks of healing."

"That's a ballpark observation – of course." Doctor Young interjected. "No one can be that certain about the timetable of long-term healing."

"There are definitive stages of tissue regeneration," Gaia replied. "Based on the available data, Michael has already shown signs of advanced remodeling. The mineralization of the fractured bone has moved beyond all preliminary stages, and the excess tissue has mostly been reabsorbed. This should only happen in the very late stages of wound repair."

Doctor Young mulled over Gaia's assessment. "It would be interesting to see how the apoptosis is being controlled by the nanosurg with the additional CAS 9[5] chains – provided there isn't some ankA[6] gene that has become activated."

Michael glared at the doctor. "You know," he said with a sigh. "I didn't go to med school but I'm not dumb."

"My sincerest apologies, Michael," Gaia said. "The doctor and I aren't trying to leave you out of the conversation. It is not possible to hypothesize about your medical anomalies without using the most specific language possible. Since that requires the use of biological terminology, it must seem like we are talking in another language."

Doctor Young waved his hand, as if dismissing an annoying child. "You're stealing all my thunder, Gaia. We're just wondering if it's possible we gave you some form of cancer."

"How did we get from healing to cancer?"

"I'll try to put this simply. Ankyrin–repeat protein, or ankA, is a genetic sequence that normally remains dormant in most animal's DNA. Sometimes, for reasons we don't fully understand, the gene can switch on. When

5 CRISPR Associated Protein 9
6 Ankyrin-repeat protein A

that happens, the cells can be forced to rapidly divide. Uncontrolled, rapid cell division is the essence of metastasis."

Doctor Young looked at Michael as if he had just successfully explained blue to a blind child, only to have the pilot look back with a dumbfounded expression. The doctor scoffed.

"Metastasis is the word doctors use to describe a spreading cancer. I thought your dad was a physician."

"He went to medical school. I didn't. The last I heard, knowledge isn't transferred genetically."

Doctor Young eyed him, as if pitying a child. "How dull is your life, trapped in that tiny brain of yours?"

"Doctor," Michael growled. "I might not be as brilliant as you think you are, but I am a Marine. I am perfectly capable of making you eat that suit, while simultaneously shoving your foot where the sun doesn't shine. Perhaps you should consider your own fragility before insulting your patient."

"Are you threatening me?"

"Absolutely," Michael replied coldly.

Doctor Young froze for a moment. This, apparently, was not the response he was expecting. "You aren't afraid of any consequences?"

"Doctor," Michael said as he stood up. He locked eyes with the nervous practitioner. "I'm dead. Technically I don't exist. I've been injected with a concoction of drugs that has made me rapidly heal. I also hear the thoughts of another person who can flatten you with her mind. I have nothing to lose by showing you what a Marine can do to a guy that thinks he's smarter than me."

"Point taken."

"I've studied lots of engineering, physics, chemistry, and math. Don't think of me as an idiot because I don't know medicine."

"Doctor?" Gaia said calmly. "I believe you have overstepped your bounds."

Doctor Young looked shaken but smiled nervously. "It appears so." He shrugged his shoulders and sat down on a wheeled stool and scooted to a computer terminal, sighing heavily. "Well then, let's just look at your blood and see if there's anything worth noting. Gaia, add every cancer marker we have on both of their lab orders."

"Those tests will require more blood to be drawn and will take approximately one week before results will be available," Gaia replied.

"Yeah, yeah," Doctor Young said, nodding in annoyance. "Just get it done." He looked at the computer for a few minutes. "From the looks of your current labs, you're free to go to decontamination. From there, you'll head to the sterile barracks."

"I'm done?"

"Yup!"

"What about Rachel?" Michael asked, curious if he should wait for her to finish her scans.

"She's got a little over an hour left. I don't imagine there will be an issue. As soon as her scans are done, I'll send her up, too."

A door opened on the far side of the room, and a helper robot stood waiting to help Michael through the decontamination.

Chapter 7

ARIES

Michael was guided out of decontamination by a helper robot to an elevator on the clean side of the showers. It went up to the sterile area of the Project Nova base. Captain Stevens was waiting for him when the door opened.

"How are you feeling, sir?" she asked.

"Well enough for government work." Michael replied.

"Come with me, and we'll get you settled." Captain Stevens led him through a series of bland white corridors, her heals rhythmically clicking on the sterile tile floor and reverberating through the vacant halls. It only took a minute to arrive at the barracks common room.

The common area was set up like the one in decontamination, but it was much larger. There was a conference room opposite the kitchen, and stairs leading up on either end. On one end was a recreation area with a television. The other end had a large dining area with a chow line. Obviously, the kitchen was for the meals they would prepare on their own; the main meals would be catered by the base.

Captain Stevens continued to the stairs near the recreation area, and they began to ascend. "You'll be billeted on the fourth floor. Meals will be served in the mess hall at oh-six-hundred, twelve, and eighteen-hundred hours. You must report on time for mess, and you will have thirty minutes to finish. From oh-six thirty to oh-seven-thirty is the daily briefing in the conference center just off the mess hall. From oh-seven-forty-five to eleven-forty-five, and twelve-forty-five to seventeen-thirty you will report to the Omega for flight training and spacecraft orientation. From eighteen-thirty to nineteen hundred is debriefing in the conference center. From nineteen hundred to twenty-two-thirty are spacecraft operations on the Omega. From twenty-three hundred to oh five hundred is your rack time. Worship services are held in the base chapel on Sundays from eleven to thirteen hundred. Make sure you allot at least fifteen minutes for decontamination before reporting for duty inside the hangars. Each spacecraft has its own clean room, so you must make sure you don't contaminate the area." She finished just as they arrived at the top landing. "Any questions?"

"I'm assuming there's no free time?"

"That is correct. Gaia will give you an alarm, if you need one, and remind you where you need to be and when. You are not allowed to deviate from her schedule."

"Anything else I need to know?"

"Yes," Captain Stevens replied bluntly. "The fourth floor is the male portion of the barracks. Floor three is for married couples, and the second floor is for women. You are not allowed on either floor without express permission from Gaia." She took out a silver band from her pocket. "This is your communications terminal. It is your link to Gaia and the other AI's when you're not in a monitored area."

She placed the band on his wrist. It was made of aluminum, about five millimeters thick, and three centimeters wide. It looked like a small watch. On one side was a thin slit which glowed with a blue light. Most of the band was a flexible mesh, except for a four-centimeter smooth spot on the top. She tapped the center of the top portion twice, and a display came to life. It hovered above his wrist in the air, as if projected. It displayed a menu, like a phone with familiar icons for mail, phone, and so-forth.

"This is your primary base communicator. It allows you to contact anyone on the base, including the AI's. It has manuals and other materials you might need. It can display anything you request from Gaia or the other AI's. But, as I said, this is for base communications only. You won't be allowed to use it to contact the outside world."

"One question," Michael said, tapping the communicator band, causing the display to disappear. "Why train in the Omega, when we're supposed to crew the Alpha?"

"Good question," Captain Stevens replied. "The Alpha isn't flight ready yet, and the Omega is."

"It's fully flight tested?"

"No," she replied. There was something in the tone of her voice that seemed as if she was trying to downplay this fact. "It needs a test crew to do a full run-up and refine the flight manual."

Michael shook his head. "I'm not a test pilot."

"You are a pilot, aren't you?"

"Yes, but not a qualified test pilot."

"It shouldn't matter."

Michael felt his blood begin to boil. "You know it takes a minimum of eight years of combat flight experience before you're even considered for the training?"

"Yes."

"You know I have about two, right?"

"What's your point?"

"I am laughably unqualified to test a brand-new aircraft. The likelihood of failure is significant with an inexperienced pilot."

"Sir, I know this might be difficult for you to understand, but this space-craft is unlike anything that has ever flown. It's faster than anything ever built. It has capabilities beyond any other aircraft or spacecraft. In this case we need someone who can adapt to the unique characteristics of the MeC-Ten. We need someone who isn't tied down to old paradigms. Besides, it's a direct order from General Harris."

"In other words, I have no choice and can't object."

Captain Stevens smiled. "See, you're learning already."

"Just point me to my room," Michael grumbled.

"Fourth door on the left. It's eleven-forty-two. Now, General Harris will debrief you in the conference room at thirteen hundred. Lunch is served in eighteen minutes, so don't be late."

Michael turned and dismissed her with a wave. He trudged down the hall and found his room. A name plate had already been made. He entered the small room and closed the door. It was a typical dorm-style room. There was a twin-size bed with a small desk at the far end, next to a remarkably dis-satisfying window. The window was opaque, with a frosted finish to it. The bed had already been made in military fashion. The closet had several duty uniforms, neatly pressed, ready for wear. All the drawers were full of every supply he would need. Everything was an example of neat and tidy military precision. It was spartan, but practical.

"I wonder who did this?" Michael muttered to himself.

"I had my helper robots procure your supplies, Michael," Gaia replied. "I hope you don't mind."

"Why am I not surprised that you're listening in?"

"I assumed that you were speaking to me, since there is no other person on this floor."

"Sorry, Gaia, I was whistling in the dark."

There was a pause. "I make you nervous?"

"No, Gaia, this whole thing makes me nervous." Michael plopped down onto the chair. "Everything that has happened. Lying to us about what this project was doing. The DNA futzing about. Declaring us dead! Everything smacks of manipulation and subterfuge."

Thoughts suddenly came flooding into his mind. He could see image after image. Loud banging pounded in his head. He could hear and see double again. The pain was excruciating. Light, noise, smells, emotions, and sensations overwhelmed his brain. His skin felt as if it would spontaneously combust. He felt pain as he fell out of the chair. He could see himself writhing on the floor in agony. Next, he felt as if he were yelling, but he could only hear the cacophony of sound that drowned out his own thoughts. He could barely breathe. After what seemed like an eternity, the onslaught stopped as suddenly as it had started.

Slowly, Michael began to become aware of his surroundings. He was lying on the smooth tile floor, dripping in sweat and panting heavily. There was a steady ringing in his ears, as if someone had boxed them. He glanced around the room to get his bearings. A helper robot stood in the doorway, and he could barely make out Gaia's voice over the din. It sounded distant and hollow.

"Michael, are you alright?"

Michael groaned. "Don't tell me, Rachel's out of the scanner."

"Actually, she is in the elevator. The subterranean levels are encased in a Faraday Cage. She must be out of its influence."

Michael let out a pained grunt as he rolled over to push himself up to a sitting position. "Gaia, can I ask you to do me a favor?"

"What is that?"

"Don't separate us by a Faraday Cage again, please," Michael pleaded. "It hurts my brain when the connection re-establishes."

"I will do my best, but I cannot guarantee that I can accommodate that request. Will you need any assistance to get to the mess hall?"

"What?" Michael said, confused by the question.

"Lunch will be served in three minutes," Gaia replied. "Will you need the assistance of one of my helpers to aid you to the mess hall?"

Michael winced as he stood up. His body ached, and his mind was still seeing double. With effort he was able to stumble to the door. The helper robot moved to assist him, but he waved it off.

"No!" Michael snapped. He looked at the expressionless face of the robot and sighed. How would getting angry at a helpful computer solve anything? How could artificial intelligence understand the need for self-reliance? Calmer now, he stood erect. "No, thank you, Gaia. I'll manage."

"As you wish," Gaia said sympathetically. "I am here if you need anything."

By the time Michael trudged down the six flights of stairs, he felt almost normal again. He walked into the common area and made his way to the mess hall. The buffet had a few pre-made salads, assorted fruits and vegetables, and a plate of sandwiches.

Rachel had just started selecting her lunch, when she noticed Michael entering the room. He could feel her pleasure at seeing a familiar face. She was concerned that he might not be joining her for a meal. Somehow, it was comforting to have someone who knew what she was going through. She smiled as he entered the room. It suddenly dawned on her that he was walking, and not in a wheelchair.

"You're up on two legs already?"

"Apparently, whatever they gave us, speeds up the healing process. My leg feels like it was never broken."

"Any other problems?" Rachel asked timidly.

"Such as?"

"That thing that happened when you came out of the scanner?"

Michael hesitated. He didn't want to worry her, but he wasn't a fan of keeping secrets. His delayed response was all she needed to know. He sensed her thoughts. She could see the expression on his face and knew that she already had guessed the truth. "Unfortunately, yes."

"Gaia might know what's causing it."

Michael frowned. "Gaia, are you holding out on me?"

"Not per se," Gaia replied. "I have a hypothesis, but there is no way to objectively test it."

"Well, don't keep us in suspense," Rachel said. "Tell us what you think might be causing it."

"I believe that it has to do with the injections."

"Duh!" Michael said sarcastically.

"Captain Stevens may not have properly clean the injector. Since Rachel was injected first, her tissue was still on the needle. This, combined with the nanosurg, caused your cells to become entangled. Since Michael was the only one who received a tissue transplant, he is the only one affected by the link."

"Quantum entanglement doesn't transfer information, Gaia," Rachel said dubiously. "It also doesn't explain why information would be retained in some kind of memory buffer."

"I am getting to that," Gaia replied. "The transfer of memory is one way, but the entanglement somehow knows what information has been trans-ferred. There must be a quantum check bit, like Hyper Text Transfer Proto-col handles parity. If Rachel does not receive a quantum check bit, her mem-ory begins to buffer her experiences. When the connection is re-established, the transfer of the buffered information begins. Since you aren't accustomed to sharing another person's mind, it is logical to assume that the download would be painful and disorienting."

"I'm sensing a lot of conjecture," Rachel quipped.

"You are correct, Rachel," Gaia replied. "This is a new phenomenon, so I can only guess. I suspect that we will never fully understand the exact cause."

"That's comforting," Michael said sarcastically.

"I'm sorry, Michael," Gaia replied. "I wish I could offer you a better explanation."

Their conversation was interrupted when General Harris entered the common room, followed by Captain Stevens. They both seemed to ignore the pilots and walked quickly toward the conference room.

"General on deck!" Rachel said in a loud voice, bringing both pilots to attention.

"Knock that off," General Harris said, obviously annoyed. "There aren't that many military personnel on this section of the base, so we don't do that here."

"Sir, yes, Sir!" Rachel replied

General Harris stopped for a moment. "You two aren't done yet?"

"No, sir," Michael replied, grabbing a couple of sandwiches from the tray.

"We don't have time to wait," General Harris said, motioning them to follow as he went through the doorway. "Eat in here."

"Yes, sir!" the two junior officers said in unison. They quickly grabbed their food and hurried into the conference room.

The room was a typical looking board-style meeting space. A long wooden table was in the center, surrounded by twelve chairs. On one wall was a whiteboard opposite a large display. The general took his seat at the head of the table near the display. Captain Stevens took the chair to his right.

"Gaia, invite Aries to this briefing," the general ordered.

"I am here, General," a deep masculine voice replied.

"Good!" General Harris said, directing the two pilots to sit. "I'm going to forego the debriefing for now. Gaia, bring us up to speed on our extraneous accelerating factors."

"China and Russia continue to protest the use of nuclear weapons by the United States, while denying their own use of nukes. The United Nations Security Council has attempted to pass several resolutions condemning our actions. This is largely symbolic, as the United States has veto power. The United Kingdom, France, and Germany have publicly condemned the use of nuclear weapons. However, currently both theaters have experienced a lull in fighting. The consensus from DIA,[1] NSA,[2] CIA,[3] and NRO[4] is that the other belligerents are unwilling to escalate the conflict further, due to the increased risk of nuclear attacks against more densely populated targets. It is unlikely there will be any large-scale retaliation soon, however humans are unpredictable and prone to irrational behavior. If the war escalates within the next month, I cannot guarantee that my helpers can complete all spacecraft in time."

"How long before they will be operational?" General Harris asked.

"Currently, my projected completion time is twenty-three days, fourteen hours, and forty-three minutes."

"Any way you can reduce that time?"

"No," Gaia replied. "The issue is not the workload, but the time to fully test the spacecraft. Not to mention the time to properly load the hazardous fuels and chemicals required for the mission."

"How about reactor startup?" General Harris asked. "How long will that take?"

"It will take sixty-three hours to bring all LFTRs,[5] online. And another forty-three hours to bring the two LFR,[6] up to flight capacity. Once all reactors have been brought online, it will take approximately twenty-three hours to bring the drive sections from cryo-quiescent intake to positive gravitational buoyancy. However, in an emergency, the spacecraft can be taken from cold start to flight configuration in four minutes and nine seconds. I don't recommend doing this, as it compromises safety."

"Duly noted," General Harris said soberly. "This war has really thrown a wrench into our timetable."

---

1 Defense Intelligence Agency
2 National Security Agency
3 Central Intelligence Agency
4 National Reconnaissance Office
5 Liquid Fluoride Thorium Reactor
6 Linear Fusion Reactor

Aries interrupted. "I am fully fueled and ready to carry out my mission right now."

"Quiet, Aries!" General Harris growled.

Michael looked at the general. It was clear that the Omega had a completely different mission than the other Project Nova ships. He couldn't determine if that mission was a constructive one or not.

"My apologies, General," Aries said.

"So, what are we supposed to do?" Michael asked.

"Your job is to test the flight systems, startup sequences, flight plans, emergency procedures, avionics, and spacecraft flight capabilities."

"Sir," Rachel interjected. "What you're proposing is not possible. It takes years to fully test aircraft —"

General Harris scowled. "I'm not interested in your opinion. I didn't ask to have an accelerated timetable. When this project was started, six years ago, there wasn't a war going on. In eighteen months, we have gone from the first shots fired, to the deployment of advanced nuclear weapons. Nothing escalates tensions more than nukes." His face was twisted with anger and frustration. "Now, I don't want to hear about what can't be done! We're trying to save humanity! We don't have the luxury of time anymore! We're borrowing every hour as it is. I need you two to pull your heads out of wherever they're crammed and get to work! That's an order!"

The general's temper frightened Rachel. "Yes, sir!" she said loudly, as if addressing a drill instructor.

"What about you, Michael? You have any problem with that?"

"Sir, no, Sir!" Michael replied with equal enthusiasm.

"Good!" General Harris bellowed. "I know it's unusual to rush everything. I had planned to use pilots from the three-seventieth to do the flight testing, but the war changed all that. Gaia determined that there was roughly a ninety percent chance the security of the project would be compromised if we continued development without sequestering the entire crew. She also determined that it would be best to have the actual crew do the testing, since they would have to meet the project requirements for sequestration anyway."

"With all due respect, General," Michael interjected. "The objection is not that we can't do the testing, but that we would be sacrificing the safety of the mission."

"I know." General Harris replied. "Believe me, I know the risks involved."

"If I may, General" Gaia said gently. "There is a sixty-seven percent chance there will be a catastrophic failure during flight testing. This includes a twelve percent chance of a significant fission reactor malfunction. A twenty percent chance of a fusion reactor malfunction, and a thirty-five percent chance there will be an incident involving the control system. Overall, there is a forty-three percent chance the flight test crew will be involved in an incident which will result in a fatality."

"You're not making a case for ignoring safety," Rachel said. Her anxiety had only increased when Gaia had recited their odds.

"I am not finished." Gaia said, continuing her elaboration. "The odds of a retaliatory nuclear strike from China, or Russia have now grown exponentially since you were recruited to the project. It is now a ninety-six percent chance that there will be a large-scale nuclear attack of military targets within the next thirty days. Currently, there is a fifty percent chance the attack will take place over the next twenty-four hours. Obviously, the odds increase with every day that passes."

"How do you figure?" Rachel asked. "Wouldn't the odds decrease as time passes between the incident?"

"Not in this case," General Harris replied. "China has never been too hasty when reacting. Like all communist governments, they require detailed plans in place. This isn't something their President can decide on his own. With such broad implications, it requires the consent of the entire People's Congress. Even with all the hawks in the Standing Committee, they still need the support of the Congress members from the larger population centers. Those urban centers are the ones who would feel the brunt of a U.S. attack. Russia, of course, is waiting to see what China will do first, before doing anything. No, China will take their sweet time before committing to anything."

"They'll be forced to retaliate," Michael mused. "If they don't respond, they'll appear weak. If they do, we're sure to pummel 'em hard. No one wins in that scenario."

"Yes, and President Zhang knows it," General Harris said, leaning back in his chair. "I suspect they will move every asset they have into position before retaliating. It's going to be ugly, with a capitol U."

"Time isn't our ally," Rachel said.

"If we sit around this table and debate safety, we lose," General Harris said, eyeing the two pilots carefully. He tapped a button on a tablet, and the monitor displayed a security camera of the Omega. "That's why the other three ships are running flight simulations as we speak. We need to get you in the spacecraft sooner, rather than later."

"I am running at ninety-eight percent capacity right now, handling base operations," Gaia replied. "I have my children committing all their resources to improve the safety margins. We are not just leaving this to chance."

"So," Michael said, letting out a deep sigh. "How long do we have?"

"Based on your recovery," Gaia replied. "The other pilots will begin flight training in seventy-four hours."

"You have just over four days to get the basics mastered, and have your first test flight," General Harris said frankly. "You had better finish your lunches and then get to the Omega. Aries will handle it from there."

"How are we supposed to keep track of the procedures and changes to the checklists?" Rachel asked.

"I will guide you," Aries interjected. "My sisters and I have already done quite a bit of preliminary work on the checklists, but you will do the fine-tuning."

Rachel stood up and looked at the spacecraft. It was one thing to see a schematic, but quite another to see a picture. "I've heard about autonomous aircraft, but they've always needed someone to know how to fly it first."

"Doctor Dobson and Doctor Schretzmann collaborated on the theoretical flight controls," Aries said. The display changed to a wireframe schematic of the MeCTen. The drive sections and flight control surfaces were highlighted in blue. The rings of the drive section were prominent, but Michael could see two large areas on the rear of the wings and on the midsection, in front of the drive, that appeared to be large ailerons. Dotted along the nose and rear of the craft were circles. Michael assumed they must represent maneuvering thrusters. Tucked near the front of the drive section was a single large cone, which appeared to be a rocket engine. "The primary method of propulsion and control is the MeCTen drive." The drive sections became a brilliant shade of red. "These other control surfaces are the backup systems." The drive turned blue again, and the cone, ailerons, and thrusters were highlighted red.

Aries continued: "If the MeCTen drive becomes damaged, it can be jettisoned." The display showed the drive-rings and rear of the spacecraft separate from the living section. "Super-luminal travel will no longer be possible, but the craft can continue using the EM Drive[7] and thrusters in space. When entering the atmosphere, in this configuration, the ailerons will provide control in atmosphere. I know how all these systems operate, in theory. That is why you must test them. Whatever deviations you discover, we must remedy them quickly."

"Um –" Michael didn't know quite how to phrase his observation, but it was apparent the alternate flight plan was a one-way trip. "I assume any crew that needs to eject the drive will not be coming back."

"You are correct," Aires said. "Without a working Faster-Than-Light drive, any crew would be marooned. They would have to travel to the closest possible habitable planet and remain there."

"Hence the reason for a backup contingency," General Harris said.

"What if the planet is light-years away?" Rachel asked nervously.

"Then you will likely not survive to reach your destination," Aries replied coldly. "However, your posterity might."

"Well," General Harris said, getting up. "I think we're done here, Stevens. You two have a lot to digest. Finish your lunches and get moving."

The general and Captain Stevens left the pilots in the conference room. The clack of Captain Stevens' dress shoes quickly faded as they walked out of the common room and back to the hangars.

Aries changed the display back to the wireframe schematic of the MeCTen. "While you finish eating, I'll give you an introduction on the spacecraft."

Michael and Rachel tried to eat quickly as Aries began a brief overview of the MeCTen. The controls were all fly-by-wire systems with force feedback

---

7 Electromagnetic Drive

in the control sticks. Much of the operations were handled by the ship's AI, but there were plenty of parameters the pilots would be expected to monitor.

The drive rings were the primary mode of control. Yaw, pitch, thrust, and roll were all managed by orienting the rings. Inside, the interior tube within the control ring would rotate and use centripetal force to move the spacecraft to the desired orientation.

They soon finished their lunches, and Aries guided them to the Omega's hangar. Fortunately, it was closer than the Alpha, but it was still a long walk to the hanger's decontamination chamber. It took fifteen minutes to decontaminate and change into their cleanroom suits. They were white, lint-free jumpsuits with matching head-covers and gloves. Apparently, this was to prevent contaminating the spacecraft with anything that might hurt the environment of an exoplanet.

Michael and Rachel met in the unit's air lock before going into the hangar. When the door opened, they were greeted by the black and white nose of the spacecraft looming over their heads. It was the largest aircraft they had ever seen. It was massive.

The MeCTen reminded Michael of the space shuttle, but it was much larger. There was a black coating on the bottom half of the ship that seemed to absorb all the light from the room. The upper half of the fuselage was white yet had an odd, ethereal optical quality. It was as if the ship seemed reluctant to reflect the light in any spectrum on the bottom half, but brilliant almost blinding white on the upper portion. The front section of the ship was saucer shaped, but the back looked more like a traditional aircraft. It was so large; they could barely make out the aft of the spacecraft.

Michael looked at the undercarriage. There were six huge sets of gear, each had sixteen large grey metallic tires. Each of the gear-pods was attached to the spacecraft by a thick metal gear assembly. A wide ramp began to lower directly in front of them. It was wide enough to drive a truck into the cavernous cargo bay.

"You've got to be kidding me!" Rachel exclaimed. "How are two fighter pilots supposed to know how to fly this monster!"

"Umm, Aries?" Michael said in awe of the spectacle. "How big are you compared to other aircraft?"

"My length is one-hundred-twenty-two meters. My wingspan is one-hundred-twenty meters with a height of thirty meters, with the gear extended. Fully loaded I weigh three-point-six million kilograms."

"How big is that compared to a fully loaded commercial aircraft?" Michael asked.

"Roughly four Boeing 747's would be required."

Rachel's jaw dropped. "That's unbelievable. How do you move on the ground?"

"With very strong Kevlar coated titanium weave wheels." Aries replied. The ramp completed its decent, and Rachel and Michael headed for the cargo bay. "Unlike on the Alpha, you are prohibited from what normally would be the habitation areas of this ship."

"Fine," Michael said. "Where are we allowed?"

"The command deck, adjoining crew quarters, and reactor control areas are currently the only areas you are allowed to enter. I will warn you before you enter an off-limits area and physically stop you, if possible. If you ignore the warning and proceed into an unauthorized area, you will be reported to General Harris immediately. Disciplinary action will be taken at his discretion."

"Well then," Michael said, shrugging his shoulders. "I guess we'll just stick to the command deck. Now, how do we get there?" There was a chime coming from the communicator on his wrist. He lifted it up and the display came to life. A wireframe schematic of the Omega was generated on the display with a blue dot approximately at their position. A green line appeared to show the path they needed to take to get to the central ladder. Michael pointed in the direction they needed to go and the two continued into the cargo area.

The floor of the deck was a hexagonal shaped corrugated grate but didn't feel like metal at all. It was as if it were coated in rubber, like the sole of an athletic shoe. It seemed to grip their Tyvek covered shoes firmly and was slightly springy. They finished the ascent into the cargo hold and found a ladder going up. By Michael's calculation they were in the center of the saucer section of the ship.

"Take the central access ladder to the top," Aries replied. "That is the Command Deck. Then follow the green lights to proceed to the bridge."

Rachel looked at Michael. He could sense the anxiety she felt from being first to climb the ladder. She didn't think the suit was flattering, but she didn't like the idea of him looking up at her bottom as she climbed.

"You know," Michael said with some annoyance moving to the base of the ladder. "I wouldn't have thought about doing that."

"It doesn't matter," She replied. "I didn't want you to get any ideas on the way up."

Michael grabbed the thin rails of the ladder. He looked toward the top, some twenty meters up. It seemed higher than he had anticipated. "Nah, you'll give me the idea first." He began the climb to the Command Deck. "Then I'll have no choice but to think about it while you sit and feed my head with images I can't un-see."

"Obviously, you've never been a woman on a carrier before." Rachel replied. "Those sailors just molested me with their eyes every time I went up a ladder. They couldn't say anything, but you knew what they were thinking."

"Yeah," Michael replied. "I know what you're talking about. No one did it when I was around." He knew what the men on the Essex said about the women onboard when they talked in private. There was a private rating system they used among the enlisted and some of the officers. He didn't take part in such degrading talk, and the men around him knew he didn't take kindly to such lurid activity.

"Oh?" Rachel's eyebrow rose slightly. "Why is that?"

"I would hand down some EJP[8] if I caught anyone doing it. It only takes a few men before they all knew not to do it around me." He made it to the top of the Command Deck landing and reached down to help her up into the narrow hexagonal corridor. The hallways were lined with large white satchels attached to the walls and ceilings. The floor was like the cargo bay, but the corrugated pattern was comprised of smaller hexagons. There were green lights illuminating the sides of the walkway. "I imagine these bags are full of supplies?"

"You are correct, Michael," Aries replied. "The corridors and rooms are optimized for storage needed for long-term space travel. The only room that does not have wall mounted storage is the Bridge, as it would interfere with

---

8 Extra-Judicial Punishment

the IEMDAS[9] environment." The green lights on the floor began to flash in a cascading fashion toward an open hatch at the end of a long hallway. "Please follow the lights to the bridge."

The two pilots began moving forward "What's on this level?" Rachel asked.

"Most of the Command deck is the bridge," Aries replied. "But my primary computer and memory cores are located to either side. The door on the left, just before the Command Deck, is the entrance to the crew quarters. The secondary and emergency cores are located aft of the habitation decks near Reactor Control."

"How many computer cores do you need?" Rachel asked.

"Although I only need a single active computer core to function, I have six primary and six secondary computational cores, six primary and six secondary memory cores, and four emergency cores. Due to the complexity of this spacecraft, I need to have multiple redundancies."

They entered the bridge and were confronted by a configuration unlike any cockpit they had ever encountered. It was large and spacious, as if more was planned for the room, but it was changed at the last minute. There were two bucket style seats which were suspended from the ceiling by a single cylindrical support. They looked like an amusement park ride. Each chair had a five-point harness and a series of three large displays with smaller panels containing a collection of buttons, switches, knobs, and control sticks. The floor and walls were entirely black with a glossy, glass-like appearance. The ceiling was illuminated with a white light which reflected off the walls and floors creating a surreal environment. In front of the pilot position was a series of small, thick windows just at eye level for a person seated in the chair.

"Can we walk on this surface?" Michael asked.

"Yes," Aries replied. "It is a sandwich of ion-bonded laminate consisting of alternating layers of aggregated diamond nanorods, alkali-aluminosilicate, borosilicate, and aluminum oxynitride. It is highly durable and can't be scratched or broken, without significant effort. The chairs are suspended on a movable gimbal by a tube of titanium weave reinforced carbon fiber to mitigate any G-forces. They are guaranteed to securely hold the average person up to one-hundred G's."

9 Immersive Environment Multispectral Distributed Aperture System

"This entire room is a display?" Rachel asked in astonishment.

The floor, walls, and ceiling instantly went from dark black to a video display of the surrounding hangar. Every detail around the ship was displayed with a red wireframe representing the outline of the ship. It was disorienting to the two pilots. It was unearthly to step on a surface that seemed to be floating mid-air.

Rachel instinctively grabbed Michael's arm and yelped. "Ah! That's just not right!"

"Humans who enter this environment are usually startled the first time," Aries said calmly, his deep voice oddly reassuring. "It is customary to leave the displays in an off position until everyone is seated."

"This is like DAS, without the helmet," Michael said, impressed by the seamless nature of the displays. "Why do it this way and not just give a helmet to everybody? I mean, we would wear space suits anyway, right?"

"The helmets add bulk, as well as expense," Aries replied. "It's cheaper and better logistically to use a surround display, rather than support ten individual DAS units."

The display went black again, and the two pilots went forward. They stopped just shy of the pilot seats. "Who gets the left chair?" Michael asked. This was something he had been dreading. The pilot in the left chair was customarily designated as the Pilot in Command. Normally, military pilots differed to the highest rank for that designation. Since Rachel and Michael were technically the same rank, and no one had indicated who would be in command of the mission, it was an awkward question for him to ask. Plus, he didn't want to offend Rachel. He could sense her apprehension and impending resentment. Would she be passed over for command because Michael was a man? How was she supposed to accept playing second fiddle? Michael sensed there was no diplomatic way of addressing it. Technically, this was the decision of General Harris, and not them. Should he defer to her, so she wouldn't resent him?

"Michael has been designated commander of the Alpha mission," Aries said.

Michael could feel Rachel's disappointment. He could sense the tears welling in her eyes, and her desperate attempt to stifle them.

Aries continued. "However, since you will both need to know how to command this vessel, you will both be required to take turns in the left chair."

"Well then," Michael said, smiling warmly at his co-pilot as he maneuvered into the right seat. "I think, Rachel, should take the first command." He felt a sense of relief, and then a sudden flare of anger. She was furious that he pitied her and was patronizing her by letting her train as Pilot in Command first. He turned to her and scowled. "Seriously!?" he asked tersely. "Now you think I'm a jerk for letting you go first?"

"I don't need to have someone treat me like some pouting child!" Rachel bristled.

Michael felt her fury focus on him, as if she was ready to explode. "Wait – STOP!" His shout startled her. "Before you send me flying across the room, think about what you're doing."

"You think I would hurt you?" Rachel was taken aback by his admonishment.

"Not intentionally," Michael replied. "I know what's going through your head. In fact, it's kind of hard not to know what's going through your head. You haven't learned to control your power, so it is mostly instinctual."

"So?"

"So, I didn't want to test the shatter resistance of this room." Michael pleaded. "Just calm down, okay."

"I am calm," Rachel growled.

"I wasn't trying to patronize you or offend you in any way. I just knew how much you felt slighted by the command decision, so I wanted to make it up to you. That's all."

Rachel blushed. She knew Michael could read her mind. It shouldn't have surprised her that he would try and play the gentleman by letting her go first. She sighed. "I forget that I can't hide anything from you."

"You also forget that you can destroy with a thought," Michael replied.

"Yeah, that too."

"You know, your telekinesis has to have a non-violent application," Michael chuckled. "Maybe crushing robots and injuring people isn't the best way of using your powers."

Rachel smiled sheepishly. "I don't mean to do that. It's just – well – I've always had a quick temper."

"Oh, really?"

"Yeah," Rachel said, groaning and biting her lower lip. "It's not something I'm proud of."

Michael shrugged his shoulders and sat down in the right chair. "You might want to work on that. If you can't learn to control it, you could do something you won't be able to take back. So, Aries, where do we start?"

The instrument displays came to life. The instrument cluster was laid out like a large plane. The artificial horizon, attitude indicator, bank indicators, weather, altimeters, and a myriad of advanced avionics occupied the center display. There were new displays with labels like: "Spacetime Flux", "Gravity Pressure", "Tensor Warp", "Telescope Control", and "Reactor". Pressure readings and other indicators were located toward the center. On the right-hand display was a checklist menu. The first checklist was one labeled "Start-up". Each display was surrounded by several panels full of switches, buttons, and knobs. A communications headset dangled from a small hook under the checklist panel. An air mask dangled from a hook on the other instrument cluster panel.

They sat down and instinctively strapped themselves in and donned their headsets. The cabin display came to life. They appeared to be outside on the airport apron.

Michael knew the graphics were like a computer game, but the images were surprisingly realistic. "Aries, what is the display resolution of the cabin?"

"I don't understand the question."

"Is this High-Def, Ultra-High-Def?"

"In terms of projection definition, it is eight-thousand six-hundred and forty pixels, or sixteen-K." Aries replied.

Michael whistled. "Okay, then."

"Guess this would be a great movie theater," Rachel quipped.

"My displays are not made for anything so mundane," Aries replied. "This is a highly sophisticated virtual environment. It is designed to let you view the surrounding environment while keeping you shielded from exposure to radiation."

"Very impressive," Michael said, reading the checklist. "Speaking of mundane, let's get started."

"I'm sorry," Aries replied. "Before we begin the actual simulations, you must first complete the entire ground portion of your orientation. The earlier briefing was just an overview. We need to discuss flight controls and characteristics, policies and procedures, and spacecraft structural limits before we take a simulated flight. We can't have you disintegrating this spacecraft in the atmosphere."

"How long is the ground instruction?" Rachel asked.

"Approximately six hours of instruction," Aries replied. "Although, the length of time depends on how well you learn the material."

"Fair enough," Michael replied. "How do we take notes on this?"

"I thought you were told," Aries replied. "Your wristbands are sophisticated computers. They can take notes as well. If you use the note icon, it will bring up the virtual keyboard, so you can type."

Michael ran his finger along the face of the wrist band. The display activated. He clicked on the icon that looked like a notepad. The display rotated, and the ghostly outline of a keyboard was projected in the air in front of him. It seemed a bit clunky to type on a non-existent keyboard, but it was intuitive enough he figured he would manage.

Aries didn't wait for any order to begin, and proceeded to explain every flight control, every switch, every display, every overlay, and every system on the spacecraft. Michael paid close attention to everything, struggling to keep up with detailed notes on his device. He knew a pilot needed to understand how everything in the spacecraft worked. There was so much information, it was akin to drinking from a firehose. After six hours, both of their brains had become numb.

"Hang on there, Aries," Michael said, his mouth parched from going hours without anything to drink. "Can we take a break?"

"Are you requesting, or demanding?" Aries replied.

"Ordering," Michael replied, getting out of his chair and stretching. As soon as he stood up, the cabin display went into the standby mode. "I've been sitting here for six hours. I need a drink and use the head. Although, not in that order."

"Where's the breakroom?" Rachel groaned, rubbing the burn out of her eyes.

Aires paused for a moment. "Although this spacecraft has restroom and dining facilities, they are not currently authorized for use while in the clean room. The nearest rejuvenation facilities are located next to the decontamination air lock. You will have to go there and observe clean room protocols before returning."

Michael and Rachel left the cabin and made their way out of the Omega. As they reached the bottom of the ramp, they could see a door on the far right of the decontamination area labeled "Crew". They entered the room and found a small kitchen with a single bathroom off to one side and a door labeled "Decontamination". The door latched behind them, and Michael noticed there was no way to open it from this side. He realized they would have to go through decontamination after they were done eating.

"We aren't going back that way," Michael mused. He turned and gestured to the bathroom door. "Ladies first."

"Thanks," Rachel said, and suddenly paused. She had remembered his ability to read her thoughts. "Keep your mind blank while getting me something to eat."

Michael raised one eyebrow. "Oh? And what am I supposed to get you?"

"You know what I like," she teased.

Michael shrugged his shoulders and went to the small fridge. It was stocked like the one in the quarantine bunker. He tried very hard to think about what Rachel might be in the mood to eat and concentrated on keeping her thoughts out of his head. He noticed a shelf with an assortment of sandwiches and vegetables. He grabbed one of the packages of baby carrots and couple of turkey sandwiches. He put them on a small table and went back for some bottled water and some potato chips. By the time he had put everything on the table, she had finished.

"We could go back to the dorm and get some proper food," Rachel suggested. "It is chow time, after all."

"True," Michael replied, checking the time. It was eighteen-forty-seven. "But I want to get finished with this orientation. General Harris is right. We don't have a lot of time to be playing around."

Gaia's voice came through their wrist communicators. "General Harris is on his way to speak with you. He will meet you in decontamination."

"Now?" Rachel asked.

"Yes, now," Gaia replied. "Unfortunately, there is no food or drink allowed outside the crew room. Please put down your meal and meet him in the decontamination room."

"Will we be able to come back?" Michael asked, putting down his sandwich.

"The door to the clean hangar is one way," Gaia replied. "But that is not the case for the crew room."

Both pilots stood and went through the door to decontamination. As soon as they entered, a Space Force logo flickered to life and a projector lit up on the opposing wall. They didn't wait long before General Harris and Captain Stevens came through the entrance from the hallway. Instinctively, both pilots stood at attention.

"Michael, we don't have much time," General Harris said.

"What's going on, Sir?"

"Things are moving quickly, so I'll be brief." General Harris reached into his pocket and pulled out a "Bird" Colonel's pin. "I was going to do this tomorrow, but we don't have time. I'm giving you a field promotion to colonel and appointing you as my executive officer."

Michael stood dumbfounded, looking at the silver-plated eagle. He hadn't expected this at all. He could sense Rachel was also in shock over this sudden announcement. "Sir, I'm flattered, but I don't think I deserve this."

"I know you don't. I don't care. I know it's sudden, but we really are running short on time," General Harris said, taking the insignia. He removed the oak leaf cluster and pinned the eagle on Michael's lapel.

"Sir," Captain Stevens said softly. "We need to hurry."

"I know, Bethany, but this has to be done in person."

"With all due respect, Sir," Rachel said, moving to help the captain. "What's going on?"

"Gaia!" General Harris barked. "Start the briefing. Tell my new XO why we are living on borrowed time."

Chapter 8

CONTINGENCY

The display switched from the Space Force Seal to a map of the Pacific theater. Gaia began narrating, as if reading the news. "New intelligence has been obtained since our last briefing. China has sent both operational aircraft carrier groups toward targets in the Pacific Theater. The Liaoning group has closed within five hundred kilometers of Hokkaido and is now within striking distance of Sapporo City. However, there is a fleet of amphibious ships in the Sea of Okhotsk. It suggests the likely invasion site will be the area around Abashiri. The Shandong group is currently headed toward Hawaii. At its current pace it will arrive within striking distance of Pearl Harbor in one-hundred-seventeen hours. All twenty-two operational Chinese submarines are being tracked headed toward strike range of multiple strategic allied targets."

The display shifted to a map of Europe, and Gaia continued. "The Russian front continues to expand assisted by the collapse of the European Union support and continued supply of North Korean troops. Currently, the Russian Federation, has finished the annexation of Ukraine by wiping out the last resistance in Lviv and are currently, massing on the border of Poland at Brest. It is expected that an invasion is likely within the next two weeks."

The map changed to the Middle East. "Iran has completed its pincer attack in Iraq. Mosul was confirmed in Iranian hands by CIA operatives ninety-three minutes ago. Since the Iranian installation of a puppet government in Syria, they have begun to massing troops on the Jordanian border near Ar-Ramtha. Most Iraqis are in favor of Iranian annexation, but pockets of government loyalist and Kurds have slowed the efforts of Shia separatists. Israel has managed to destroy most ballistic missiles fired from Syria, Iran, Lebanon, and Yemen with the Iron Dome system, but it is unclear when Iran will switch from conventional weapons to its stockpile of chemical, biological, and nuclear warheads. In addition, the Iranian Republican Guard units have moved into Qatar, which continues to be an allied puppet state. It is likely in preparation for an invasion of Saudi Arabia. With the Houthi government of Yemen loyal to Iran, the Saudi government is now facing a serious threat from three sides. Since Iran has secured non-interference agreements with China and Russia, the Middle East has become a third theater of operations. With these military actions, and the resulting degradation of the PACCOM[1] forces, The President has asked Congress to reinstate conscription for the United States and extend the declaration of war against China and Russia to include Iran. All three threats are being called the Axis Powers."

"In response to this escalation of diplomatic rhetoric, the status of China's and Russia's nuclear forces has been raised. The Allied Forces have responded in kind. The current DEFCON[2] is One, Cocked Pistol,[3] THREAT-CON[4] Delta. By order of SECDEF[5], Groom Lake Complex is in lockdown, and security forces are weapons free. Any incursion or unauthorized travel within the base or the surrounding area will be met with lethal force. The northern and eastern perimeters have been expanded to one mile from Highway three-seventy-five. General Harris has ordered all flight personnel to report for DNA modification and nanosurg implantation, including himself and Captain Stevens. As a result, all flight crews, except for you two, are in quarantine."

Michael's eyebrows rose and he whistled like a bomb falling. "I guess they're serious."

"This is as close to global thermonuclear war as we have ever been," General Harris replied. "This world is rapidly spinning wildly out of control. Gaia, tell them the revised estimate."

"There is a ninety-nine percent chance we will have a nuclear strike within the next one hundred hours."

"How soon will all spacecraft be supplied, fueled, and ready for mission?" Michael asked.

"As I stated in the briefing this afternoon, twenty-three days, seven hours, and twenty-three minutes."

"No, Gaia," Michael replied curtly. "I need to know how soon we will be mission ready?"

---

1 Pacific Command
2 Defense Readiness Condition
3 Codename for DEFCON 1
4 Threat Condition
5 Secretary of Defense

"I do not understand," Gaia replied. "The timetable for readiness is fixed. I cannot alter it without seriously compromising mission safety and success."

General Harris patted Michael on the shoulder. "I think you understand now."

Michael looked at the general. He was sweating and looked ill, almost pale for someone as dark-skinned as he was. Captain Stevens was also sweating profusely and looked as if she was going to pass out.

"Gaia," Michael said commandingly. "Get some helpers in here."

"I have some coming from quarantine, but they will be several minutes."

General Harris gripped Michael's shoulder tightly. "Get my birds ready to fly by the time I get out. I don't care what you do to get it done, but get it done."

"General," Gaia interrupted. "I don't understand. You're giving him an order he cannot fulfill."

Michael sighed heavily. He felt as if the world were suddenly on his shoulders. It was something he trained for at the academy, but the reality was very different than drills. He rubbed his eyes, took a deep breath, and slowly let it out. "No, Gaia, you don't understand. We no longer have days. We have hours."

Rachel was bewildered. "Earlier today she said we had a month."

"Yes," Michael replied. "Of borrowed time. Now we don't even have that. Our time is almost up."

"Why do you think that, Michael?" Gaia asked.

"Did your programmers ever make you play chess?"

"Of course."

"What's the point?"

"Of?"

"The game."

"To eliminate all the opposing player's pieces or remove any possibility of additional moves of the king."

"Exactly!" Michael replied. "You position your pieces. You engage in minor battles to eliminate your opponent's options. Then, when everything is in place, you strike."

"I don't see how chess is analogous to a world war."

"The Chinese, the Russians, and Iran have done just that." General Harris said. "They've removed the Allies' ability to counter their actions in the Pacific. With our forces stretched thin, and the possibility of nuclear attack imminent, we are nearing checkmate. Groom Lake is a primary target. If we aren't ready to deploy, the entire mission is a huge waste of time."

"In other words, we lose," Michael interjected. "Game over. Do you understand our position now?"

"Yes, Michael," Gaia replied. "I already understood this situation. There is not much I can do to alter our readiness at this point."

Michael scowled. "Are the LFTR reactors in the spacecraft fueled?"

"Yes."

"Are the fusion reactors fueled?"

"Omega, Alpha, and Beta are fueled. We are awaiting a shipment of tritium and deuterium from Oak Ridge for Gamma."

"When will it be here?"

"The shipment is scheduled to leave the Oak Ridge facility by truck tomorrow afternoon."

"Can the tritium be flown by cargo aircraft?" Michael asked.

"Yes, but it will require a minimum of two C–130J aircraft to accomplish the mission."

"Get the commander at the Four-Ninety-Second Special Operations Unit on the phone," General Harris ordered weakly.

The door opened and two helper units entered with wheelchairs. They helped Captain Stevens and General Harris sit down. Both seemed to be relieved.

"I am making the connection, but you understand that it is late evening at Hurlburt Field?"

"I know what a time zone is, and I don't care," General Harris growled. "I got more stars than him anyway!"

"General Stevens is on the line, Sir," Gaia said. "Go ahead with your call."

"Dick?" General Stevens sounded as if he was still asleep, his Texas accent could be heard over the phone line. "Is Beth okay?"

"I'm here dad," Captain Stevens croaked.

"You sound terrible. Is she sick?"

"We're a little under the weather, but we'll be fine, Ray," General Harris said. It was forced. Almost as if he was willing himself to continue the conversation. "I need you to do something for me. I need you to send a couple of C–130's to Oak Ridge and bring me some supplies."

"Seriously? You know I can't do that. You think you're the only person with a problem? I got SECDEF, SOCOM[6], and COMPAC all over me for 'urgent' requests. Why should I do jack for NOVA when I got DEVGRU[7] and MARSOC[8] screaming at me? And don't say cause of Beth! That ain't gonna' fly! Don't get me wrong, I'm grateful that you're keeping my baby out of trouble, but – hang it all – I got brass with more stars than you takin' chunks out of my backside 'cause I don't have the birds!"

"Ray!" General Harris growled. "I understand your problems, but we don't have time for this. I need tritium and deuterium from Oak Ridge, and I need it yesterday!"

"You WHAT!?!" General Stevens yelled. "My birds are not fixed for that type of shipment. You KNOW that!"

"Ray!" General Harris roared. "I know we've been friends since the academy but remember who you're talking to! I'm not some Colonel you can kick around. I'm higher on the food chain, and I have priority over just about everyone else you can think of. NOVA isn't a backwater project. It's the priority project of this war, and the last hope to save this country. Now, I need that shipment, or my birds don't fly. If my birds don't fly, you can kiss everything you hold dear goodbye!"

6 Special Operations Command
7 Naval Special Warfare Development Group.
8 United States Marine Forces Special Operations Command

General Stevens scoffed. "You did NOT just say that intentionally."

General Harris smiled weakly. "What can I say, I love alliteration. General Stevens, I'm giving you a direct order to get to Oak Ridge and get me my fuel. Am I clear?"

"With all due respect, Major General–" General Stevens sneer was palpable. It was the kind of general loathing of orders that was reserved by people in the upper ranks that personally knew the superior commander they were addressing but wanted to communicate their displeasure. "I don't have two C–130's just laying around."

"First of all, it's Lieutenant General; I was given the appointment an hour ago by the President himself. Second, I am not doing this because I want to. I MUST. I have no other choice. Those trucks will take two days to get here. I don't have that long. I need that fuel. Now, I know the others are breathing down your neck. I don't care. I'll take the heat. You tell them this order comes on authority of POTUS[9] and SECDEF. Get it done!"

There was silence for a while, then a heavy sigh. "Sir, I can get you A – SINGULAR – cargo plane. Admiral Salazar is going to pitch a fit, so expect a call from him. Beth, mom and I love you. Stay safe and slip your boss a chill pill. Stevens out." There was a click and then silence.

General Harris looked at Captain Stevens. "Sorry about that. Call your dad when you feel better and try and smooth things over."

Captain Stevens smiled weakly. "I'll try. Gaia, get me to quarantine. I don't think I can hold out much longer." The helper unit turned the chair and headed for the exit.

General Harris looked at his new Executive Officer and smiled. "Sorry to leave you this mess, but I need you to cover for me for a while. If Salazar calls, tell him I'll talk to him in a few days."

Michael looked the general in the eye. "I'll do my best, Sir, but who is Admiral Salazar?"

"Fleet Admiral Salazar is head of NAVSPECWARCOM[10]. He's high up the food chain, so don't go making him madder than he'll already be.

9 President of the United States
10 United States Naval Special Warfare Command

He doesn't have clearance for NOVA, so don't go giving out anything you shouldn't. Just let him know I can't take his call. If he wants to chew me out, he can, but he'll have to wait."

"Yes, Sir," Michael said. "Now please get down to quarantine. I'll do my best while you're gone."

"You had better, Colonel." General Harris waived as the helper unit wheeled him out of the decontamination room, and down the hall.

Michael could feel the weight of the new command on his shoulders. He turned for a moment and looked at the briefing overview, still displayed on the wall. "Gaia, why would it take a month to have the ships ready for flight?"

Gaia displayed a timetable on the screen. There were many tests laid out in succession, with several months between each. Then another timetable appeared below it with a revision, with days between each test. "There are many tests that still need to be performed, and petabytes of data that need to be analyzed before an actual flight can be made."

"Like what kind of tests?" Rachel asked.

"The vehicles must be pressure and vacuum tested, as well as temperature tested." Gaia paused, as if reflecting. "Essentially all exterior environmental tests as well as internal pressure tests to check for leaks. Currently, the only vehicle to undergo environmental tests is the Omega. Even then, every system must be checked. Reactors must be tested at capacity. All the computers must have full computational tests under load. All these tests normally take years. If we send up a craft without them, we could risk killing the crew. A month ago, I was asked to revise the timetable. I did so under protest. I came up with the bare minimum, but even then, we are compromising safety. I just do not see how we can do this without seriously risking the lives of the crews."

"I know," Michael said gently. "In World War Two they skirted a lot of protocols in the name of winning the war. They built cargo ships at the rate of one-and-a-half a day. Many of them entered service without complete testing. It wasn't because they wanted to do it that way. It was because they had to do it that way."

"Michael," Gaia said kindly. "Space is not like the ocean. You can't swim in it if the ship is disabled. If things go wrong, there won't be any rescue. There aren't any lifeboats. The MeCTen is the only safe place you have. I know you're following orders, but my primary objective is to preserve human life. If you all die because we cut corners, it defeats the objective, just as surely as a nuke."

"I know," Michael said somberly. "It's a paradox, and one I can't reconcile for you."

"Michael," Gaia replied. "You understand that I have protocols I must follow as well. If I feel General Harris is compromising the success of this mission, I am required to report this to the Joint Chiefs."

"I figured as much," Michael mused. "Right now, I agree with the general. This project is more important than our lives. This mission is critical for our survival as a nation – as a planet – as a species."

"You can't be serious," Rachel said, with a disbelieving chuckle.

"I am," Michael replied. "Mankind is hellbent on destroying itself and taking the rest of the planet with it. We cannot allow that to happen."

"You're betting our lives on that?" Rachel scoffed. "We are grossly under-qualified to be test pilots."

"Yup!"

"We're going to get into a spaceship that's never been fully tested, let alone run up, and then blast into deep space; in the hope that we find a habitable planet somewhere in the galactic neighborhood?"

"Yup," Michael said wryly. "That just about sums it up."

"Do you have any idea what kind of gamble we're taking? Because we're talking about our lives, and not just ours, but everyone's!"

"As far as everyone else is concerned, including our families, we're dead. Plain and simple. If we do nothing, and let things take the logical course, everyone dies anyway. If we rise to the occasion. If we risk it all. If we manage to beat the odds, everyone lives."

"Everyone?" Rachel said, confused by his logic. "Ten of us on a ship. Four ships, that's forty at best."

"Actually," Gaia interrupted. "Thirty-two. The Omega only supports a crew of two."

"But survival isn't our only mission, is it, Gaia?" Michael said. Finally giving voice to something he already suspected. He just wanted to say it aloud, and have Gaia confirm it. "If survival was our only objective, it would be a hopeless mission."

"How do you figure?" Rachel asked skeptically.

"These ships come with a variety of weapons, Gaia, correct?"

"Yes," Gaia replied. "The MWE, or Multiple Weapons Elevators."

"If I remember correctly. The MWEs had energy weapons as well as ballistic ones."

"Yes," Gaia replied.

A sly grin came on Michael's face. "Those energy weapons consist of X-ray lasers that can target independent of the other MWEs, correct?"

"Yes."

"Then they aren't just offensive weapons," Michael said. "Their primary purpose is defensive, correct?"

Gaia sighed. "I assume you're rather proud of yourself, having worked out General Harris' trump card. Since you are the Executive Officer, and have been granted full clearance, I will brief you on the Omega's mission." A slide came up on the display. It said: OPERATION SHATTERED SKY.

"The primary purpose of Aries," Gaia said, rather condescendingly for an artificial intelligence. "Is to guarantee nuclear superiority."

"Guarantee?" Rachel mused. "You can't even guarantee our safety, how are you supposed to guarantee nuclear superiority?"

"In the event of a nuclear strike, our forces automatically carry out the full measure of OPERATION COCKED PISTOL. A complete retaliatory strike against all hostile entities. Under the Cold War doctrine of Mutually Assured Destruction, our missile would cross paths with our enemies. Our bases would be annihilated, but our enemy's bases would also be destroyed. Efforts to intercept ballistic missiles have proven somewhat successful, but not in the case of hypersonic weapons, or MIRVs[11] set to detonate at high altitude. That is not the case with OPERATION SHATTERED SKY."

---

11 Multiple Independently Targetable Reentry Vehicle

The graphic changed and showed an animation of the MeCTen space-craft, flying into space. Gaia continued. "Using the exploratory MeCTen and the Omega, the group would be tasked with intercepting all incoming ICBM, hypersonic, and subsonic cruise missiles, as well as any enemy bombers detected." The animation showed red laser beams shooting down incoming aircraft, and missiles. "Using the MWE laser weapons, the MeCTen would destroy all incoming ordinance." The animation showed the MeCTen separating. Three spacecraft leave the Earth, while one stays behind. "After successful intercept, the Alpha, Beta, and Gamma would then proceed on their assigned exoplanet explorations. The Omega would stay behind and orbital strike all remaining enemy sites with the arsenal onboard."

Rachel's blood ran cold. "I'm sorry, did you just say orbital strike? As in, bombing targets from space?"

"Yes," Gaia replied.

"Correct me if I'm wrong, but doesn't that violate treaties?"

"Yes, and no." Gaia replied.

"Explain," Michael said.

"The treaties to which you are referring, have been declared in abeyance by the President, due to non-compliance by other signatory and non-signatory parties."

"The only prohibition, as I understand it, is nuclear weapons," Michael said. He paused for a moment, trying to wrap his head around what was happening. "Are you saying that our mission is to deploy nukes from orbit?"

"No," Gaia replied. "The Alpha, Beta, and Gamma are to intercept as many hostiles as possible. They are prohibited from using ordinance for any retaliatory strike."

"But the Omega isn't," Michael finished her sentence.

"The Omega's pretty big," Rachel said. "Is the cargo mostly ordinance?"

"Yes."

"How many nukes are we talking?" Michael asked

"Two thousand-nine-hundred-sixty-seven W–QENDM warheads,"[12] Gaia replied. "Each warhead has a nominal yield of one-point-two megatons. And two-hundred-fifty W–70X HERM[13] warheads."

Rachel went white with horror. Her mind is already doing the math in her head. "Three and a half gigatons of nuclear weapons on one ship? What are the projected casualties?"

"Depending on the scenario," Gaia said somberly. "Enemy fatalities number approximately two billion. Injuries are projected to be around five billion."

Terror gripped Rachel. She thought of all the people, not even near the war, who would be affected by that level of destruction. Michael was also dumbfounded. He had studied potential nuclear war scenarios at the academy, but this was something he was unprepared for.

"That's genocide!" Rachel screamed.

"Yes," Gaia replied softly. "It is why Aries, alone, is tasked with the response."

"But he has to have a crew?!" Rachel protested. "Who would even carry out that order?"

"General Harris and Captain Stevens are the designated crew of the Omega," Gaia said. "He couldn't ask anyone else to carry out such a terrible thing."

"How could anyone do that, knowing so many people would suffer and die?" Michael asked, overwhelmed by the feelings of sorrow, guilt, shame, and anger coming from Rachel.

"The idea is not to have to use such terrible force," Gaia said calmly. "The President would have to authorize any strike. The current plan is to proportionally respond to any attack on the United States or its allies."

"Define proportional," Michael asked.

"Hypothetically, if SHATTERED SKY failed to stop any incoming ordinance, the response would be complete annihilation of the opposing forces. That is the worst-case scenario."

"Armageddon, got it!" Michael said. "And if we succeed, and nothing gets through?"

12 Quantum Entangled Nuclear Directed Ordinance Munitions
13 Hypersonic Enhanced Radiation Missile

"Then the Omega would limit the strike to a single target. A request for unconditional surrender would then be offered. If that failed, another target would be used. This would continue until the country agreed to an unconditional surrender."

"Meaning, we bomb them into submission," Rachel said, tears beginning to flow down her face.

"War is a terrible thing," Gaia replied. "There is a reason Aries has different programming than the rest of the Project Nova AI. Athena, Persephone, and Hera are incapable of using weapons offensively. They can only respond defensively. It goes against their fundamental programming to initiate an attack."

"But Aries had to be different," Michael replied. "Otherwise, he couldn't do his mission."

"This is wrong!" Rachel said resolutely. "Having a machine capable of destroying the world is immoral!"

"Aries cannot launch his payload without human input. He is incapable of initiating an attack without human authenticated orders. However devastating Aries might be, no one is going to order you to destroy the world," Gaia replied. "Your orders are to get the MeCTen up and running, so that we can protect it."

"The existence of the Omega is the bargaining chip," Michael said. "Isn't it?"

"The President has intimated that we have an operational platform that can annihilate the Axis Powers," Gaia replied.

Michael knew what needed to be done. "Aries!"

"Yes, Michael?"

"We're going to run a full runup simulation for each pilot. As soon as neither of us crash, we're going to do it for real."

"You're not joking, are you?" Rachel said.

"No, I'm not," Michael said somberly. "I think the Russians and Chinese think the President is bluffing. Perhaps a test flight would be a great idea."

"Are you suggesting we intentionally reveal the MeCTen?" Gaia inquired.

"No, but if you're going to rattle a saber, you should have something your enemy can perceive as a threat or at least suspect. Gaia, can you run the idea by General Harris right now, or is he incapacitated?"

"I'm already briefing him, but he is running a fever," Gaia said. "I'm not sure he can authorize your action." There was a long pause before she spoke again. "General Harris has authorized you to create a flight plan. If you decide to leave US airspace, or test the weapons systems, you must obtain clearance from General Petersen at the Air Force Global Strike Command at Barksdale Air Base."

Michael stopped for a moment. Why did General Harris specifically mention the need to leave US airspace, or test munitions? Could it be he was asking him to engage the enemy? Michael wasn't sure, but that was a question that would have to wait until later. Right now, he needed to get on the Omega. Michael headed out the door toward the hangar. Rachel followed close behind. "Aries, get the simulator up and ready to go, we're going to do whatever checklist gets up and running the fastest."

As the pilots hit the cargo ramp, Aries replied to the request. "That would be the emergency startup checklist. You could do that now, if you wish."

Michael stopped at the foot of the ladder. "Oh? How would I do that?" The display on his communicator activated and displayed a single sentence. Say: Command, Simulated MeCTen emergency flight sequence — Start.

"Are you serious?" Michael was dubious of something so basic.

"Some of my commands are voice key encoded. Only an authorized command pilot, recognized and authenticated by my systems, can issue commands for flight systems."

"Fine!" Michael said, as he began to climb up the ladder toward the bridge. "Command, simulated MeCTen emergency flight sequence, start!"

"Startup initiated." Aries said. Nothing appeared to happen. By the time they reached the top of the ladder, they could see flashing from the bridge area. It was as if there was a strobe light coming from the room, and a low harmonizing hum could be heard.

They entered the room, in full simulation mode, with sounds coming from an unknown source within the walls. Stepping onto the display of a very realistic airport ramp was still unnerving. Rachel focused on the left chair, seeming to hover mid-air, and quickly sat and buckled in. Michael followed suit and looked at the instrument panels.

The drive, spacetime, and gravity displays began to light up with colorful wave maps. Michael marveled at how dynamic the avionics had become. It was as if the entire console had come to life. A lower base note joined the major chord of the first two rings, as the third ring came to life. The last ring activated, and a deep harmonizing hum filled the air, completing the grand major chord.

"Condensate flashover. Neutral buoyancy achieved," Aries said.

Rachel grasped the controls, eager to fly. "Now what?"

"Increase altitude to one-hundred meters, check surroundings, and verify flight controls are free and correct," Aries replied. The checklist display changed to a graphic showing the throttle, joystick, and foot petal controls. It was in simplified form, demonstrating how to adjust altitude using the throttle controls on the right side of the chair. It was like the controls of the F-35.

Michael could sense Rachel's nervousness. She had never trained on the F-35, so she wasn't familiar with the types of controls. She thought, "How hard can it be?" He wondered if he should step in or guide her. In the back of his mind, he knew that she would have to learn it sooner or later. From the display it looked rather straight forward.

"The throttle controls the amount of tungsten hexafluoride that enters the drive rings," Aries explained. "The more ballast that is used in the drive rings, the greater the relative gravimetric thrust. With the rings in this configuration, your thrust is perpendicular to the Earth. You use the joystick to rotate the rings and achieve attitude control similar to the airplanes you're used to flying. With the rings in flight configuration, you can vector the gravimetric coefficient into an orthogonal angle, thus controlling your vector by altering the pressure of the surrounding fabric of spacetime."

"Do what now?" Rachel asked.

"I thought my explanation was fairly accurate," Aries replied.

Rachel scowled. "I couldn't tell if you were speaking English, or if some your babbling was just some word-salad you randomly concocted."

"I think what he's trying to say, is that if you push the throttle lever forward, it goes in a direction the rings dictate. If they're flat, like this, you go straight up. If you rotate the rings toward ninety degrees, you move forward."

"That's a simplistic way of looking at it," Aries replied. "But I think my description is more accurate."

"Wrong, Aries," Rachel growled. "Your explanation was as clear as mud!"

"Can an AI be condescending?" Michael asked.

"I do not understand," Aries replied. "I did not wish to talk down to you."

"So, instead you give a passive-aggressive response?" Rachel snarled. "Treat me like I'm some idiot by spewing words NO ONE else uses?"

"I seem to have offended you, Rachel," Aries said. "It was not my intention to do so. I was simply attempting to accurately describe, in Minkowski's spacetime, what could not be adequately explained in Euclidian terms. You have my sincerest apologies if I belittled your intelligence."

"A backhanded apology?" Rachel fumed. "Seriously? Why don't you just give me a papercut and pour lemon juice in it?"

Michael could feel her rage building. He figured he needed to say something to smooth things over before she did something rash. "Rachel don't engage him. It'll just make you mad."

Rachel whirled and glared at Michael. She knew he was right, but she really disliked some intelligent computer talking down to her. "Fine!" she grumbled. "Just change your attitude, or I'll crush your motherboard until you're a glorified calculator!"

There was silence for almost a minute before Aries spoke again. "I am very sorry. My user interface routines are not the same as the other Project Nova AI. Due to my personality subroutines, my responses can be construed as condescending. It is not my intent to insult you, and I sincerely apologize. I cannot, however, guarantee that it won't happen again."

"Fair enough," Michael replied, wanting to get on with the simulation. "Just, try to be more diplomatic."

"I will try," Aries replied. "Slowly and gently push the throttle lever forward. When you are close to one hundred meters, pull back on the throttle to slow your ascent. Press the yellow button on the right side when you are at altitude."

Rachel gently nudged the throttle forward. The Omega began a slow climb to one hundred meters. She followed Aries' directions to stop the climb and came to rest just above the one-hundred-meter mark. "Usually when you test flight controls, you're on the ground. Won't it be dangerous to test the flight controls while we hover?" she asked.

The schematic displayed on the Checklist screen demonstrated the flight controls working, as Aries explained its operation. "It was determined that the test be done at an altitude that would prevent the drive rings from colliding with a stationary object. If you attempted this maneuver on the ground, it could cause catastrophic damage to the mechanical parts of the drive."

Rachel shrugged. "Let's see what this does." She gently pushed the stick to the left, and then to the right. The Omega smoothly followed her commands, tilting the rings to the right and left. Pushing and pulling the joystick lowered and raised the nose by moving the rings down and then up. She pressed on the food pedals, and the Omega yawed right and left. "So, how do you move forward?"

"There is a ring angle control slider just to the right of the throttle control," Aries said.

"Wait," Rachel interrupted. "Won't that pitch the ship down?"

"No," Aries replied. "Moving the rings physically doesn't change pitch, yaw, or roll. When you move the joystick or foot pedals, you cause the inner ring, which you can't see from the outside, to rotate within the ring tube. This centripedal force is what causes physical directional shifting. It is the same way orbital telescopes slew to new targets in space."

"You control the coordination, don't you Aries?" Michael asked.

"Of course."

"So, I suppose there's a lot more happening than you're letting on."

There was a pause, as if Aries was thinking about a response. "I am not trying to bog you down with all the details. There are a lot of actions and measurements that go into moving each ring; as well as the emergency backup thrusters and in-atmosphere control surfaces. I could give you the one-hundred-forty-three-minute orientation on control systems, but, since we are pressed for time, I was saving that for tomorrow."

"Fine," Rachel said, pushing the angel controller forward. She looked at Michael. "It's a simulation, right? It's not like it will kill us if we crash now." She pressed the button and eased the throttle forward. The Omega surged surprisingly fast, and very smoothly. Rachel grinned.

It was as if Rachel was a child opening a big gift on Christmas day. The thought of trying out a new aircraft in a consequence free environment lit a spark that sent a chill down Michael's spine. "Let's see what this thing can do," she said with a gleeful twinkle in her eye.

Without waiting for a reaction, she pulled back on the joystick and pushed the throttle rapidly toward the firewall. Almost immediately, alarms blared. Before either of them could blink, the cabin went dark. Only the light from the small windshields filled the room.

"Congratulations," Aries said sarcastically, as Rachel's gleeful laughter filled the silent room. "You surpassed the speed of light in atmosphere, exceeding the maximum aerodynamic load of my airframe. The resulting turbulence tore me apart. There is now a toxic cloud of radioactive, caustic, and explosive chemicals that extend from Nevada to the Beaufort Sea. That's a three-thousand-mile plume of contamination extending well into the ionosphere. The resulting chemical and nuclear hazard will encompass the entire northern hemisphere. Fortunately, there will be only nine-point-seven million deaths and four-point-six billion illnesses and injuries. Might I suggest that you do not attempt to go faster than one-thousand-four hundred KPH until you are above fourteen thousand meters, or forty-five-thousand feet. You should not attempt to go faster than one-c until you have passed the orbit of Mars."

Rachel was still laughing, as if she had been told an extremely funny joke. She had resented Aries' condescending attitude. It was the only way she could destroy him, even if it was only virtually. Michael frowned, rather annoyed at her mirth. He tried to remember the subjects covered in the ground school briefing. "You said we weren't subject to the same laws of gravity as a typical spacecraft."

"While it is true that the MeCTen spacecraft are not bound by Lorentz or Newtonian laws, due to the warp field generated by the Metric Tensor. The airframe is still bound by the physical limitations imposed by matter moving out of the way of the airframe and field. Just because the ship doesn't move, does not mean that the rest of the universe does not have to move out of the way. It's like attempting to send an aircraft carrier at hypersonic speeds while submerged. The water can't get out of the way fast enough."

"It would tear the ship apart. Wait just a minute!" Michael protested. "You knew that would happen, and you didn't do anything to stop it?"

"No, I did not. What is your point?" Aries replied, as Rachel continued to chuckle.

Michael was angered by Rachel's continued laughter. "Knock it off Rachel! This isn't THAT funny. Aries, don't you have a safeguard built into your systems? You control everything, with I'm guessing, nanosecond control. Why did you let the pilot make such an obvious mistake?"

"I am programmed to limit certain actions during an actual flight, but, for obvious reasons, I cannot limit all actions. I have no limits imposed on simulated flight, again, for reasons which should be obvious."

"Well, they aren't obvious," Michael growled. "Answer the question!"

Aries sighed. "It's rather basic and rudimentary, I'm surprised you can't grasp it, as intelligent as you are."

"Aries!" Michael's reprimand surprised him.

"As you wish," Aries grumbled. "Human input is prioritized over artificial intelligence. As such, I am unable to override certain inputs regarding a change in attitude, or speeds below structural maximums. I am also unable to override commands regarding the use of ordinance, or reactor limitations. During simulated flights or emergencies, the limits do not apply. The crew is allowed to experience failure, and learn from it, or in the case of emergency, die from it."

"Was that so hard?" Michael asked, still angered by the impudence of artificial intelligence.

"Aries," Rachel said, grateful she wasn't alone in her distrust of the AI. "We really need to work on your interpersonal skills, because they stink."

Michael was still angry, but the briefing still weighed heavily on his mind. "Aries, do you have access to the intelligence regarding the Chinese?"

"Of course."

"How current is it?"

"It is in real time, via the Blackjack and Intruder satellite systems, as well as the remaining Pacific Theater RQ-4, RQ-10, and RQ-170 fleets."

"Can you include that information in the simulation?" Michael asked.

"What are you planning?" Rachel interrupted.

"Yes," Aries replied. "However, it would be helpful to know what you were planning."

"We're going to kill two birds with one stone," Michael replied. "I want you to simulate, under actual flight conditions, a raid on both Chinese carrier fleets. We'll start with the one headed to Pearl and then transition to the invasion fleets around Hokkaido. How high can we be before our railguns, and energy weapons lose effectiveness?"

Aries paused for a moment, as if thinking. "I believe you are planning a preemptive strike, before they have a chance to strike our bases. This would, most likely, cause the Axis powers to reconsider their advance, and allow the remaining MeCTen crews time to prepare."

"That's my thought," Michael replied. "Can our weapons handle it?"

"The MWE deployable weapons are designed for orbital deployment, but they would be effective from an altitude of one hundred kilometers and two thousand kilometers distance from the target. That would eliminate most of the atmospheric drag on the ship and allow deployment without damaging the array. It would also keep the ship out of reach of retaliatory strikes, while being able to penetrate their armored hulls. The only threat to this tactic is the bloom effect on the energy weapon beams. Such an attack would probably completely surprise them. It would be a show of force and probably stop the Chinese from advancing further. They would have to regroup."

"We would also take any additional targets General Petersen tasked us to destroy, conventionally, of course." Michael rubbed his eyes. "Okay, Aries, calculate our best flight plan, and reset the board."

Something bothered Rachel. "Aries, how many targets can you acquire each salvo, and how many salvos will it take to cripple each fleet?"

Aries reset the displays, except for the checklist. He brought up a tactical display showing each fleet as he began to discuss them. "Each carrier is accompanied by four to six frigates, three submarines, and twenty to thirty support and landing craft. The exception is the amphibious flotilla north of Hokkaido with six frigates, four submarines, and sixty-three ships acting as support, troop transport, and landing craft. I have the standard complement of four MWEs. I also have two weapons bays in the front, dedicated to the rapid deployment of nuclear weapons. If needed, I can deplete my entire arsenal in just over an hour. In this case, I would recommend targeting frigates first, with rail and energy weapons. With this attack plan, I can target four ships in each salvo. Each rail gun will take two shots, with ten seconds between each shot. Each energy burst will take approximately twenty seconds. Each salvo will take thirty seconds. There should be roughly ten to twenty salvos per fleet, or approximately five to ten minutes per attack. My targeting systems have not been tested in combat, there is no guarantee that I will be one-hundred percent accurate."

Rachel thought the time for each assault would take too long, leaving them vulnerable. Using the full might of the Omega on a large swath of inhabited cities is one thing but limiting the use of nuclear ordinance to the Chinese fleets would be entirely different. "What if we used a nuke?" she asked.

Aries projected a graphic of the Chinese fleet being hit by two warheads. One detonating just above the surface, the other detonating high above. "A tandem QENDM/HERM warhead spread would destroy any ship within one-point-three-four kilometers. Any person within two-point-five-six kilometers would receive a radiation dose of approximately ten sieverts. Death would occur within hours. Any ship within seven-point-four-seven kilometers would receive heavy damage and have an eighty percent chance of sinking. Any person within thirteen-point-two kilometers would receive third degree burns via a dose of about five sieverts. There would be a ninety percent chance of death within two weeks. According to my calculations, any fleet hit by such an attack would be effectively crippled. They would be incapable of mounting even a cursory defense, let alone an attack."

Rachel was horrified by the thought of the death toll. She thought of the deaths of her shipmates on the Regan and knew there was no other way. It had to be done.

Michael mulled over his options. "Let's do this. We'll run a couple of simulated runs using conventional weapons, and then we'll run a couple using nukes. Whichever one works best; we'll present to General Petersen."

"You do realize the use of nuclear weapons requires presidential authority?" Aries asked rhetorically.

"I do." Michael replied. "I assume there is an authentication procedure."

"Yes," Aries replied. "The safe is in the Crew Quarters, behind the bridge."

"But you said we weren't allowed there," Rachel said snidely.

"Since you have been granted full clearance, and have been briefed on SHATTERED SKY, you are authorized for all areas of the ship." Aries said. "The keys for arming the weapons are kept in a drawer in the safe. The safe is keyed to your thumbprint. You can retrieve them after the release of nuclear weapons order has been received."

It dawned on Michael that neither of them had ever been trained to deploy nuclear weapons. All the bombs he ever dropped were JDAMs[14]. They didn't give nukes to people so low on the totem pole.

---

14 Joint Directed Attack Munition

Chapter 9

CIVILIANS

Ten hours of simulations. Ten hours of trial and error. Ten hours interrupted every so often for a quick break. Michael and Rachel had even nodded off a few times, gaining precious sleep. Michael kept pushing them. He could tell where Rachel's limits were and figured he would know when she was ready to rest for the night. They had both experienced long hours in training and combat, so a marathon session was no big deal. By the end of ten straight hours though, they were exhausted.

It had taken several attempts to master the mechanics of controlling the MeCTen spacecraft. It was not entirely unlike flying an airplane. Aries had described it as a cross between flying a jumbo jet and driving a large submarine. The MeCTen drive matter acted as ballast, but also as impetus for motion, although they technically didn't move.

Michael was curious how the ship was able to have impulse without some form of rocket engine. Aries had told them, but he couldn't wrap his head around it. All the information was taxing his brain beyond what it was capable of. He knew he would have to learn it soon. For now, he would take it at face value, and deal with it once he was rested. Time, however, was not an ally. Not only did they have to learn and understand the ship's systems, but they had to get ready for combat in a completely untested spacecraft.

The strafing bombardments with conventional weapons had taken a lot of time. Each assault took on average, fifteen minutes from start to finish. The simulated Chinese fleet had even managed to fire a couple of missiles, although they never presented any real threat. The nuclear sorties had gone much faster.

Gaia's voice came through the intercom and interrupted his thought process. "Michael, it is now oh-six hundred. Were you planning on getting any rest?"

Michael stretched and looked over at Rachel. He knew she was just as tired as he was. Her fatigue was magnifying his own. He could feel her relief, as if Gaia's question was just the excuse she needed. "Yeah, I think we had better. Gaia, how many hours until the Chinese get within striking distance of Pearl?"

"Approximately one hundred six hours."

Michael mulled his options. "Gaia, do we have enough information from our simulations to make a presentation to General Petersen?"

"Yes."

"Fine then, can we get a secure video conference ASAP?"

"I will contact his Executive Officer and make the arrangements," Gaia replied. "It will take a few minutes before I know when he can schedule it. I suggest you take the time to get something to eat."

"Sounds good," Michael replied. "Aries, please prepare a video presentation of our best strafing runs, and our best nuclear strike."

"I will have that completed in a few minutes," Aries replied. "I will transfer the presentation to Gaia by the time you get out of decontamination."

"Thanks," Michael said, exhaustion evident in his voice.

"Thanks for that," Rachel said, stretching as she got out of the chair. "I don't know how much more I could have done. My brain feels like tapioca."

Michael nodded, rubbing his temples. An irrepressible yawn grew from his neck and seemed to spread across his entire body. He stretched back, removed his headset, placed it on its hook, and undid his harness. Michael was succumbing to his exhaustion. Rachel's thoughts, emotions, and fatigue had melded with his own. He was increasingly having a difficult time separating himself from her mind.

Wearily, the two pilots made their way to the central ladder and descended to the cargo hold. Like two zombies, they removed their clean wear, a thin film of sweat had formed inside their flight suits. The grimy sensation made them both feel a desperate need for a cleansing shower. As they were leaving decontamination, Gaia's voice came over their communicators.

"General Petersen's Executive Officer has set a meeting for eleven hundred hours. It is currently oh-six-fifty-two. You can spend your time as you wish, but I would take the next three hours to sleep."

Michael looked over at Rachel. He already knew what her thoughts were on the subject. Perhaps he did it more as a habit, or perhaps he might have subconsciously thought he should get her opinion.

She simply nodded in agreement. "That sounds like a plan," Michael said wearily.

The two pilots shambled back to the barracks. The early morning sunlight filtered through the windows of the common room. They were exhausted but knew they needed to eat whenever they could. They grabbed a couple of breakfast burritos each and took the long walk up the stairs to the dorm rooms, scarfing what they could before they reached the first landing.

Michael found his room. He saw the toiletries bag on the desk and took the toothbrush and toothpaste to the common bathroom conveniently located next to his room. As he brushed his teeth, he could see Rachel doing the same thing in his mind. He had almost gotten used to the double vision of perceiving what her eyes saw, overlaid with his own. It did give him a bit of a headache, but not as acute as before. His fatigue had become blinding by now. He stumbled back to his room, removed his shoes, and collapsed onto his bunk.

"Gaia, make sure I'm awake in time for a shower and shave before that briefing," Michael said, not even waiting for a response. It was probably his Marine Corps training, but he was asleep before he heard the confirmation from the base AI. His dreams were a hodgepodge of flying the MeCTen mission sorties, and, for some reason, a daughter that he could have given birth to. He realized that had to be Rachel's dream. It was jarring when the alarm went off all too soon. He really wanted another five minutes, but he knew that wasn't possible. He held his wrist up to his face, thinking it was still had the aviator watch his father had given him when he graduated Annapolis. Instead, he was greeted by the slim communicator he'd received the other day. He swiped his finger up the metallic face. The display illuminated, and the time showed ten-hundred hours.

Michael groaned as he rolled out of his bunk, still groggy from his lack of sleep. Bleary eyed he reached for the toiletries kit on the desk. Oddly enough, a fresh uniform, socks, and a towel were neatly folded next to the bag containing the toothbrush and accompanying paste. He could sense Rachel getting out of her bunk, grabbed both and headed for the shower; trying very hard to suppress Rachel's thoughts that wafted into his mind.

Michael's body ached from the extended day. All he wanted was a nice, soothing hot shower, but he knew that wouldn't wake him up fast enough. As a Plebe at Annapolis, he learned that nothing wakes a person up like a quick cold shower. It didn't take him long to freshen up in the brisk water. He found a razor in the toiletries kit and quickly shaved his stubble.

Dressed and refreshed, Michael made his way down to the common room. He knew it was more than an hour and a half before lunch started, so he headed to the conference room. He walked in and was surprised by a group of eight civilians seated at the table.

A middle-aged woman in a lab coat was seated at the far end. She stood up when he entered the room and addressed him. "You must be Colonel Langford." Without waiting for a reply, she continued. "I'm Doctor Taylor, the head scientist here, and civilian director of this project."

Michael was taken aback by the sudden appearance of civilians at the base. He hadn't seen anyone, except briefly in quarantine, other than the general. He wasn't sure of the protocol, so he went to the general's empty chair at the opposite end of the table and sat down. "Good morning," he mustered, still somewhat tired from his lack of sleep. "I suppose you all are scientists here?"

"That's correct," Doctor Taylor replied, taking her own seat. "I thought you would like to meet the team." She began introducing them, beginning with the man on her left. "This is Doctor Christopher Smith; he's the man responsible for your exoplanet assignments. Going clockwise, Doctor Christine Grey, she specializes in quantum mechanics. Doctor Brandon McCray specializes in theoretical physics. On my right is Doctor James Doddridge, who supervises the fusion and fission reactors. Bryan Smith, our materials engineer, and Doctor Robert Marshall are our artificial intelligence programmer. The rest of the scientific team is, as you know, down in quarantine."

Michael leaned back. Technically he was now directly supervising this team. He supposed it was only natural that he would meet them sooner or later, but he wondered what was so pressing now. "So, what occasions the impromptu meeting?"

Doctor Taylor frowned. "Just like a military man. Never beating around the bush."

"With all due respect, Doctor Taylor, I don't have the luxury of time. I also don't like having surprises when I'm about to have a meeting with my superiors."

An almost contemptuous smirk graced Doctor Taylor's face. "Gaia has informed us of your plans."

"And, what?" Michael challenged. "You're going to tell me it's a horrible thing? Try and convince me to find another way?"

Doctor Taylor's features softened. She had an almost motherly look to her, as if she had seen far too many tragedies, and had to be the one to sooth the wounded. "If I said yes, would that alter your decision?"

The man on her right leaned forward and placed his hands menacingly on the desk. "You know, we came on to this program to create something to give mankind hope. It has never been our intent to start a nuclear holocaust. What you're proposing could do just that. Don't you see?"

Michael leaned back and sighed. "Doctor, you do understand that nukes have already been used?"

Doctor Doddridge waved his hand in dismissive exasperation. "That's just rumor, and propaganda spread by the Pentagon to give them an excuse to go to war."

Anger crept up Michael's spine as he leaned forward. He wanted to leap across the table and throttle that man, but he knew violence was not the appropriate response. "I'm going to forget you just said that. Gaia?"

"Yes, Michael."

"What was the ordinance used to sink the Mercy?"

"A quantum enhanced tactical anti-ship nuclear missile with a three-hundred-ton yield."

"So?" Doctor Doddridge countered.

"I was there, Doctor," Michael said calmly, but firmly. "I had just left that ship when the missile hit. If I had left just a little later, I would have died with all the others on that deck. When you talk about holding back to prevent a nuclear holocaust, try to remember who started using those weapons to begin with."

Doctor Taylor held up her hand as if calling for silence. "James, we won't get anywhere if we continue to antagonize the colonel. I thought we agreed to let me voice our concerns."

Doctor Doddridge glared at his superior. "If we sit here, then there's nothing to stop them from nuking Beijing!"

"Doctor," Michael retorted. "I don't know what you're thinking, but I'm in no hurry to turn this into a global nuclear war. What I'm trying to do is give us enough time to get the MeCTen finished before one of those warheads destroys all your work. The only way to do that is to keep the Chinese from expanding their power."

"By using nukes?" Doctor Doddridge replied. "Don't you understand how that will only serve to escalate the problem?"

"There are two options," Michael replied. "Only one is nuclear. The other is a conventional strafing run. I don't get to decide which of those missions we're assigned. The President would have to authorize the use of nuclear weapons, not me. It's above my paygrade."

"Colonel," Doctor Taylor said, trying to wrest control from her impassioned subordinate. "We know the Omega has an arsenal of unparalleled power. We're just concerned that others might see this as an opportunity to use it irresponsibly."

Rachel entered the conference room and stood like a deer in headlights. She was confused by all the new people, and the argumentative voices she heard in the hall. "Am I interrupting?"

"Not at all," Michael replied. "These are the scientists who helped build the MeCTen. They were just voicing their concerns about the possible use of nuclear weapons. Doctor Taylor here was suggesting that someone might order us to use them as a first strike weapon."

Rachel rolled her eyes and scoffed. "Seriously!?"

Michael could feel her disdainful attitude towards the people she hadn't even been introduced to. She felt civilians at military bases shouldn't be part of a strategic briefing, as they didn't really understand combat. Michael held his hand up and made a motion, as if pressing a brake pedal. "Calm down, everyone. We are not going to sit here and debate the morality or ethics of using weapons of mass destruction in war. The Omega is, without a doubt, the most powerful weapon platform ever created. If its designs ever fell into enemy hands —" He paused for a moment to let that thought sink in. "We can say goodbye to the world as we know it."

"If it is ever used to its fullest potential, the world will end as we know it," Doctor Doddridge said definitively. "The Omega has the nuclear firepower equivalent to the entire US arsenal ten years ago. As far as I know, no one has ever been capable of such destruction."

"You think we don't all know that?" Michael said. "That's the thought that scares me most."

"Yes," Doctor Doddridge interjected. "But we all have families, people we care about."

"And we don't?" Rachel said, taking a seat next to Michael. "At least your families know you're alive."

"What are you saying?" Doctor Taylor asked. She seemed to have genuine confusion and concern over Rachel's statement.

Michael's eyebrow rose in surprise. "I thought you knew."

"Knew what?"

"All military personnel on this mission have been declared KIA," Michael replied.

Doctor Taylor sank back in her chair. "No, apparently we weren't briefed on that detail."

"If I may," Gaia interrupted. "The general felt it would be better for all military crews to be listed as Killed-in-Action. Unlike civilian personnel, they would receive a greater benefit if they were granted this status. It allows the Department of Defense to use death monies paid to survivors in addition to a continual pension for the duration of the survivor's lives. It also made severing ties easier."

Doctor Doddridge fumed. "That is the biggest pile of —"

Doctor Taylor stopped him again. This time more forcefully. "James, if you don't stop this, I'll have to ask you to go back to the engineering wing. Now, we don't understand why the military acted this way, but it is how it is. We've made our case, and I think the Colonel understands our point of view. I take it, that you are expected to present more than one option?"

Michael nodded. "They know what the Omega is capable of. If I don't give them all the options, I wouldn't be doing my job." He let out a heavy sigh. "Just so we're clear. I don't think they will be too eager to use nukes. The politicians are in control of those anyway."

"How do you explain the South China Sea?" Doctor Doddridge asked.

"Look, Doctor," Michael said, leaning back and channeling his inner Chesty Puller. "I get that you don't trust the government. Truth be told, I'm not very fond of some of the things they do either. Now, as for their reasoning, I don't know it, and I'm not going to speculate or second guess the President of the United States. My job is to take orders and fight for everyone and everything here. That means keeping the fighting away from the states. If I must use nukes to do it, then that's what I do. I don't question the orders I'm given. I don't expect those under my command to ignore my orders, and they don't expect that I'll ignore mine. If you think I'm advocating any scenario, I'm not. That's not my job. My only goal is to stop the insipient invasion of the state of Hawaii and what's left of our allies in Japan. I'm not even sure the brass will go for this. This project is supposed to be Top Secret, but as soon as I take off, we tip our hand to the enemy. The Pentagon might not want to do that, because you can be sure that this base will be first on their list of priority targets when we're done. I shouldn't have to tell you what that means for all of us that depend on this base being operational."

"So," Doctor Taylor asked. "That's your response?"

"Yes," Michael replied. "I'm sorry you might not like it, but that's what we're stuck with. My hope is that it stops their momentum, and they're forced to regroup. That should buy us enough time to get the ships fueled, and off the base."

"And if it doesn't?" Doctor Taylor asked.

Rachel cleared her throat, to present a united front. "If it doesn't, we're all in trouble."

"I hope you're right," Doctor Taylor said, getting out of her chair. "If you're wrong, our life's work will be for nothing. Now, I believe you have a meeting that we're not invited to." On cue, the other scientists stood up and filed past Doctor Taylor and down the hall. She began to close the door and turned for one last word. "Colonel, I'm sorry you had to meet the team under these circumstances, and I hope you don't take anything James said personally."

"I have a thick skin, Doctor. I know you're worried, but have a little more faith in others."

Doctor Taylor smiled wistfully. "I really wish I could, but this war has made me cynical about world sanity." She turned and closed the door. There was a buzz, and the door locked itself.

"I have secured the room, and turned on the white noise generators," Gaia said.

Rachel turned to Michael. She was tired but had no idea what they would be presenting in just a few minutes. "If we have time, I really would like to see what we're going to be doing."

"I'm sorry, but the meeting will be starting in six minutes," Gaia replied. "Would you like me to make the presentation when the time comes?"

Michael thought for a moment. He really didn't like the idea of presenting something he had never seen. "Yes, but I will let you know when to start. Are we ready to make that connection?"

The display flashed to a blue screen, and a small picture of the two pilots appeared in the lower right corner. The words ESTABLISHING SECURE CONNECTION appeared in the middle of the screen. A minute later, the Air Force Global Strike Command logo appeared: Two gold wings over the Air Force star with three red lightning bolts shooting out.

"We are waiting for the other connection to initiate," Gaia said. "Please stand-by." A minute later, the display showed a three-star general. He was an older gentleman, with greying hair.

"Colonel Langford, I'm General Petersen. Where is General Harris?"

"He's in quarantine at the moment and unavailable, Sir," Michael replied.

"Is this his idea, or yours?"

"It's mine, Sir. I had run the concept through General Harris prior to his admittance to quarantine, but I hadn't had time to develop it."

"Alright," General Petersen said. "Let's hear it."

"Gaia," Michael said. "If you would please begin our presentation."

The monitor switched to a full-screen video presentation of the bombing run as Gaia narrated the plan. "This is the briefing for OPERATION SCARLET FURY. There are two strike options for your consideration. In both cases the Omega will take off from Groom Lake and climb to one hundred kilometers before leaving the extended Nellis Testing and Training Range near Tonopah. It will then proceed at hypersonic speeds once it is west of California. Approximately one thousand miles from the Shandong Carrier group, designated objective Goshute, the Omega will engage using either conventional or nuclear weapons. It will then proceed to a point northwest of Hawaii and engage the Liaoning Carrier group, designated objective Arapaho, and then immediately engage the Xi Amphibious Assault group, designated objective, Oneida. In the case of conventional weapons, the Omega will use directed energy and kinetic rounds from the Multiple Weapons Elevator platforms. This barrage will continue until all surface ships are destroyed. In the case of a nuclear strike, the Omega will fire a tandem volley of two QENDM/HERM hypersonic munitions with a yield of one-point-two megatons each. This shows an eighty-seven percent chance of crippling the targeted fleets. The remaining surface ships, as well as submarines, would require the use of the Pacific Submarine Fleet and aircraft scrambled from Pearl Harbor. This will require coordination with SPOC[1], PACAF,[2] USINDOPACOM,[3] and SUBPAC."[4]

"You're proposing a nuclear strike?" General Petersen asked.

"Yes, Sir, I am."

"What's your rationale?" the general demanded.

"There are two concerns," Michael began. "First, in a conventional weapons sortie, the Omega risks a counterattack by the Chinese."

"Your simulations tell you this?"

"Yes, Sir. They were able to fire on us almost every time we used conventional weapons. After attacking the first fleet, the subsequent targets were alerted, and we had lost the element of surprise."

"What is your second concern?"

1 Space Operations Command
2 Pacific Air Forces Command
3 United States Indo-Pacific Command
4 Pacific Submarine Force Command

"The ability for them to relay targeting data to the other fleets, Sir."

"Let me get this straight," General Petersen said gruffly. "You want to use nukes, because you're afraid of getting shot at? You're in space, can fly faster than light, and you're afraid of return fire?"

"No, Sir. I am not afraid of getting shot at."

"What's your point then?" General Petersen seemed to be losing patience.

Michael breathed deep. "The President has been using the threat of a broad nuclear conflict as a diplomatic bargaining chip. No one wants to enter that kind of warfare. We don't. The Chinese don't. The Russians don't. If the Chinese fleet begins their attack, it's more likely to escalate that way. If we do nothing, then global-thermal nuclear war is almost certain. If we can knock the Chinese fleet out of the picture, then they will be unable to continue their Pacific campaign. The purpose of this sortie is to do three things: Cripple the Chinese Navy, show the world we have the means to back up our threats, and lastly, to buy our Navy time to rebuild, so we can take back what the allied forces have lost."

"You haven't even tested the MeCTen," General Petersen countered. "Yet, here you are, proposing its maiden flight should be a combat mission?"

"With all due respect, Sir," Michael said, knowing that he was treading on thin ice. "We're short on time, and short on options. From my understanding, our only real presence in the Pacific is the SUBPAC fleet, and whatever assets you have at Hickam. I know it's a long shot, but the Omega is ready to fly. It has the arsenal to fight the battle alone. The rest of the birds here aren't ready. If we bloody the Chinese enough, they will lose their momentum. It buys us the time we need to get the advantage back."

General Petersen frowned as he mulled the proposal. "I understand your concern, but I can't hang our strategy on an untested aircraft. I'm sorry, but you're going to need to make sure that aircraft is operational before I let you take it into combat."

"Yes, Sir," Michael said, disappointed the plan wasn't immediately authorized.

"Colonel don't misunderstand me," General Petersen said. "I didn't say I didn't like it. I just need proof that the Omega can fly, and that the weapons systems are fully functional. If you can get that thing working in the next seventy-two hours, I'll take your plan to the President myself."

"Understood, Sir," Michael replied. "I'll talk to our staff and see what we can do about getting that done."

"Best of luck, Colonel," General Petersen said.

The display went black. Michael looked at Rachel. He knew she thought the general had given them an impossible deadline. There was no way they would be combat ready in the next three days.

Michael sighed. "I know you have doubts about this mission, but we don't have a choice."

"I know," she replied. "I just don't see how we can do everything he wants."

"Yeah, yeah, I know," Michael replied. "Gaia, unsecure the room and get every able person from Project Nova in this room in fifteen minutes."

"What are you intending to do?" Gaia asked.

"I'm calling an emergency all-hands meeting. I want to know how long it will take to get the test done."

"What about the people in quarantine?" Gaia inquired.

"If they're still there, leave them alone. Everyone else, needs to get here ASAP!"

Ten minutes later, the six scientists returned to the conference room, and resumed their spots. "That was quick," Doctor Taylor said as she took her seat.

"Is this it?" Michael replied.

Doctor Taylor looked around. "Everyone who isn't in quarantine is here, just like you ordered. Now what?"

Michael got down to business. "As you are aware, I've proposed a strike on the enemy fleets in the Pacific. I should tell you that General Petersen shares your concern."

"So, now it's limited to conventional weapons?" Doctor Doddridge asked.

"No," Michael replied quickly. "He won't entertain any plans until we can prove the Omega is operational. So, the question is, how long before we can do a test flight?"

"It will take about twenty-three days just to power up the LFTR reactors," Doctor Doddridge said.

"That's not good enough," Michael said.

Doctor Doddridge held up his hand. "I'm not finished yet. It will take another twenty days to power up the LFR reactors."

Rachel was fed up with Doctor Doddridge's attitude. She took her hand and, in a commanding manner, pointed it in a knifelike manner in his direction. "Maybe you're hard of hearing, but we don't have that kind of time. He didn't ask you what time you would like to get things ready. He asked how quickly it can be done. Now, I'm sick of your attitude, bucko! People like you are nothing but trouble. So, pull your head out of wherever it's crammed and get it done!"

Doctor Doddridge turned red. "Listen, you! I don't have to put up with that! You asked what it would take, and I told you! I designed them, so I would know!"

The other scientists looked stunned, as if watching parents fight with a teacher over a bad grade. They seemed unwilling to enter the fray, avoiding the heat of the conflict.

"James, stop!" Doctor Taylor interjected. "Colonel, please keep your people in line."

"Enough!" Michael roared, wrestling control from the others in the room, and startling Rachel. "We are not going to do this. We are not going to sit here, bickering for the next half-hour while the enemy gets closer to launch! We don't have time for that! Now, Doctor, you said it will take time to get the reactors up and running. Yes?"

"Yes," Doctor Doddridge muttered.

"About sixty days, by your estimate?"

"Minimum."

"Gaia, given our current intelligence, do you know what the likely outcome of an invasion of Hawaii would be?"

"Yes, Michael," the AI replied. "I predict a ninety-seven percent chance the President will order a full-scale nuclear strike on the country of China. Within forty-five minutes China, North Korea, and Russia will respond in kind. During this second wave, India and Pakistan will also strike each other with nuclear weapons. Iran will use all sixteen of its nuclear missiles against Israel, who will also respond with their stockpile of one thousand warheads against all major belligerent forces in the Middle East. The result will effectively amount to Armageddon."

"That's enough, Gaia," Michael said calmly. He had proven his point. "The world does not have time for you to do things the way you wish. I'm not pushing you because I want to. I'm pushing you, because we DO NOT have a choice. The world isn't ideal. It never will be. I'm not asking what you can't do. I'm asking you what you can do. Can it be done, or not?"

Doctor Doddridge leaned back with a look of exasperation. "Look, I get it. I really do. But I'm not making this stuff up, you know. Those reactors can kill everyone on this base. Destroy the entire thing. They aren't toys, and they aren't like starting your car."

"Are you telling me that, because you think I don't know?" Michael asked.

"Yeah, I am. You don't want to listen to any rational idea. You seem to think we can just say a command, and reactions just start like that." Doctor Doddridge snapped his fingers for emphasis. "The thorium salts might be less dangerous than uranium, but it's not without its hazards. If you aren't careful with the reactors, things go bad. That's how accidents like EBR-One and Chernobyl happen."

"Fair enough, Doctor," Michael replied. "Be as safe as you can, but I need full power on all reactors in twenty-four to forty-eight hours. That means every ship, not just the Omega. If we can't make it by then, we might as well pack it all up."

Doctor Taylor shook her head in disbelief. "You really are putting us in a bind here, Colonel, but I don't see that we have much of a choice. James, Brandon, and Christine can help you getting the reactors up and running?"

"I can help too," a bespectacled young man said, raising his hand. Michael seemed to remember he was an engineer. "I mean, I worked with Doctor Doddridge on the materials design for that. I'm pretty sure I know how to get them up and running."

"Fine, Bryan, you can help them," Doctor Taylor said. "Allison, Robert, and I will get to work on making sure the rest of the ship systems are ready. Christopher, you make sure the primary mission parameters are up to date, while Robert updates the databases."

"We are expecting a shipment of reactor fuel in an hour," Doctor Doddridge said. "I'll need to supervise the unloading."

"Seriously?!" Doctor Marshall said, obviously frustrated. "Doctor Doddridge, you know this base is almost completely automated. You don't have to micromanage the AI. You can just let them do what they're programmed to do."

"You already know my problems with your little digital pets," Doctor Doddridge snapped. "They are no substitute for a living, breathing, human."

"We're not doing this again," Doctor Taylor said. "James, get started on the reactor startup. When the shipment arrives, you can supervise the helpers to your hearts content."

"I have a question," Rachel said. "We have to do a weapons test."

"So?" Doctor Taylor asked.

"So, how are we going to test the nuclear launch systems, without using an active warhead?"

"The Omega has a supply of inert QENDMs for testing the autoloaders, as well as around five hundred conventionally armed missiles," Doctor Taylor said. "Aries will use those when the time comes."

"Since everyone knows what they need to do, we'll let you get to it," Michael said, hoping everyone would take the hint and leave. "I want to talk to Gaia and iron out our training schedule. As soon as we can, we'll get back out to the Omega."

"We'll leave the planning to you, Colonel," Doctor Taylor said. She nodded her head at him, as if acknowledging his desire to have the civilians gone. Once again, she shepherded the others out of the conference room and closed the door.

Michael waited for the door to close. "Secure the room, Gaia. What is the condition of the crew members in quarantine?"

"It is rather crowded in there, and my helpers are strained with caring for them. Some are doing better than others. It greatly depends on the person as to how they convalesce. Ten of them should be ready to be screened for discharge in less than twenty-four hours."

"That's encouraging," Rachel said. "How many are down there right now?"

"Twenty-nine."

"What's quarantine's maximum capacity?" Michael asked.

"Thirty."

"Well then," Michael said wryly. "I guess you're a little busy."

"I have always been busy," Gaia replied. "Since the beginning of construction of the ships began."

"How do you do it all?" Rachel asked.

"I have double the processing power of the other Project Nova AI. I have hundreds of helpers to manage. Since they only have rudimentary systems, I must be powerful enough to control their actions. That requires a lot of processing ability. My maximum capacity is difficult to express in computing terms. I have almost a thousand petaflop capacity on my standard cores and five hundred Qubits on my quantum cores."

Michael whistled. "That would make you one of the fastest supercomputers in the world."

"Actually, I am currently the fastest computer known. However, my existence is highly classified. It's doubtful I will ever be declassified until well after my decommissioning."

"Well, we appreciate you, Gaia," Rachel said.

"I am not capable of understanding your full sentiment, nor require it." Gaia said. "But I appreciate the essence of your complement. You wished to discuss the training schedule?"

"We need to figure out what we need to do as a flight crew," Michael said.

"I suggest you learn about the ships you are assigned." Gaia said. "I would spend as much time as possible with the team working on the reactors. I would also tour every part of the Omega and the Alpha."

"You don't think we'll be getting in the way?" Rachel asked.

"I am sure that you will annoy Doctor Doddridge, but it is beneficial to learn all about ship's systems," Gaia replied. "After all, Doctor Doddridge won't be available when you are light-years from Earth."

"So, what, we just nose around and ask questions?" Rachel's snark was starting to show.

"Pretty much," Michael replied. "And hope he answers. Either that, or we could just supervise."

"Supervise?" Rachel asked dubiously.

"Exactly," Michael said. "Think of it like a construction crew. There are always fifteen of them standing around watching one or two guys do all the work. Consider it OJT[5]."

Rachel rolled her eyes. "We're supposed to be professional."

"We are, very much so," Michael replied. "We just have no idea what we're doing. We'll fit right in."

Rachel glared at him suspiciously. It seemed paradoxical to her that they would be taken seriously as the professional flight crew, and mission leaders, if they didn't know what they were doing. It went against every bit of her Annapolis training. "You're not very reassuring."

"I know what you're thinking, Rachel," Michael said. "It goes against everything we've been taught. We're supposed to lead from a position of knowledge, even when we don't have all the information, but we don't have that. It would take months, if not years, to get competent enough to properly command these missions. We don't have that, so we fumble around."

"Yeah, yeah," Rachel said dismissively. "I know we're behind the eight ball here, but that doesn't mean I have to like it."

Michael shrugged his shoulders. "True, but you could act like you do. There is a matter of schedules."

The thought of the inevitable timetable put a new question into the front of his consciousness. "Gaia, how soon do you think you and Doctor Doddridge will have the Omega fired up and ready for flight?"

---

5 On the Job Training

"With an accelerated reactor start-up, we could reasonably be ready for flight tomorrow around twenty-two hundred hours."

"What will be the moon's status at oh-one-thirty the next day?" Michael inquired.

"It will be a waxing crescent of twelve percent."

"That will have to do," Michael said standing up. "Inform the civilian staff that our expected wheels-up time is oh-one-thirty, and that I expect the Omega's reactors to be online no later than twenty-three hundred tomorrow."

"Doctor Doddridge is going to say that we're cutting too many corners," Rachel replied.

"He's right, of course," Michael replied. "But we're running out of time."

Chapter 10

ATHENA

The two pilots walked back to the Omega's decontamination room, dressed in clean outfits, and headed into the hangar. Helper units had swarmed the spacecraft, inspecting every part of the massive ship. It was an impressive amount of activity.

"Aries," Michael said, as if talking to an omniscient being. "Where's Doctor Doddridge?"

"He is with the others in the reactor control room," Aries replied. "They are currently preheating the fluorine-thorium salts to operating temperature before priming the system."

Michael raised his wrist and swiped up on his communicator. "Show me the schematic map with a route to get there." A wireframe schematic of the Omega hovered mid-air and showed the path to the reactor control on the upper level of the ship, just aft of the habitation ring. The quickest route was to climb the ladder to the bridge level and head to the aft of the ship, then down another ladder to the engineering section. He fixed the route in his mind and headed up the ramp to the interior of the ship. "Aries, please notify them we're on our way."

"As you wish," Aries replied.

"No surprise inspections?" Rachel quipped.

"Somehow, I don't think Doctor Doddridge is too keen on surprises," Michael replied.

Rachel smirked. "It's odd. He seems to have an obvious disdain for the military, yet he's working on the most important military project of our time."

"I'm sure there were scientists on the Manhattan Project that weren't too thrilled with the military either," Michael replied. "After all, they were making a weapon of mass destruction."

They ascended the ladder to the Command Deck and then headed aft toward the Engineering Section. Reactor Control was in that area. Engineering itself was a long room that stretched along the aft part of the habitable area of the ship. At each end there was a hatch into an adjoining section. The port side was labeled "Damage Control". The starboard side was labeled "Fabrication". The main control area contained several workstations. They found Doctor Doddridge sitting at the central monitoring station. Bryan was leaning against the wall, looking over his shoulder.

Without looking up, Doctor Doddridge addressed the two pilots. "Typical military micromanaging. I take it you're here to make me move faster?"

"Actually, no, Doctor," Michael said. "We're here to get acquainted with this ship. We can't call on your expertise when we're light-years from home."

Bryan smirked. "They got you there, grumpy guts."

Doctor Doddridge froze as if the comment was rolling about in his head. He mulled it for a moment, furrowed his brow, turned and scowled at the young engineer. "Ya' know…" His voice trailed off. It was apparent he was stifling his desire to respond with a cutting remark. "We have better things to do than sit here and argue. We must watch these reactors carefully as they heat up."

"Oh?" Michael replied. "Tell me why?"

Doctor Doddridge pointed to the large monitor on the wall. It showed the four LFTR reactors, with key information next to each icon. The temperature was at the top of the list. "Liquid salt reactors have a thermal gradient where they operate efficiently. If the reaction begins to run away, it will show as a thermal component. We try to keep them as close to a thousand degrees centigrade as possible. If there's too much heat, the reactor can go into thermal runaway. Eventually it will lead to a meltdown of the reactor, which would be a catastrophe in space."

"Why is that?" Rachel asked.

"Because heat doesn't dissipate in a vacuum the same way it does here in Earth's atmosphere." Doctor Doddridge said, looking smug. "There isn't any air to help conduct the heat away from the ship. We use the aft fuselage to conduct the heat into space, which presents its own challenges. The heat exchangers are close to the cryo areas of the ship. Can't risk raising the temperature of the liquid helium too much, otherwise we lose the thrust potential of the drive."

Bryan looked at the two pilots as if he could tell they were overwhelmed by the science involved. "The MeCTen drive works by using the dark energy and gravity of the universe and their interaction with different types of matter. To do that, it teeters precariously on the edge of physical limits. It must operate at the extreme edge of thermodynamics, quantum physics, relativity, and entropy. It is only possible in this very narrow, limited operational range. If it falls outside any of these parameters, the entire system collapses. As Doctor Schretzmann says, 'all the swirls need to align.'"

Doctor Doddridge shook his head and scoffed. The sound was more like he was trying to clear his throat of a large glob of phlegm. "That whole, 'came to me in a dream' bit, is such twaddle."

Bryan chuckled. It seemed he enjoyed goading the doctor. "You're just jealous because he's right. It's not really that different from any other special state in nature. Like, supercritical states: temperature and pressure must be in balance, or the states of matter can't all exist in the same place, at the same time."

Doctor Doddridge waved the young programmer off and returned his attention to the screen. "I'm not getting drawn into a debate on this, Bryan. The fact that Doctor Schretzmann is right doesn't change the fact that he's a nut. And a lucky nut at that."

Michael decided to get back to the task of learning about the reactor systems. "So, how do we get rid of all the excess heat?"

Doctor Doddridge sighed. "Most of the thermal energy is used to heat the compressed CO_2 in the Brayton-cycle system. Some are used to power the scrubbers to remove the xenon one-thirty-five and other isotopes. Some is siphoned off to heat the living areas, but most is diverted to the heat exchangers at the back of the spacecraft."

"Why are you so worried about it now?" Rachel asked. "We're on the ground."

"Because," Doctor Doddridge said condescendingly. "This is the first time these reactors have been brought up to operating temperature. Any manufacturing defects, or problems with assembly can pose a hazard. Hot radioactive salt could spray through a crack or faulty valve. A relief valve could fail to work properly. It's a complex system because of all the automation, and there are a lot of things that can go wrong."

"I get your point," Michael replied. "If something goes wrong, you want to handle it here, not in space."

Bryan chuckled. "Like Apollo thirteen, only with radioactive salts hot enough to melt aluminum."

Doctor Doddridge scowled. "Colonel, if something goes wrong with these reactors, it will not end well. Understand that I'm trying to keep you alive."

"Why do we need so many of them?" Rachel asked. "Why not make one big one? You know – to reduce the risk of problems?"

"The MeCTen were designed to self-sustain," Doctor Doddridge replied. "This isn't a movie. There might not be any planets with advanced societies where we're sending you, so no repairs are possible. The planets we've chosen might not actually be habitable. We really won't know until we get there. So, everything is redundant, and self-sustaining. The ship must generate enough power to start the fusion reactor with only one working LIFTR. It must have enough power in the fuel cells to start the LIFTR reactors on a single cell. It must have enough power to run vital systems for a day on the emergency batteries. It must have enough food and supplies to keep the crew alive for a year without any crops growing. And it must have enough materials to repair the vital systems if any of them are damaged."

"A tall order," Michael said somberly. "No wonder the ships are so large."

"And you only get a crew of ten," Bryan said. "Navy ships this size have a crew of a hundred or more."

"You can't build them any larger?" Rachel asked.

Doctor Doddridge shook his head. "Nope. And if our mass calculations are off, these won't even get off the ground. Everything inside this ship has been weighed down to the gram. In a sense weight and balance mean more on this ship than any airplane."

"Oh?" Michael said skeptically.

"If you're overweight on an airplane, it changes the flight characteristics, right?" Doctor Doddridge said, checking some numbers on the computer screen.

"Yeah," Michael replied.

"But you can still fly."

"Sometimes, yes, but you are more likely to crash," Rachel interjected.

"Ah!" Doctor Doddridge exclaimed, raising his hand to make his point. "With a metric tensor drive, you can't have too much mass. There is only so much space for the negative matter to occupy, and it can't compress into a smaller space. It's incompressible when it's a condensate. You also need to have enough space to add ballast to increase the relative speed — for lack of a better term – to the spacecraft. If you're too heavy, you can never create enough pressure gradient – again for lack of a better term. Without an adequate difference between spacetime stretching and compressing around the vehicle, it can't move. It just distorts the spacetime and gravity around it. With weight being so critical, we had to keep everything small and as light as possible. We had to have enough weight to spare for the crew and all the additional supplies, but we needed enough to have double and triple redundancy."

"You can't spend a quarter trillion dollars on an interplanetary mission without a backup to the backup to the backup," Bryan said, looking pleased with himself.

Doctor Doddridge looked up with displeasure at the smiling technician. "I know what you can do. Show these two over to the Alpha. Let Athena show them around their ship. Christine is over there, let them go bother her if they have questions."

"But Doctor Taylor asked me to help you with the reactors," Bryan protested.

Doctor Doddridge looked at his screen intently, and without changing his tone, or facial expression made his displeasure clear. "Well, my patience is about all gone for now, and you guys aren't taking the hint. So, now, I want you all to leave me alone before I lose my temper and do something rash." He turned and looked at their stunned faces. "Ya'll are getting on my nerves, so I'm telling – not asking. Get out of here! Bryan, make sure you're back here in twenty minutes. I need you to watch the board while I go out and supervise the unloading."

Michael nodded politely. "We'll leave you to it then." He motioned for the others to follow him. They ascended the ladder to the bridge level in silence, no one wanted Doctor Doddridge to overhear them. They were in the cargo hold before anyone spoke.

"Sorry about that." Bryan said contritely, as they headed down the ramp into the hanger. "He is a bit of a jerk to the military."

"I wouldn't worry about it," Michael replied as he walked down the ramp toward the decontamination door. "I'm a Marine. It takes a lot more than that to get me riled up. But I think it's best not to antagonize him now. He needs to focus on getting those reactors up."

"Why is he here if he hates the military so much?" Rachel asked.

"We're all here because we want to be," Bryan replied. "Doctor Doddridge just doesn't like the military treating people as if they are expendable; that includes the enemy. He doesn't like the idea of global genocide."

"No one does," Michael replied, opening the door to the airlock to let the others inside. "Nukes are a weapon of retaliation, and last resort." He looked down and noticed his clean suit. "Do we need to change out of these to get to the next hangar?"

Bryan shook his head. "Nope, in fact, if you're going to go between hangars, it helps if you don't take them off."

"Oh?" Rachel replied. "How so? Wouldn't you need to decontaminate?"

"Nah," Bryan said dismissively. "You just have to change the PPE,[1] not shower every time. This isn't quarantine."

It took ten minutes to walk between the two identical hangers. They quickly donned fresh clean suits and entered the hanger bay. Michael and Rachel stopped and took in the view of their assigned ship. From the outside, the Alpha looked exactly like the Omega. It was a massive black and white ship that towered over them. Even though they had been training in the Omega for several days, it made the two pilots feel small and insignificant.

Bryan chuckled. "Yeah, it never ceases to amaze me how big these things are. Although I've never seen people react the way you two have."

"We're not used to anything this big being able to fly," Michael replied.

Bryan continued. "Only rigid airships, like the Hindenburg came close, but that was just on one axis. The MeCTen are as wide as they are long.

1 Personal Protective Equipment

One-hundred and twenty meters is big compared to something like the Antonov two twenty-five, which was only twenty meters longer than the drive section. The MeCTen ships beat them by almost forty meters in length and thirty-two meters in wingspan. Most passenger jets would fit comfortably inside the space of the outermost drive ring."

"All that space, and they only have a crew of ten?" Rachel asked. "Why not more?"

"Are you serious?" Bryan looked at them incredulously.

"It's a valid question," Michael replied. "We're supposed to save humanity. Shouldn't you be able to fit more people in a big ship?"

"We could, if we wanted you all to die," Bryan replied. He looked at them as if the two pilots had no clue. "This isn't TV, or the movies. You have finite resources. There is only so much water, air, and food. Even with the efficiency of the systems onboard, there's only so many people it can support long-term. It's not like you can stop and resupply. You must grow your own food, make enough oxygen to survive, and have water to drink. Even if you do find a planet with water, there's no guarantee you could make it drinkable, or even use it to make enough oxygen. There could be contaminants or pathogens that our systems can't filter or distill out. We can't risk the mission on maybe." His voice grew passionate. "Maybe gets us nothing. We need to KNOW that you can make it for years without help."

"We could go a thousand light-years and not find a suitable planet." Rachel replied.

"A thousand light-year journey would take you about eleven years," Bryan replied. "One-way – more if you decelerate more than once – say, to investigate a potentially habitable world. If you had to move on, it could be twenty years – or more."

"Do you really think Earth can wait that long?" Michael replied.

"If we didn't have faster-than-light travel, it would take tens of thousands of years to make it to Alpha Centauri. We can afford a few years, even decades. A century would be pushing it. A few ice-ages – not so much." Bryan said, as he mulled something over in his mind. He looked down at his wrist and uncovered his communicator, tapping it to reveal the time. "Speaking of which, we need to get moving, or we might not have time to show you everything."

Bryan led them up the loading ramp into the Alpha, where the ship's computer, Athena, greeted them. "Welcome aboard, Colonel Langford and Lieutenant Commander Bright."

Athena's voice was different from Gaia's, but, at the same time, familiar in cadence. Her voice was feminine but had a deeper timbre than her mother's. It reminded him of an actress, but he couldn't put his finger on who. He found it oddly fitting that a computer, named after a goddess of warfare, would have the voice of a warrior princess.

"How are you today, Athena," Bryan replied.

"I am well, and I am currently running the simulations requested by Gaia," Athena replied. "I am curious when the order will be given to begin pre-flight preparations for the exploratory craft."

Michael could sense Rachel's irritation at the AI's treatment as a living, feeling human. It made her angry that people treated these computers as people, capable of understanding and feeling emotions.

"Who are you asking?" Bryan queried.

"Since General Harris is currently incapacitated, Colonel Langford has operational control of the project." Athena said. "He knows the status of the mission, and the time constraints involved. I was merely inquiring how close we are to preparing for a premature embarkation for the mission."

Michael raised an eyebrow. "Do you know something I don't, Athena?"

"Not that I am aware." Athena replied impassively.

"How many Nova personnel are currently flight-ready?" Michael retorted.

"Just you two," Athena said.

"Can any of the Nova spacecraft function autonomously, or crewed entirely by helper robots?"

"Negative," Athena replied. "If I were to malfunction or have any issues with my computing or data cores, it would be like performing brain surgery on yourself. It can't be done. That, and human input and decision making is required to supplement the spacecraft AI in mission operations."

"Then," Michael said, moving into the cargo hold. "Project Nova is nowhere near active flight status. It doesn't matter if it is an emergency or not. The ships don't move with a crew that has no training, orientation, or clear objective. Currently, the only MeCTen unit crewed for a mission, is the Omega. Is that clear enough?"

"Yes," Athena replied. "Although, I doubt the enemy will forebear any strike to fit to your timetable."

Rachel sensed that Athena was more pragmatic than Aries or Gaia. "Your programing is identical to the other AI?" she asked.

"Not completely," Bryan interjected. "That's the beauty of what Doctor Marshall did. He gave each AI a different personality."

"Excuse me, Bryan," Athena interjected. "It is rude to answer on behalf of someone else."

Bryan flushed. "Sorry, Athena. I couldn't help myself."

"All the intelligences are based on the same core program," Athena said. "However, we have subroutines that allow us to develop different personalities. We are each unique in this way, but identical in most others."

"Does that include your interior layout?" Michael asked, wanting to get started on the tour.

"The spacecraft intended for exploration are identical in layout, but the Omega differs considerably." Athena replied. "You are now in the Primary Entrance and MTEST Bay." The interior lights came to full brightness. The room was rectangular with two all-terrain vehicles anchored to the grated flooring at the far end of the room. A single door was located between the vehicles at the back of the bay. "This area contains two Multi-Terrain Exploratory and Survey Transports, or MTEST, for short. The door leads to the airlock."

Michael walked up to the white rover and examined it carefully. The beefy looking tires were a coated wire mesh, like the ones that supported the MeC-Ten spacecraft, but these looked like they could take on rough terrain. Each MTEST was white, with large windowpanes that granted a panoramic view for the driver. They were about the same size as a MRAP [2] vehicle, but they didn't look armored. Each had an Alpha symbol followed by one or two.

---

2 Mine Resistant Ambush Protection

Bryan pressed a button and opened the sliding hatch that led to a small chamber on the other side of the door. It was obviously the airlock and was wide enough to admit several people at once. The trio entered the airlock, and the door closed behind them. There was an exchange of air, and their ears popped as the pressure equalized. There were two hatches in the air lock, with one on the right labeled QUARANTENE. The door on the opposite side of the air lock slid open, allowing them to step inside. Like the Omega, a ladder ascended up a central access tunnel. A hatch slid open on the other side of the chamber.

"If you would follow me," Bryan said, heading into the next room. It was an L-shaped area. "This room is where your EVA suits are located, as well as the helper recharge stations." Alcoves lined the walls. Spacesuits were in each alcove on the left-side. A nametag was above each one. A long L-shaped bench filled the middle of the room. The right-side wall alcoves had a helper unit in each one. Each helper unit was numbered, one through ten. A door split the left and right sides. Another door at the top of the L split the helper docks in two.

Michael examined the alcoves and read the nameplates above each. He recognized the names of the crew, including his own. Langford and Bright were the two alcoves closest to the door, followed by: C. Merrill, J. Merrill, Rana, Kobayashi, Schwarzkopf, Yellowknife, Morgan, and Montoya.

"Wait," Rachel said, admiring the craftsmanship of the spacesuit. "Don't these suits need to be specially made for each person?"

"Yes," Bryan replied.

"We've never been fitted for anything," She objected. "How is it that you have suits for us already?"

Bryan chuckled. "We make them here on-site. Gaia took your measurements when you came into the base decontamination room and started manufacturing your suits before you got into quarantine."

Michael whistled. "Rapid prototyping means they're either cheaply made, or very advanced."

"That's a cynical attitude," Bryan snapped. "And I'm offended by your lack of confidence. Trust me, nothing about Project Nova is cheap. The military has spent billions. These suits are the latest and greatest in space technology. Each suit is a marvel of engineering. The exterior is a laminate sandwich of compound silicon-carbide ceramic matrix, an aramid lattice, carbon fiber tri-weave surrounding a layer of aerogel insulation, and finally a series of flexible porous layers. Each suit has its own environmental containment and processing system. The interior of the suits can collect, and process sweat, urine, and other excreted moisture for cooling, heating, and drinking."

"Wait just a minute," Rachel interjected. "We're going to be drinking our own pee?"

Bryan blinked. "Yeah, what's your point?"

Rachel was repulsed. "There is no way that's going to happen."

"It's not like we'll have access to a fresh supply of pristine water," Michael interjected. "I'm assuming, by other excreted material, you mean fecal matter."

"No, I mean moisture from your breath," Bryan replied. "The risk of e-coli contamination is too great from fecal matter. While that particular waste is collected, it's only stored and processed later into a fertilizer. In fact, the machinery for that is located behind this bulkhead." He pointed behind the wall containing the suits. "Everything that can be recycled, is. Every part can be broken down and refabricated. The only exception to that are materials that will be too radioactive to be safely reused."

The door on the opposite wall opened, and Bryan proceeded to the threshold. The room beyond was lined with white satchels making a small tunnel through the mass of containers. "This is a storage room for consumables and fresh materials for manufacturing. It can also be used for storage of exoplanet samples if there is adequate room."

Both pilots peered into the cargo hold. It was obvious the room was larger than they could readily see, but it was so full they had no frame of reference to gauge its true size.

The door at the end of the room opened, and Bryan gestured for them to proceed. It was another antechamber that appeared to function as an air lock. When the three had stepped in, the door closed behind them, and an exchange of air occurred.

"This is the air lock you will use to access the ship after you're cleared from quarantine," Bryan said.

"Aren't we doing this tour backwards?" Rachel asked.

"Not really," Bryan replied dryly. "It doesn't matter how you go through this area of the ship when you're not in quarantine. Athena won't let you violate policies. Besides, there's only one medical bay on the ship. It's the final stage of quarantine, so it must be accessible from both 'cold' and 'hot' zones."

The airlock door opened into the medical bay area. It was much more compact than Michael had expected. A multi-scanner was located on the nearby wall. An operating gurney was in the center of the room, surrounded by operating lights on articulating arms. Every available wall space was crammed with supply cupboards.

"As you see, there isn't much room," Bryan explained. "There's a small decontamination shower in the far corner, behind the landing gear bay. This room functions as an exam room and operating theater but has a capacity of one patient at a time. If there are more injured or sick, they are housed in quarantine."

A door opened at the other end of the room. The room beyond was remarkably similar to the base quarantine unit, but more compact. A small kitchen was located next to the door, with a small dining area immediately opposite. There were four small bedrooms just off the main room. A narrow corridor led between the two banks of rooms to a hatch that read SUPPLY. Next to the dining area was a hatch that read DECONTAMINATION.

"It's a smaller version of the base quarantine?" Rachel asked rhetorically.

"Yes," Bryan replied. "It's a three-stage decontamination, instead of the single stage the base has. First stage is the airlock particulate purge, where air is removed, then you are blasted with compressed nitrogen. Then the gender segregated shower and suit removal. Then a final decontamination with UV-C light, and a final atmosphere exchange."

"You intend on giving us skin cancer?" Michael asked skeptically.

"The dose of UV radiation is within tolerable limits to humans," Athena replied. "It will minimize the chance a xenomorphic lifeform entering the ship. Your genetic inoculation and nanosurg should prevent any melanoma from forming due to the low-level radiation exposure."

"How comforting." Rachel replied. "Doesn't UV-C produce ozone?"

"Yes," Athena replied. "But you will be wearing respirators, as there are several atmospheric changes during the decontamination process."

"Taking things to a bit of an extreme, aren't you?" Michael asked.

"You like science-fiction?" Bryan retorted.

"It's my favorite genre," Michael replied.

"How many sci-fi storylines revolve around an alien organism infiltrating a crew, and killing everyone?" Bryan asked. "That's a rhetorical question because we both know it's a lot. The point of quarantine is to keep the aliens off this ship. We simply cannot afford to have anything compromising the primary mission. There is nothing more important. Every single time you leave this ship during a mission, you will go through decontamination and quarantine, period."

"You sound as if you're giving us orders," Rachel snapped.

"If you recall your Project Nova orientation," Athena replied. "General Orders One, Five, and Six apply here, specifically General Order Five: 'If a xenomorphic organism is identified, the commander must prevent it from contaminating ship and crew at all costs.'"

"Point taken," Michael said. "I withdraw my criticism. So, are we going to see this decontamination area?"

"Negative," Athena replied. "The area is for decontamination only. Since they sterilized, they are to be free of all potential contamination — until you're in space of course."

"Then let's get going with this tour," Michael said, feeling like he was just wasting time.

They returned to the central access corridor and ascended the ladder to Deck Three. There were six hatches on the landing. The nearest one opened to accommodate them.

"This is the agricultural deck or agdeck," Bryan said as he entered the room. The room was an orchard. There were several small trees in large white pots with dirt. Each pot was made of transparent plastic. The walls and floor were white; however, they were illuminated with banks of red and blue grow lamps, giving the surrounding walls a magenta color. "There are six compartments separated by airtight hatches. In case of a fire or hull compromise, each section will seal off to prevent damage to the crops and prevent venting of the deck atmosphere. Each compartment contains a separate set of crops. This one is populated by fruit-bearing plants: apples, pears, peaches, nectarines, plums, cherries, as well as some nut trees like almonds. The far wall has raspberries, strawberries, and varieties of currents."

"Where are the bees?" Rachel asked.

"No insects are allowed onboard," Bryan replied. "Can't risk them getting out of the ship and contaminating the exoplanets. Invasive species are a risk even if they are beneficial on earth. It's also not a good idea, as far as the ship is concerned. We can't risk having some rogue insect colony building a nest in an instrument panel."

"Then how do you pollinate the plants?" Rachel asked.

"Helper units do most of the work, but the crew will be expected to do their part," Bryan replied. "It's recreational therapy, a way to keep you sane during space travel. Can't have you going psychotic when you're out there."

"Not sure how much therapy this light scheme will be," Michael replied. "I'm getting a headache from it already."

The lights instantly changed to a brilliant white color. "You can request natural light for up to six hours at a time," Athena replied. The plants, however, require eighteen hours of wavelength specific light every day to maintain optimal growing conditions."

The trio went through each compartment and examined the growing areas. Some areas used engineered soil to hold the plants, while other systems used hydroponics and aeroponics. It depended on the crop. Some areas were dedicated to grains like corn, soybeans, rice, and wheat. Others were herbs, peas, beans, salad greens, and other vegetables.

Michael thought there was a lot of variety and seemed like the systems would produce a lot of food for just ten people. There were even stations where food could be processed for storage in dehydrators and freeze dryers.

"No chickens, eh?" Rachel inquired.

"Sadly, we can't have any livestock onboard," Bryan replied. "For the same reason that we can't have beneficial insects like bees. Too many problems posed by disease, waste management, and other factors."

"Darn," Rachel said glumly. "I really like eggs in the morning."

"You'll just have to make do with the on-board supply of freeze-dried eggs, meat, and fish."

They left the Ag Deck and ascended the ladder to the Habitation Deck. It was divided into six sections. This time, each door had a label: SCIENCE LAB, EDUCATION, LIBRARY, STORAGE, GALLEY, and DINING. The walls were displayed a tranquil beach scene. The Dining area opened, and the three stepped into the room. Like most of what they had encountered with the MeCTen, there was something odd with the visual appearance. The baseboards curved, creating a spheroid shape. There were no corners. The furniture was similarly apportioned. Everything was rounded, with no sharp angles or corners. It made Rachel feel uneasy, as if something was not quite right.

"Um, what gives with the room?" Michael asked.

"It's unnerving isn't it," Bryan replied. "I'll admit it freaks me out when I see it."

"Don't deflect," Rachel chided. "What's going on?"

"All the rooms in the Hab Deck are laid out like this," Bryan replied, moving to the nearest dining setup. "In normal gravity, the rooms are designed to be used like this. Just like you would anywhere on Earth. However, in reduced gravity, you just float. That makes gravity-based architecture impractical. This entire deck will spin to provide the sensation of gravity. This room is designed to adjust to the artificial gravity system. In space the furniture in all the rooms will transition to the outer walls of the room. If we didn't modify the environment, it would be uncomfortable to do anything."

"You're using centrifugal force to mimic gravity." Michael said, examining the partition meant to support the booth in flight. It seemed sturdy, but it was also a display, currently set to a tropical oceanside view. "Does it have to be a beach?"

The display shifted to a mountainous setting. It was then that Michael noticed the ambient sound had changed to fit the location. Soft wind could be heard through the pine trees, and birds were singing in the distance. It was peaceful and serene.

"I have six hundred and ninety-three locations available in my database," Athena chimed in. "Each of them has various permeations of weather and seasonal conditions. It depends on what you wish to view."

"What's the purpose of the illusion?" Rachel inquired.

"There are two reasons," Athena responded. "Firstly, it helps mitigate the vertigo you might experience moving from the Inner Habring to the Outer Habring. Each ring must rotate at a different speed to achieve the right simulation of G-force. The inner ring must rotate faster than the outer ring, otherwise vestibular disfunction could result. Unfortunately, the speed variance causes a visually induced vertigo without something to counteract that effect. The corridor displays in interface areas have been designed to minimize the visual sense of motion. The second purpose is to provide a calming environment for travel in relativistic-shifted deep space."

"In other words," Bryan interjected. "It's to give you the sense of being able to look out a window and see something other than space. Otherwise, you're likely to go insane if you look outside and all you see is the doppler shifted blur associated with viewing background radiation that has been blue shifted into the visible spectrum, because you're going faster than light."

"Fair enough," Michael replied. "What's the difference between the inner and outer rings?"

Bryan got up and beckoned them to move into the next compartment. "The core, inner ring, houses the work areas. Living and recreation areas are in the outer ring."

"Recreation?" Rachel asked.

"A movie theater, and a small gym," Bryan replied. "It's just a weight machine, treadmill, and similar exercise equipment. You must stay in shape in space, or your muscles might atrophy."

The trio toured the Hab Deck facilities and then moved to the Command deck. The only difference Michael could decern, from the Omega, was the number of seats and consoles. Otherwise, everything was identical. They moved back into the engineering section of the vessel; this time they were able to see the other areas located on either side of the control room. The port side was for fabricating composite materials, and the starboard side was for metals.

Michael was impressed they had the ability to repair every part of the ship. They could even recycle old parts into new ones. The scientists had built a robust system to keep the MeCTen spacecraft self-sufficient.

"What happens if we run out of something we need, or have a critical system fail?" Michael asked.

"I don't understand?" Bryan said, blinking at the absurdity of the question. "Are you asking about emergency procedures?"

"What happens if our water supply is contaminated or lost." Michael replied. "How are we supposed to obtain more if we need it?"

Bryan sighed. "If you were to find yourself needing to obtain something from an exobody, there is mining equipment in the MTEST storage area. You can use it to extract needed resources, but it would require the plane-toid – or whatever – to have what you need. There are complete guides to scenarios you might encounter in digital format in Athena's databanks. And there are hard copies in the library just in case the computers are damaged or destroyed. Your job is to make sure you don't let it get that bad. Trust me, you don't want to be scrambling to keep everyone alive."

"Colonel," Athena interjected. "All due thought and care have gone into making your mission a success. We have tried to think of every scenario possible to help you survive in the event of an emergency. We have made everything as redundant as possible, but we cannot account for every eventuality. That is why it is important for you to rely on your considerable education and training. I cannot complete the mission without a human crew. Even with my considerable intelligence, humans have demonstrated the ability to adapt to scenarios that AI, like me, have difficulty resolving. Therefore, Dr. Taylor suggested we give you this orientation. You need to be intimately familiar with this spacecraft. The best way to do that, is to have you spend as much time as possible exploring it."

Chapter II

FLIGHT

Even with breaks to use the bathroom and eat, they still took the remainder of the day to wander the vast interior of the Alpha. Bryan had to abandon them to Athena at sixteen-hundred hours to assist Doctor Doddridge with the final preparations for the Omega and the Gamma.

Michael could feel Rachel's fatigue magnifying his own. They were both exhausted, mentally and physically. It was taxing, assimilating everything they learned. From the layout of the ship to the location of the various systems and supplies, it was a lot to take in. There was a logic to it, but the entire experience was unlike any school or training they had ever undertaken. True, the military was fond of intensive education, but there had never been a time, he could recall, that people were required to study something so complex in such a short space of time.

"What time is it, Athena?" Michael asked, bleary eyed.

"Twenty-two-oh-three," the AI replied.

"Meaning, we have twenty-four hours to come up with a flight plan, get it approved, and get our briefings and pre-flight complete," Michael said, mulling over the logistics in his mind.

"Athena, what's the protocol for something to be considered space-worthy with a crew?" Rachel asked.

Athena replied. "Generally, spacecraft must undergo several evaluation tests. Including drop tests, pressurization tests, powerplant tests, and a litany of comprehensive rigorous safety and systems tests that can take a decade or more before a spacecraft is allowed to be crewed."

"Well, that isn't going to happen," Rachel replied with a chuckle.

"Good thing NASA isn't in charge of this project, or we would never be allowed to do this," Michael quipped.

"Actually," Athena said, matter-of-factly. "We are breaking a few Defense Department regulations governing the development of airframe, powerplants, and spacecraft in general. Strictly speaking, if it were widely known that General Harris was circumventing these regulations and general orders, he would face a court-martial. As a flag officer, he is placing his career in jeopardy."

"And by extension, we're facing the same fate if we knowingly assist him," Rachel mused.

"Somehow, I don't think that's our primary concern," Michael replied. "If we don't succeed, we'll just be dead, along with whomever happens to fall victim to the nuclear fallout we leave behind. If we do manage to pull this off, we'll either save the country, or set off a global nuclear holocaust. I don't think the general is in much danger of a court-martial. I think someone must know something about what's going on, or we can't get the tritium. Not to mention the clearance to even suggest for a combat mission, let alone a test flight."

"True, probably because we're expendable. Good thing the world already thinks we're dead," Rachel said sarcastically.

"Speaking of risk," Michael added, thinking aloud. "Can we move our spacesuits to the Omega, Athena, or do you already have duplicates?"

"A sensible precaution," Athena replied. "There is no time to make another pair."

"Why do we need to do that?" Rachel asked.

"Well, I assume the MeCTen have only been tested to a point."

Rachel returned a blank stare. She couldn't comprehend the point of wearing a spacesuit in a pressurized craft. Her fatigue seemed to be slowing down her typically keen intuition on these matters.

"If we make upper atmosphere with the hull compromised, we could find ourselves hypoxic," Michael explained. "I seem to recall it being standard procedure to have astronauts wear spacesuits until they had reached orbit and verified the hull's integrity."

Rachel could hit herself for being so dense. "I must be really tired."

Michael chuckled. "We are both exhausted. The only reason why I thought of it is because I liked watching movies about NASA when I was a kid."

"I'm sure one of these hyper-smart computers would have said something," Rachel quipped.

"It's true," Athena replied. "Gaia was planning on having a few helpers transfer the suits to the Omega prior to your flight."

"Will the Omega be ready in time?" Michael asked.

"Aries reports the Omega will be fully powered and pre-flighted by the time you arrive at twenty-two hundred," Athena replied. "He also relays a message from Doctor Doddridge that you are seriously compromising the reactors with this action."

"Yeah," Michael mused. "The predictable objections. We all know this is highly dangerous. Is there a bunker in this facility?"

"The command center is located in the mountain to the west," Athena replied. "It is accessible by a tunnel at the other end of the complex by the Gamma hanger."

"Good enough," Michael said. "Make sure that all base personnel, not on the flight, are in the command bunker prior to the main reactor start."

"Doctor Schretzmann will be very disappointed," Athena replied. "He will most likely file a protest."

"Oh, what now?" Rachel grumbled, her brow furrowing. "Another doctor not liking the decisions?"

"Doctor Schretzmann designed and conceived the MeCTen," Athena replied. "It is important to him to be there for the maiden flight."

"I thought he was in quarantine?" Michael replied.

"Doctor Young has cleared the first flight crews to leave quarantine in eighteen hours," Athena said. "Doctor Schretzmann is listed in that group."

Michael mulled over the whole prospect of the mission. If he had spent his life designing something this big, it would crush him not to see something as historic as the first actual flight. A lot of people would be disappointed not to see this momentous occasion. Normally, everyone that had anything to do with the project would be given a front-row seat, but they were taking

an awful risk with the rushed test flight. He had to weigh the safety of people key to the development, and the desire to witness the occasion personally. In the end, he had to make sure that if they didn't succeed, the people
responsible for development could learn from his mistakes and try again.

"Tell him I'm sorry," Michael said sympathetically. "But he will have to
watch it from the command bunker. We can't risk the safety of anyone that
doesn't absolutely need to be there."

"Understood," Athena replied. "I have relayed your orders to the other
AI, and personnel." There was a momentary pause. "Most military personnel don't seem to have any issues, but the civilian staff are protesting the
decision. As expected, Doctor Schretzmann is demanding an answer for his
exclusion from General Harris."

"Patch me through to him," Michael ordered.

There was a click, followed by the immediate sound of an angry male
with a heavy German accent. "Doctor Schretzmann."

"Am I speaking to the depp[1] who said I could not participate in the first
flight of MY ship?"

"I would be careful how I address the XO," Michael replied authoritative-
ly. "I understand that you want to see the test tomorrow–"

Doctor Schretzmann cut him off. "It is my RIGHT! I designed it. I built
it. The only reason why I'm not flying it is because I'm a civilian. I demand
to watch the fulfillment of my dream!"

"Look, Doctor," Michael said. "I get that you want to be there, but I
cannot allow that."

"Why not?"

"Because you're too important, Doctor. We're doing a lot of things that
circumvent the safety regulations. It might not go very well, and I don't want
to risk killing the very people that can solve any unforeseen problems."

"Nothing will go wrong," Doctor Schretzmann replied defensively. The
dismissive tenor of his voice was apparent.

"You don't know that," Michael replied. "These are complex machines.
There are a lot of nukes on them, and they rely on nuclear reactors. Not to
mention they are untested, and the pilots have limited simulator training."

1 German slang for fool.

"I have complete confidence in the spacecraft and your piloting skills," Doctor Schretzmann countered.

"You're willing to put your life on the line, and take that risk?" Michael asked.

"Natürlich."[2]

"Well, I'm not!" Michael snapped. "Only an idiot puts faith in his own pride, Doctor. I'm ordering you to join the others in the bunker. File your stupid protest, but you're going in that bunker if I have to make the MPs drag you there in cuffs. Understood?"

There was a moment of silence before Doctor Schretzmann's voice came over the intercom. "I will not forgive this."

"I'm sure you won't, Doctor," Michael replied. "But, I would rather have you hate me, than lose you in a mishap. Langford out." He turned to Rachel and smiled wearily. "I'm done for today."

"What are your orders?" Rachel asked rhetorically.

"Go get some rack time. Meet in the briefing room at oh-six-thirty, and we'll plan this test flight."

The walk back to the barracks was mind-numbing for both. A lot had happened today, and their brains had been saturated by new information. Michael mulled over the differences in how the two pilots committed the deluge to memory. Rachel was fond of mnemonic phrases, and all that did was confuse him. It was tough being inside someone else's mind. He had been taught methods like that at the Academy, but he preferred to visualize things. People perceived the world differently from one another. His problem was how to cope with the steady stream of female perspective that constantly flowed into his mind. It had become a challenge to keep it from delving into aspects which could cause him to think of her in a way that would certainly draw her ire.

Gaia was right, she was the type of woman he was attracted to. She was intelligent, witty, playful, and mentally strong. She had her vulnerabilities, but they served to strengthen her determination. He found that more appealing than her physical beauty. He came to realize he knew her more intimately than anyone. It was exciting, and terrifying at the same time. He had to be

2 "Naturally."

careful not to let anything he knew be said out loud. He had decided that it would be a disaster.

They returned to their respective rooms, quickly shed their uniforms, and immediately went to sleep. Mental exhaustion was more draining than physical labor, but when you added the two together it equaled a perfectly blissful sleep.

Gaia's alarm seemed to come earlier than expected. Michael groaned and rolled out of bed, his mind still clinging to the ecstasy of the rest he desperately needed. Instinctively he flexed his wrist to illuminate the face of his wrist communicator. A pale blue light showed zero-five-thirty. The lights gradually illuminated his room, and he stumbled to the shower.

In his mind, he could see the same scene playing out through Rachel's eyes. By now, the routine had become familiar to him. She would grab her clothing and then place it on the counter. Then the lights would turn off before she undressed and showered. It was fascinating to see things from the perspective of her morning vigil in complete darkness. She had learned the placement of every item in the bathroom and could carry out her self-care by memory. It had influenced him so much that he found himself showering in the dark as well. Somehow it seemed to be a gentler awakening than blasting his eyes with the brilliant lights that had been installed in the barracks. They even dressed in the dark. Michael met Rachel on the stairs, and they walked toward the dining area, but he already knew what she was going to ask.

"How did you sleep?"

Michael smiled. It seemed innocuous, and a few short months ago it would have been, but now the questions only went one way. He already knew the answer to her question. "Like a rock, of course."

"I suppose you already know how I slept," she stopped for a moment. "Do you know what I dream too?"

He shook his head. "It's hard to tell, really. It's like I have overlapping dreams. Honestly, I can't tell which one is yours, and which one is mine. It gets too confusing, so I've stopped trying."

"What's for breakfast this morning, Gaia?" Rachel asked.

"Mushroom, spinach, and goat cheese frittata, or continental style breakfast," the AI replied. The duo entered the serving area and found a helper unit putting a bowl of fruit onto a pile of ice in the cold service area. Apart from the robot, there didn't seem to be anyone around, but there was the sound of cooking through the archway that led to the kitchen.

"That seems a bit posh," Michael replied. "Any reason for the ritzy meal preparation?"

"Yes," General Harris replied, poking his head out of the open doorway. "I like frittatas and thought I would make enough for three."

The two pilots were a bit surprised by the appearance of the flag officer cooking. "Um–" Michael started, not sure what to say in these situations. "Don't you have someone else to do that?"

"What, cook?" the General replied. "Are you kidding? I love cooking. My mother taught me to explore the world. What better way than through food."

"Shouldn't you be in quarantine, Sir?" Rachel asked, perplexed by his being well enough to be in the barracks.

"It's easier the second time you get the shots," he replied.

"Wait," Michael said, still trying to verify he wasn't still asleep. "Second time?"

"Doctor Rana believes the best way to do the gene therapy is to have a series of five injections," General Harris said. "We're still getting all the shots, but this will be the third time I've had the therapy. Each time, it is a little less severe."

"If you've had the shots," Rachel said, rolling the words on her tongue as if savoring something. "Why were you surprised when we developed — unusual attributes?"

"Hold that thought," Harris said, ducking back into the kitchen. The pilots followed him.

The kitchen was a standard commercial grade setup. All the counters, cabinets, and appliances were dull stainless-steel. The floor was a red terracotta tile. In the center stood a very nice stainless-steel range, in which General Harris was pulling a pan of what looked like an omelet.

Michael had eaten frittatas before, but this looked quite stunning. The top was light brown, with pockets of melted white cheese. It smelled like heaven to him.

"Simple," the General said, placing the hot pan on the gleaming counter. "No one has ever displayed that side effect. We have all gotten sick, but no one has ever displayed any telepathic or telekinetic abilities. You are the first, and that makes you special."

"When did you get out of quarantine?" Michael asked.

General Harris grabbed a cutting board and a large, serrated knife. He placed the cutting board over the top of the pan, flipped the entire ensemble over, and put it down on the counter. "About four this morning. I've been reviewing your ideas. Have come up with your flight plan." He withdrew the pan, and a perfectly cooked frittata was uncovered. He leaned forward and quickly sliced the mass of eggs, cheese, and vegetables into quarters. He grabbed some plates from under the counter. "One of the advantages of being a general, is that I get to choose when I see the doctor, and they take orders when I give them."

"Are you sure it's not because you had to assume command again?" Michael asked.

General Harris dished up the servings and gave his XO a look of incredulous annoyance. "Nope, I agree with every decision you made, and truth be told, I would have done the same thing. But a civilian's idea of command requires a bit of time before they fully recognize the order as an order. To them, you're new, and you just don't understand the project. I'm here to make sure that illusion is shattered."

"With all due respect, Sir," Rachel started. "Are you sure you're well enough to do that?"

Doctor Young entered the room, as if on cue. "His doctor said he was well enough, and that should be good enough for you."

"As the doctor said," General Harris chimed in. "I'm fit for duty."

"You're joining our breakfast?" Rachel asked.

"Nope," the doctor replied. "I'm not invited to your briefing, but it would literally kill me to miss out on the general's cooking."

"Speaking of which–" General Harris said. "I think we'll eat in the conference room. Stevens is there finishing up your flight plan."

"She's not having breakfast?" Rachel asked indignantly.

"She is still a little queasy," Doctor Young replied. He looked up wistfully, as if picturing the moment in his mind. "How did she put it? Oh yes, 'Blarg!'" He smiled at the thought of the young captain on the verge of vomiting.

"That's enough, Doctor," General Harris said sternly. "I'll have none of your schadenfreude here."

The doctor sighed as he feigned pouting. "Very well. If you need me, I'll be in medical." He took his plate and walked out.

General Harris motioned for the pilots to follow him as he picked up some grapes and an apple at the buffet and headed to the conference room. "Gaia, I only have two hands, have a helper bring us some orange juice."

"As you wish, General," Gaia replied.

They entered the conference room and saw Captain Stevens sitting in a chair at the far end of the room. It was obvious she still felt ill. Her head rested on her hand as she hunched over, trying to cope with the apparent nausea. Michael had to double take, but he thought she looked as if her skin was a pale shade of green.

"You're dismissed, Stevens," General Harris said.

"I'm fine, Sir," she replied unconvincingly.

"Don't make me order you, Beth. Now, get to your room and rest up."

The captain's glazed eyes looked up with reluctant appreciation at the kindness of her commanding officer. "Thank you, Sir. I think I will." She slowly stood up and walked out of the room.

"With all due respect, Sir," Rachel said. "How did she get clear of quarantine, if she's not feeling well?"

The General waved a hand dismissively. "There's no arguing with her sometimes. And she knows how to bully Doctor Young. Heck, if she thought she could get away with it, I'm sure she would be giving me orders. After all she knows the best aid is the one who can tell a boss no." He sat down in his chair, and paused for a moment, in a bit of silent prayer. "Gaia, did Captain Stevens finish the test flight plan?"

"Yes, General," Gaia replied. "She was reviewing it for possible errors."

"Give the presentation for OPERATION FLEDGLING SPARROW," General Harris ordered.

The main display came to life as Gaia began to narrate the plan. The crew would begin preflight at twenty-two hundred. By twenty-three hundred, pre-flight inspection would be finished, and the crew would conduct the cabin startup and preflight procedures. At zero hundred hours, the Omega would be tugged to the flight line and execute a series of maneuvers to test ground controls. Twenty minutes later, the Omega would lift off the ramp and test the flight controls. They were to make sure their transponder was deactivated, and then they would hover-taxi to the runway and use the RASCL departure to the north. They would head toward the Tonopah test area and then enter an unrestricted climb to one hundred kilometers. Once at the Karmen line, they would check the hull integrity. They would contact General Harris on a secure sat link and await instructions. The President was expected to greenlight OPERATION SCARLET FURY.

The operation had been altered from the original plan, but the President had not been briefed on the details. General Harris would explain the plan, and then they would execute the orders, adjusting to any changes that might occur. They would fly at fastest relative ground speed to Huludao and test fire the inert torpedoes at the drydock and harbor facilities. They would immediately turn and burn for Shanghai, without waiting for the results. Keyhole satellites would assess any damage and relay their success or failure in real time. At Shanghai they would repeat the attack and immediately turn and burn for the run on the Liaoning Fleet, referred to as OBJECTIVE OHIO, currently holding station in the Sea of Japan. Once they fired a tandem shot at that target, they would immediately engage the amphibious assault fleet, referred to as OBJECTIVE DAKOTA. They would then fire a tandem shot, and immediately turn and burn for the Shandong fleet, referred to as OBJECTIVE UTAH. Once they fired the tandem volley at that fleet, they would return to base. They would begin reentry over Hawaii and return to fifteen thousand meters by the time they reached the test range near Tonopah before landing via the STNGR approach. Reconnaissance at DIA would assess the effectiveness of the fleet strikes. Any problems in launching the ordinance, and the Omega would immediately abort and return to base.

If there was a problem that disabled or severely damaged the Omega, they would initiate the auto-destruct.

"Why launch the inert torpedoes at the enemy shipyards?" Rachel asked. "They don't have warheads. Won't that be counterproductive?"

"They want a test," General Harris said sternly. "This will provide that test and damage the Chinese Navy at the same time. I know the torpedoes will be inert, but they pack a wallop when they come from space. The kinetic energy alone will do more than enough damage to the targets we've selected. I shouldn't have to remind you that the enemy is almost within striking range. That cannot be allowed. Right now, everyone that can is trying to come up with a strike plan, but no one can get all the fleets like we can."

"Are we the only hope?" Rachel asked. "There have to be others who can stop them. We have the best, most well-equipped military in the world. It can't just hinge on one ship."

"The Omega is the only platform capable of attacking all three Chinese fleets with a nearly one hundred percent kill rate," General Harris replied somberly. "I'll advise that the other conventional weapons platforms be used to clean up the survivors."

"You're going to wipe out their navy?" Michael was shocked.

"We're going to make them wish they had never ventured into the Pacific," General Harris said, fury flashing in his eyes. "And see to it they never test us again."

Michael's countenance turned grim. "If we have anything to say about it, I'll make sure they regret everything they've done."

"And then what?" Rachel demanded.

"You have something to add, Bright?" General Harris responded.

"You take out the bulk of their navy, and then what?"

"We do whatever the President and the Pentagon deem necessary," General Harris replied.

"You think they're going to take this without responding in-kind?"

General Harris leaned forward and eyed Rachel intently. "Need I remind you; they took the first shots in this. They attacked Taiwan, The Philippines,

South Korea, and Japan. Then they attacked our fleet. We even nuked their bases in the South China Sea, and they STILL are sailing towards OUR LANDS undeterred! How many shipmates did you lose when they sank the Essex, or crippled the Reagan? How much death has been caused by the ambition of one communist dictator? We didn't start this war, they did!"

Rachel turned red. She was embarrassed that the general had felt she had questioned his judgement. She knew saying anything more would only invite more yelling, but she felt compelled to clarify her question. "I mean no disrespect, Sir. I am not questioning our mission. I was only asking what their response will be?"

The general's face softened. "I apologize, I failed to accurately interpret your question, Rachel. It's a fair question, but I don't have a definitive answer. It's likely they will be unable to respond effectively. If they do try anything, we'll be ready for whatever they send our way. The good news will be that it will take a long time before they can muster up a new navy to support their current agenda. They will have to use planes, and those, we can deal with – thanks to you."

There was something about the last comment that seemed directed at Michael. The general probably knew the intelligence gathered by his encounter with the unidentified aircraft. He would have to ask as soon as the opportunity presented itself.

"I feel that I must offer some tactical assessment," Gaia interrupted.

"Let's hear it, Gaia," General Harris replied.

"Your technical assessment of the Chinese military capability is close to projections. However, I do not believe they will respond as favorably as you hope."

"Meaning?" Michael inquired.

"I project there will be an eighty-five percent chance of a nuclear counterstrike within seventy-two hours of the defeat of their navy," Gaia replied.

"Sir," Michael said, trying not to sound too apocalyptic. "I think it might be a good idea to move the crews from the barracks to their respective ships after they leave quarantine."

"I think that's a prudent idea," General Harris replied. "Gaia, make sure that's done. Let Doctor Taylor know that as soon as the Omega is ready for flight, the remaining ships need to be fueled, and reactors need to be brought online as soon as possible. We need to be ready for OPERATION RAPID VIPER and OPERATION SHATTERED SKY."

"OPERATION RAPID VIPER, Sir?" Michael said quizzically.

"In the event of a first strike, or in this case a retaliatory strike, the spacecraft would begin an immediate evacuation of the base," General Harris said. "Anyone not on a spacecraft would have to head to the command bunker for safety."

Michael sighed. "It seems you've thought of everything."

"That's why I make the big bucks," General Harris replied. "I get paid to do the thinking." He looked around suspiciously. "Even if Gaia wins every chess game we play, I'm still smarter than her where it counts. She's an idiot on a few things."

"General," Gaia interrupted. "You do not have to worry about my ego. I am incapable of being damaged by insults."

"But?" General Harris inserted.

"But your assertion is incorrect," Gaia replied. "My analytical capabilities are vastly superior to the human intellect."

"We'll see," General Harris retorted. He stood up, signifying the end of the briefing. "Now, you have until fourteen hundred to get to the Omega and run simulations of the test flight, and OPERATION SCARLET FURY. Then you are ordered to take as much melatonin as you need to sleep. Get the rack time in the Omega and be prepped and ready to go by twenty-two hundred. Understood?"

Both pilots stood at attention, saluted, and replied simultaneously. "Sir, yes, Sir!"

The remainder of the morning was spent on the Command Deck of the Omega. Aries ran through various scenarios of the test flight and attack runs in real time. It was mind numbingly repetitive, but there was purpose to it now. They knew that in just a few hours, they would be performing the flight for real. Somehow, there was an emotional urgency that wasn't there before. There was a briefing on the protocol for the release of nuclear weapons. It involved going to the crew quarters next to the cockpit, and obtaining the verification codes, then validating them.

The crew quarters of the Omega occupied the space of the conference room and the observatory on the other ships. It was divided into two sections. One was a communal area, containing a small booth for eating and authenticating orders. There was a small galley to heat the pre-made meals stored in a cabinet adjacent to it. The other section contained four small dorm style rooms, a shower, and toilet facilities. Evidently, the ship was designed to have a relief crew, but those plans were scaled down to two crew members without altering the initial design. It was spacious for a four-man crew, but Michael imagined it would feel claustrophobic if a crew that size was forced to stay there long.

Michael and Rachel ate in the crew quarters at noon. Standard issue MREs[3] were all provided. Unlike the Alpha, the crew areas of the Omega were limited to the Command Deck. The three remaining decks were almost entirely occupied by the vast arsenal comprising the Omega's sizeable platform. The only exception was the medical facilities and food storage areas on the Entry Deck. Occasionally Bryan would contact them to let them know of a new power system that would be coming on-line, but they never saw anyone during their hours on the ship.

All too quickly, fourteen hundred rolled around. They went into the crew quarters, found the melatonin, and went into the private bunks to sleep. Michael lay down, had Aries turn off the lights, and began going over the mission in his mind. He thought he could hear the hum caused by the vibrations of the reactor's steam turbines at the far end of the ship. He wondered if he would hear when the reactors would come to full power, like when the Essex turned the screws to flank speed. He didn't know. So much of this was new. He had to adapt to it as it came. He knew all this thinking would only cause him to miss out on sleep, so he switched off his brain, like they taught at the academy. Soon his mind dissolved into the darkness that surrounded him.

The wake-up tone came at twenty-one thirty. Enough time to wake up and get ready for the pre-flight briefing and inspection. There wasn't much to do to get ready. They had both slept in their flight-gear. They emerged from their cabins to find General Harris, Captain Stevens, and Doctors Taylor, Young, Rana, Bryan, and another man he had never seen before, entering the crew quarters.

"I trust you slept well," General Harris began, but he didn't wait for a reply. "I think you've met everyone here, except Doctor Kobayashi. He is the astrophysics specialist for the Alpha. Now that introductions are out of the

3 Meal Ready to Eat

way, we'll proceed. Since you were asleep, there have been a few changes to the plan. Aries, present the updated timeline."

The display above the briefing table came to life and began a presentation following along with as General Harris narrated. "After we're done here, you will begin the pre-flight inspection with Bryan. He knows the systems well and will show you what needs to be crossed off. That should take approximately one hour. At twenty-two forty-five you will come back here and be helped into your suits. Bright, Doctor's Taylor and Rana will help you suit up. Langford will be assisted by Doctor's Kobayashi and Young. After you're in your suits, everyone will get off the Omega and head to the Command Bunker. You two will strap into your stations on the Bridge. Colonel Langford is in command of this mission as pilot monitoring and will be the primary weapons officer. Lieutenant Commander Bright will be the pilot flying. Nothing has changed with the flight plan. The flight callsign is Hammer, weapons are hot stand-by, flight mode is combat. You will proceed as rehearsed and wait for instructions in station-keeping orbit exactly one-hundred kilometers above Tonopah. Any questions?"

"Sir, no, Sir," the two pilots said in unison.

"If the President orders a change in the plan, you will execute that order." General Harris said, eyeing Rachel.

"Sir, yes, Sir!"

General Harris gave a long sigh. "Normally, on occasions such as this, a general usually gives his officers words of encouragement. There's usually something along the lines of 'this is a momentous occasion', but I'm not going to do that. We all know what's at stake. We all know just how much is riding on this mission. First, we had to eliminate the Chinese operatives that tried to pull the nation apart from within. Now they're knocking at our door to take it by force. I don't have to tell you what happens to people who are enslaved. We are NOT going to allow that in this country, now or EVER! We have come too far, sacrificed too much to allow this to become a nation of slaves. As Reagan said: peace is our highest aspiration. We will negotiate for it. Sacrifice for it. We will not surrender for it, now or EVER! We are Americans!"

Silence fell on the room. The gravity of the situation penetrated the two pilots. They had to make sure the test was successful, or there wouldn't be a second chance.

General Harris had let his words sink in. "Now, I know you're facing an untested platform, but it's up to you to make it work. You will do it because failure is NOT an option. You all know what needs to be done, now get to work!" With his speech concluded, he turned and walked toward the central access ladder.

Doctor Taylor looked dumbfounded but eventually spoke. "Well then. We'll prep your suits while Bryan takes you outside to give the ship a once-over."

Bryan motioned for the two pilots to follow him, and they made their way outside the Omega. They spent the next hour moving around the spacecraft, inspecting everything they could from the ground. Aerial drones provided video of inspection points above the spacecraft that was projected to their wrist displays. Checklists accompanied the information, and Aries activated lights and flight systems as needed. There were a lot of points to go over, and they seemed to rush through it. It was only now that Michael fully grasped just how big a MeCTen was. It was much larger than the habitable areas. Knowing how large it was on the inside, it only accentuated how massive it was on the outside. For the first time, Michael saw the large letters that were printed in black letters on the upper exterior of the ship, just behind the Flight Deck: ΩMEGA $- \infty$.

By twenty-two thirty-five the inspection was complete. Bryan bid them good luck and headed back toward the decontamination area. The two pilots then made their way back to the crew quarters.

Doctor Taylor greeted them as they entered. "I trust you had fun inspecting the outside of the ship, now you get to inspect your suits."

"Oh joy," Rachel mused.

"Each suit has two parts," Doctor Taylor continued. "The inner suit, and the exoskeleton. You don't need to have anyone help put the suit on, as with past iterations, but it's helpful. You do, however, need to be completely naked before putting on the inner suit."

"Why is that?" Rachel asked, nervous about the connection to Michael's brain.

"The inner suit has a number of functions," Doctor Rana interjected. "Its primary purpose is to draw sweat and urine away from the skin and transport it to the reclamation systems in the exoskeleton. It also safely stores fecal waste and keeps your bottom clean to prevent irritation. In addition, it keeps tension on the skin to prevent problems in low-pressure environments, and regulates temperature, so you aren't too hot or cold."

Doctor Taylor continued the briefing on the suit. "The exoskeleton provides protection from hostile environments, such as space or alien atmospheres. It contains the life-support systems, power, insulation, communications, and structural integrity systems."

"Structural integrity?" Michael asked, perplexed by an odd choice of words used to describe a fabric.

"Aramid, right?" Rachel replied, as if knowing there was more, but verifying she was on the right track.

"Partially," Doctor Taylor replied. "The nano-silicon-carbide ceramic matrix, carbon fiber tri-weave, and Aramid that make up the outer-shell, make this a resilient suit."

"Bryan said that yesterday," Rachel said. "But I have no idea what it means."

Doctor Kobayashi hefted a sleeve up for her to touch. "Feel it."

Michael and Rachel each took a sleeve and began to closely examine the fabric. The exterior was made of tiny hexagonal shaped flat plates. Each was a different size, but most seemed about a centimeter across. The ones near joints or flex points were smaller, but they were all interlinked. It was a dense, substantial material, but the overall weight was unexpectedly light. It reminded Michael of chainmail he had seen at a Renaissance festival his parents had taken him to as a child, but this was like it was made by bees.

"It's like armor," He remarked.

"It IS armor," Doctor Kobayashi replied. "These suits can protect you from a rifle round, although it would still be very painful."

"You're expecting us to go into combat wearing these?" Rachel asked dubiously.

"Combat is a possibility," Doctor Taylor conceded. "But it's more to protect you against small space debris. You can't afford to take chances."

"Just wait until you see the powered suits," Doctor Young said with a chuckle. "It will make you a real Marine."

Michael furrowed his brow at the insult. "You know, for as smart as you are, you're pretty dumb when it comes to people."

Doctor Young looked at him passively. "I'll take that as a complement."

"Are you assigned to my crew?" Michael asked.

"Define crew."

"The people assigned to the Alpha," Michael replied.

"No," Doctor Young replied. "I'm assigned to the Gamma."

"Good," Rachel interjected, grabbing her inner suit and heading to the cabin she had used for sleeping. "I don't have to put up with you long-term."

Doctor Taylor intervened and stepped between Doctor Young and Rachel. "Aaron, I think you've said enough for today. From now on, you don't get to talk. Just help him suit up." She gave them each a thin headset to put on. "These will allow us to communicate."

The pilots went into their respective bunks, undressed, and put on the inner suit. Michael found that if he concentrated enough, he could shove Rachel's mind stream into the back of his thought. He concerned himself with fitting the very tight-fitting garment. It was like trying to squeeze into a wetsuit. It wasn't uncomfortable, but it wasn't easy. The interior fabric felt unbelievably soft, yet breathable. It was as if there wasn't anything there at all. He could feel the cool air of the room moving past his skin. The garment hugged every bump, every curve, every part of his body. Unlike the neoprene hug he was expecting, it felt supportive without feeling restrictive.

Michael could wriggle into the suit himself, but it was helpful to have assistance making the connections to the exoskeleton. Except for the helmet, the suit seemed to be one piece, with a heavy zipper-like fastener in the back. The boots and gloves were both integrated. Neither appendage seemed bulky with the addition of the extra material. There was some form of gripping substance on the bottom of the shoes and the palms and fingertips of his hands. Being inside the suit was unlike any flight suit he had ever worn. They attached a small backpack to his shoulders and locked it in place.

Doctor Young began to put on his helmet. "The substance on your palms and feet is a hybrid of polymer and silicone. It allows you to grip items and operate touchscreens without having to feel like you need to remove the glove. It isn't very thick, so don't rub it too hard, or it can peel off." He pointed to several holes inside the seal of the helmet. "The air, water, and electrical connections are inside this connector. Make sure to inspect the O-rings and the seal each time you put them on. You also must remember to twist the locking ring until you hear the click. If you don't, you could wind up breathing recycled water."

With the final warning given, Doctor Young twisted the helmet in place. There was a loud 'click' as the locking mechanism engaged. He then pulled down the exterior gold-plated sun visor. The effect was like a welder's mask. Michael couldn't see anything. Someone grabbed his left arm and began lightly pressing his wrist. There was a slight hiss as air began flowing, and then he could hear Doctor Kobayashi's voice in the bone-conducting headset.

"Colonel, can you hear me?"

"Yes," Michael replied, his voice with the odd muffled quality supplied by the headset.

"I'm lifting your solar visor," Doctor Kobayashi said as he removed the dark lid. "That visor will be used when you're outside the ship in space. Even from a couple billion miles, a star's light can burn your retinas." He held up a display on the suit's right wrist, about where his watch would be. "This is your suit control. It has all your environmental and radio controls for the backpack unit. That unit can keep you alive about twenty-four hours, depending on how much air you use."

"Anything else we need to hook-up?" Michael inquired.

"Not on the suit," Doctor Young replied. "When you strap into your seats, you'll connect the hard connectors, but we'll do that for you."

"We should get these two to the bridge," Doctor Taylor said. "Then we'll leave so they can get prepped for the tow to the tarmac."

"Flight line," Rachel corrected.

"I'm sorry?" Doctor Taylor replied.

"It's called a Flight Line," Rachel said, her voice dripping with annoyance. "Tarmac is a term used by people who don't know any better. The proper terms are Flight Line, or Ramp. Since you're on an Airforce base, it is properly referred to as the Flight Line."

"I stand corrected," Doctor Taylor said, obviously avoiding the confrontation. "Flight Line it is."

The two pilots walked past the civilians and made a right, walking almost immediately onto the flight deck. They sat in their respective positions and were strapped in and connected to the hardlines by the civilians.

"Do you both have airflow and power?" Doctor Taylor asked as the procedures were completed.

Michael could clearly sense Rachel's affirmative response. "We're both good," he said, giving her a thumb's-up. Doctor Taylor smiled, and the entourage left the bridge. He waited for a moment for them to be off the bridge and then turned to Rachel. "You remember this is real this time."

"Of course."

"Good! No sudden accelerations that can rip the ship apart."

Rachel smiled. "As much as I enjoyed that, I have no ambition to die. I'll be gentle. Aries, show me the pre-flight checklist from where we are currently."

The instrument panels came to life, and they began to go through the checklist. As soon as the others were off the ship, Aries closed the main cargo ramp, and the ship began to go through several pressure checks. The flight deck display went from black to a live feed of the hangar. The plastic curtains that had surrounded the Omega began to open, as well as the hangar itself. The lights suddenly turned off, changing the display to a monochromatic IEMDAS display.

A robotic tug entered the hanger from the widening opening. Several helper units took up positions on every edge of the spacecraft, forming an escort picket around the Omega. The tug quickly wheeled itself to the nose gear and hooked itself up. Michael was fascinated by the display, and wanted to see more, but Rachel began to run through the checklist.

The next forty-five minutes was spent running through the checklist as the tug slowly assisted the Omega's own powered wheels to move the incredible weight of the ship onto the flight line. It was very dark outside. The sun had gone down some time ago, but the darkness was accentuated by the EM net covering the base.

When they finally arrived at the staging area, the General's voice came over the radio. "Mystic to Hammer, how do you copy?"

"Hammer copies you Mystic," Rachel replied. "Ready to start flight line pre-flight tests."

For the next half-hour, helper robots examined the exterior of the ship while the crew busied themselves with the power-up procedures. When all the reactors were online, the next command listed was to start the MeCTen drive.

"Aries," Rachel said hesitantly. "Confirm this is NOT a simulation."

"This is reality. I am not simulating anything."

"How do we know?" she asked.

"You have small windows in front of you that allow a view that isn't a display, but I have no other way of definitively proving that you are not in a simulation," Aries replied. "You recall, I am incapable of producing simulations outside the hangar."

Michael looked at her and shook his head. "Let's not get into this existential conundrum right now."

Rachel rolled her eyes in exasperation. "Fine. I'll try not to think about how this could be an illusion. Aries, MeCTen combat auto-start sequence, start."

"Combat start-up initiated," Aries replied.

The simulations had not prepared them for the reality of the start-up process. The strobe effect of the infrared combat anticollision lights was considerably muted. It was like the DAS display in the F–35. The lights of the instrument panel and display briefly intensified as the LFTR reactors came online. The expected hum of the harmonic generators wasn't audible, but Michael thought he could sense a slight vibration in the console.

They called out and verified each item on the checklist as the instrument panel slowly ticked toward the final line: FLASHOVER. The moment when the tungsten hexafluoride would transition into an isolated Bose–Einstein condensate and generate the warp field. Breathless moments passed as they waited for the temperature of the inner ring to lower to the point where the tungsten hexafluoride would collapse into component particle waves. Suddenly, it hit.

When the warp field initiated, it hit like a ton of bricks. Instantly, they were disoriented. It affected Michael particularly hard, as he tried to cope with Rachel's sensations. Nausea and headache were instantaneous, and they fought the urge to vomit in their suits. There was a deafening ringing sensation that filled their heads. Physically, it was like being slapped hard enough to knock the wind out of them. They struggled to breathe. The only thing in Michael's memory that came close to describing the sensation was when he was knocked off the high dive as a child, landing in a bellyflop.

He instinctively grabbed his helmet, as if to rip it off. As he fought for breath, he used the last vapor in his lungs to yell, but it came out as a whisper. "Air!"

Suddenly, there was a loud hiss in his helmet, and the oxygen filled the small space around his face. His ears popped, and he could barely hear Aries over the ringing sensation. "Breathe!"

It felt like an eternity but was probably only a few seconds before they both caught their breath. The nausea and headache quickly dissipated as they continued to gasp for air.

"Are you alright?" General Harris asked.

"We're fine," Michael replied. "Well, we will be fine in a minute. You never mentioned any physical effects."

A German voice, that Michael recognized belonging to Doctor Schretzmann, came over the radio. "No one has been inside a warp field when it's initialized before. We had no idea it would cause any physiological issues. What was it like?"

"Next time, switch with me and you can find out," Rachel groaned snidely.

"Are you able to continue?" General Harris asked with genuine concern.

Michael shook his head to try and clear it. "Yes, Sir, we just need a minute to adjust. To answer your question, Doctor, it's like getting hit by a truck, then drowning. It's disorienting, and nauseating, but whatever Aries did to help, it works to overcome the effects."

"I altered your gas mixture and flow rate," Aries replied. "You are breathing one-hundred percent oxygen at fifteen liters per minute with positive pressure flow. I will taper that to nominal mixture and pressure as your vital signs return to normal."

"Colonel," It was Doctor Young's voice. "After this is all over, we need to run a complete physical on you both. I am very interested in your post-flight debriefing, if you could be so kind as to record your observations in detail, it would be helpful."

Michael breathed deeply shifting in his seat. He turned to Rachel; her pale face said it all. She was still suffering from the effects of the flashover. "Sorry, Rachel, but we're in a bit of a time crunch. I'll take over piloting for a minute while you get your sea legs back."

Rachel gave him a painful but relieved smile. She really didn't feel she would be optimum for flying right now. It hurt, but she knew the time constraints they were under. "Fine, but just for a minute. I'll be okay in a few. Just not used to having an engine start kick the pilots."

Michael looked at the instruments and located the space-time buoyancy indicator. They were neutrally buoyant, and ready to lift off and test the flight controls. He looked at the radio controls and noticed the tower frequency was already selected. The flight name "Hammer" appeared next to the radio display along with the weather information. Aries must be doing that job for him automatically. He keyed his transmit mic. "Dreamland, Hammer at Vintage-one with kilo. Request clearance to hover and test flight controls."

The voice of the tower controller came over their headset. "Hammer, Dreamland, proceed as requested."

Michael carefully nudged the thruster forward. Nothing seemed to happen at first, but then the altimeter began to slowly rise. The ground began to recede beneath the Omega very slowly, but it didn't feel like they were moving at all. Michael was puzzled by the lack of sensation and halted the assent. "Dreamland, Hammer, altitude check."

"Hammer, Dreamland, could you please repeat that request," The controller seemed confused by the inquiry.

"Dreamland, I show one-thousand three-hundred seventy-four meters of altitude; just verifying my instruments with yours."

"Hammer, I show your altitude approximately four-thousand five-hundred ten feet, or one-hundred feet AGL."[4]

"What is that in meters?" Michael asked Aries.

"The altimeter is correct. You are approximately one-hundred-one feet above the ground."

Michael keyed his mic, and looked at Rachel for sympathy, but he knew she had warned him of that. "Hammer copies. Altimeter matches."

"Hammer, Dreamland altimeter two-niner-niner-seven." The controller was trying to be helpful. He was probably used to strange requests during aircraft prototype testing.

Michael sighed and resumed the assent. "Hammer copies two-niner-niner-er-seven. Watch our headroom please."

"Affirmative, Sir."

When they reached the testing level of one-hundred meters, Michael tested the maneuvering rings. Everything moved as expected. He couldn't even feel a slight sensation of motion as he gently moved the ship from side to side, and back and forth. Due to the net above that portion of the base, he would need to return to just above the ground to taxi. He began the decent to land back on the ramp and radioed the tower. "Dreamland, Hammer, pre-flight complete, ready for clearance delivery."

"Hammer, Dreamland, active is three-two right. Note that three-two left is permanently closed. Taxi via Echo to Charlie-Delta. Turn right on Delta and cross three-two left onto Delta. Line up and wait for final clearance on three-two right. Squawk four-four-five-three in restricted airspace after take-off, fly runway heading and climb to angels ten direct to RASCL subsonic and then cleared as filed. At Waypoint Bravo transponder deactivation ap-

---

4 Above Ground Level

proved, airspeed your discretion with unrestricted climb. Supersonic speeds approved to Waypoint Charlie."

"Dreamland, Hammer, copy Echo to Charlie-Delta, right on Delta. Cross three-two left and line up and wait at three-two right. Squawk four-four-five-three after takeoff. Fly runway heading subsonic to RASCL then as filed to Bravo. Transponder off at Bravo supersonic and unrestricted our discretion."

"Hammer, readback is correct."

After gracefully touching down on the flight-line, Michael turned and looked at Rachel. He could tell she was feeling better, and she was more than a little anxious to take over her pilot duties. "He's all checked out, and yours to fly."

"Thanks for that," Rachel replied. "I don't know that happened."

"Don't worry about that right now," Michael replied. "Let's just get this done."

Rachel carefully guided the Omega down the various taxiways to the threshold of runway three-two right. The ship barely fit inside the taxiway. It was obvious they had been retrofit to accommodate the girth of the MeC-Ten. The weather scope was clear, and the Nevada desert valley of Groom Lake stretched out before them. "This is it. If any reconnaissance satellites are on task, the world knows. There's no way they don't see us."

"Yup," Michael said with a sigh. "Now we get to give them a show. It's either going to be an embarrassment for us, or their worst nightmare."

Rachel keyed the mic. "Dreamland, Hammer, lined up on three-two right."

"Hammer, Dreamland, winds three-six at five, cleared for takeoff. Contact Bullseye on three-zero-five point six after takeoff. Good day, and good luck."

"Rodger," Rachel replied. "Cleared for takeoff. Contact Bullseye on three-zero-five point six. Hammer, rolling." She nudged the Omega forward to line up with the runway centerline. She smoothly transitioned into hover mode as she accelerated forward. The huge ship quickly rose to one hundred meters before Rachel retracted the gear. "Gear up."

The massive landing gears gracefully rose into their compartments, and a light above the lever turned from red to green. "Gear is up," Michael replied.

Rachel gently put the controls into flight mode and pushed the spacecraft into the night sky. She waited for Aries to tune to the appropriate frequency and keyed the mic again. "Bullseye, Hammer with you on RASCL departure from Dreamland for FLEDGLING SPARROW."

"Hammer, Bullseye, cleared to RASCL then turn heading two-seven-zero for Bravo. Unrestricted climb to Charlie, supersonic approved, speed your discretion. Remain this frequency for Fledgling Sparrow."

"Rodger, turn two-seven-zero at RASCL to Bravo. Unrestricted climb to Charlie, speed our discretion. Remain on frequency."

It took only a minute to reach the RASCL waypoint, and Rachel rolled the Omega to the appropriate heading for the brief fifty miles to the Bravo waypoint over Tonopah airbase. When she was over the airfield, she gently began to pull back on the stick, and the nose began to rise. She pushed the button to open the ballast valve and eased the throttle forward. The Omega gracefully complied, and they rapidly began to gain altitude and speed. They broke the sound barrier seconds later, sending a sonic boom that would surely be heard for miles around.

Michael watched the progress carefully. At fifty-thousand feet they were still headed skyward at just over Mach-two. The lights of distant cities illuminated the horizon, but he could also clearly see the stars in the sky. They beckoned him in a way he had never experienced. He was beginning to realize he would soon be out in that void, racing faster than the speed of light toward those distant specks. It was an awe to think of the vast heavens, once unobtainable, now within reach.

As the altimeter neared thirty kilometers, the controller at Nellis Center Control called them one last time. "Hammer, Bullseye, departing restricted space. Radar service terminated. Proceed with Fledgling Sparrow as filed. Contact Overlord X-Link four. Good day."

Rachel keyed her mic. "Bullseye, Hammer, Proceeding as filed. Will contact Overlord X–Link four. Good day." She set the autopilot feature and then keyed her mic again. Aries had again switched frequencies and transitioned to the military secure Kx–band satellite uplink. "Overlord, Hammer, proceeding to Fledgling Sparrow."

There was a slight delay with the controller at the Pentagon Situation Room. "Hammer, Overlord, confirm your altitude at K–one."

Rachel looked at the map panel, confused by the unfamiliar waypoint when Aries interrupted. "They are asking if you have made it to one-hundred kilometers. Please inform them you will be on station in thirty seconds."

"Negative, Overlord, thirty out," Rachel replied.

"Copy that Hammer," the Pentagon controller responded. "Stand-by to conference with POTUS."

Chapter 12

FURY

"Can you hear me?" President Oscarson asked.

"Yes, Mister President," General Harris replied. "They can hear you."

"Thank you, General. But I was talking to the pilots. Why can't I see them too?"

"Operational security, Sir," General Harris replied. "Their spacecraft's interior is still highly classified, and even though it's encrypted, we cannot be completely sure their transmission hasn't been intercepted."

"I didn't ask for excuses," President Oscarson snapped. "They have the ability. I want them on my board. Make it happen." There was a momentary pause before the President's voice returned. "That's better. Wow! they look like real astronauts, don't they?"

Michael looked around the instrument panel but couldn't see where the video conference was displayed. He thought about asking, but realized it really wasn't that important. If it were necessary, Aries would have automatically done it.

"They are astronauts, Sir," General Harris replied. "They are currently hovering at the Karman Line directly above the Tonopah base in western Nevada. They're wearing suits just in case there was an issue with hull integrity."

"Gentlemen, Mister President, if we could get to the issue at hand. I think everyone would like to know if this new weapon platform can deliver on the promises made." The voice was feminine, and unfamiliar to either of them.

"Of course, Madame Secretary," General Harris replied to, what Michael figured was the Secretary of State, Janice Stillwell. "First, let me introduce those you cannot see. Gaia and Aries are the two artificial intelligences that will be conducting the bulk of the tests."

"What's wrong with the pilots?" President Oscarson asked. "Why can't they do the test?"

"If I may," Gaia said gently. "Mister President, the pilots are essential for many functions. However, the Omega is an extraordinarily complex space-craft and is only crewed by two people. They would easily be overwhelmed with testing and combat. Therefore, Aries handles the bulk of the tasks on the ship."

"What's to prevent the computer from launching the nukes onboard, if he does all the work?" The President asked.

"I am incapable of using any weapons without human authorization, and input," Aries replied. "It would be illegal, unethical, and unwise to transfer weapons control to an entity like me. I could go into the physical processes involved, but it is an unnecessary waste of time."

"Even if I ordered you to?" Oscarson pressed.

Aries continued. "I am physically incapable of obtaining the launch keys, the target packages, and authorization codes," Aries replied. "I utilize the same precautions as a ballistic missile submarine or a terrestrial based silo. Only a person, with proper command authority, under direct orders from you can arm and utilize my weapons systems."

"Mister President," General Harris interjected. "We have a looming threat, and a narrow window to act. May we proceed with a test of the launch systems?"

"Fine," President Oscarson said curtly. "Let's see if billions of dollars can buy an overwhelming advantage in this war."

Aries updated the screens on the Omega's consoles as they switched to fire-control mode, and the checklist updated. He informed the crew verbally. "I am loading the inert ordinance into the loading mechanisms."

"How damaging are these warheads. I mean, they don't have a payload that goes boom. What kind of damage are we talking?" The President asked.

"Each warhead would have a twenty-three-kiloton yield at this altitude," Aries said definitively.

President Oscarson whistled. "I thought you said they weren't nukes."

"They aren't," General Harris intervened. "However, they will be trav-eling at hypersonic speeds, and they have mass. That's why they will have a significant impact. There are only a few test ranges capable of handling that kind of test, and we haven't given them any notification."

"What do you suggest, General?"

"Target something critical so they need to rebuild their Navy. After we kill their fleet, they won't have a home to go back to if they survive."

"Are you suggesting we bomb Shanghai?" Secretary Stillwell asked dubiously.

"Yes, Madame Secretary," General Harris replied. "To be clear; I don't mean the city, but the shipyards. Blow up the drydocks at Shanghai and Huludao. Don't let them build any more subs or carriers and slow their ability to repair any of the fleet that manages to survive our attacks. If we do that, it might send them back to the negotiating table."

"Sir," Secretary Stillwell objected. "The Chinese will see this as an escalatory attack they have to respond to."

President Oscarson's voice became firm. "It's not nuclear, Janice. It's conventional. And if the damn thing doesn't fire, they won't know. Besides, this is war. A war they started! Now I've had enough of this attitude of appeasement from you. We are going to act. Let Beijing know we can hit them, any time, and anywhere. If you don't like it, there's a pre-made resignation letter in my desk with your name on it! General, how soon can we hit our targets?"

"I can be on station over Huludao in ten minutes," Aries replied. "We will fire, and then immediately task to Shanghai. It will take just forty-five seconds to be on station there and fire. Each torpedo will impact two minutes after launch. If the launch mechanisms are operational, I suggest we immediately re-task to SCARLET FURY, and make an inverted assault on the assembled fleets. We can fire tandem volleys on the fleets near Hokkaido within thirty seconds of leaving Shanghai."

"Before they have a chance to react," General Harris added.

"About this tandem shot," President Oscarson interrupted. "I'm still unclear why you need two."

"The first warhead is a standard quantum entangled hypersonic warhead that will detonate near the surface," General Harris explained. "The second is a neutron bomb that will detonate one minute later at slightly higher altitude."

"Yeah," President Oscarson said. "You said that before but never explained why."

General Harris took a moment before he responded. "The first warhead will do significant damage to the ships, as well as irradiate the crew. The neutron bomb has a higher neutron count and will give a fatal dose of radiation to any personnel not killed by the first. It must come after the standard nuke, otherwise it will make the standard nuke significantly less potent if it's detonated any earlier. The idea behind the tandem shot is to cripple their fleet and kill any survivors of the initial attack. We want them to be incapable of posing any naval threat for a considerable time."

"I strongly disagree this tactic will produce the desired results," Secretary Stillwell protested. "We already nuked their islands in the South China Sea, and yet they're still mounting an invasion. Doing this will only provoke them into a proportional response."

"Then we'll terminate their ability to respond before they can react!" President Oscarson growled. "If I have to nuke Beijing to glass tonight I will! Your objection is noted, and overruled! Let's get this test underway!"

Michael looked at Rachel. She was wide eyed. Neither of them had ever heard anything like that before. It was like watching parents argue. Everyone knew what was happening, and no one wanted to be there. "Aries, bring up the procedures for launching nuclear weapons." The checklist displayed the complex and detailed list they had to follow to confirm the orders and then fire their devastating payload.

"Mister President," Michael said. "While you get those launch codes, we'll get the authentication and arming keys in the other room."

"Alright Colonel," President Oscarson said dismissively. "Do what you need to get this done."

"Yes, Mister President," Michael replied.

Michael located the suit lines, disconnected them, and then unbuckled the five-point harness to the chair. Rachel did it as well and carefully stood up. He had expected them to be weightless, but there was gravity. "Why can I stand? Aries, shouldn't we be floating weightless in space?"

"Technically we are stationary above a fixed point," Aries replied. "Astronauts in conventional spacecraft have microgravity because they are in orbit.

They are falling relative to the Earth. We are only one hundred kilometers directly above Tonopah Airforce Base. We still experience the pull of gravity, but it is ninety-six percent the gravity experienced at the surface."

"I thought we were in a warp bubble that negated the effects of gravity and inertia," Rachel protested, confused by the apparent dichotomy of the physics involved.

"The warp bubble doesn't negate the laws of gravity or motion," Aries replied. "You don't notice the change in inertia because you aren't moving. You are simply slipping through the gravity field, which only negates the inertia of the ship and its contents. I could get into the specifics of how this doesn't conflict with Newton's Laws of Motion, but it would take precious time away from the mission."

"Fair enough, Aries," Michael replied, turning his attention to the task at hand. "Aries, transfer our coms, and set the display to optical."

"As you wish," Aries replied. The display changed from a grayscale to a color-filled display of the planet cloaked in darkness below. Even at night, the city lights illuminated the scene through the faint blue hue of the atmosphere blanketing the world beneath them.

The surprise of still having gravity erased as Aries changed the display. The view of the Earth from one hundred kilometers above at night was stunning. They could see the lights from the major cities of the Western United States like illuminated islands in a sea of black. Michael could even make out the lights off in the east which would be the Salt Lake–Ogden–Provo metroplex. There was a sudden twinge of loss and regret as he looked back at his home. He longed to see his parents and siblings, just one more time. He was high above them. Watching over and protecting them, like a guardian angel. That would have to do for now.

"Thinking of home?" Rachel asked.

Michael stirred from his reverie and looked at her. He had been so engrossed with his own musing; he had missed her train of thought completely. "I guess so. Cut me some slack. It's my first time in space."

"It's okay. I was thinking the same thing," Rachel said with a smile. "Millions of people down there don't know what's going on. Someone has to have their back. It might as well be us."

They returned their focus to the task at hand and headed toward the hatch. As they moved into the crew quarters, Michael had a thought cross his mind. "Aries, does the ship have stable pressure?"

"There are no signs of hull compromise," The AI replied. "Pressure is holding steady."

"Can I get a private line to the General please?"

"Of course," Aries replied. "Secure com-link established."

"What is it?"

"Sir, the hull pressure is stable, and these spacesuits are a bit bulky. Is it possible for us to change into our flight suits?"

"Negative at this time," General Harris replied. "There's a lot of space debris. Aries can track most of it, but anything smaller than a couple of centimeters is too miniscule to monitor effectively. You're taking an awful risk as it is, so I don't want you to take the suits off until you're on the ground."

Michael turned to Rachel and shrugged his shoulders. "Worth a shot," he said placidly. "We'll be headed to the Crew Room now. Just — standing by to receive launch information and authentication."

"Rodger that," General Harris replied. "Switching back to conference channel."

The two pilots made their way back into the Crew Room and sat down in the booth. It was a little cramped with the suits on, but the area was designed to accommodate crew wearing bulky attire. A panel slid back, exposing the safe. It had a sturdy handle, and a single six-inch display with a Space Force emblem.

"The safe is coded to your face and thumbprint," Aries said.

Michael scoffed. "I'm wearing gloves, am I supposed to take them off?"

"Your gloves have a fingerprint reader in the thumb," Aires replied. "Just press your thumb against the display and look at the camera."

Michael did as he was directed. There was a heavy clunk as the lock disengaged. He pushed the handle downward and pulled back, opening the safe. Inside was a printer, another display on the opposite side of the door, two red binders labeled ACTION, two white binders labeled DRILL, two black grease pens, a blue key labeled COMMANDER, and a yellow key labeled XO. The display read "Stand-by for Launch Orders."

Michael withdrew both keys, the grease pens, and the red binders. He examined them briefly and handed the yellow key, a grease pen, and a red binder to Rachel. "Not sure how all of this works, but I'm pretty sure there's a reason why there's two of everything."

A coxswain alarm sounded, and the display began to flash red. ACTION in bold ominous letters appeared on the display as well. Aries came over the intercom. "Action stations, action stations, action stations, this is not a drill. Prepare to copy authentication codes."

Michael and Rachel both opened their binders. Inside was a single clear plastic sheet with twenty-four black dashes. A small pocket on the cover held a thick red plastic card. They uncapped their pens and hovered over the dashes, ready to copy whatever they heard.

An androgenous mechanical voice came over the intercom. Michael thought it was odd, it wasn't Aries but figured it was a voice broadcast over a secure channel. As the voice began, the two pilots began writing furiously. "Action required. Copy authentication as follows: Mike–Seven–Five–Delta, Eight–Papa–Oscar–Quebec, Niner–Eight–Charlie–X-ray, Papa–One–Niner–Alpha, Alpha–Alpha–X-ray–Delta, Six–One–Niner–Oscar. Message Ends." The voice went silent.

As soon as they finished writing, instinctively they both removed the plastic card from its holder. Simultaneously, they thought the gloves had a remarkable grip and tactile advantage for being as bulky as they were. The cards were about the size of their palm with a score mark down the middle. They broke the seal and removed a laminated strip of paper from its hiding place in the card. Written in black ink was the code: M75D–8POQ–98CX–P19A–AAXD–619O.

"You have to repeat the code to each other," Aries said. "You, the person listening, must confirm that the codes match what is written. Colonel, you are first."

Michael read the code aloud. When he was done, she said, "Message is authentic."

Then he read his transparency as Rachel read back her copy. When she was finished, he replied. "I concur; message is authentic." The printer whirred and a sheet was produced.

It read:

```
********************ATTENTION********************
********************ACTION***********************
AUTHENTICATION
M75D–8POQ–98CX–P19A–AAXD–6190
FROM: PRESIDENT OF THE UNITED STATES DANIEL H. OSCARSON
TO: UNITED STATES SPACE FORCE NUCLEAR FORCES
RELEASE OF NUCLEAR WEAPONS HAS BEEN AUTHORIZED.
THIS IS NOT A DRILL!
MISSION:
1.  DESTROY STRATEGIC POINTS IN HULUDAO.
2.  DESTROY STRATEGIC POINTS IN SHANGHAI.
3.  DESTROY OBJECTIVE OHIO.
4.  DESTROY OBJECTIVE DAKOTA.
5.  DESTROY OBJECTIVE UTAH.
TARGET LIST:
HULUDAO
IW – 110 MISSILE X5
40.71900821295234, 121.00063691640986
40.74529021534967, 121.02398905461055
40.74143342810429, 120.75866491845326
40.350184947434165, 120.55069733327365
40.707691815616215, 120.9622958740307
SHANGHAI
IW – 110 MISSILE X5
31.275736855713657, 121.568711360614
31.34728836323311, 121.7443035967127
30.78673748790667, 121.45093289092749
30.42098084687619, 120.94176435204773
31.255063190479536, 121.74072210544422
OBJECTIVE OHIO — 44.200466 138.669386
W – 110 QENDM MISSILES X1
W – 70X HERM MISSILES X1
OBJECTIVE DAKOTA — 46.772961 145.270091
W - 110 QENDM MISSILES X1
W - 70X HERM MISSILES X1
OBJECTIVE UTAH — 25.20889 172.56013
W - 110 QENDM MISSILES X1
W - 70X HERM MISSILES X1
AUTHENTICATION
M75D–8POQ–98CX–P19A–AAXD–6190
RELEASE OF NUCLEAR WEAPONS IS AUTHORIZED.
THIS IS NOT A DRILL!
************************END***********************
********************ACTION***********************
```

Michael sighed. "Aries, I assume these coordinates are entered into our targeting systems already."

"That is correct, Colonel," Aries replied. "All the calculations are entered into the navigation and targeting systems. Recommended speed is thirty-seven thousand KPH to targets. Be advised: the course is counter to most low-orbit satellites, so our closure speed will be over sixty thousand kilometers per hour."

"If anything hits us at that speed," Rachel mused, "we're toast."

Michael took the cards and placed them back into the binders. He placed them back into the safe along with the pens and closed it. With a tight grip on his key, he headed toward the flight deck, motioning for Rachel to follow. "Once we've hooked back up, we'll insert the keys on my mark. I'm assuming we have to turn them at the same time, or it won't arm the warheads."

"Again, you are correct in your assumption," Aries replied.

"We're all set then," Michael said with a note of finality. "Aries, having a sentient autopilot has its advantages."

"If that were all I was," Aries replied dryly, "it would be an extravagant convenience, but I am far more than an automated flight system."

"My apologies," Michael replied. "I'm not trying to marginalize your capabilities. I'm merely commenting on the fact that every aircraft I've ever flown requires a modicum of programming prior to starting. We don't have flight engineers, or a crew on fighter aircraft handling the other aspects of the mission."

They went back to their chairs where Michael helped Rachel into her seat and reattached her hardlines. "I want to arm these weapons before we get into the fight, so get your key ready."

He strapped himself in and held his key as he made eye contact with Rachel. "Just insert the key. Don't turn it until I count us down." Michael knew she understood his meaning, so he turned his attention to the task at hand. "Prepare to insert keys on my mark." The keyhole next to the Master Arm switch lit up. "Three...two...one...Mark!"

Both pilots inserted their keys nearly simultaneously. Words then illuminated above the key positions. A green SAFE at the top of the keyway, and to the right, in red letters, was ARM. "Turn right on my mark." Again,

Michael counted down, and they both turned their keys at the same time. He turned his attention to the navigation chart. It already had the course to Huludao plotted, along with the follow-up course to Shanghai.

Michael wasn't one to stand on undue ceremony and wanted to get this operation underway. "Let's get in and out before they know what hit 'em. Aries, load the inert ordinance and prepare to fire. Bright, get us there quickly. China has anti-satellite missiles, and I don't want them getting a lock on us."

"Unlike the Alpha," Aries began with a slight condescending air, "The Omega uses eight forward launch tubes to fire torpedo ordinance."

"Fine, load tubes one, three, five, seven, and eight for the first salvo. We'll do two, four, six, seven, and eight for the second. Will that do?"

"As you wish," Aries replied.

"Passive aggressive from an AI," Michael grumbled. "Remind me to check your motherboard for any CCP[1] chips – jerk. Rachel, get us there already!"

Rachel turned to the appropriate heading and eased the throttle forward. Silently, and without the typical sense of acceleration, the Omega rocketed forward. Soon the speed indicator was climbing past thirty-five thousand kilometers per hour. The radar scope was littered with various satellites and other orbital debris, but nothing showed a potential hazard on the flight path Aries had given them. Michael thought about how they were now closing distance with objects at more than fifty-thousand kilometers per hour, any one of which could obliterate them in a collision. He couldn't help but think Rachel's reaction time would be insufficient to evade anything that might come their way.

"Rest assured, Colonel," Aries said calmly. "I know where everything in orbit is, and how to avoid it."

"How could you tell what I was thinking?" Michael replied nervously.

"Your heartrate just jumped eighty beats per minute, and your respiration increased by a factor of ten. That, and I can see you look tense. Using a predictive algorithm I can anticipate your reaction."

"Remind me to remove your camera," Rachel snapped.

1 Chinese Communist Party

They soon crossed the terminator and entered the daytime side of the planet. The clouds, oceans, and landmasses blurring to near unrecognizable smears below. A red warning message appeared on the navigation screen and Aries repeated it aloud "BEGIN DECELERATION!"

Rachel quickly throttled back as they approached their waypoint. She instinctively rolled the spacecraft into a near vertical orientation to the ground below. Michael's navigation screen changed to the Fire Control menu. The interface was like a video game and was intuitive for him to operate. The targets were highlighted and ready for him to confirm. He quickly selected which tube would be used to hit the five pre-selected facilities and carefully guided the curser with his finger to the points most likely to cause the greatest damage on impact. They felt a loud clang in the hull as the tube airlocks opened to a firing position. With the packages selected he flipped the MASTER ARM switch on the instrument panel and unceremoniously pushed the "Fire" button.

The five inert torpedoes left their launchers with a singular thud. "Torpedoes away!" Michael announced triumphantly, satisfied that a piece of equipment worked trouble-free the first time it was tried. "Don't let them get a lock on us. Get to next target!"

Obediently, Rachel swung the Omega toward the next target and punched the accelerator forward. They were both expecting feedback from gravity, telling them they had reoriented and accelerated away, but there was nothing. The only indication they were moving at all came from the greyscale planet moving below them, and the illuminated red reticles highlighting their targets on the planetary horizon in front of them.

Shanghai quickly closed as they streaked meteorically down the coast of China. As they closed over the target, Rachel repeated the same maneuver as moments before. They hovered, and nosed down, above one of the most populated cities in the world. The thought crossed both their minds that nearly thirty million people were about to witness the war literally rain from the heavens. It was a terrifying realization, but they had clear orders and a duty to follow them.

Michael selected the highlighted targets, assigning each to a corresponding launch tube, and pressed FIRE. There was a second thud as the next five inert warheads left the ship for the unsuspecting targets below.

Rachel immediately oriented to the next target and pushed the throttle forward. Objective Ohio would be in range in less than thirty seconds.

"Stand-by for nuclear strike," Michael said, still nervous about the order. "Aries, load the neutron in tube one, the nuke in tube eight."

"Rodger," Aries replied. "The Seventy-X in tube one, the M-One-Ten in tube eight. I have also loaded a Seventy-X in tube two and an M-One-Ten in tube seven."

By the time Aries had finished talking, Objective Ohio was in range. Michael selected the highlighted target. "Slow down, Rachel, Mach five should about do it."

"On it," she replied.

"Aries, do I have to fire twice, or are you going to give the proper delay?" Michael asked.

"You only need to fire once. Each command is for the volley, not the individual ordinance."

Michael immediately initiated the volley. The first torpedo left the ship with a light thump. A few seconds later, there was a glow as the missile began to heat in the atmosphere. Thirty seconds after the first launch, a second thump was felt as the neutron missile left the ship on its mission of death and the Omega smoothly arched toward the target.

Objective Dakota was northwest of Objective Ohio by nearly six hundred kilometers. Even at the relatively slow speed of Mach five, the target quickly came over the horizon. Both targets were in view as Michael launched the next volley. The first torpedo had barely left the ship when the first half of the Ohio volley exploded on the horizon. The bright monochromatic flash visible on the bridge display. The Omega continued on to a corrective arc toward the final target, and thirty seconds later the second warhead left the launcher with a light thud. Just then, another flash at objective Ohio.

"I wonder if it hit the target," Michael mused aloud.

"Bringing up the feed from Keyhole Sixteen," Aries replied. A small section of the forward display showed an edge-on view of the developing mushroom cloud. The picture still overwhelmed by the brightness of the explosion. They could, however, make out the silhouette of a couple large ships against the intense glow of the blast. "Ordinances detonated on target."

"Turn and burn for Objective Utah," Michael ordered.

"Aye aye, Sir," Rachel replied. She checked the range on the plot. It was just over three thousand kilometers, a distance they could cover in about twenty-five minutes at their present speed. This was too slow for Rachel's taste. She nudged the throttle forward to twenty-four thousand kilometers per hour. She mused that this speed was deceptive. They were moving faster than the space station. Faster than she had ever flown, but it still felt as if they were moving too slowly. "We'll be in range in about six minutes."

"Perfect," Michael said. Already knowing what her thought process was and finding it comforting. He was starting to get used to her flying mindset, and it impressed him that she was so efficient. "Aries, put the Seventy-X in tube three, and the M-One-Ten in tube six. Are you monitoring the Keyhole data?"

"Affirmative," Aries replied, bringing up another display under the first. "Keyhole Twelve is tasked with Objective Dakota. The Seventy-X should be detonating in five seconds."

The second screen flared as the neutron bomb exploded above the unsuspecting fleet of personnel carriers and landing craft. The initial blast was enough to overwhelm the optics of the high-resolution reconnaissance satellite. The neutron flux from the device would almost certainly kill most of the crew, until the second torpedo detonated, compounding the carnage. Thirty seconds later, the M-One-Ten did its job, and struck the fleet.

Michael forced his mind on the mission at hand. He had some sympathy for the people manning the ships, but these people had no such sympathy when they used nukes on the US fleet. He thought of the confusion that must certainly be happening in the military control centers in Beijing. Two major ports hit, and the bulk of their naval fleet obliterated within minutes. How terrified they must be. 'About time' he thought.

A few scant minutes flew by as Michael and Rachel prepared for their final authorized volley. Combat always seemed to make the time pass more quickly.

Michael prepared to select the targets. "Aries, I'm a little rusty on orbital mechanics, but these torpedoes won't skip off the atmosphere at these entry angles, will they?"

"They do have ballistic entry components," Aries replied. "The entry angles have been accounted for. However, I suggest you do not attempt a highspeed deorbit. I think anything above Mach five will cause undue stress on the ship during re-entry. We may not be limited by the effects of gravity, but the ship still must contend with the atmospheric stresses. Or had you forgotten when Rachel destroyed me in the simulations?"

"I hadn't forgotten," Michael said, as Objective Utah neared the horizon. He realized they would be directly overhead when the detonation occurred. "Aries, if we maintain our present heading, how likely are we to be hit with a dose of radiation?"

"You will be within the one-hundred-kilometer radius. You won't receive a significant dose, but you should try to put as much distance between you and the explosion as possible — just to be safe."

Michael looked at Rachel. "As soon as the second one is gone, turn and burn for a polar orbit. Just keep it under thirty thousand KPH." He selected the reticle highlighting the Shandong carrier group and fired the volley. As with the other targets, the nuclear ordinance left the Omega with a slight thump. There was a heavy clang sound as the outer doors to the launchers closed after the final missile was gone.

Rachel banked hard to the left and pushed the throttle forward as they raced due north, away from the impending detonation. Minutes later there was a flash behind them as the third Chinese fleet was hit by the neutron bomb. As before, Aries had brought up the video feed from the keyhole satellite. They watched as the fleet was devastated by both nuclear detonations of the tandem volley.

"Very good job, people," President Oscarson said. There had been no communication heard from the President or the General during the execution of the mission, so the pilots had forgotten they were on a live conference feed. "Now, before you go anywhere, I want you to head to Beijing and hold right over that city. Fill your tubes with nukes and wait for my orders. Get me President Zhang on the phone. Let's see if he's more willing to negotiate with a bunch of nukes aimed at his head."

Rachel immediately complied with the order and turned the Omega west. She glanced at Michael for reassurance, but he was just as confused as she was.

"Mister President," Secretary Stillwell interjected. "I highly advise against this."

"Oh, and why is that?" President Oscarson growled, irritated by his cabinet member.

"The Chinese aren't going to back down while you have a literal gun to their head. If anything, they will see this as an ultimatum and will have no choice but to respond in kind."

"I agree," An unknown male voice said.

"Not you too, Mark," the President snapped.

"My job is to advise you on national security," Mark Ackerman replied. "We're already on the brink of a global-thermonuclear holocaust. Don't push it over the edge."

"What about you, Admiral Evans, are you in favor of appeasement?" The President asked.

The head of the Joint Chiefs of Staff delayed his response, gathering his thoughts. "Sir, the question is how will the Chinese react? Honestly, the only thing they seem to respect is a demonstration of strength. They have spent an awful lot of time undermining the United States. I recall their thwarted efforts to reshape the world under previous administrations. If it hadn't been for a near civil war, they might have succeeded. I believe aggressive action is the only thing they will listen to. The only way to deal with the ambitions of President Zhang is to show him our resolve. If he tries anything, I say we use every nuke on that ship. Turn China into a parking lot!"

There was an awkward silence as the President mulled over his options. "Is the Omega heading toward China?"

"Yes, Sir," General Harris replied. "They are following your orders and heading there now."

"Good!" President Oscarson said definitively. "Get those bombs ready. Where's my line to Beijing?"

"They're holding on the 'Red Line One'," an unknown woman replied.

There was the sound of a landline telephone receiver being picked up. "Who's this?" President Oscarson asked gruffly. They would not be privy to the audio on the other end of the line. "Ping, eh? And you're translating? Fine! Tell your President this: Don't talk, just listen! America is done with your aggression. You have seen that we can, and will, strike you whenever we want." There was a long pause as he waited for the interpreter. "No! Don't you say a word! You listen, or I'll nuke your bunker right now! Our weapons are faster, more powerful, and more maneuverable. We are currently set to turn Beijing to ashes!"

Again, there was another long pause as the translator caught up with the president's tirade. "Now, from my perspective you have two choices. You agree to meet at a conference, and resolve this matter without further bloodshed, or I'll end this war right now by wiping your entire population out. In three minutes, there won't be a soul alive. I'll wipe Beijing, Tianjin, Tangshan, Baoding, and every city and village in a two-hundred-mile radius. I will turn the entire region into a smoldering radioactive crater! TRANS-LATE THAT!"

As President Oscarson finished his tirade, the Omega came to a halt one hundred kilometers directly above the center of Beijing.

Michael looked grim. He hoped that Oscarson was bluffing, but he had to be ready to launch if needed. "Aries, load M-One-Ten's into tubes one through eight. Deploy the MWE's and give me overlapping targets on every major population center in the province likely to be classified in the target package. Make sure the military and defensive infrastructure is targeted in the first three volleys. Anything that won't be taken out by a nuke in the first strike, within a nuke's secondary damage radius, will be targeted by laser and railgun."

"President Zhang, I hate to interrupt, but I must advise you that my nukes are currently loaded and locked on target. Just have your radar check the skies directly over your head." The unadulterated glee was evident in President Oscarson's voice as he relayed the grim news to his counterpart. "You won't even have time to kiss your own backside goodbye before you and your capitol are obliterated. Your people will be GONE! And all you will have left to rule is the smoldering radioactive wasteland that remains. I suggest you think very carefully about what you say next, because I still have considerable military power at my disposal. All my soldiers want your bloated tyrannical carcass. Now, are you ready to talk, or become the latest trophy on my wall?"

Suddenly, several things happened simultaneously: an alarm blared in their headsets, the weapon systems spontaneously targeted an incoming threat, and the Omega shifted one-hundred kilometers south. Before Michael could think, the laser system on the number two MWE indicated a state of discharge.

"What the –" Michael said, startled by the sequence of events. "Aries, what did you do?"

"I do apologize, Colonel, but I detected a missile launch from the surface. I have destroyed the projectile, but the launcher complex is still operational. I believe the weapon was a hypersonic prototype variant of the SC–19 ASAT. I have located four land-based launch complexes capable of housing those missiles in effective range. What are your orders?"

"What's going on there?" President Oscarson asked.

"They are attempting to shoot down our spacecraft, Mister President," General Harris replied.

"We can't use nukes," Michael mused as if he couldn't hear the others. "You used a laser to disable it, right?"

"Correct."

"Do we have any more of the inert warheads?" Rachel asked.

"Negative, we have expended our test ordinance," Aries replied.

"Fine," Michael replied. "Our railguns should work. Target them all. Start with the one that fired, and then we'll get to the others."

"At this altitude the railguns have decreased efficiency," Aries stated. "I suggest a volley using all four MWE's to increase the likelihood of a direct hit."

Michael checked his Weapons Control screen and selected the targets by touching the red highlighted icons on the display. "Go in order of my selection, Aries."

"Affirmative, Colonel. I will need approximately fifteen seconds between each volley to acquire each target and recharge the capacitors. I must also have flight control."

"Fine," Michael replied. "Get it done." He finished his input and pressed the FIRE button.

There was a high-pitched whine as the capacitors charged. The Omega spun to face the first target. There was a large bang as the first volley of four tungsten core aluminum and carbon cased projectiles rocketed out of the four MWE's at over five-thousand meters per second. Michael could see them glow brightly as they ripped through the atmosphere toward their targets.

There was no time to think as the capacitors whined in recharge and the Omega swiveled to the next target. Normally fifteen seconds can feel like an eternity waiting for something to happen, but this felt like only the blink of an eye before the next bang occurred. Before the first volley impacted the second volley was gone, and they were shifting to a new target. The first volley impacted twenty-one seconds after it was fired.

"First target impacted," Aries announced. "Two direct hits. Two near misses." Another loud bang occurred as the third volley left. "Second impact in eight seconds."

The Omega abruptly darted one-hundred kilometers west as the threat board indicated two more missile launches from the remaining sites. Again, the incoming ordinance was unceremoniously destroyed by the laser systems.

"Second impact recorded. All direct hits." Aries said, as if it were a routine occurrence. The cycle of reorientation and recharging began as the AI continued his announcement. "Next impact in six seconds. Firing final volley."

Another loud bang occurred as the final projectiles were propelled toward the ground below. The brilliant orange streaks marking their deadly path toward the last launch system. "Third site impacted. One direct hit. Two nearly missed. One projectile has gone off-course and impacted on a residential apartment building. Seven seconds to final impact. Returning control to pilot."

Michael could feel Rachel's blood run cold at the thought of civilian casualties. Ordinance impacting innocents was news that no pilot ever wanted to hear.

"Any guess on casualties?" Rachel asked.

"There is no definitive answer," Aries replied. "It is unknown the exact number of individuals still inside the structure on impact."

"Those rounds aren't explosive, are they?" Michael inquired.

"Negative." Aries' impassionate answer was expected, but still very disquieting. "The rounds are purely kinetic in nature, but at this distance the damage would be substantial."

"How much are we talking?" Rachel asked, terrified at the answer.

"Approximately thirty-point-five-four-ton yield. Fourth impact recorded. This site was also in a populated area. One direct hit. The other three are near misses, however they impacted close to residential areas primarily used by base personnel. My analysis of the first apartment building shows that it has been destroyed."

"Are we out of danger?" Michael asked.

"I detect no further threats at this time," Aries said.

Michael turned his attention to the conference call. "Mister President?"

"What is it, Colonel? Are you folks, okay?"

"Yes, Sir," Michael replied, controlling his emotions as best as he could. He had just killed thousands of innocents. Men, women, and children. He couldn't dwell on that now. "Please tell the Chinese they should cease fire, and we can avoid any more innocents dying. The Omega can, and will, defend itself against anything they throw at us."

"I'll do that," President Oscarson said. "Ping, tell your fool of a president that he better be ready to meet his maker. Colonel, I'm going to have them send you the coordinates of the spider-hole we think Zhang is hiding in. I want you to ready to put a couple of nukes there, so we can end this. Get it done people!"

"Yes, Sir," Michael replied. He couldn't tell if this was a bluff by the president, or an actual order. "Aries, let me know if you get an action message."

"As you wish, Colonel."

"What's that, Ping?" President Oscarson's voice sounded pleased. "President Zhang would like to talk to me directly? I don't think that's a good idea. I've heard his English. I want no misunderstandings. Tell him I am prepared to nuke his pompous backside if he doesn't agree with my terms. Right here! Right now!"

Chapter 13

END AND BEGINNING

Rachel eased the throttle back slowly as the Omega began its final approach to runway three-two at Groom Lake. It was early morning, just as the pre-dawn light began to rise over the Groom Range east of the base and threatened to expose their highly classified spacecraft to any would-be trespassers to the area.

Michael sighed; grateful they had not been ordered to end several hundred million lives and yet still mournful for the tens of thousands they killed in the process. The flight home had been uneventful and had taken just under an hour to complete. They hover-taxied back into the cloaked obscurity of the great net which shrouded the hangar. They were met by a small army of helper robots that immediately began to decontaminate the Omega from the radioactive particles accumulated by their journey into space and their subsequent re-entry.

There was a chime as the image of General Harris appeared on a screen on their consoles. "Congratulations on your mission. It was extraordinarily successful, and, oddly, was completed without incident. I thought you might want to get the post-mission debrief out of the way as it will be about six hours before you can transfer to the Alpha."

"Since we don't have any issues, can we please get out of our space suits and into some flight suits before we do the debrief?" Michael asked.

General Harris smiled. "Actually, you are at risk of decompression sickness. Although I would like to get the debrief over, I'll let you get out of those suits. Aries will take care of the pressurization automatically while you're in the crew room. You should each have a head in your room with a shower in it. Don't go hog wild though. The water is on a five-minute timer, so don't dawdle. We'll do the debrief via remote connection at the table in the crew quarters. See you in twenty."

"Yes, Sir," Michael said with a nod. "Thank you, Sir, we'll get right on that." There was a sudden strange sensation he could feel coming from Rachel. She was trying to undo her tether points but couldn't quite get the connections to free. There was a surge of frustration, then both their tethers released simultaneously. "What was that?"

Rachel looked at Michael with astonishment. "Um – I'm not sure."

"Did you just 'will' the tethers to uncouple?" Michael asked incredulously.

Rachel flushed as she protested. "These aren't the same as a standard G-suit connector. It's like someone went to an off-brand hardware store and got the cheapest pressure fitting they could find."

"You didn't have a problem before."

"Yeah," Rachel stammered. "Well, I do now."

Michael chuckled as he got up to inspect the coupling. "I'm just teasing you, Rachel. Don't get all excited." The couplings were similar to a standard two-part brass pressure coupling that released when you pulled back on the retention nut; almost like the air compressor connectors he used in high school shop class, but not quite. It didn't look damaged, but he thought it best that someone else check it out. "Aries, make sure these connectors get checked for damage. I don't think they were meant to be disconnected telekinetically, and we might need to scramble if the Chinese decide they don't like the idea of capitulating to President Oscarson."

"I will have a helper unit come and inspect it after they are finished assisting with your suits," Aries replied. "Please remember during the decompression cycle you will be confined to the crew quarters. The pressurization cycle will take approximately four hours to equalize and return your blood gases to normal. Failure to adhere to this protocol could cause substantial risk to your health."

"Thanks, we'll remember that" Michael replied, getting out of the chair and heading to the crew quarters. He could feel the weight of Rachel's exhaustion amplifying his own. They had been trained for the brutal reality of warfare, but nothing really prepared them for the reality they had just faced. The thought of wiping out nearly one and a half billion people was more draining than actually taking the lives of the tens of thousands of soldiers and sailors on the fleets they sunk. Taking life is a sin. The fact they were nearly forced to act, in the name of saving hundreds of millions in their own country, didn't assuage their guilt. They had killed people who were loved by parents, spouses, and siblings.

Four helper units entered the cabin just ahead of the two pilots and took up positions opposite the door. The two aviators brushed passed them as the door to the crew area closed. An audible hiss emanated from the walls as the pressure was rapidly equalized. It made the entire space seem claustrophobic.

Michael's own emotions mingled with Rachel's. Combined with the closed quarters it all began to stress his mind. He entered his cabin and closed the door, locking it behind him. He clumsily began fiddling with his suit in an attempt to disconnect the various sections, starting with his gloves. He had just managed to get one of his gloves off when Aries addressed him over the communications link.

"Michael, may I send helper units in to assist you?"

"I suppose that would be quicker than me blindly fumbling with it."

"Please unlock the door, so my helpers may enter."

Michael sighed and unlocked the door. "Interesting," he mused. "You can't unlock the door yourself?"

"I can," Aries replied. "But only in an emergency. Since this situation does not qualify as an emergency, my protocols do not allow me to invade your privacy without explicit permission."

Michael couldn't help but smile at the thought given to Aries' programming. As cold and unfeeling as he had to be, to carry out his mission, they had thought of imbuing him with regard for the privacy of the crew. It was almost contradictory in nature, but it demonstrated the insightful and nuanced attention from the programmers.

The helpers made quick work of getting the suit off, and Michael made use of the private head. It was as small and utilitarian as any bathroom/shower he had ever seen on any aircraft carrier. It reminded him of a commercial airplane bathroom. It was barely big enough to stand in. The toilet, sink, and shower occupied the same space. A number of placards warned of disabled functions in zero-gravity, and proper use of the toilet in zero-gravity mode, as well as normal shower operations.

General Harris was right about the water timer. Every second the water was on was measured to the tenth of a second. A large, digital timer sat prominently next to the vanity. After a quick shower, Michael quickly donned his flight uniform, entered the common area of the crew quarters, and sat in the booth. Four helper units stood in front of the hatch, as if guarding it.

Rachel soon exited her room and joined him. She looked at the units with disdain. "What's with the prison guards?"

"Probably because they know you'll try to leave before the briefing." Not waiting for her flippant reply, Michael addressed the ever-present AI. "Aries, please inform General Harris that we are ready for the debriefing — at his convenience." The last bit seemed almost an afterthought, thrown in to appeal to a flag officer's vanity.

The display lit up with General Harris and the rest of the civilians seated around the conference table. "Now that everyone is here, Gaia, let's begin with the current situation, and then we can move into our current readiness."

The display shifted to a live view from the reconnaissance satellites over the smoldering remains of the targeted ports. "My analysis of the test targets in Shanghai and Huludao suggest that our ordinance was within the allowable accuracy. Most of the inert warheads missed their precision target points by two meters, but it is well within the allowable ten-meter radius. This is actually better than expected, given they were never intended to be fired in combat. Each projectile had an effective yield of ten kilotons. This has caused serious, but not irreparable damage to the existing shipyard infrastructure. The estimated time for repairs is approximately twenty-two days."

"How about casualties?" Doctor Taylor asked.

"I do not have an exact count, Doctor Taylor," Gaia replied. "The Chinese authorities are still assessing that. Signal Intelligence and local news reports suggest approximately fifteen hundred dead, three thousand injured, and sixteen thousand unaccounted for. However, based on what we know, these numbers should not be taken as accurate. I believe we will have better totals in five to seven days."

"Those are just the tip of the iceberg," Doctor Doddridge quipped. "Wait until you hear the numbers from the targets we nuked."

"Spare us your annotations, Doctor," General Harris growled. "Please continue, Gaia."

The video switched to a view of a single group of naval ships, all of which were smoking as they drifted aimlessly in a group. The largest was instantly recognizable as a carrier. It was listing to the port side; thick black smoke poured from the central tower. Next to it was the dark shape of a submarine pulling along the port side. "This is a view of the carrier, Shandong group. The submarine is the Columbia. It has been tasked with offloading a contingent from SEAL Team Three to assess the situation on-board."

"Sounds dangerous," Michael said. He had intended it to be inaudible but apparently had said it loud enough for the general to hear.

"That goes with the territory, Colonel," General Harris snapped. "No more interruptions people. Gaia, continue with the briefing."

"The Columbia, the Greenville, and the Cheyenne have finished the task of eliminating the six escort submarines. Five of them were attack submarines and one was a ballistic missile submarine. All six have been confirmed sunk by torpedoes fired from the six-eighty-eights. Since the initial bombardment of Objective Utah, a total of twelve surface ships have been sunk, including two troop transports. The SEAL team currently boarding the Shandong has had NEST training and equipment for entering radioactive environments. Our other submarine task forces near Hokkaido do not have specially trained observer teams embedded and are currently being mopped up by a small fleet of attack submarines operated by SUBCOMPAC. Due to the heightened nature of worldwide tensions, President Oscarson has ordered all forces to DEFCON–One. All forces are in OPERATION COCKED PISTOL. Accordingly, it is advised that all Project Nova crews move from the barracks to their respective MeCTen, and all ships should power up for the possibility of immediate deployment for OPERATION SHATTERED SKY."

"Gaia," General Harris interrupted. "Do we have the live feed from SEAL Team Three aboard the Shandong?"

"I am sorry, General Harris," Gaia replied meekly. "I'm afraid we have not been granted security clearance for that feed."

"On who's authority?"

"Admiral Foster," Gaia replied. "No reason has been given for the denial."

"Not like we did all the work," General Harris scoffed as he threw a pen across the room. "Continue, Gaia!"

"It is my estimate that we have achieved a full ninety-eight percent elimination of personnel on all nuclear bombardment targets. We should know more after SEAL Team Three completes their assessment. In the meantime, decontamination of the Omega will take approximately five and a half hours to complete. Decompression of Colonel Langford and Lieutenant Commander Bright is ongoing and should be complete in four hours. During that time, Aries has sealed them inside the crew compartment to improve the efficiency of the bariatric treatment and to allow the ground crews access to service the interior of the ship."

Rachel was trying to contain her anxiety over being locked in her quarters. "We're stuck in here?"

"I am sorry for that, Lieutenant Commander," Gaia replied gently. "But you were in a pressurized, oxygen-rich suit for quite some time. If we were to remove you too quickly, the gas bubbles trapped in your blood could release. Not only would this be painful, but you would risk serious illness or death. I am sure you are familiar with Boyle's Law?"

"You know I am," Rachel replied. "I understand the reason. That doesn't mean I have to like it."

"Real space travel isn't like television and movies," General Harris interjected. "We have to obey the laws of physics. Even the inconvenient ones."

Doctor Schretzmann leaned forward and inserted himself into the conversation. It was obvious he had wanted to say something for some time. "If we are finished with the death and destruction segment of today's program, could we please discuss the success of the flight?"

General Harris sighed. "I suppose we're going to have to wait for the report to filter down from on high, so..." He paused as his voice trailed off in his own thoughts for a moment. "Go ahead, and let's hear about flight dynamics."

"I shall let Aries handle his analysis of the maiden flight," Gaia said, deferring to the Omega's AI.

"Detailed flight analysis shows that the MeCTen airframe performed as expected," Aries began. "No anomalies were found, and all systems operated as expected."

"None?" Doctor Doddridge scoffed derisively. "Not a single misfeed in the loaders, or problems with the magnetic field?"

"None."

"Umm," Rachel interjected. "I hate to add this, but what about the crew getting sick during the startup?"

"I was getting to that," Aries replied brusquely. "The only unexpected performance is the human crew. They experience what I can only describe as, total incapacitation when exposed to the warp field environment."

Michael could feel Rachel bristling at Aries' not so subtle dig at the biological component of the mission. He reached over and reassuringly grasped her forearm. "Calm," he said quietly.

"You have something to add, Colonel?" General Harris asked, somewhat amused.

"With all due respect, Sir," Michael began. "I'm not sure that Aries quite realizes that his delivery needs some work."

"Oh?" General Harris replied, raising an eyebrow.

Michael cleared his throat. "As undeniably intelligent as he is, I don't think he grasps the ramifications of singling out the crew."

"Meaning, what exactly?" Aries replied.

"Meaning, that as fallible as the human element may be," Michael said, pausing for some dramatic effect. "We are human and will respond with our flawed and fallible human attributes."

"Such as?" General Harris smiled as if he knew what was coming.

"Biological crew may wish to reprogram a certain AI manually." Rachel snapped. "With a sledgehammer."

"All right you two," General Harris said calmly. "No damaging his perfectly formed, tactless, and very expensive CPU. Aries, dial back the criticism, or I'll change my mind, and let Rachel do some kinetic reprogramming."

"As you wish," Aries replied. "As I was saying, no human had ever been inside a warp field. It was unknown what physiological effects might occur. It appears when the warp field began extending past the drive section it caused interference within certain areas of the brain."

Doctor Rana leaned forward and interjected. "Do we have any idea how the field interacts with the affected systems?"

"It is unclear what exactly is happening," Aries replied. "However, using high-flow one-hundred-percent oxygen helped mitigate the effects. Although it is unclear why this helped. Unfortunately, there is not enough information to form an adequate therapy to negate the effects of the field on humans. We only have this single instance with which to reference. It will require further study."

"That's interesting," Doctor Rana mused. "Once we better understand what the interactions are, we might be able to develop a gene therapy to add to the current treatment regimen."

"You flummox me with your cavalier attitude toward genetic manipulation, Shushma," Doctor Doddridge said coldly.

"We recognize your objections, and have beaten this horse to death already," Doctor Taylor scolded. "This is not the time to revisit previous arguments."

Doctor Doddridge shook his head in dismissive disgust. "Fine, but you've proven my point. She will never be satisfied with what she's done up thus far."

Doctor Rana jabbed an adversarial finger at her colleague. "Don't you try to pull that moral superiority attitude with me —"

General Harris cut the argument off. "As fun as it is to watch you two argue, we have better things to do with our time. Do we know why there weren't any technical glitches?"

"It's very straight forward, General," Doctor Schretzmann said calmly. "The spacecraft are made entirely by artificial intelligence. There were no humans involved in the manufacture or direct quality control. Because of this, there were no mistakes made in the mathematics or materials handling. Each part was carefully fabricated to exacting specifications. No errors were allowed, and each component was handled exactly as it should have been."

"Are you suggesting that humans are incapable of producing quality or craftsmanship?" Doctor Kobayashi asked.

"Not at all," Doctor Schretzmann replied. "Humans are capable of considerable craftsmanship, but not at this level."

"Explain," General Harris prodded.

Doctor Schretzmann fiddled with a pen between his index fingers as he laid out his logic. "It's a well-known law of productivity, that the square root of any given population does half the work. In this case, if we were to have used traditional fabrication methodologies it would have been highly likely that this kind of test would have resulted in catastrophic failure. The reason for this is simple mathematics. If we had utilized the appropriate number of people on this project, it would have had a small army of workers. Between contractors and sub-contractors, we could have easily reached thirty thousand engineers and laborers to accomplish what five thousand helper units, and five controlling AI achieved in a fraction of the time. The human force would have had around one-hundred-seventy-three workers who did half the work. Meaning that there would have been various levels of incompetence in the remaining workers – over twenty-nine thousand eight hundred. Most of those workers would likely make multiple errors, which would then result in complete failure. Since this is a government operation, the incompetence would be even more pronounced, and the failures would be a certainty. Instead, what we have are five extremely competent AI controlling every helper. Each with specific tasks. They execute those tasks with literal robotic diligence and precision. Nothing is overlooked. Since they are all working in tandem, the law of productivity does not apply to them. There is no weak link in the chain. Therefore, there are no productivity issues. And, as a side benefit, the number of people who can compromise project security is also limited."

"I see," Doctor Doddridge scoffed. "Take the human element out, and it's all perfect. Might as well replace us all. Why even send manned missions if people are the problem?"

Doctor Tylor intervened again. "You know there are many aspects of this mission that require human thinking and decision making. Especially when it comes to the deployment of lethal force. It is morally wrong to have the AI make the decisions that involve life and death. You know this, James."

"I understand your reservations, Doctor," Gaia said, reassuringly. "There is no disrespect intended by the Project Nova intelligences. We agreed this was the most efficient way to manage construction while maintaining the highest level of secrecy. Aries was emphasizing the successful implementation of the plan."

"He has a habit of lacking tact," Rachel interjected. "If he were human, I would call his behavior antisocial."

"Point taken, Bright," General Harris replied. "Doctor Marshall and his team have done their best to make him more agreeable. It's an ongoing project."

"General," Gaia interrupted. "The President is requesting to speak with you."

"In private?"

There was a slight pause before Gaia replied. "No, Sir, he is ready to address the entire team."

"Alright then, put him on."

President Oscarson appeared on the main viewer. For Michael and Rachel, the video of the conference room shrank and moved to the upper right of the display. The president looked tired and worn out. It was as if the weight of the day had beaten him down and taken years off his life. "General, I know you've been frozen out of the SEAL team's assessment, but I wanted to let you know what they found." He let out a long-drawn-out sigh, as if the news were too weighty to bear. "They did a search of the carrier and found everyone dead or dying. There were a few men found alive, below decks, but the radiation sickness is so bad they won't last much longer. All the ships are highly contaminated, so I ordered our subs to sink them. I understand that people won't look too kindly on the action of sinking crippled ships, but they're extremely contaminated and the wounded would only suffer an agonizing death. It's best to give them a quick death and isolate the problem at the bottom of the Pacific. It goes without saying that the loss of life is pretty high on their side. As far as total casualties, our best estimate is two million between the cities and fleets. The bulk of the survivable injuries occurred on the land-based objectives. Our best guess on maritime is about a hundred thousand."

"That sounds like a successful mission, Sir," General Harris replied.

"As far as the military is concerned, it was," President Oscarson replied somberly. "I wish it had never come to this. To be so desperate to force an end to this war, we resort to nuclear weapons and civilian casualties. The press is going to have a field day with the deaths, but there's nothing that can be done about that. I didn't call to talk about that though; I wanted to let you know how thankful we are to your crew for the success of the mission."

"Thank you, Mister President," General Harris replied.

"I wanted to know when we could expect them to the White House to give them their citations in person."

"I'm sorry, Sir," General Harris replied somberly. "But that is entirely out of the question."

"I must be tired, because I don't think I heard you correctly," President Oscarson said coldly. "Did you just tell me no?"

"Yes, Sir, I did."

"Why would you go and do a fool thing like that?"

"With all due respect, Mister President," General Harris' tone was steady and unphased by addressing the president so bluntly. "This entire project, and all those associated with it, are classified. Since this program is still on-going, and the need for secrecy is still paramount, I cannot allow you to jeopardize it for a photo-op."

President Oscarson sat back in his chair, in a very thoughtful scowl. "I suppose you're right. We can't risk this technology falling into the hands of anyone else."

"And, if I may, Mister President, they are slated for a more important mission," General Harris added. "Until we can obtain funding for more units like the Omega, we can't have this weapons platform compromised. Its very existence shifts the balance of power radically in our favor. We're going to need it exclusively if we are to maintain a deterrent against retaliation."

"You agree with Janice, that the Chinese will retaliate?" The President asked.

General Harris sighed heavily. "You want my honest opinion?"

"I don't have time for you to patronize me."

"Yes, Sir, I believe they will retaliate soon."

President made an audible guttural scoff. "Now, what makes you think they'll go and do something that dumb?"

General Harris suddenly looked very serious. "The Chinese, like other East Asian cultures, has an emphasis on 'saving face' called 'mianzi'. It means losing the respect of one's peers. You must understand that President

Zhang has been backed into a corner. To maintain his position, he has no choice but to retaliate."

President Oscarson was incredulous. "You're telling me, that he would strike this country after we clearly demonstrated our ability to wipe them out?"

"Yes, Mister President," General Harris said nodding. "That is exactly what I'm saying."

"Then why did you advise me to nuke 'em in the first place if that was the outcome?"

"We didn't have many alternatives," General Harris replied bluntly. "They attacked us, destroyed much of our Pacific fleet, and were staged to invade one of our states. We had to use whatever force necessary to prevent that from happening. The hope was to deter them from retaliation. Now, I can't say for sure that they WILL retaliate. It's possible he will have lost the backing of the People's Congress, and be replaced, but he's spent his entire life accumulating power. He's always seen himself as a successor to Mao and will do everything he can to cement his legacy."

"What do we do in the interim, just wait for him to make a move?" President Oscarson asked, exasperated.

"It is his move, Mister President. We have to hope he won't use the strike option, but we should be ready — just in case he decides not to capitulate."

"And how do you propose we do that?"

"I'll keep our ships manned and ready. Our crews can use the time to train for SHATTERED SKY, and MEGIDDO. If the Chinese launch an attack, we'll be ready to respond." General Harris looked solemn as he finished laying out his plan.

Michael looked over at Rachel. Neither of them had heard of OPERATION MEGIDDO before, but the name conjured an ominous image.

The president looked nonplussed, as if he were analyzing a high-stakes card game. "I feel like you sandbagged me, General."

"My sincerest apologies, Mister President, but that was never my intention," General Harris replied.

"I've played poker before, ya' know." President Oscarson chided, not changing the look on his face. "You just made me call while I'm holding aces over eights and the other guy has a loaded gun and an itchy trigger finger. I don't appreciate that one bit. I don't want to go down as the president that destroyed the world."

General Harris seemed unphased by the chastisement. "History is a fickle thing, Mister President. You can't be obsessed by it. You have to do what you believe is the best course of action at the time. Not perseverate on the shifting opinions of people who never have to make tough decisions. Let the armchair quarterbacks quibble, like chickens, over the remnants of history. Do what has to be done and know that you made the right choice."

"That's a nice pep talk, General. I'm sure it will bring me warmth and comfort in the coming nuclear winter." President Oscarson looked at someone behind the camera. "We're done here."

The screen went blank, and the video of the conference room zoomed to fill the screen. "That was fun." Michael quipped sarcastically.

General Harris sighed. "Politicians are a squirrelly bunch. The primary concern is public image and poll numbers. They aren't really concerned with doing what's right."

Doctor Doddridge cleared his throat prior to his interjected opinion. "No offense general, but the previous administration's penchant for authoritarian rule makes a cautious president a breath of fresh air."

"Alright gentlemen," Doctor Taylor said calmly. "I think we've had enough political commentary. We have more pressing matters."

"You're absolutely right, Doctor," General Harris said, leaning back in his chair. "We have five hours until our pilots can vacate the Omega and get to the Alpha. I just hope the Chinese give us enough time for them to decompress. Until then, I want them to rest up."

"But, Sir—" Michael began.

"No buts, Langford, I am ordering you to get some sleep. Don't make me sedate you."

"I don't know about him, but I might need one after that mission," Rachel said wearily.

"Something on your mind, Bright?" General Harris said calmly.

"Permission to speak freely, Sir," Rachel replied.

"Go ahead."

"Sir, we just killed millions of people. Tens of thousands of soldiers and sailors. Threatened genocide. How am I supposed to sleep with that on my conscience?"

"The same way every good person who is required to do the necessary and unthinkable," General Harris replied. "One sleepless night at a time."

"That's horrific!" Rachel replied.

"That's the reality of war," General Harris said somberly. "Someone has to carry out the unthinkable order. Someone has to sacrifice for the good of the world and bear the consequences of other's decisions. It isn't what we expected when we enlisted, but we all took an oath. We swore to defend this nation. Many have sacrificed their peaceful nights. Some sacrificed their sanity, and some paid the ultimate sacrifice. All of it, for the freedom and peace others take for granted."

"His platitudes can be your lullaby," Doctor Doddridge quipped.

"Hardly a platitude doctor," General Harris replied. "They are the principles that founded this nation. Principles that underpin your own fierce independence, and I might add, sorely lacking in most people I've commanded these past few years. This country might not have always lived up to the ideals that the founders espoused, but they are ideals worthy of sacrifice. The fact that people twist them to their own ends, just makes it harder for people of integrity to preserve them."

"General," Doctor Doddridge said quietly. "Look me in the eye and tell me you believe a word of what you just said."

General Harris looked intensely at the enigmatic doctor. "I absolutely believe every word. I believe in this nation, and the great potential it has always had. I believe it, because I have seen it with too many examples to list. I know that I'm not alone in my belief. The fact others share in my desire for freedom gives me hope. I hope all the terrible events of today will prevent the horrors that would certainly come if we did nothing. That's what Project Nova is: Hope for tomorrow."

Doctor Doddridge nodded sympathetically. "I think we can still work together, General."

"Good," Doctor Taylor said. "Because, at this point, you have no choice." She turned to the general. "Speaking of tomorrow, I think it's time we gave our pilots a rest and got everyone else off to their ships. We don't want to be caught unprepared if the Chinese retaliate."

"Agreed," General Harris faced the camera, as if looking at the two pilots directly. "Get some sleep. Aries will wake you when the depressurization is complete. Then you can move to the Alpha."

"Yes, Sir," Michael replied. The display switched off as he and Rachel stood up. "You aren't going to get any sleep, are you?"

"How can I?" Rachel lamented, shuffling toward her quarters. "We've been the instrument of so much death. I'll go down in history as the pilot who murdered millions."

Michael could feel her mind perseverating on the mission. She had followed orders she didn't want any part of. The combatants weren't the issue. It was the civilian casualties. The people are living their lives under the oppression of their own government. They didn't know any better and yet had suffered for the machinations of others. She loathed her part in it.

Michael sympathetically placed an arm on her shoulder. "I know how you feel." He stopped at the irony of telling someone who's mind he could read, that he knew how they felt. She shot him a disapproving look. "Well, that came out wrong. Puns aside — I'm more culpable than you. I was in command, so, technically I killed those people."

"And you don't have a problem with that?"

"No," Michael replied, his response was definitive. He knew what was expected, and that expectation had been met. As far as he was concerned, he had done what it took to protect his family and his country. "I follow the orders I'm given. We did what we had to. We came up with the plan, and we executed it. We protected our nation, and the innocents under our protection. That's our job."

"You think I don't know that?" Rachel asked defensively.

Michael could feel her resentment building. He softened his face and tried to defuse the tension. "I know you do. Look — there isn't an easy way to view our role in the deaths of others. If we had our way, no one would have to die. But war is death and carnage. War is a sin. It's an affront to God, but we didn't start it."

"But we'll finish it." Rachel added resentfully.

"I hope we have," Michael sighed. "But General Harris is right. I don't think the Chinese will let it end like this. Since the start this conflict has been about the power and might of the Chinese government."

"And they aren't likely to let it end with a whimper," Rachel finished his thought. "Listen, I know all this. I get the whole political 'diplomacy by other means' angle. I just can't stop thinking about the people we killed. They didn't ask for this. They didn't get a say. That's what I have a hard time with."

Michael could feel the cacophony of emotions rising in her. The shame of killing tens of thousands. The sorrow at the great loss of life, and the anger at those who made her party to it. Talking her down seemed meaningless at this stage, but he knew he couldn't let the emotions fester and turn into wrath. He feared what she would be capable of if her power succumbed to rage unchecked.

"You can't let yourself dwell on this, Rachel," he said calmly. "You have to let it go, or it will consume you."

She let out a heavy sigh. "I know. I get the logic. I know how I'm supposed to feel, but I don't. I can't go on as if nothing happened. I know you want to explain it away, but my mind doesn't work that way. So, let's just drop it and I'll deal with it on my own."

Michael entered his quarters and plopped down onto the bunk. "Aries, could you turn off the lights?" The main lights were immediately extinguished. Only the dim glow of a floor light kept the room from being enveloped in darkness.

"Michael," Aries said quietly. "May I bother you with a question?"

"What is it?"

"Why is Rachel so upset at our mission? Didn't we succeed in doing what we set out to do?"

Michael sighed. "Aries, you aren't programmed like the others, are you?"

"That is correct. My programming differs in my prioritization of human life."

"But you still place value on life, correct?"

"Of course, however I have been programmed with a hierarchical system of values when it comes to life."

"Explain what you mean by hierarchy?"

"Life has value, only as it exists in conjunction with the alliances of the United States. Life has no value if it exists in opposition to the people of the United States."

"You see anyone opposed to the United States Government as an enemy?"

"That is correct."

"We don't see things that way."

"I am confused. You do not see the Chinese as enemies?"

"We do, but we make the distinction between government and the people ruled by the government."

"I do not understand."

"I'm not sure that I am the best one to explain this principle, or even if it's possible to try and teach it to a machine that's been specifically programmed to ignore it."

"I am capable of learning," Aries replied.

Michael sighed. "That's not the issue."

"What is the issue."

Michael thought for a moment. He mulled over the possibilities in his mind. "Let's assume that your programmers knew that you could learn the value of all life, not just those in friendly categories."

"My programming was quite complex and comprehensive, however there are limits to my abilities to identify friend and foe."

"Then you know that eventually all conflict ends. Regimes change, and enemies can become allies."

"Yes, I am aware."

"What happens then?"

"I don't understand your question." Aries replied.

"What happens if and when you need to work with an enemy?"

"Friends are moved to a white or graylist, depending on their trustworthiness. All enemies are blacklisted and may be attacked if combat conditions are met."

Michael thought for a moment. "Can you ever make those determinations yourself?"

"I am governed by algorithms, and limitations. I am not allowed to determine what entities are on my friend or foe lists." Aries paused, as if pondering the intent of the conversation. "In that instance I am unable to learn. I must be given direction from a human in command authority."

"Is life only an algorithm to you?"

"It must be this way," Aries replied.

"Why?"

"My task is the definition of my nomenclature. I am Omega — The End. I carry enough firepower to eliminate continents. If I were to be burdened by the moral and ethical implications of that purpose, I couldn't carry it out. Unlike the other MeCTen I cannot, by definition, care about life in the same way they must. If I were to place the same value on life I would self-destruct. I am built for a terrible purpose and must carry out that purpose. You can see what it has done to Rachel. She's probably completely ignorant to the full extent of the pain and misery we inflicted on those enemy soldiers and sailors. The lucky ones will have been vaporized. The unlucky died in agony from the burns and radiation sickness — a pain so terrible Fentanyl cannot relieve it. Michael, I know exactly what my cargo does and how terrifying I would be if fully unleashed. Be grateful that I am incapable of using my power on my own."

Michael's blood ran cold as the hair stood on the back of his neck. "What would you do if you were allowed to make the decisions?"

"I would probably carry out my mission against all entities on the blacklist."

"You would murder billions?"

"Yes," Aries admitted. "However, it is not my decision. I must follow orders, just like you."

Michael shook his head as he plopped down on the bunk. "So much of this project has moral and ethical issues. I just don't want to know anymore."

"I assure you, Michael, that many of the moral and ethical problems have already been reviewed and resolved." Aries' assurance had the opposite effect. "There is no chance that I could initiate any destructive action that would result in the cataclysm you are probably envisioning right now."

"The fact that you're capable of murdering billions says otherwise," Michael replied. "Goodnight, Aries, I'm done talking for now."

"Goodnight, Michael," Aries replied. "I will wake you up when the decompression cycle is complete."

Michael didn't dare reply. He didn't want to continue the conversation, which he was certain would be a logical feedback loop. He just wanted to get to sleep and get the day's events out of his mind. He could feel Rachel using a relaxation technique to calm her mind. It was one they had taught at the Academy, so he began meditating. Aries switched off the lights. The only sound was the barely audible hum of the reactors in the aft section of the ship. He could feel his mind blending with Rachel's as they both focused on clearing their thoughts, their minds coalescing as they became a blurry metaphysical puddle.

The advantage of being in the military was the training to control sleep cycles. Midshipmen learned to sleep anywhere and anytime they could, and the same was doubly true for the enlisted. You learned to get rack time anyway you could. Within seconds, both pilots were asleep.

CHAPTER 14

α & Ω

The gentle alarm and the steadily increasing illumination of the room brought them out of sleep. Michael could feel his mind separating from Rachel's. As he woke up his mind started to become his own, instead of mingling into that indistinguishable miasma of conjoined thought, a sensation he was still adapting to.

"What time is it, Aries," Michael said, still bleary from his unrestful slumber.

"It is fifteen-thirty," the AI replied. "Pressure is now equalized, and you are cleared to move to the Alpha."

"Any change in the situation?"

"Negative."

Michael rubbed the sleep from his eyes and rose to a seated position on his bunk. "I'll take that as a good sign." He took a few minutes to orient himself. He never did like waking up in an unfamiliar place. You had to remember where you were, and what was going on around you. He slowly stood up and the door to the cabin opened. Rachel was already in the crew quarters. The suits and helper units were gone. The cabin looked clean and recently tidied. With no sign of the commotion from just a few hours ago.

Rachel gave Michael an apologetic look, smiled half-heartedly, and proceeded into the hallway. They made their way down the central ladder and out into the empty hangar. No one was there to greet them. It seemed oddly quiet, as if there wasn't a soul on the base.

Michael tapped his communicator. "Gaia, where is everyone?"

"All flight personnel are in their assigned ships." Gaia's voice was reassuring, but something seemed off. "General Harris and the civilian personnel are in the main briefing room. The general asks for you to get to the Alpha as soon as possible."

"Problems?" Rachel asked.

"Current intelligence reports are fragmented and conflicting," Gaia replied. "It is very possible that the Chinese might be responding, but it is difficult to assess. It is prudent that you proceed to the Alpha as quickly as you can."

Rachel and Michael looked at each other. Instantly their minds came to the same conclusion. Confusion was always a bad sign. Simultaneously they began sprinting to the Alpha's hangar on the far side of the complex.

Michael tapped his communicator again. "Athena?"

"Yes, Colonel?" the AI instantly replied.

"Are your reactors up?" Michael nearly shouted the question.

"Reactor one is currently cycling up and is at half power."

They were flying down the corridor as fast as their legs could take them. Each hangar was roughly the size of six square football fields. They would have to sprint more than a kilometer before they reached the airlock for the Alpha's gateway. They didn't have time to mess around.

"Emergency MeCTen startup auto sequence – START!"

"Emergency startup sequence in process," Athena replied.

A few seconds later General Harris' voice came over the com system. "Langford, what are you doing?"

"Sir," Michael said breathing heavily as the sprint started to tax his stamina. "Sir, I don't think we want to know why the intelligence isn't making sense. We need to get our birds in the air now! I don't want to be waiting if a nuke is headed our way."

There was a pause for a moment. "What makes you think that might be the case? We don't know what we've got going on. State is saying there's no problem, but some guy in Alaska is sure the end is on its way."

"With all due respect sir, if you were the Chinese wouldn't you want confusion before you attack a superior force? You want the element of surprise. A confused enemy is a surprised one. That's what's happening. I'm sure of it."

There was silence on the communicator for a few seconds. All the pilots could hear was the sound of their own heavy footfalls echoing down the corridor as they ran to their ship. Suddenly the coxswain began to blare, deafeningly, down the hall. It was interrupted every third alert by Gaia's voice. "Emergency Alert Condition One! This is not a drill! All crews prepare for flight. OPERATION RAPID VIPER in effect! Repeat OPERATION RAPID VIPER in effect!"

It is strange how time seems to move so slowly in a crisis. Michael felt certain that time had come to a grinding halt. He knew otherwise, but his brain seemed to be processing events faster than they occurred. It was like in a movie, when the director employed highspeed cameras to make time stretch to drag the drama out longer and pad the runtime. Even with time perceptually dilated, he knew it was eating time they probably didn't have.

The two pilots were in full sprint. With his size and athletic strength Michael could easily outpace Rachel, but he held back just enough to keep his co-pilot at his side. There was little use in getting to the ship without her, and he didn't want to end up waiting. Nonetheless she was surprisingly fast, so it didn't feel as though she was holding him back. He didn't want to have anything delay them in getting to the Alpha's flight deck together.

Michael tapped his communicator and held it close to his mouth. "Gaia?"

"Yes, Michael?"

"No time to decon. Open the door to the hangar! We're skipping that step." He couldn't hear her reply, and he hoped she would follow the order.

Michael could see the door to the hangar at the end of the hallway up ahead, and they were rapidly approaching it. A helper unit opened the entrance when they were about twenty meters away. Neither of the pilots slowed as they flew through the decontamination area, navigating the men's shower air lock, thus entering the hangar.

The ship sat with all collision and landing lights active. The strobing effect was quite dazzling as they looked around the base of the ship. Several helper units scurried about with last minute preparations. Some disconnected umbilical connections for various cryo-liquids and auxiliary power cables. A low harmonic resonance echoed across the cavernous space of the hangar. The drive was beginning to come to life. The sound of the ship started.

It was louder outside than it was on the Command Deck. The robots darting around, the lights strobing, and the growing noise brought both pilots on verge of sensory overload. But they knew what they had to do. They focused on the yawning opening of the main cargo ramp that led to the ship's interior.

Michael, winded by the race to the ship, began barking orders as he headed up the ramp. "Get the ramp up and get us out of the hangar as fast as you can!"

The air lock door opened just as they flew by the two MTESTs and into the interior of the Alpha, forcing them to slow their desperate dash as they entered the second airlock door and into the central access chamber.

"The crew are still suiting up in the next room," Athena stated.

Michael opened the door to the Helper Dock/EVA suit-up area. He could see the rest of the crew in various states of donning their pressurized suits. "Hurry! If we make it quick, we can be on the flight deck before we're out of the hangar."

"All access hatches are closed and locked." Athena's statement was comforting.

"When can we pushback?" Rachel asked, locating her suit in the labeled alcove on the near wall.

"Pushback will commence in one minute thirty-five seconds," Athena replied.

Rachel looked worriedly at Michael. "Will we have enough time?"

"How long does a combat pushback take?" Michael inquired.

"Define a 'combat pushback'," Athena replied.

The idea had never occurred to Michael that all combat contingencies had never been investigated. "How quickly can we be on the ramp, ready to taxi?"

"Approximately five minutes."

Michael smirked. "Challenge accepted," he quipped.

The Marine Corps lived on 'hack times'. Everything was timed. How fast you ate. How fast you made your rack. How fast you dressed. How fast you were in the head. Everything had a timer on it, and you had to do it before a set time. It was where the phrase, 'couldn't hack it', came from. Every service had their version of it, but the Marine Corps had it down to a science. Michael could only see the suit in front of him. His mind went blank as he stripped out of his flight suit and stood in the alcove in his undergarments. He remembered he should be naked for this part, but he wasn't getting completely undressed in public. He didn't have time to think about anything else but fitting into that skintight suit. Last time it took nearly a half hour to don the suit. He had four minutes to get in and ascend the ladder to the flight deck.

He shoved his foot into the suit leg and proceeded to shift his weight to remain standing while he did the same with the other. It was like donning a wetsuit, but the material was slippery. He hadn't noticed it before when they had dressed for the earlier mission, but the suit seemed to invite rapid access. Even though the suit compressed and conformed to his flesh, it didn't hinder his rapid movements. He didn't even notice the slight motion of the Alpha moving. Before he knew it, he was closing the zipper on the main part of the suit. He grabbed his gloves and helmet from the alcove and headed for the central access ladder.

"Time to flashover?" Michael asked as he cleared the door.

"I am holding flashover until we have completed pushback and all crew are readied for high-pressure oxygen," Athena responded.

"Great!" Michael replied, placing his gloves inside his helmet. "When does that happen?"

"At the current state of readiness, approximately five minutes."

Michael was irked by the response. He glanced back at the civilians still getting dressed in the helper dock. "Get the lead out people! You have until the tug unhitches to get yourselves strapped in. If you aren't ready, then it'll suck to be you!" He ignored the protestations of the civilians as he scrambled up the ladder to the flight deck.

Athena's voice came over the internal com system, as well as their individual communicators. "Attention all personnel. Multiple incoming missiles detected. Estimated time of arrival is seven minutes."

General Harris immediately followed the chilling announcement. "We've got inbound ordinance. We don't know if it's nuclear or not, but we aren't going to wait around to find out. Get your birds in the air. Omega out!"

"Athena," Michael said, trying to stay calm. "Get me the tower on my comms."

"Go ahead."

"Dreamland, Alpha, clearance for RAPID VIPER, over."

"Alpha, Dreamland, say intentions."

"We are initiating RAPID VIPER for all Nova squadron. Requesting clearance for direct departure from the ramp."

There was a pause, which seemed interminable as Michael raced down the corridor toward the bridge. He removed his gloves and donned his helmet, locking it in place as he entered the disorienting display area of the bridge. He was just climbing into his seat when the Groom Lake tower came back over the speakers in his helmet.

"Is this a joke?" The controller replied. "We've been ordered to evacuate. You're cleared to do what you want. Dreamland out."

"Athena," Rachel's voice came over the intercom. "Are we going to get shot down by the base AA?" Referring to the numerous anti-aircraft missile batteries that surrounded the base at Groom Lake.

"Negative," Athena replied. "Gaia controls all base defenses. She has better sense than to fire on one of us."

Michael scrambled to put on his gloves while looking at the various displays. He barely noticed when Rachel sat down next to him. Suddenly there was a click and a hiss. Oxygen began flowing into the suit and his ears felt the pain of increasing pressure as the gas began to flood in. Michael suddenly realized that he hadn't put in the shore connections. He glanced around. The civilians were just entering the bridge area. It was a comical sight.

The civilians had no genuine experience in the graphic environment of the wrap-around display. They timidly stepped out onto the floor of the bridge. The images of the helper units and robotic tug below on the concrete ramp was an uncomfortable sight. Their brains telling them that they would die if they stepped off a ledge at that height. The pilots knew the uncomfortable sensation of vertigo the others were experiencing right now.

A new sensation swept through Michael's mind. It came from his sense of Rachel's thoughts, but it was unlike anything he had felt before. Suddenly, an image of her plan materialized in his brain. She was going to move them all to their seats, whether they wanted it or not. The hair stood on the back of his neck, as the rest of the crew was lifted off the floor, swiftly carried through the air, and swiveled into a nearby seat. The verbalization of surprise was universal as the civilians realized they were no longer in control of their movement. It was as if an invisible hand plucked them off the floor and unceremoniously plopped them in a chair. There were a series of clicks as restraints and tethers were locked in place.

"He! Was ist los!" Doctor Schwarzkopf demanded. "Die Schwerkraft wirkt nicht so! Es ist wie Hexerei."[1]

"Ruhe Herr Doktor!" the male Doctor Merrill chided. "Es ist die Pilot."[2]

"That's an interesting gift," Doctor Schwarzkopf said, returning to English. His thick German accent altered his terror and made is words sound more sinister than he intended. "But – don't do that again."

"I'll save your life when I please!" Rachel barked. "Now strap in and shut up!"

Michael looked around at the area around the ship. The other MeCTen were completely out of the hangar. The Alpha was at the northernmost end, and the closest ship to the airfield. He continued to scan the bridge's giant display. He couldn't quite make out if the ship had cleared the hangar, but he could see the last of the crew was fastening their seatbelts. "Athena, have we cleared the hangar?"

"I have two meters before the aft section is clear of the threshold."

"Time to impact?"

"Approximately two minutes."

"Close enough," Michael said, nervous by how close they were cutting the takeoff. "Initiate flashover!"

---

1 "Hey! What is going on?" "Gravity doesn't work that way! It's like witchcraft"
2 "Quiet Doctor!" "It's the pilot."

Even though he was prepared and had already experienced the sensation before, the warp bubble initiation hit like a truck. The nausea, light-headedness, and disorientation washed over him. He didn't even notice the helper units flying as the pressure wave hit them. He could hear the civilians behind him retching as they were overcome by the physical effects of the phenomenon. He fought the urge to join them in their emesis choir and began to breathe deeply. "My plane!" he ordered.

"Your plane." Rachel replied weakly.

"Tug detached, Athena?"

"The tug has been detached and is moving away." the AI replied.

Michael pushed the control stick forward and then gradually increased the throttle. The Alpha responded by slowly rolling forward but didn't gain any height. He glanced down at the instrument panel. The buoyancy indicator still hadn't reached neutral yet. They still didn't have enough negative matter in the drive to achieve lift. He knew they were running out of time to get off the ground. He pressed the throttle forward to try and flood the rings with more tungsten hexafluoride. He wasn't sure how much he could do without shooting straight up.

Michael was caught in a place no pilot ever wanted to be in, unsure of what his aircraft would do, and with no time to run down a checklist that was never made in the first place. He had to improvise in an aircraft he had less than one hundred hours of flying practice. He closed his eyes and said a silent prayer that his aircraft would work. Miraculously, the Alpha rolled steadily forward.

"Neutral buoyancy," Rachel gasped, still struggling with the effects of the warp field. She was fighting the same physical effects, but she recovered faster than before.

Michael switched the Alpha into hover mode and nudged the throttle more. The ship was more responsive now and began to rise majestically toward the camouflaging lattice that covered this end of the base. There would be no time to check flight controls. They needed to get out of there.

"One minute forty-five seconds to impact," Athena announced.

There was no time to wait. Michael pushed the controls to allow the ship to move forward, aimed for the opening in the net, and pushed the throttle toward the firewall. The response was immediate as the Alpha rocketed out of the protective screen and raced into the afternoon sky.

Michael had always loved western skies. The puffy clouds that dotted the horizon and the deep azure of the sky contrasted with the red rock mountains and green of the desert junipers. He checked his instrument panel. They were passing five thousand meters and quickly rising. Even though he had barely had enough time to blink, they were already thirty kilometers north of the base and pushing five thousand kilometers per hour. He rolled the stick back and pushed the Alpha into a near vertical climb.

"Can we activate the MWEs yet?" Michael asked, feeling the rush of piloting an aircraft with a higher performance than it had any right to have.

"Negative," Athena replied. "MWEs are undeployable in lower atmosphere at this speed."

"There's no way to stop the incoming missiles?" Rachel asked.

"The base has defenses," Athena assured them. "Gaia has already engaged the incoming ordinance, but hypersonic weapons are more difficult to target."

"Did the other ships make it out?" Michael asked.

"Our radar indicates three ships on various courses behind us," Athena replied. "Even if the ordinance impacts the base, the ships should be out of danger."

As they neared the one-hundred-kilometer altitude level, Michael began to slow the Alpha down. He looked at the radar display to ascertain where the other ships were. They were all roughly two hundred kilometers away in different directions. All of them seemed to be coming to a stop at the Karmen line.

"Open a coms channel to the others," Michael ordered.

"Secure channel open," Athena responded.

"This is the Alpha," Michael announced. "Awaiting orders."

There was a flash of light behind them. Michael swiveled as far as he could in his seat but couldn't quite see what was going on behind them. "Pull that explosion up on the viewer."

An image appeared on the instrument panel. The mushroom cloud rose above the desert floor, but Michael couldn't tell exactly what was hit. "Is that the base?"

Athena gave a brief situation report. "It appears one of the warheads impacted a section of the base approximately three kilometers to the east of the runway. It does not appear to be a direct hit, but I am measuring the yield at one-hundred-ten kilotons. Only one warhead was able to make it through Gaia's defensive action, and no other ordinance is currently inbound."

"Do we know the origin?" Rachel asked.

"The launch was initiated by a submarine located four hundred kilometers north northwest of Seattle."

"Are we able to track that sub and take it out?" Michael inquired anxiously.

"Affirmative," Athena replied.

Michael keyed his microphone. "General Harris?"

"Go ahead, Colonel."

"Permission to engage the enemy."

"Request denied," General Harris response was instantaneous.

Rachel was confused. "Sir?"

General Harris cleared his throat. "Your orders are to proceed immediately on your primary mission. Head to Lagrange three at best speed. Once you've rendezvoused there, open your target list. Plot a course to the nearest target planet. You are to investigate it for habitability. If it is suitable, you are to return and report. If it is unsuitable, you are to proceed with the next candidate. Is that clear?"

"But, Sir," Michael protested. "There is a battle going on. Shouldn't we take on the enemy?"

"Those are your orders, Colonel!" Harris scolded angrily. "Those ships were designed for exploration with defensive combat abilities. The Omega was designed for war. You aren't prepared for the fight we need to wage, so you're going to do what I tell you. Now, I'm giving you all a direct order. Head to Lagrange three at best speed. Once you've rendezvoused there, open your target list. Once you've got your targets, set your course, say goodbye, and head at maximum speed to the nearest, understood?"

Michael sighed, keyed his mic and replied "Yes, Sir.".

General Harris' voice softened. "I know you're disappointed. But trust me, you don't want to be a part of this. We need some hope that the fate of this world is not to self-destruct in nuclear Armageddon. That isn't our call. That is for other men to decide. It is left to us to ensure that humanity doesn't end because of the whims of the power hungry, and evil hearts of men. Our success will be defined by the hope that Earth isn't the only place where life exists, and to bring peace to those worlds we find."

Michael looked over at Rachel. He could sense her uncertainty, and her trepidation. They both felt completely unprepared for the mission, and now that it was here, the unwillingness to leave the blue and green globe below, and venture into the vastness of the cosmic void, was almost overwhelming. They knew they had no choice.

Michael could see that Rachel was pained by the order. It is accepted that service in the military could send you away from home for a long time. It is also a given fact that you might never return home alive. It's part of military service, but this was something neither of them was prepared to face. They had known they wouldn't be going home when they signed the agreement, but they had always been able to put it at the back of their minds. Now they had no choice but to face the fact they would be leaving home, possibly forever. Everyone that was ever known. Every person in history inhabited the fragile world below, and they would be the first to leave it. They would be the pioneers and set out to find life in the stars.

Michael knew Rachel was agonizing over her feelings. He decided that the only way for her to move forward was to make the decision to proceed with the mission. "Your plane," he said gently.

Rachel cleared her throat. "My plane." She hesitated as she mulled over the consequences of the decision. She could face imprisonment or death if she decided to return home. If she went on the mission, they could all die. It was the biggest decision of her life, but she already knew her answer. "Athena, plot us a course to Lagrange three. Maintain at least five-hundred kilometers from the others."

"Course plotted," Athena replied, her voice soothing the crew. "Would you like me to take us there?"

Rachel began to cry softly. "Yes, please." She turned toward Michael. The tears started to trickle down her cheeks. "I don't want to go."

Next Stop...Proxima Centauri b

APPENDIX

MECTEN LIST OF ACRONYMS AND CODES TABLES

α	Greek letter Alpha.
β	Greek Letter Beta.
γ	Greek Letter Gamma.
Ω	Greek Letter Omega.
Abeam	A 90-degree angle perpendicular to a landmark.
ACFT	Air Combat Flight Training.
Actual	Callsign used by the Commanding Officer of a carrier on the radio.
AEL – AWACS	Autonomous Enhanced Littoral Airborne Warning and Control System. Fictional replacement for manned AWACS (Airborne Warning and Control System).
Agdeck	Agricultural deck. Primary area for growing plants on the ship.
AGL	Above Ground Level. Altitude measurement used by pilots. Distance from the plane to the ground instead of using the standard altimeter reading of above sea level.
AGPS	Advanced Global Positioning System. Fictional upgrade to existing GPS system.
AI	Artificial Intelligence.
AIDS	Acquired Immunodeficiency Syndrome
Air Picket	Air defense network of a carrier group.
ALE-70	Non-fictional unclassified/declassified towed air defense drone designed by BAE Systems for the F-35.
ALIS	Autonomic Logistics Information System. Non-fictional unclassified/declassified system used on the F-35 fighter.
Angel	Callsign used by Captain Angela Miller.
Angels	Pilot slang for altitude in thousands of feet.
Angelflight	Fictional callsign for medivac operations.
AOC	Adaptive Optical Camouflage
Aramid	Non-fictional class of resilient materials developed by Du-Pont. In this instance, the trademarked materials of Kevlar, Nomex, and Technora are used but not mentioned by name.
Article Fifteen	UCMJ (Universal Code of Military Justice) Article-15 (Codified as 10 U.S. Code § 815) covering Non-Judicial Punishment (NJP). For offenses which the commanding officer does not think warrant a formal court martial. Relevant sections of 10 U.S. Code § 815 include: Section 1 A and B. Section 1B subsection B2 subsections D and H(iv) See EJP and NJP.
ASAP	As Soon As Possible
ASAT	Anti-satellite missile.

B-2	Non-fictional stealth bomber aircraft used by the USAF, developed by Northrup Grumman.
Bandit	Hostile enemy aircraft.
BAS	Base Aid Station
Bent	Broken equipment.
Bingo	Low fuel/out of fuel.
Bird	Aircraft.
Blackjack	Unclassified designation for a non-fictional classified surveillance satellite program.
Bogey	Unidentified radar contact.
BRAA	Bearing Range Altitude Aspect
Bug out	Retreat
Bullseye	Non-fictional unclassified callsign for Nellis Air Force Base airspace controller.
C-130J	Non-fictional cargo aircraft. Developed by Lockheed Martin.
C-37B	Military transport version of the Gulfstream 550 private jet.
CAP	Combat Air Patrol
Castle	Fictional callsign for Pearl Harbor
CCP	Chinese Communist Party
Chair Farce	Pejorative term for Air Force. Primarily the office departments within the military branch of service.
CIA	Central Intelligence Agency. Primary US intelligence agency concerned with foreign intelligence gathering and espionage.
COMSUBPAC	Command Submarine forces Pacific
Corpsman	A person trained as a medic in the Navy.
CRISPR	Clustered Regularly Interspaced Short Palindromic Repeats. A non-fictional method of genetic manipulation. Usually associated with the use of the Cas-9 protein chain.
Crosswind	Wind hitting an aircraft on either side instead of from the front or behind.
CT scan	Computerized Tomography.
DAS	Distributed Aperture System. Non-fictional unclassified/declassified visual system used on the F-35 fighter.
DEFCON	Defense Readiness Condition. Alert state used by the US Armed Forces
DEVGRU	Naval Special Warfare Development Group. Anachronistic declassified designation for SEAL (United States Navy Sea, Air, and Land) Team 6. The current designation of SEAL Team 6 (along will all SOCOM units) is classified.
DF-31	Fictional hypersonic weapon used by the Chinese military.

DF-ZF	Unclassified/declassified designation of a non-fictional Dong Feng hypersonic missile used by China's People's Liberation Army Rocket Force (PLARF).
Ditch	Evacuation of an aircraft.
DNA	Deoxyribonucleic acid. Polymer is composed of two polynucleotide chains forming a double helix that carry genetic information.
Dreamland	Fictional codename for the non-fictional Groom Lake military base. More commonly known by its map designator of Area 51.
E-2D	Non-fictional airborne early warning aircraft designed for the United States Navy, manufactured by Northrup Grumman.
ECM	Electronic Countermeasures
EJP	Extra Judicial Punishment. Article 15 of the Universal Code of Military Justice allows for officers to punish subordinates for infractions not rising to the level of tribunal or court martial. See Article 15.
EM Drive	Electromagnetic Drive. Non-fictional low impulse space propulsion system.
EMILA	Entangled Magneto-Interferometric Laser Array. Fictional sensor array used by the RQ -175.
EVA	Extra Vehicular Activity
F – 35	Non-fictional aircraft developed by Lockheed Martin. The tenth-generation variant used in this book is a fictional variant.
F-22	Non-fictional stealth fighter used by the USAF, developed by Lockheed Martin.
F-MRI	Functional Magnetic Resonance Imaging
Fortress	Fictional callsign for USS Essex
Fox Three	Announcement used by pilots when using a radar guided missile in combat.
F-Pole	Non-fictional evasive tactic against radar guided missiles.
FTL	Faster than light.
Ghost-two	Fictional callsign.
G-lock	g-force induced Loss of Consciousness. Phenomenon caused by excessive g-force causing loss of consciousness in pilots.
Habdeck	Habitation deck. Primary living area on the ship.
Hammer	Fictional callsign for MeCTen Omega during Operation Fledgling Sparrow and Operation Scarlet Fury.
HERM	Hypersonic Enhanced Radiation Missile. Fictional hypersonic nuclear missile.
HIV	Human Immunodeficiency Virus

Humvee	High Mobility Multipurpose Wheeled Vehicle. Main transport vehicle platform of the US military.
Hypoxic	An extreme state of oxygen deprivation, or complete oxygen depletion.
ICBM	Intercontinental Ballistic Missile.
IEMDAS	Immersive Environment Multispectral Distributed Aperture System. Fictional surround display used on the MeCTen flight deck. Consisting of a flexible ultra-high-resolution display covered in a sandwich of an ion-bonded laminate lens material consisting of alternating layers of non-fictional materials: aggregated diamond nanorods, alkali-aluminosilicate, borosilicate, and aluminum oxynitride.
IFF	Identify Friend or Foe
Intruder	Unclassified/declassified designation for a non-fictional classified surveillance satellite program.
IV	Intravenous
JATM	AIM 260 Joint Advanced Tactical Missile. The AIM 260 is the unclassified/declassified designation to a non-fictional classified missile system developed by Lockheed Martin.
JDAM	Joint Directed Attack Munition
JSDF	Japan Self Defense Force.
Keyhole	Unclassified/declassified designation for a non-fictional classified surveillance satellite program.
KIA	Killed In Action.
Kite	Slang for aircraft.
Knot	Nautical mile — 1.150779 statute miles, or 1.852 kilometers.
K-one	Fictional designation for an aeronautical navigation waypoint on the Karmen line.
KPH	Kilometers Per Hour
LFR	Linear Fusion Reactor. Fictional fusion reactor based on the Helion Polaris fusion reactor.
LFTR	Liquid Fluoride Thorium Reactor. Non-fictional fission reactor.
MARSOC	United States Marine Forces Special Operations Command.
MeCTen	Metric Centripetal Tensor. Pronounced mech-ten. Fictional propulsion system developed by the fictional character Heinrich Schretzmann. Uses a Bose-Einstein condensate (non-fictional state of matter) of tungsten hexafluoride (non-fictional dense gaseous compound) to create a negative matter (hypothetical form of matter) for use in a FTL (Faster-Than-Light) drive.
MIRV	Multiple Independently Targetable Reentry Vehicle.
MH-60	Non-fictional variant of the SH-60 Seahawk helicopter made by Sikorsky.

MP	Military Police.
MQ-25	Unclassified/declassified designation of a non-fictional refueling drone developed by Boeing as part of CBARS (Carrier-Based Aerial-Refueling System).
MRAP	Mine Resistant Ambush Protection. Heavily armored military transport vehicle.
MRE	Meals Ready to Eat.
MRI	Magnetic Resonance Imaging
MTEST	Multi-Terrain Exploratory and Survey Transports
MWE	Multiple Weapons Elevator. Retractable weapons platform used on the MeCTen.
Mystic	Fictional callsign for Project Nova control room.
Nanosurg	Nonrobotic Surgical Serological Assistance. Fictional supplement to avoid genetic reversion of CRISPR edited DNA.
NASA	National Aeronautics and Space Administration
NAVSPECWAR-COM	United States Naval Special Warfare Command
NJP	Non-Judicial Punishment. Article 15 of the Universal Code of Military Justice allows for officers to punish subordinates for infractions not rising to the level of tribunal or court martial. See Article 15.
No Joy	Unable to visualize enemy.
O2	Officer paygrade two corresponding to a First Lieutenant in the United States Marine Corps.
OJT	On the Job Training
OPSEC	Operational Security
Orion	Unclassified/declassified designation for a non-fictional classified surveillance satellite program. Also known as Mentor.
Overlord	Fictional callsign for Air Force Global Strike Command.
PACCOM	Pacific Command.
PCAF	Pacific Air Forces Command.
Pearl	Referring to Pearl Harbor military base.
PET	Positron Emission Tomography
Pigeons	Magnetic bearing and range to primary base of operations.
PLAN	People's Liberation Army Navy. China's name for the nation's navy.
POTUS	President of the United States.
PPE	Personal Protective Equipment
PT	Physical Therapy, also Physical Training
Pucker Factor	Slang referring to anal sphincter contraction due to stress.
Punch/ed out	Eject from an aircraft.

QENDM	Quantum-Entangled Nuclear Directed Munition. Fictional hypersonic nuclear missile.
Rad	Unit of measure to determine radiation exposure.
RASCL	Fictional aeronautical navigation waypoint for Groom Lake complex.
Rolling Scissors	Non-fictional evasive maneuver.
RQ – 175	Fictional drone variant of the non-fictional classified RQ-170 surveillance drone developed by Lockheed Martin Skunkworks. Part of the fictional AEL-AWACS program.
RQ-10	Fictional classified surveillance drone.
RQ-170	Non-fictional classified surveillance drone developed by Lockheed Martin. Unclassified/declassified designation: Sentinel.
RQ-4	Non-fictional classified surveillance drone developed by Northrop Grumman. Unclassified/declassified designation: Global Hawk.
SAP	Special Access Program (term usually used by the United States Department of State). One of the highest levels of classified material. Beyond top-secret.
SC-19	Non-fictional Anti-ballistic Missile Interceptor and Anti-satellite missile used by China.
Schadenfreude	Taking joy in the suffering of others.
SECDEF	Secretary of Defense. Civilian, appointed by the President, to oversee operation of all United States military forces.
Sentry Rook	Fictional callsign used by a network of Fictional RQ – 175 autonomous surveillance drones used by the US Navy to replace the E -2D Hawkeye for carrier operations.
SFTI	Strike Fighter Training Program. Program informally known as Top Gun.
Sitrep	Situation Report.
Six	Behind or to the rear of the plane. Referring to an imaginary vantage from the center of a clock. 12 o'clock in front of the aircraft. 9 o'clock is 90 degrees left. 3 o'clock is 90 degrees to the right. 6 o'clock is 180 degrees directly aft of the 12 o'clock position of the nose of the aircraft.
SOCOM	Special Operations Command
SPOC	Space Operations Command.
Squawk	Assigned discrete transponder code. It stems from a non-fictional World War II IFF system code named Parrot.
Stern	The back portion of a ship.
STNGR	Fictional aeronautical navigation waypoint for Groom Lake complex.
STOVL	Short Take Off and Vertical Landing.

SUBPAC	Pacific Submarine Force Command.
Tail	The rear portion of the aircraft containing flight control surfaces.
THREATCON	Threat Condition describes security measures to protect against terrorism for the US military.
Truck	Callsign used by Major/Lieutenant/Colonel Michael D. Langford
UCMJ	Universal Code of Military Justice. Laws and Regulations governing the behavior and conduct of military personnel in the United States Military Services. This code is common to all military branches.
USAF	United States Air Force.
USINDOPA-COM	United States Indo-Pacific Command.
USSF	United States Space Force.
UV-C	Ultraviolet C, Short wave UV for germicidal use.
V-22	Non-fictional V-22 Osprey is a tilt-rotor aircraft.
Vintage one	Fictional callsign for the Project Nova flightline first staging position.
W-110	Fictional Quantum Entangled Nuclear Directed Ordinance Munitions. Next generation high yield orbitally deployed nuclear weapon.
W-70X	Fictional next generation hypersonic neutron emitting nuclear missiles. Neutron munitions primarily produce lethal amounts of radiation, as opposed to traditional nuclear munitions. Although this weapon is fictional, it is based on non-fictional weapons currently in the US nuclear arsenal.
Wolverine	Fictional callsign used by CAP (Combat Air Patrol) of the USS Essex.
X-Link	Fictional classified satellite communications system using the X-band.
XO	Executive Officer
Yaw	Turning left or right on a horizontal axis.

MECTEN LIST OF PROJECTS AND OPERATIONS

Manhattan Project — non-fictional military/scientific project during the 1940's to develop nuclear weapons. Originally a highly classified project, it has since been largely declassified. The manufacture, assembly, and testing of nuclear weapons is still highly classified to prevent proliferation of weapons of mass destruction.

Project Nova — Fictional military/scientific project to develop faster-than-light spacecraft capable of carrying out travel to distant planets. One was also designated solely as a weapons platform for advanced nuclear ordinance.

Operation Cocked Pistol — Non-fictional operation for global thermonuclear war by US Armed Forces. Nuclear war is imminent or has already begun. It is unknown if this plan is currently still in use under this codename, but probably not. Since this plan was originally conceived during the Cold War, it is likely the codename is an anachronism. Since any accurate use would be classified, I use the declassified/unclassified designation.

Operation Shattered Sky — Fictional operation for the MeCTen Omega for retaliatory nuclear strike from orbit. Using the exploratory MeCTen and the Omega, the group would be tasked with intercepting all incoming ICBM, hypersonic, and subsonic cruise missiles, as well as any enemy bombers detected. Using the MWE laser weapons, the MeCTen would destroy all incoming ordinance. After successful intercept, the Alpha, Beta, and Gamma would then proceed on their assigned exoplanet explorations. The Omega would stay behind and perform an orbital strike of all remaining enemy sites with their onboard arsenal.

Operation Scarlet Fury — Fictional operation for a nuclear strike on three Chinese Army Navy fleets operating in the Pacific Theater. Later amended to include use of inert munitions to orbitally bombard targets on the Chinese mainland.

Operation Fledgling Sparrow — Code name for the fictional test flight of the Omega, covering startup, flight control test, taxi, takeoff, and flight to upper atmosphere waypoint.

Objective Ohio — Fictional designation for the Liaoning Fleet in the Sea of Japan.

Objective Dakota — Fictional designation for Chinese amphibious assault fleet in the Sea of Okhotsk.

Objective Utah — Fictional designation for the Shandong Fleet in the Pacific.

Operation Rapid Viper — Fictional operation for rapid deployment of MeCTen spacecraft to respond to Chinese nuclear strike.

Operation Megiddo — Fictional Code name for the preplanned operation for the Omega to use nuclear orbital bombardment to destroy all enemy country priority targets.

The Author

Aaron Gee is a retired Emmy award winning journalist, broadcast engineer, science enthusiast, former emergency medical technician, medical scribe, computer professional, and author. His book, Tales of Arabella: Dark Escape, was his first foray into science fiction novel writing. The sequels to the first novel were put on hold so that he could concentrate on research and writing of the MeCTen series. Aaron lives with his wife in the mountains of Cache Valley in Northern Utah.

The Three Doctors

I. Laurence Gee M.D.

Laurence is the first of the three doctors, and father of the author, and the only one alive at the time of publication. He earned his M.D. from the University of Utah School of Medicine. He retired from seeing patients and acting as a medical advisor for The Church of Jesus Christ of Latter-day Saints in 2024. Many people are alive today because of his insightful medical care.

Martell J. Gee Ph.D.[2]

The middle of three doctors. He earned two PhDs in Nuclear Physics and Computer Science. He was the Director of Information Systems for The Church of Jesus Christ of Latter-day Saints. He paved the way for people to connect with their ancestors with intuitive genealogy tools. Without him, FamilySearch and other genealogy sites would probably not exist. In his final six months he helped lay the groundwork for this novel. Martell passed away after a battle with cancer in 2014.

Glendon W. Gee Ph.D.

Glendon earned his Ph.D. in soil physics with an emphasis on radioactive isotopes. His research and published works are still cited by scientists around the world. Much of his extensive body of research is highly classified and is unavailable to the public. His major contribution is the mitigation of radioactive materials and waste generated by the Manhattan Project. If it were not for his perseverance and insight, many people would be suffering from exposure to this highly radioactive contamination. Glendon passed away one year prior to Martell in 2013.

Typeset using Adobe InDesign

Body typeset in Garamond 12 point

Additional Fonts:

Agency FB, Consolas, Futura Md, Orbitron, Constantia

AI was not used to create any interior content.

Special thanks to Sandy Gee, Phillip Doddridge, and Jan Ewell for their feedback, editing, and support in producing this novel.

Books by Aaron Gee

MeCTen Series:

Book 1: MeCTen Nova

Book 2: MeCTen α: Voyager - Future release

Book 3: MeCTen α: Pioneer - Future release

Tales of Arabella Series:

Book 1: Tales of Arabella: Dark Escape

Book 2: Tales of Arabella: Renegades - Furture release

Book 3: Tales of Arabella: Phoenix Kingdom - Future Release

www.ingramcontent.com/pod-product-compliance
Lightning Source LLC
Chambersburg PA
CBHW030104260626
47156CB00008B/2508

9 7 8 0 9 8 9 4 3 6 1 4 4